Praise for J

Murder at Buckskin Joe

I admire J.v.L. Bell's clever way of dropping in historical facts while keeping the story fast-paced and the mystery convoluted. Action and humor jump off every page and make me even more of a fan of this author.

-Vicky Ramakka, Award Winning Author
of *The Cactus Plot*

Millie Drouillard is as precocious and strong-willed as the unsettled town of Buckskin Joe in the Colorado Territory. She keeps her six-shooter in her apron pocket and is prepared for everything except the bottom of a mine shaft with little hope for escape. This book is rich in historical detail with characters you won't forget. Excitement at every turn of the page.

-Nancy Oswald, Award Winning Author

The Lucky Hat Mine

The Lucky Hat Mine, filled with period detail and real-life pioneers such as Mountain Charley, Green Russell and the Tabors, is a spirited...tale.

-Sandra Dallas, *The Denver Post*

J.v.L. Bell has written an unusual murder mystery with a romance angle set during the Civil War period. The dialog and narrative, which is humorous at times, fittingly captures life in a gold mining town. The inclusion of strong female characters, such as a freedwoman, adds to the appeal of the story... The novel is an entertaining read.

- Waheed Rabbani, *Historical Novel Review*

Hilarious, endearing and intriguing, this book has everything for everybody to enjoy it. It made me laugh, it made me cry, and I am sure it will stay with me for a long time.

-Audiobook Reviews

Denver City Justice

What the author chiefly delivers in *Denver City Justice* is an amusing, suspenseful, well-written story that will tug at your heartstrings and tickle your funny bone.

-Colorado Book Review

Denver City Justice is a slapstick romp through early-day Denver with an assortment of characters both real and imagined.

-Sandra Dallas, *The Denver Post*

Murder at Buckskin Joe

Murder at Buckskin Joe

A Colorado Historical Novel

J.v.L. Bell

A Mexican Arrastra

REVERBERANT
M E D I A

ISBN: (Paper): 978-0-9969144-4-4
ISBN : (EBOOK): 978-0-9969144-5-1
ISBN: (Audio): 978-0-9969144-6-8

Cover design: Nikki Rasmussen
Cover photograph © 2021 Clifford M. Conklin
Title Page Artwork: Annie Carter
Cover photographed in the Stamp Mill at the Western Museum of Mining & Industry in Colorado Springs.

Reverberant Media, LLC
Louisville, Colorado
Author Website: www.JvLBell.com

Library of Congress Control Number: 2021914527

For my extended family of friends. I couldn't write without your love, support, and encouragement!

Author's Note

Although this novel is fiction, I love researching history and I try to be as accurate as possible. Gold was discovered at Buckskin Joe in August of 1860 and the Phillips Lode was discovered soon thereafter. The Phillips Lode was extraordinarily rich, attracting over 1000 men (some sources say up to 3000 men.) By the summer of 1862, Buckskin Joe had transformed from a rough mining camp to a full-fledged town with nine stamp mills, two hotels, a bank, and numerous stores. It became the county seat of Park County, and in 1862, over 300 men were employed by just the Phillips Mine. Unfortunately, by the fall of 1863, the Phillips Lode played out and almost overnight, Buckskin Joe became a ghost town.

The descriptions and history I've used throughout this novel are from Buckskin Joe's boom years, between 1861-1863. I apologize for changing the dates of the history in this book, but South Park is one of my favorite areas in Colorado and I couldn't resist resurrecting Buckskin Joe and letting Millie and Dom (and my readers) enjoy its boom days.

As always, I apologize for any historical mistakes, especially mining details. Thanks for being a reader and please email me at Julie@JvLBell.com or send me a comment through my website at www.JvLBell.com and let me know what you think of *Murder at Buckskin Joe!*

-Julie

Murder at Buckskin Joe

ONE

April 18, 1865

Fried Porcupine Cutlets

"**I** swear, the tomfoolery of those children will drive me to murder," Millie said, her Southern accent rolling her a's and stretching tomfoolery into five syllables. Her husband, Dom, mumbled a nonverbal response as he used her dish rag to wipe off a white and black speckled rock with small blue crystals, something he'd called Fluorite and Sphalerite. He sat at their rough wooden table, his back to Millie, his tools neatly laid out as he prepared to do a fire assay. Millie shook her head knowing Dom hadn't heard a word she'd said.

Sighing, she turned her attention to the slab of bloody flesh lying on her prized Charter Oak cookstove. None of her beloved cookbooks offered advice on porcupine, but Millie had seen the pride in the eyes of their adopted son, Hosa, when he presented his kill. He'd even offered Millie the raw heart—a cherished morsel in his Arapaho culture. Millie had politely accepted the kill but refused the morsel, looking away as he eagerly devoured it.

To Millie, the porcupine heart was just one more example of the difficulty of raising an Arapaho son. Last November, she'd saved Hosa's life after Colorado soldiers massacred his mother, along with most of his peaceful tribe. Millie brought the eleven-year-old boy home, but she often wondered if her skills as a mother—or lack thereof—were adequate to raise the boy, no matter how much she loved him. The thought brought another and she turned back to Dom. "Has Hosa talked to you about wanting a horse?"

"Course." Dom rose and stretched, his wide shoulders flexing under his flannel shirt in a way Millie found particularly mesmerizing. They'd been married just over a year and Millie never tired of admiring Dom's muscular frame. "Just about every day."

"He thinks his father is still alive." Just this morning, after devouring the porcupine heart, Hosa had reminded Millie he planned to join his people in the fight against white soldiers. His words had broken her heart. With Lee's surrender at Appomattox, the War of the Rebellion would soon be done, and America would turn its attention to its Indian problems. The Plains Indians didn't stand a chance.

"Hosa's father may still be alive." Dom turned and gave Millie a one-armed hug. "We can only do our best. Keep the boy focused on schoolwork and chores. You know, mother stuff."

"*Mother stuff?*" Millie eyed her husband with annoyance. He knew she'd been raised in an orphanage. Motherhood terrified her. "Dominic Drouillard! Hosa needs a mother *and* a father. You could teach him how to assay gold. Maybe we should get him a horse."

Dom gave her a long kiss that made her toes curl. "We're both doing our best, but we have to be prepared. If his father is alive and comes looking, we can't stop Hosa from leaving."

Tears pricked Millie's eyes, but she swallowed hard and decided there was no use borrowing trouble. Hopefully, it would never come to that. Dom returned to his assay and she turned and poked the firm, dark meat with her knife, deciding it cut a bit like chicken. Fried porcupine cutlets seasoned with salt and mace shouldn't taste too bad, especially if she rolled them in flour, egg, and breadcrumbs.

The meat was soon sizzling on the stove, although Millie found the smell rather unappetizing. Considering what else she could add to the meal, she retrieved turnips and set them in a pot to boil, but her thoughts were interrupted by a heavy hand striking their door. Dom glanced at her and asked, "You expecting anyone?"

Millie shook her head. As Dom rose and walked toward the door, she slipped her hand into her apron pocket and wrapped her fingers around the smooth grip of her six-shooter. After almost two years of living in the Colorado Territory, she'd learned to carry her gun everywhere—even inside her own home.

Another reverberating thump shook the door, causing the leather hinges to stretch. Dom jerked it open and a huge fist came down, striking his chest with enough force it would have sent a small man to the floor. Dom just grunted and staggered backward.

Millie drew her gun as a large figure stomped into the cabin, bringing in snow from yesterday's late spring storm. The stranger's salt-and-pepper beard stuck out in all directions, looking slightly frozen as it tangled with the man's long gray hair. He wore a lynx fur hat that had been fashioned so the animal's ears stuck straight up, the nose hung over his thick forehead, and the legs dangled on either side of his face. A hairy, buffalo skin robe completed his ensemble, giving Millie the impression of a spring grizzly just crawling out from his cave.

"You Dominic Drouillard?" The stranger's voice carried the distinct twang of a French-Canadian trapper, but it was the man's nose and eyes—or what Millie could see of them—that caused her to gasp and almost drop her weapon. Although his eyes were dark brown—not the blue of a Colorado sky—his big bushy eyebrows and the shape of his nose were awfully familiar.

"Who wants to know?" Dom snarled, stepping forward until his nose was inches away from the stranger's.

"Your uncle," bellowed the man. The newcomer wrapped his thick arms around Dom and lifted him off the ground. "*Merde*, last time I saw you, nephew, you were knee high to a grasshopper and playing marbles with your brother, Johannes. You forced me to waste an entire afternoon while you showed me every stone in your blasted collection." He released Dom, dropping him with a thump, and stepped back. "I'm George Drouillard. *Mamam* named me after my papa, your grandpapa."

Millie saw the family resemblance. The stranger looked fit, but he had to be sixty, or maybe older. Perhaps when he was younger, he'd been as handsome as Dom, but now this Drouillard looked hard-used and had an unpleasant, pungent odor wafting off him.

Dom—apparently unbothered by the smell and unable to see the likeness—scowled and narrowed his eyes. He fisted his hands on his hips and bellowed, "I don't have an uncle."

"Still as stubborn as a jackass, are you?" The man slammed the door and stripped off his heavy coat, getting it tangled with a long, beaded knife sheath. He carefully untangled his coat before dropping the snowy garment onto the floor. He thumped Dom's shoulder. "Don't you remember my visit?" Casually he added his gloves and hat to the wet pile.

Millie narrowed her eyes. Did he expect a servant, or maybe a slave, to clean up after him? Even the children had better manners. "Sir," she said curtly, "wet—"

"Your father was my half-brother," the newcomer spoke over Millie. "While traveling with Captains Lewis and Clark, my papa spent time with my *Maman's* people, the *Nay Persay*, or Nez Perce as you Americans call them. They're a friendly tribe and *Maman* was obviously very, very friendly. She weren't the only one." The big man chuckled. "There were several light-skinned children born nine months after Lewis and Clark's visit. I used to play with Clark's son, Hal-lah-too-kit."

"Gramps Drouillard traveled with Lewis and Clark?" Dom asked as Millie blurted out at the same time, "William Clark fathered an Indian son?"

"Papa was Lewis and Clark's hunter." The man casually thumped Dom's back again, grinning. "I'm your long-lost Uncle George."

Millie felt a shiver run up her spine. This stranger was indeed a Drouillard, no doubt about it. She was equally certain his arrival boded trouble.

TWO

April 18, 1865

Uncle George

Dom looked dazed and didn't respond as George bent down and untied the lace on his thigh-high boot. Casually he pulled the boot off and tossed the dripping leather toward his clothing. Millie narrowed her eyes, but before she could ask him to clean up his wet attire, the leather strap of his other boot snapped. *"Maudit!"* he spat out, adding a volley of French as he angrily flung the broken strap onto the floor.

"Sir!" Millie said sharply. "There is absolutely no swearing in this house." She might not have understood a word of what he'd said, but the man's intonations were just like Dom's when he used improper language.

George replied with an ugly, *"Putain!"* and jerked off the second boot, throwing it against the cabin's wall. "That was my last seal-skin strap."

"Sir," Millie said louder, "There is no swearing in my home. And throwing—"

"Gramps was Lewis and Clark's hunter?" Dom asked,

interrupting her. "Pa never spoke about my grandpa, but surely he'd have mentioned something like that."

"Doubt it." The big man kicked the wet pile of clothes toward the wall. "Your grandpapa was the son of a Shawnee and a French-Canadian trapper. Hell of a man, but I doubt your papa ever mentioned him." His expression softened. "I stayed with your family for a month when you were a little pup. Your *maman* was a *real* lady. She come from blue blood. The kind of family that wouldn't want a mixed breed for a son-in-law. Bet your pa never mentioned he was part Indian. Man had enough trouble convincing her family to let him marry her. He were just a poor miner, way beneath them."

Millie had never met any of Dom's family, but he'd told her numerous stories about growing up near Harrods Creek, Kentucky where he and his brother, Johannes, had run wild, sounding even worse than Hosa. After their parents passed, Dom and his brother came west together and settled near Idaho Springs. Dom had moved on, traveling to mining towns to do gold assays, but Johannes had made Idaho Springs his home. He'd advertised for a wife and Millie had answered. She'd arrived in Idaho Springs days after Johannes' death, murdered as it turned out.

"My pa wasn't poor," Dom said slowly, his brow furrowing. "Maybe he weren't rich, but he worked hard and provided a good home for Ma and us boys. He told me his grandma raised him. Said his pa died when he was young."

Dom's uncle nodded and strode past the kitchen table, reaching above Millie's cookstove and grabbing the morning bread. Speechless, Millie watched as the man ripped off the end of the loaf—his hands filthy—and shoved it into his mouth. Speaking as he chewed, he said, "When I was twelve or thirteen—*Maman* weren't never sure when I were born—I took off looking for my papa. Found out he went trapping in Blackfeet country and never came back. Heard he'd been a hell of a backwoodsman, but *putain*, Blackfeet are devils."

"Sir!" Millie jammed her six-shooter back into her apron so hard she heard a seam rip. "In this house there is *no* cursing, we hang wet clothing on the nails by the door, and we use knives, forks, and plates like *civilized* people. This is a home, not a pigsty."

George turned and raised his thick eyebrows as his eyes tracked down every inch of her body. Millie felt her face heat and her temper flare. He was examining her like a merchant considering a purchase. "Fine looking woman you got here, Nephew. Which house you find her in? There's this strumpet in—"

"Mr. Drouillard!" Millie's mouth snapped shut and she sucked in an angry breath. "How dare you?"

"Uncle George," Dom quickly hurried to Millie's side. "This is my wife, Millie. She's—"

"Guess her fine figure overcame that flaming red hair, but that Southern accent." George shook his head and shrugged. "Women are scarce, but still."

"Uncle George!" Dom snapped. "Millie's my wife. She's a lady and you'll treat her as such."

Millie appreciated Dom's harsh words, but she wanted Dom to throw the buffoon—kin or not—out of her house. Knowing Dom's soft spot for family, she turned to her stove and picked up the bloody meat cleaver she'd used on the porcupine. Spinning around, she poked George's filthy, rawhide covered chest with the knife's point. "You, sir, are rude. I don't care if you're related to President Lincoln himself. In my presence you will act like a gentleman or—"

"Glad I ain't related to our murdered President," George said cheerfully, stuffing the last of the bread into his mouth, looking totally unconcerned by Millie and the knife. "Else I'd have to pretend to be in mourning."

"Our murdered President?" The tip of Millie's cleaver dropped, leaving a trail of blood down the man's fringed, buckskin shirt. "What do you mean, murdered?"

"Reb shot him." George brushed away the knife like it was an annoying mosquito and helped himself to another chunk of bread. "At least there won't be no more quaint stories. I shudder whenever I hear the words, 'That reminds me...' That man's stories were awful. I—"

"President Lincoln can't be dead!" Millie's voice rose shrilly. She'd been raised in New Orleans, but since arriving in the Colorado Territory, she'd become friendly with her neighbor, Mary, a free black woman. Millie wouldn't have survived without Mary's friendship and help. Over time, Mary had changed Millie's attitude toward slavery and the south. "Lincoln's celebrating Lee's surrender to Grant. He's—"

"He's deader than a worn-out whore. Killed while watching a play at Ford's Theater. Your sheriff read the story aloud last night in Diefendorf's saloon. Said it had to be true since it was printed in the *Daily Mining Journal*."

"No!" The cleaver dropped from Millie's numb fingers, stabbing into the wood floor inches from George's stockinged foot. The big man jumped backward, but Millie barely noticed. President Lincoln couldn't be dead. The country needed him. His wisdom, his compassion, and even his homey stories. Without Lincoln, America, divided by the War, might never heal. "He's really dead?"

"Yep. Move, tart." George stepped around the knife and pushed Millie aside. "Hope she keeps you happy in bed, Nephew," he said, reaching for the stove. "It appears her cooking is challenged." He moved the frypan off the heat. "This porcupine almost burned, although it still smells mighty fine. I'm starving."

"Uncle George." Dom sounded exasperated. "I'm pleased to meet kin, but you need to apologize to Millie. You'll treat her like a lady or you'll have to leave."

Despite her shock over Lincoln, Millie felt infuriated and frustrated. With his entire family dead, she knew Dom was thrilled to discover an uncle. Still, family or not, this George Drouillard wasn't the kind of man she wanted in her cabin.

Narrowing his eyes, George glanced from Millie to Dom, his expression suddenly blank. In a solicitous tone he said politely, "My apology, *Mrs. Drouillard*. I assumed, well, never mind. No offense meant." Like a polished gentleman—or an excellent actor—he took Millie's hand, bowed down, and kissed it. "It is a pleasure to make the acquaintance of my nephew's wife."

Millie felt the hairs on the back of her neck rise. Rude, loud behavior she knew how to handle—she was married to Dom after all—but this sudden personality shift felt sly and practiced. Why had this man looked them up? Millie doubted it had anything to do with *him* seeking a family. Still, if he could act politely, she could too. "Your apology is accepted, Mr. Drouillard." She pulled her hand from his. "You may address me as Mrs. Drouillard. I expect polite behavior and allow absolutely no cursing." She stepped over, bent down, and jerked the cleaver from the floor, slapping it down on their wooden table. "Finally, I will tell you once, and only once: my hair is *auburn* with a *few* red streaks!"

George threw back his head and roared. His laughter cracked like a gun, shaking his whole body. When he finally got his mirth under control, he turned and slapped Dom on the back. "*Ayoille!* Folks said you married a hellca—ah, a lady. But enough about her and our dead president. I came around because kin helps kin and I need help."

"You need help?" Millie asked. More forcefully, she added, "What did you do?"

"Nothin'," George said, averting his eyes. "I got a mine called the Three Rings. It's located near Buckskin Joe, in South Park. Mined it with my partner, Wandering Will, for nearly a year. Last month we uncovered a promising gold lode, one that would make us rich. Then Wandering Will got murdered. Townsfolk come after me with a lynching rope, saying I killed him. They forced me from town." He shook his head in disgust, his beard jerking with the motion. "They just wanted me gone so they could jump my claim."

Untrustworthiness wafted off George stronger than his unpleasant odor. "Why didn't the local miners' court help you?" asked Millie.

"The miners' court," George snarled. "Buckskin Joe's miners' court deliberately looked the other way, as did its sheriff. *Maudit!* Sheriff Finch would rather bake pies than keep the law. None of them objected when them Odd Fellows tried to string me up."

"They tried to hang you without a trial?" Dom asked indignantly.

"What do you mean, Odd Fellows?" Millie found most miners odd, but George made the term sound specific.

"The Order of the Odd Fellows. One of them so-called gentlemen's clubs. The kind that promises to bury you if you die. Them Odd Fellows claimed Wandering Will left his half of the Three Rings to them and then they run me out of town. They wanted it all." He flung his arm casually over Dom's shoulder. "I ended up in Georgetown and heard talk of an assayer named Drouillard. Thought I'd take a look-see and find out if we were related. What do you say, Nephew? Help me prove my innocence and we can go into business together. You can become my new partner."

Dom grinned and looped his arm over George's shoulder, obviously forgetting George's rude words toward Millie. "Family always helps family. *Of course*, I'll go with you to Buckskin Joe."

Millie scowled. Dom wouldn't be going anywhere without her, especially not with this untrustworthy new relation. But she knew her husband. Before either of them began planning a trip, she wanted some details about George's partner's death. Lifting her own eyebrows, she asked, "Mr. Drouillard, *you* didn't murder your partner, did you?"

THREE

April 18, 1865

A Lady Never Swears

Dom didn't give George time to answer Millie's accusation. "Course Uncle George didn't kill his partner, Millie. He's family." Dom pulled George toward the table. "Have a seat. Millie's a great cook, but she's never cooked porcupine." Dom smiled and shook his head. "Imagine, another Drouillard. Who'd have thought? After Johannes died, I assumed all my kin were gone. We need to celebrate. I've been saving some Taos Lightning for a special occasion. You just sit tight, and I'll get it from the root cellar."

Millie watched Dom stride toward the back door, idly wondering where he'd hidden his whiskey. As the door slammed, Millie lifted her eyebrows and nodded toward the growing puddle surrounding George's clothing. "Mr. Drouillard, coats are hung on the nails near the door; boots are set by the stove; the shelves are for wet hats and gloves. Here's a rag to wipe up the floor."

"Course." George winked at her. "I like your

directness, *Mrs. Drouillard.* Please, call me George."

Millie ignored the invitation. Despite living in the rough mining town of Idaho Springs deep in the Rocky Mountains, she always tried to emulate her heroine Florence Hartley, the author of *The Ladies' Book of Etiquette.* Of course, past experience had taught her that when it came to murder, proper etiquette and well-bred behavior wasn't always possible, although one could try. Politely she asked, "Mr. Drouillard, did you murder your partner?"

He choked as he bent to pick up his coat. "I'm family, ma'am, just like your husband said. Would I come here and ask for help if I—"

The back door banged open. "Heat some water, Millie. Hurry!" Dom's booted feet shook the cabin's rough plank floors as he rushed into the room, a bottle cradled in one arm and their six-year-old daughter, Rachel, in the other. The little girl was Dom's illegitimate daughter and had arrived soon after Hosa, leaving Millie, who had never wanted children, suddenly the mother of two. Dom left a trail of snow as he carried Rachel toward Millie, the child's mittened hands wrapped around the wooden bucket Millie used for hauling wash water.

"Dom, take her back outside and shake off…" Millie's words petered out as she saw the child's profile. Rachel's tongue was out of her mouth, stuck against the iron hoop that held the oak staves of the bucket together. The child's blue eyes, the same color as her father's, sparked as she grunted and tried to free her tongue. She looked madder than a wet hen.

"I see." Millie shook her head and frowned as Buttercup, her pet goat, hurried inside, every inch of her covered in snow. Millie itched to brush them all off, but that would have to wait. "Hold Miss Rachel over my dish bucket, Dom." She tested the water in the kettle, added cold water so it wouldn't scald, and began pouring warm water down the child's face.

"Did Hosa make you do this?" Dom huffed, struggling not to drop the writhing child or his bottle of whiskey.

"Shoo." George waved his hands at Buttercup, looking almost afraid of the little goat.

"Leave her be," Millie said over Rachel's loud gurgling sounds. "My goat is allowed in the cabin, but I'd appreciate if you'd brush the snow off her."

"You let a goat into your cabin?" George shook his head and moved closer to Dom, squinting at Rachel. "Who's the kid? She's got Drouillard eyes, but folks said you two ain't been married but a year."

Millie didn't intend to explain the history of Dom's illegitimate daughter or why Buttercup was allowed in the cabin, so she ignored both questions. Pouring more water over Rachel's head, Millie winced when the child's tongue ripped free.

"I gonna kill that boy," Rachel said, her speech gargled. She added several crude curses that caused Dom to start. He dropped his bottle and George deftly caught it.

"Rachel," Dom said sharply. "Those are *very* bad words. Did Hosa teach them to you?"

Rachel squirmed from his arms, landed with a thump on the floor, and shook out her black, curly locks, sending water and snow everywhere. "No, Pa," she said, scowling. "I learned them words from you."

Dom blanched, but Millie had almost four months

experience dealing with Rachel and Hosa. Distraction, she'd found, was her best weapon. "Miss Rachel, you are never to use those words again. Now explain why you licked the iron hoop around my bucket?"

"That Hosa!" The little girl's face burned red, and her expression turned murderous. Millie had no doubt Hosa had goaded—or dared—Rachel to lick the frozen metal, but unlike Dom, her sympathy for the little girl was limited. Hosa was rough-and-tumble trouble, direct and impetuous, but a poor liar. Rachel, on the other hand, had an angelic face that hid a rabble-rouser with a devious mind, and the child lied better than a professional gambler.

Behind Dom, George pulled the stopper from the whiskey bottle and took a healthy swig. Millie scowled as she squatted in front of Rachel and used her sternest schoolmarm voice as she said, "Miss Rachel, swearing is always inappropriate. After what you did to Hosa yesterday, you can hardly blame him for getting even. You will change into a dry smock and afterwards write fifty times in your daybook, *A lady never swears.*" Millie rose, took the child's hand, and led her toward the children's bedroom. "Dom, brush the snow off Buttercup and out of the cabin."

"You got any children?" Dom asked George.

"None I've been told about." Millie heard sounds of Dom sweeping as George asked, "What's with the goat? Fattening her up for tomorrow's dinner is fine, but why let her into the cabin?"

"Buttercup is Millie's pet goat." Dom laughed. "She's sort of like a dog, but when trouble shows up, instead of protecting the house, she faints. She and her daughter,

Hosa's goat Nanko, live in the cabin with us. Don't worry, they're usually good about going outside for their business."

"You let your wife keep goats in the cabin?" George sounded truly horrified. "That one ain't even cute. She's got bulging eyes and floppy ears."

Millie ground her teeth. Buttercup wasn't beautiful, but she'd been Millie's only companion when Millie first arrived in Idaho Springs. Her family might not be typical, but she loved Rachel, Hosa, Dom, and Buttercup.

"I wouldn't make fun of Buttercup, George, and don't ever mention roasting her." Dom spoke in what he considered a whisper, although his words carried clearly throughout the three-room cabin. "Millie's a little sensitive in that area."

"You know, boy, letting your wife wear the trousers makes you look like a milksop." George burped loudly. "A good wallop usually solves any problems."

"What's a milksop?" Rachel asked in her high-pitched voice.

"Come," Millie said, barely keeping her temper under control. "You need to write *A lady never swears.*" Although she was having difficulty following her own good advice. "You'll write it fifty times." Millie stomped from the bedroom and ran into Hosa and his goat Nanko. The two were pressed against the wall in the walkway to the back door, the boy peeking around the corner at George and Dom.

"You are in *so* much trouble," Rachel said angrily. "When you sleep, I'm gonna—"

"Miss Rachel!" Millie said sharply. "Get your daybook and sit down at the table. Hosa, you will retrieve your daybook and write *A brother always treats his sister with respect.* Fifty times. Neatly. I'll write the first sentence for both of you." Neat was an exaggeration, but Millie tried. Hosa's English had improved remarkably in the past few months—sometimes it was better than Rachel's—but his letters looked like chicken scratch. Still, the work would keep them both busy.

"Who is that?" Hosa asked, pointing at George as they walked toward the kitchen table.

"This is your Uncle George." Dom lifted his cup and downed his whiskey before rising from the table and stepping over to the children. Gently he rested a hand on Hosa's shoulder. "This is Hosa and his goat, Nanko." Ruffling his daughter's hair, he added, "And you haven't been properly introduced to our little girl, Rachel."

"That boy ain't yours," George said flatly. "I know Arapaho filth when I see it."

Hosa let out a war hoop, jerked his hunting knife from its sheath, and dove at George.

FOUR

April 18, 1865
Death by Crinoline?

M illie grabbed for Hosa's arm, but Dom was quicker. He caught the boy mid-stride and lifted him off his feet. Hosa's knife arm flailed wildly. Millie stumbled backward, but not quick enough. The sharp blade sliced through her long, bell-shaped sleeve, cutting the material halfway to the elbow. Millie cried out and both Buttercup and Nanko tumbled to the ground in dead faints.

"Easy does it, son." Dom held Hosa's knife arm firmly and glared at his kin. "Uncle George shouldn't be so rude. He's part Indian too. He'll apologize *right* now."

"He is enemy," growled the child, struggling against Dom's hold. "I will—"

"Look what you did to my sleeve!" Millie held out her arm.

Hosa froze, his eyes widening. Dom took a step back, tripped over the comatose Buttercup, and dropped Hosa. The boy landed on his feet, but his knife arm swept downward, and he sliced off Nanko's beard. Crying out in horror, he dropped to his knees and cradled his goat, gently probing for damage.

For an instant, the room went silent.

"Got yourself a nice, cozy little family," George said into the quiet.

"Now you is really in trouble," Rachel said to Hosa. "After Miss Millie skins you alive, we can punish Pa's kin."

"Miss Millie?" George laughed. "Your kid don't even call you *Maman*?"

Millie wanted to throttle the lot of them—starting with George—but she felt hurt along with her anger. Rachel called Dom, Pa, but she'd never called Millie, Momma. Millie had never said anything, but the more she'd grown to love the child, the more it hurt.

Hosa slipped his knife back into its sheath, helped Nanko onto her feet, and turned to Millie. "Sorry, Miss Millie."

Millie knelt in front of the boy. "Hosa, you *must* control your temper. If your knife had landed differently, you could have killed Nanko. You can't fly into a rage just because someone insults you."

"Sure are careless with knives 'round here." George took a swig from the whiskey bottle. "Course allowing goats and savages into your home is part of the problem."

Millie stood and strode over, grabbing the bottle from his hand. "Shut up you dunderhead! One more word and you're out of my cabin. Permanently."

Behind her, she heard Dom and the children gasp. Millie closed her eyes and took several deep breaths, feeling a bit calmer when Dom moved beside her and wrapped his arm around her. "George, if you can't be polite to my family, kin or not, you'll need to leave."

George's expression turned sour. He muttered a curt apology, not even trying to make it sound sincere. After an awkward silence, Millie placed the Taos Lightning on the shelf above the stove, took away Hosa's knife as punishment, and settled Hosa and Rachel at the table—as far from George as possible. The children began writing and Millie turned to her stove to mash turnips. Behind her, chairs scraped as Dom and George sat at the table. For the next few minutes, other than her meal preparations, the room was silent.

"Supper's ready," Millie said curtly. "Children, please put away your work and set the table." She glanced at George. "Mr. Drouillard, we do not have extra cutlery or dishes. Do you have a pack or provisions?"

"Out with my burro in the barn." He sullenly rose and retrieved his boots. "I'll grab what I need. I'll plan to bed down in your barn, unless you have room in here?"

Dom opened his mouth, but Millie was quicker. "The barn will be fine, sir." Normally they invited guests to sleep near the cookstove, but Millie saw no reason to extend an invitation to George. In addition, with George outside, she might hear if Hosa opened the door and tried to sneak out. The boy wasn't mean, but his Arapaho honor would require retribution. Millie would need to keep a close eye on him.

After everyone settled around the table, she served the burnt cutlets and mashed turnips. Finally taking her place at the table, she sipped her tea and realized she'd have to keep her eye on Rachel too. Alone, the children fought like siblings, but as the Idaho Springs schoolmistress often pointed out, an insult to either caused both to take offense. Hosa would obey Millie's rules, but not Rachel. The little girl would bide her time, looking and acting like a little angel, but when she got the chance, no telling what she might do. Best to keep them both as busy as possible while George was around.

"After supper, Mister Hosa, Miss Rachel, you both need to finish your writing and then complete your evening chores." Hosa hated the title so Millie only used it when she wanted to make a point. "In addition, Miss Rachel will darn socks with me and Hosa will fill the wood boxes, both inside and out." She tasted her porcupine cutlet and discreetly pushed it to the side of her plate. It was barely palatable.

"Mighty generous of you to take in an orphan, Nephew." George speared a cutlet with his buck knife and bit off the end, talking as he chewed. "But when we leave for Buckskin Joe, *Mrs. Drouillard,* the children, and especially the goats, can't come. Buckskin Joe ain't civilized like Idaho Springs. It ain't a place for a *lady.*" His intonation indicated he didn't really consider Millie a lady. "Also, we got Utes in Bayou Salado, or South Park as folks up there call it. They're the sworn enemies of the Arapaho. They'd scalp the boy."

Hosa said something in Arapaho and Millie tensed. She didn't understand the words, but clearly, they were *not* polite. She turned and stopped short when Rachel responded in Arapaho. *Lor' Almighty!* Shaking her head, Millie rested a hand on Hosa's shoulder and turned to George. "Hosa became part of our family when he saved my life. Last year we were at the Big Sandy when soldiers attacked. His momma, along with most of his people, were killed in the massacre."

"The Big Sandy?" George cocked his head, looking confused. "Wandering Will told me about that Sand Creek battle. Said it were a big fight between Indians and soldiers."

Millie stared at the man, unable to hide her distaste. "I was there, sir. Uniformed soldiers massacred peaceful Arapaho and Cheyenne on their own reservation. Mostly women and children. It was a disgraceful slaughter." She thought back to that terrible day and shivered. The word massacre wasn't strong enough to describe the horror she'd seen. "After killing hundreds of Indians, the soldiers desecrated the dead. Col. Chivington and his forces should be punished for their inhumane and cowardly actions."

George scowled, stood up, and retrieved the bottle of Taos Lightning. He filled his cup, topped off Dom's, and set the bottle on the table, his eyes daring Millie to say anything. She remained silent only because she was speechless at his impudence. George grinned like he'd won and stuffed an entire strip of meat into his mouth, taking a long swig from his cup.

"You children ever hunt porcupine?" Neither child responded. "They're good emergency food. They're slow, so when you find one, all you got to do is whack it over the head and you got yourself a meal. Course watch out if your porcupine gets away and climbs a tree. They tend to pee on you if they're angry. It's mighty stinky, worse than skunk."

Maybe that was what Millie was smelling. George brought a unique odor to the table.

"*I* kill this porcupine," Hosa spat out. "You teach me

nothing. You are a killer."

The big man eyed the boy speculatively. "Least I'm a Drouillard."

"Uncle George," Dom growled.

"How many people have you murdered?" asked Rachel with more accusation than innocence.

"Murder's a strong word, little girl."

Rachel just stared and Millie realized George hadn't contradicted the child's accusation. "I've seen my share of death." George stretched. "There once was this girl—"

"Uncle George," Dom interrupted quickly. "Millie believes in proper behavior. I don't think her heroine, Florence Hartley, would advise discussing murder during a meal. At least not with the children present."

Despite the tension in the room, Millie almost laughed. She'd tried—and failed—to improve Dom's manners through readings from the *Ladies' Book of Etiquette*. He hated the book so much he'd burned Millie's first copy. For him to use Florence Hartley's name to try and deter George showed true desperation.

"Don't you worry none, Nephew. This here's an educational story for the young lady." Uncle George helped himself to the last of the turnips as he spoke. "When I was a younger man, I courted a *lady*. Sophronia Souter. On March 28 of '55—the day the first train crossed the suspension bridge at Niagara Falls—I visited Sophronia. Invited her to stroll along the cliffs near the train crossing." He speared another porcupine cutlet and dipped it into his turnips before biting off half the cutlet.

"Mr. Drouillard," Millie said, "I—"

"Sophronia's old man didn't approve of a half-breed courting his daughter," George said over Millie, "so he followed us, *chaperoning* he said." He made the word sound like something reprehensible. "Just to annoy the old man, I decided right then and there to propose. Unfortunately, Sophronia was wearing one of those ridiculous crinoline petticoats for our stroll." He paused and wagged the half-eaten cutlet at Rachel. "Never wear one of those silly things. They make you look like a school bell on a stick. My Sophronia's dress stuck out so far, I couldn't even take her arm. I got busy perfecting my proposal as we neared the rim, looking forward to seeing the old man's face when I dropped onto one knee."

He paused and Rachel cocked her head, her eyes bright. Millie knew the girl loved frilly dresses and decided it was time to change the subject. "Mr. Drouillard, perhaps you could tell us about your home in South Park."

"I've heard about gold discoveries in Fairplay Diggings, Tarryall, and Buckskin Joe," Dom added quickly. "Is it true they found gold nuggets the size of watermelon seeds near Tarryall?"

"Don't care about gold watermelons." Rachel planted her elbows on the table and glared at George. "I want to hear about the lady in the purdy dress."

"Pretty dress," Millie corrected automatically.

"Ugh!" Hosa fingered his empty knife scabbard.

"I'm teaching your children an important lesson." George winked at Dom, giving him a wry smile. "You see, by the time we reached the cliffs overlooking Niagara Falls, the blustering wind was a full-blown gale. Still, the spot was perfect for my proposal. I dropped to one knee, smiled as the old man gasped, and then noticed my girl was white as a sheet. She started backing away and I thought she were insulted by my proposal. I jumped up, more than a bit out of temper, then realized she wasn't backing up, she was being blown backwards."

Horrified, Millie interrupted. "Mr. Drouillard! This isn't—"

"I darted forward and made a grab for the foolish woman. Got close enough for a handful of material before Old Sophronia tumbled over the cliff, her petticoats flapping around her drawers. Her scream split the air, even with the roar of the falls."

"She fell into the falls?" Dom looked appalled.

"Yep." George shook the last of his cutlet at Rachel. "Let that be a lesson, little girl. Sophronia's oversized skirt became a wind sail. The newspapers called it 'Death by Crinoline.' Never did find her body."

"That's awful." Millie glanced uncomfortably at the children. She'd never worn a crinoline, but while crossing the Great Plains, she'd once been swept off her feet by a severe wind burst. Wearing a corded petticoat produced what she considered a pleasing silhouette, but it also widened her skirt's profile.

"It were unfortunate," George added, shrugging insolently as he scraped the last of the turnips from his plate into his mouth. "But it weren't murder."

"It was murder if *you* pushed her over the cliff," Hosa said.

FIVE

April 18, 1865
Murder

Relieved to finally tuck the children into bed, Millie changed into her Sunday dress and carried her sliced sleeve to her rocker. The whip-stitching that connected the sleeve to the bodice was undamaged and fortunately the cut was in the underside of the bell sleeve. Her repairs would be noticeable, but mostly hidden by her arm. She eavesdropped on the men's conversation as she worked, growing more concerned as George described the gold vein in the Three Rings and promised to make Dom rich. Millie held her tongue until Dom began making travel plans.

"Before *we* discuss *our* trip to Buckskin Joe, Dom, I believe *we* should learn a bit more about George's partner's death," Millie said, annoyed by his assumption that he would leave without even discussing it with her.

"*We* won't be going, Red. I will." Dom's tone, and his use of the nickname she disliked, raised Millie's ire. She didn't want to make Dom look weak in front of his uncle, but such rudeness could not be ignored.

"Dom—"

"You heard Uncle George." Dom cut her off. "Buckskin Joe isn't a place for a lady." He waved his hand at her as she opened her mouth. "Anyway, you need to stay home and take care of the children."

"I need to stay home and take care of the children?"

He had the good grace to look slightly abashed. Obviously trying to make amends, he added quickly, "We can't leave them here alone."

"No, but I'm sure Miss Mary can care for them while we're away." Mary and her husband Jake were their closest neighbors and friends. Their son Samuel was Hosa's best friend and Mary knew everything there was to know about raising children, or so it seemed to Millie. The children would be left in good hands. No way would she let Dom leave without her. Despite his rough edges, Dom had a heart of gold, but a gullible heart of gold where family was concerned. George felt as trustworthy as a prairie wolf. "If *you* plan to go, then *I'm* coming with you."

"Millie—"

"The only kind of women in Buckskin Joe, *Red*, are the working kind." George eyed her defiantly.

"Mr. Drouillard, you will *not* call me by that impolite nickname." She glared at him. "Understood?"

"Fine," George said sourly. "But Buckskin Joe ain't safe, especially with a killer on the loose."

"The killer is the reason why I'll be coming." Millie lifted her eyebrows and scowled. Dom jutted out his chin in defiance and Millie decided George was bringing out the worst in Dom. "Perhaps Dom failed to mention how

I uncovered the identity of two killers over the past two years. And how *I* saved Dom's life."

Dom's face turned several shades redder. "My wife and I will discuss this in private, George, but on one point I agree. I'd like to hear the details of your partner's murder."

Millie would be accompanying them on the journey. They'd have their private discussion—to keep from injuring Dom's pride—and she would win her point. Returning her attention to her mending, she asked, "Mr. Drouillard, why did folks believe you were responsible for your partner's death?"

"They said I killed him 'cause of the gold. Course I thought Wandering Will's death meant our claim were mine. We shared it fifty-fifty, after all. I didn't know otherwise until after he were dead." He gave Millie a sour look, like it was somehow her fault. "The Odd Fellows Society helped Will write his last testament weeks before he died. He left them everything, including his half of the Three Rings. The president of the Odd Fellows, Milo, was one of the men who run me off."

"If the gold lode is as rich as you say, you did have motive to kill your partner." *Motive.* Millie loved using the term. Last year, after an Idaho Springs woman was murdered, Millie watched a Denver City detective investigate the crime. He'd written everything he learned in a daybook and asked questions about suspects, motives, clues, and proof. Millie now had her own daybook and her fingers itched to write down her observations and theories. "Therefore, I must ask again. Did you murder your partner, Mr. Drouillard?"

"Why would I?" he snarled. "I can't work the claim

alone."

"You can't?" Millie was disappointed.

"To work a vertical shaft mine like Uncle George's," Dom said, "you need someone down below, pulling ore from the mine, and someone on the surface to haul the ore up and process it. George could never do it by himself. He'd need at least one partner."

George slapped Dom on the back. "Now I got a new one, right, Nephew?"

Millie shuddered, not sure which was worse: Dom becoming George's new partner or the thought of spending a day working underground in a mine. For her entire life, Millie had hated dark, closed-in spaces. She couldn't imagine working in a filthy mine. Pushing away the thought, she asked, "How did your partner die?"

"Fell down the mine shaft. Broke his neck."

"Like Miss Sophronia fell off a cliff?" Millie asked.

"I had nothing to do with Will's death," George said, averting his eyes.

Millie thought refusing to hold eye contact was a sure sign of lying. It was also interesting how he hadn't included Sophronia's death in his denial. Finishing her stitches, she knotted her thread and bit off the end.

Dom rubbed his chin and asked, "How'd he fall into the shaft?"

George shifted uneasily and Millie frowned. Why were women expected to sew, manage the household, and raise children? She loved her children and their home, but she had far more confidence in her detecting skills than her mothering ones.

"Someone tossed him in," George said. "After they stabbed him."

"Stabbed?" Dom sipped his whiskey thoughtfully.

Millie put away her thread and needle and glanced over as Buttercup rose and moved into the walkway between the back bedrooms. Millie had heard the children sneak into the hallway and had considered scolding them back into bed, but it didn't seem worth the effort. They'd just wait a bit and get up again.

"George, tell us the whole story, from start to finish." Dom refilled his uncle's tin cup and Millie noticed the bottle of Taos Lightning was now half empty.

"Fine. It happened Saturday morning, three and a half, maybe four weeks ago. I reached my claim and called out but Wandering Will didn't answer. I weren't worried none. After a Friday night, well…" He lifted his thick eyebrows suggestively. "The dancehall girls in Buckskin Joe are *real* friendly on Friday nights and the working girls, well, they can warm a man right up."

"Do these women have anything to do with your partner's death?" Millie asked sarcastically.

George opened his mouth and then closed it. "Maybe." He furrowed his brow. "Wandering Will earned his nickname. He liked variety and had a way with the ladies. They all loved him, and not just the working ones. Maybe one of the women killed him, or maybe a jealous husband."

"Anyone particular come to mind?" Dom asked.

"Well, Queeny. She's a fancy girl. Always charged Will three times her normal fee. Not that she ain't worth the price." His smile made Millie blush. "When Queeny sets her mind to entertain a man, she—"

"Uncle George!" Dom said sharply.

Millie glanced toward the back hallway, half expecting

Rachel's high-pitched voice to ask, "What's a fancy girl?" Wisely, the child remained silent.

"When did you realize something was wrong?" Dom asked, changing the subject. Millie suspected Dom had deliberately changed the subject because he, too, knew Rachel and Hosa were listening.

"You know, Nephew, Queeny would be happy to demonstrate some tips you could try with your wifey. I'll introduce you when we get there."

"Uncle George, do you want my help or not?" Dom asked impatiently. "Explain what happened to your partner."

George's grin turned down and he shot Dom a disgruntled look. "Nothing happened. I started working. Harnessed my burro to the arrastra and Wandering Will's burro to the whim. His burro always stayed with me since he ain't got no barn. Anyway, I tried to get his burro moving, intending to pull up the ore bucket, but the burro couldn't turn the drum and lift the bucket." He refilled his tin cup with whiskey and took a sip.

Millie disliked any kind of liquor, but she remained silent. George's insinuation that Dom was a henpecked husband wasn't true, but she knew it had bothered him. She was a strong-willed and sometimes headstrong woman, but Dom was just as strong. Ignoring the liquor, she asked, "What is a whim, sir, and an arrastra?"

Millie and Dom owned the Lucky Hat Mine which produced small, teardrop-shaped gold nuggets that allowed them to live comfortably, but Millie had never considered how her neighbors worked their vertical shaft mines.

"Don't you know nothin', woman?" George asked.

"The biddy at the Beebee House said you were smart."

"George!" Dom rubbed his brow and shook his head.

George glanced at Dom and sighed. "My apology, Mrs. Drouillard. I was just having a bit of fun."

Millie pressed her lips together. Florence Hartley said, "Never meet rudeness in others with rudeness upon your own part," but Millie was having difficulty following this good advice. "Please explain what a whim and arrastra are," she repeated.

"Sure. Like I said, me and old Wandering Will dug a shaft. It's maybe fifty feet deep. We use a simple wooden frame and a horse whim—a rope hoist operated by a burro. It turns a capstan, a drum, that the rope wraps around. The rope lifts and lowers the ore bucket. To drop into the mine, Will stood in the ore bucket and held onto the rope. The burro would walk in circles, turning the capstan, and lower him down. Will's burro was so well trained, I didn't even need to be there when he went down."

He paused, as if waiting for a question, but Millie just nodded. She'd grown up in New Orleans hauling water from wells and she'd seen deeper wells operated with a horse or burro. She didn't know the contraption was called a whim, but she understood the concept. "Is there a ladder? As backup?"

"Nope. Just the whim and pulley system. Wandering Will rigged it. He was smart that way, a real experienced miner."

"Did you work in the mine, too, sometimes?" Just asking the question made her skin crawl. Once she'd entered the Lucky Hat Mine—to save Buttercup. The experience still gave her nightmares. She was a firm believer that the only time a body should be underground was when it was dead.

George shook his head. "Wandering Will worked underground. That's why I wouldn't want him dead. It took me above and him below to work the mine, and he was the one with experience. He worked in California before coming here. That's where he met Queeny."

"You said Queeny hated Will," Dom said. "How'd they both end up at Buckskin Joe?"

"Queeny was one of Wandering Will's former wives." George laughed. "You might say Will introduced her to her current profession." He rubbed his head and shrugged. "Maybe she did kill him."

Millie made a mental note to add Queeny to her list of suspects, but with the thought came a tinge of apprehension. How would she investigate and interview a working woman?

"So Wandering Will worked below, clearing the ore and filling the bucket?" Dom sipped his drink. "You handled the ore on the surface?"

"Yep. We had a system. When the ore bucket was filled, Will jerked on the rope. I'd get his burro moving and haul the ore to the surface. Then I'd dump the raw ore in the arrastra channel and get my burro moving, grinding it, before I sent the ore bucket back down."

"How'd you separate out the gold?"

"Quicksilver. Later we distilled the amalgamate to recover the gold."

Millie was having trouble following the conversation. She'd heard Dom talk of amalgamating ore, but she didn't really know what it meant, although she doubted the process had anything to do with Wandering Will's murder. Still, best to be make sure. "How does an arrastra work, sir? Quicksilver is mercury, right?"

"Course quicksilver's mercury," George said, giving her a superior look.

"An arrastra's a Spanish ore grinder," Dom explained. "Lots of Hispanos in Southern Colorado. They come up from the New Mexico Territory. An arrastra is a round channel that uses a boulder to crush the ore into powder. Uncle George's burro would drag a grinding stone around the channel. The stone would crush the ore against the arrastra floor. It's cheaper than hauling ore to a stamp mill, assuming you got one."

Millie nodded. "Wandering Will spent all day in the mine?"

"Yep. Like I said, Will was experienced. He even hooked up a nice shaft-head windsail to blow fresh air down."

"If he was such an expert," Millie asked dryly, "how'd he end up falling down your shaft and getting stabbed?"

"He didn't get stabbed in the mine, Millie." Dom glanced at George who nodded his agreement. "Someone ran him through and then dumped his body down the shaft. Wonder if he was dead before someone tossed him in the shaft?"

"He were alive," George said with no emotion as he nudged his tin cup toward Dom. After Dom poured, Millie rose and removed the bottle from the table. George lifted his eyebrows and gave Dom a "you're acting like a milksop" look, but he refrained from commenting on her actions.

"He was stabbed and then dragged into the mine, alive?" Horrified by just the thought, Millie replaced the bottle's stopper and set the bottle back on her shelf.

"Yep," George said sourly. "When we pulled Will out, his neck were clearly broke. He was beat up from the fall, lots of blood, so I didn't notice the stab wounds until the sheriff pointed them out. Sheriff thought someone had run Will through with a bayonet, once in the leg and once in the shoulder above his heart. The sheriff pointed out blood and drag marks that showed Will struggled against whoever hauled him into the Three Rings."

"The sheriff was at your mine?" Millie found trying to follow George's description of the murder as difficult as understanding his mining details.

"Not at first. When the burro couldn't lift the ore bucket, I began worrying something were wrong. After messing with it for a bit, I went to town. Old Haw Tabor, the local shopkeep, offered to help and grabbed a rope. Sheriff Finch, who'd been buying flour at Haw's store, joined us." George paused, picked up his tin cup, saw it was empty, and put it back down.

"When we got to the Three Rings, Haw offered to go down the shaft. We lowered him by hand, and he hollered that Wandering Will was down there, dead." He shrugged. "I assumed Will got drunk and fell in. It happens. Weren't till we hauled the body out that I realized there were problems. Sheriff gave me a funny look and then pointed out the stab wounds and drag marks." George shook his head, his expression resentful. "I didn't realize they thought I done it until several of them Odd Fellows come round, talking about lynching me."

SIX

May 5, 1865
Uncle George's Home

Millie trudged along a rough trail and glanced again at her pocket watch before sliding it into her apron. It was one o'clock in the afternoon. George had sworn they'd reach his cabin before their midday meal, but of course by now, she should know better than to believe anything George said. Her feet ached and her skirts were filthy, dragged through so much mud they were weighed down with clumps of grime. Her nose had peeled despite her bonnet, and she smelled almost as bad as George. It was time for their journey to end. Millie wanted a bath and to live inside four solid walls—preferably free from George's unpleasant company.

Not that she hadn't enjoyed some of their travels, but after several weeks on the road, she was bone tired. They'd chosen the southern route—a bit longer than heading north but it had fewer high passes and Dom had hoped, less late spring snow. From Idaho Springs they'd climbed up Floyd Hill and over to Bergen Park, enjoying a night at the Bergen stagecoach station. From there they'd followed a decent wagon road down to Bear Creek, but then the trail turned rough. It only got worse as they passed through Bradford Junction and headed up Kenosha Hill. They'd climbed up and up and up. Millie felt like the hill lasted forever, but despite her weariness, the scenery had been lovely, filled with bubbling brooks, tall evergreens, and towering rock formations.

Finally, they reached the Kenosha House and spent two nights under a solid roof with someone else doing the cooking. Millie hadn't been impressed with the food, but she'd been happy to have a break.

They'd left the Kenosha House on a clear, crisp morning. The weather had been beautiful, although the top of Kenosha Hill was covered in deep, wet snow. Finally, they'd made the summit and began their descent and Millie got her first glimpse of South Park, or the Bayou Salado as George called it.

The view had taken her breath away.

The Bayou Salado was a wide, flat valley with pinnacles of land protruding from a carpeted, green landscape, looking like islands in an emerald lake. Silver streams flowed through the landscape and blue, pine-clad mountains surrounded the basin, their snowy summits piercing a cloudless indigo sky. It was the most magical landscape Millie had ever seen. Unfortunately, the magic slowly dissipated as they trudged down and headed across the green expanse. By the time they passed through the mining town of Hamilton and reached Fairplay Diggings, Millie was footsore and ready to be done.

She'd resupplied in Fairplay Diggings at George's insistence, although Millie couldn't imagine Buckskin Joe could have prices worse than what she'd paid in Fairplay. The Indian wars and native attacks on freight trains crossing the Great Plains had made prices soar, but in Fairplay they were downright criminal! She'd paid over forty dollars for ten pounds of flour and thirty for a bushel of potatoes. Dom had loaded her purchases on George's burro, and they'd left the lush grasslands behind and headed toward the towering mountains.

George led them along a rough road in the direction of a narrow valley situated between snowy mountains. Millie felt like she was walking toward a giant cave and George, after noticing her unease, immediately launched into the story of the Espinosa killers who had terrorized South Park in 1863. He had taken particular delight in detailing the murder that had occurred along the remote path they were now following.

"Be there within an hour," George hollered, interrupting Millie's bleak thoughts. "Buckskin Joe's down valley. Thought we'd head straight to my cabin. You can visit town tomorrow."

"Is your cabin big enough for all of us?" Millie asked for the umpteenth time, although she didn't really expect an answer. George, she'd learned, could discuss working women and gold, but little else.

"It ain't that big," George answered, surprising her. "But there's room for a tent in front and Dom's burro can stay in my barn."

Millie scowled. She wanted a roof over her head and a cabin big enough for all of them. Pausing, she turned and glanced back at the caravan behind her, shaking her head. She still couldn't believe they'd given in to the children's demands.

The night after they'd heard the details of Wandering Will's murder, Millie and Dom had had their private conversation and of course Millie had won her point. Dom had grudgingly agreed she might be useful as a cook, but his enthusiasm increased when she reminded him of a month or two of private nights. They both loved Hosa and Rachel, but Rachel had an unfortunate habit of bursting into their bedroom at the most inopportune moments.

After settling the details between themselves, they had informed the children of their decision. Hosa and Rachel had listened politely, appearing pleased as Millie explained they would spend the summer with Mary's family. Afterwards, they'd nodded and gone outside to play. Or so Millie had thought.

That afternoon, when Millie called them in for supper, Hosa had taken a bite of his meal, chewed thoughtfully, and said resolutely, "We come with you to Buckskin Joe." He'd risen and rested a hand on Millie's arm, his eyes on George. "I do not trust Arapaho enemy. I come to protect Miss Millie, but first I need a horse."

Millie wasn't sure how to respond to such a statement. She appreciated Hosa's concern for her, but not his total disregard for their decision. Stumbling, she tried a bribe, offering to bring him back a horse if he stayed home and took care of Rachel. Dom had nodded in agreement, emphasizing Hosa needed to stay to help protect Rachel.

Hearing her father's words, Rachel had stomped over and looked up at him, her hands planted on her hips. "We is both coming, Pa. If you leave us, we'll sneak out of Miss Mary's cabin and follow you. She can't lock us up forever.

The little girl had looked so sweet and innocent, dressed in a new green dress decorated with ribbons and flounce, but Millie had no doubt Rachel would do exactly as she threatened. She didn't understand it. Winning arguments with Dom and Hosa was no problem, but when Rachel made up her mind, nothing could change it.

After a heated discussion, Millie and Dom were somehow convinced that they should bring Hosa, Rachel, Buttercup, and Dom's burro, Columbine, to Buckskin Joe. Hosa chose to leave his goat, Nanko, behind, worried about the Ute threat.

Millie had finished the conversation, and the evening, by informing Hosa he would not be receiving a horse. Insurrection would not be rewarded. Now they trudged along in a line, looking as George said, like a traveling circus.

Hosa moved cautiously through the shadowed pine trees, watching and listening, pausing every couple steps to check his surroundings or drop to his knees to examine a track. Since they'd entered Ute territory, the boy had transformed into a young Indian brave. The Utes were the sworn enemies of the Arapaho and Hosa didn't intend to be ambushed.

Rachel rode Columbine and led Bluebell, the name she'd given to George's burro. Following at the end, Buttercup paused occasionally to graze, fainting dead if a deer or other animal startled her. Millie sighed. Hers was a patchwork family, but after weeks of George's company, she would take a family she could choose over blood kin any day.

"This here's my homestead," George called, interrupting Millie's thoughts. She looked up and saw Dom cringe. Resigned, she strode out from the thick evergreens into an open meadow with a grove of quaking aspen on one side and a tiny brook on the other. Turning, she looked in the direction George indicated and groaned.

"It's not that bad," George grumbled.

"Not bad? Not bad!" Millie stared at George's homestead. "That's not a cabin, it's a chicken coop!" George's home consisted of a slanted structure that looked like it might blow over during the next storm. Beside it were two smaller buildings—presumably, an outhouse and the barn. Not only did his cabin look uninhabitable, but even from this distance she could smell the barn and outhouse.

"I sleep in a tent," said Hosa. "That cabin have lice, ticks, or worse."

"Yuck! Bet the inside's a pigsty." Rachel dropped Bluebell's lead, slipped off Columbine, and landed in front of Buttercup. The little goat bleated and fainted. Columbine sniffed at the pile of fur and hooves before ambling into the meadow to graze. Bluebell followed, staying right behind Columbine's tail even though her lead was on the ground.

"We will NOT sleep in that." Millie fisted her hands on her hips and turned to face her husband. "No!"

"I'm sure it looks better inside," Dom said doubtfully.

"You can put up a tent," George added. "I'll clean it up a bit and—"

"No!" Millie turned and walked down the trail. "Come children. Miss Rachel, please pick up Miss Buttercup.

Hosa, take the leads of Columbine and Bluebell. We'll return Bluebell once we find a place to stay *in town*."

"But Millie..." Dom said.

"I'm sure Buckskin Joe has a hotel, or maybe an available *clean* cabin." She marched by Dom and George and continued down the trail. "Come children."

"I tell you, boy," George said loud enough for Millie to hear. "You got to show her who wears the trousers in the family."

SEVEN

May 5, 1865
A Duel

Millie strode down the trail, fuming. Florence Hartley advised that a wife should be "a rational friend, a cheerful partner, an interesting companion, or at least, an efficient listener." Dom wasn't a milksop, but there were times when a wife had to put her foot down. She reached the edge of the meadow and George pushed past her. Without looking at her, he hollered, "The Three Rings is near the creek, Dom. The children and Mrs. Drouillard can head on into town while I show you around my mine." Dom barreled past without giving Millie a glance and the two of them disappeared down the trail.

Men! Shaking her head, she made sure the children and animals were following, her thoughts bouncing between useless kin and unfit places to live. Minutes later she reached a Y in the trail, one path leading down toward a bubbling stream, the other heading up a rocky incline covered in mine tailings. The men were nowhere in sight, but above her Millie heard an indignant bellow—one she recognized. Lifting her skirts, she scrambled up the hill.

Five angry men stood facing off, all of them looking furious. Behind them was a structure with a burro harnessed to a long, horizontal plank. The plank formed a T over a stout vertical shaft with a large barrel mounted on top. *George's horse whim?* The rope around the barrel crossed over to a smaller frame with a pully centered over a ten-foot round gaping, black hole, obviously the entrance to George's Three Rings mine.

"Looks like you scofflaws couldn't wait for Wandering Will to get cold in his grave," George hollered. He pointed at a man with dirty blond hair and a long, drooping mustache. "You planned to jump my claim all along, didn't you, Milo."

"Wandering Will was a certified Fellow," replied the man, sneering. "After you run off like a yellow-belly, the miners' court agreed the Odd Fellows lodge inherited the entire claim." Milo looked down his nose and scowled, not quite managing to look superior since he was a full head shorter than George. "After murdering Wandering Will, I'm surprised you got the gumption—"

"I didn't murder Will!" George thundered, moving his hand over the butt of his revolver. "Me and my nephew are here to prove it! We're gonna find the real killer."

Millie stiffened. If Buckskin Joe was anything like Idaho Springs, by tomorrow everyone in town would know who they were and why they were here. Including the killer.

"We know you killed him." Milo stepped forward and shook a filthy finger at George. "You're a greedy half-breed. Wanted all the gold for yourself. Should of…" His voice petered off and his eyes widened as he noticed Millie. "You got a lady, some kids, and a goat over there."

"Gadzooks! A purdy lady." A man with greasy hair streaked in gray turned toward Millie and stared at her, his mouth gaping open. "She's got fiery red hair like a good mountain sunset."

His strong accent was neither Scottish nor British, but something that sounded a bit like both. Millie found it enchanting, until he mentioned her hair. "Sir, my hair is auburn with a few red streaks," she said sharply.

"My mistake, ma'am." The man smiled shyly. "Name's Peran. Peran Cornog. I'm a Welshman and it's a pleasure to make your acquaintance."

Dom hurried to Millie's side and rested what she assumed was a protective hand on her arm. "This is my wife, Mrs. Drouillard, and my children, Hosa and Rachel." Turning toward Millie he introduced Milo and Mr. Cornog, ending with "The boy behind them is Tex."

"I ain't no boy. I'm a man and I don't hide behind nobody." His voice was high-pitched but to prove his manhood, he stepped over until he stood beside Milo. He was short and lean, barely more than a boy Millie decided, although his hairline had receded badly. "You best remember that, stranger."

Peran doffed his hat at Millie. "Ma'am, my Angel will be mighty pleased to make your acquaintance. Ain't many proper ladies in Buckskin Joe." He looked rough and disreputable, missing all but a couple teeth, but Millie found his manners and his Welsh accent charming.

"The pleasure will be mine, Mr. Cornog." She inclined her head as Florence Hartley instructed when meeting a stranger.

Not to be outdone, the man with the drooping mustache bowed stiffly. "Michael Milo here, the Noble Grand of Buckskin Joe's Odd Fellow Lodge. I'm pleased to welcome you to Buckskin Joe, ma'am, but I'm concerned at the company you keep. This half-breed," he nodded at George, "is a killer."

"Uncle George didn't kill nobody," Dom said, releasing Millie and fisting his hands.

"Are you sure about that?" Milo's long mustache quivered. "The local lawman, Abner Finch, says otherwise."

"I ain't killed Wandering Will." George puffed out his chest. "And I'll duel any man who says otherwise."

"I'll take you on," said Tex, lifting his nose in the air. The sunlight glinted off his balding forehead and a slight breeze caused his long sideburns and scruffy beard to puff away from his narrow face.

"Fine." George pointed at Dom. "My nephew will be my second."

"No, he will not!" Millie blurted out.

Dom turned and scowled at her. "Course I'll be George's second." He waved her away. "Take the children and wait by the stream, Red. This is man's business."

Lor' Almighty she hated that nickname, but right now, it was the least of her problems. A duel killed people, and sometimes the seconds got involved. No way did she want Dom anywhere near that, especially not with George.

Milo slapped Tex's shoulder. "You're a fine man, Tex, but I'll handle this." He turned and faced George. "Tex will be my second. Thirty paces. Shotguns loaded with ball—one or more shots, as needed."

"Done," George said.

Millie's gut tightened. Last year, Editor Byers of *The Rocky Mountain News* had told her about the 1860 duel between Dr. James S. Stone and William Bliss, two of Denver's most distinguished citizens. The two old friends had been trapped into violence because of hot words and stubborn pride. Neither man intended a fatal shot—in fact one man, Mr. Stone, didn't even lift his weapon. His shot bit into the dirt at his friend's feet, but Mr. Bliss was not so kind. He wanted to make a point and aimed at Stone's legs. Later Bliss insisted he only intended to give his friend a minor wound, but his shot struck bone and ricocheted upward into Stone's abdomen. Doctors could do nothing, and Stone was racked by agonizing pain for months before finally succumbing to death.

"In the field by the school, tomorrow," Milo said. "Seconds to carry six-shooters." He gave George an accusing look. "They'll fire on anyone who cheats."

"I'll shoot *anyone* who breaks the rules," Tex said excitedly, eyeing Dom meaningfully.

"You accusing me of being dishonest, son?" Dom's tone was quiet, but Millie knew her husband. When his sky-blue eyes sparked like now, there was no talking sense with him.

"I ain't no son of yours." Tex spat at Dom's feet. "Wouldn't want to be. You're a Drouillard. That makes you a lying skunk."

"You take that back, son, or it's you and me who'll be on the dueling field." Dom took two steps forward and

Millie panicked, unsure what to do or how to stop this madness.

"I'll take you on. Any time. Any place. Or are you jest a blowhard?"

"Let's go. Tonight. At—"

"Gentlemen!" Millie hollered, her tone shrill. "Gentlemen!" She wanted to scream but instead took two deep breaths as all eyes rested on her. "You cannot duel tonight or tomorrow."

"Why not?" George demanded as Milo said, "Course we can."

Dom scowled. "Red, this ain't your business. Take the children down to the stream."

"It *is* my business, Mr. Drouillard." Dom was her life. What would she do if anything happened to him? Steeling herself, she said firmly, "You cannot duel tonight, tomorrow, or even the next day. It just won't work." Surprisingly, all the men remained silent and stared at her.

"Why?" asked Dom suspiciously.

Why indeed? Millie's mind went blank but behind her, Rachel spoke up. "Pa can't duel 'cause he's not available. We been on a long trip and Pa's got to help us settle."

Millie could have kissed the child. It was a crazy excuse, but women and children were scarce in these parts. It might work. "That's right. For the next few days, maybe even a week, Dom will be much too busy to duel anyone."

"What in tarnation are you talking about?" Dom demanded.

"I'm exhausted, Dom." Millie let her shoulder's droop and put on a suffering expression. Thickening her

Southern accent—something she'd learned was effective when dealing with Yankee men—she tried to look and sound exhausted. It didn't take much effort since she felt travelworn and weary to the bone. *"Your* children need a roof over their head and a decent meal." She hoped she didn't sound too whiny. *"You* need to find us a place to stay. To get us settled. To find the children a school, so they can continue their learning, to buy supplies, make us beds, and..." *And we need to find a murderer before he comes after us.*

"I got a cabin," said Peran in his soft, lilting accent. "Might not be clean as a whistle, but it's got two rooms and a working box stove. My Angel and me got us a baby last year. Had to build a larger place. I'm sure my Angel would be pleased to have a lady as a neighbor."

Millie thought the man looked as disreputable as George and she had little hope for the cabin, but if his offer put a stop to the plans for a duel, she'd live in a barn. "Thank you kindly, sir. Where can we find this cabin and your dear, sweet wife?" From Dom's sour expression, she decided she might be overdoing it.

"It's right near the Tabors' store." Peran grinned, showing lots of red gum and few teeth.

"That sounds just fine. Would you please be so kind as to show us the way?" She stepped forward and leaned heavily on Dom. "Can we go? Please Dom, I'm exhausted."

Dom's expression softened and all the other men— except George—looked concerned.

"Maybe we can duel day after tomorrow," Milo said uncertainly.

"Dom will be busy settling us for days. He won't have

time to duel or be a second for at least a week, maybe two."

"Fine." George scowled. "We'll duel a week from next Monday."

"Monday in a week at noon." Tex pointed at Dom. "You and me will be George and Milo's seconds. When they're done, we'll take to the field. George will be dead so you'll need to find a second."

"His wife can be his second," George said ungratefully. "She can put on trousers for the job."

Dom made a growling noise, but Milo nodded and started walking toward the path down the tailing pile. "We'll duel Monday in a week," he said, "assuming the half-breed ain't been lynched before then."

EIGHT

May 5, 1865
Buckskin Joe

Milo's words caused George to spew out a string of French curses while Dom's voice boomed out, "No one will hang Uncle George." Once again, men's angry voices filled the air. Millie wanted to pull her hair out. She glanced at Hosa and Rachel, hating how they were witnessing this ugliness.

"Gentlemen!" Millie hollered when Dom and George paused to breathe. "Dom and I won't have time to solve these issues until Monday. We need to get our family settled. Mr. Milo, I expect you and your Odd Fellows to behave like gentlemen. George, you too. Promise me you'll all stay away from each other and the Three Rings mine. They'll be no trouble until after the duel." She stared from one man to the next. "Do I have your word, as gentlemen?"

Milo grumbled and nodded. George, on the other hand, gave her an ugly sneer and stomped past her, disappearing down the trail without a word. She didn't want him hung, but Oh 'Lor was she glad to see the galoot's backside.

"No one enters the mine shaft unless I'm with them," Dom said loudly.

"Whatever." Tex kicked a shovel, causing it to clatter down into the black hole. "Mine hasn't been paying worth shit since we cleared out the lode." He strode away, but not before Millie heard him mumble, "But the murderer *will* pay."

The young man, she realized, like George, hadn't made any promises. She shrugged. There was nothing more she could do right now. "Mr. Cornog, would you *please* show us the way to Buckskin Joe and your cabin?"

Peran smiled and waved them down the trail. Dom took Millie's arm—not very graciously—and helped her down the hill, following Peran. Millie glanced behind, relieved to see the children following with Buttercup and the burros. Behind them, Milo brought up the rear, acting like he didn't have a care in the world.

Dom helped Millie cross the stream, and then waited so he could walk beside Milo. Millie followed Peran down a well-worn trail that paralleled the small creek, feeling exhausted and shaken by Dom's willingness to follow his uncle into something as crazy as a duel. Her thoughts were interrupted when Rachel called out, "Look, Miss Millie. Them miners is everywhere."

Millie looked around, surprised to see groups of miners all along the small stream. Some panned for gold, but most worked in groups, dumping dirt and sand into rickety sluices.

"Most of the placer gold is played out," Milo said, loud enough for Millie to hear. "But there's still some shallow lode deposits, like what we found in the Three Rings. Last year, Buckskin Joe had six stamp mills crushing ore twenty-four hours a day, but now we're down to just one. Most of us can't afford to pay a mill, so we use Mexican arrastras to crush our ore."

"Tex said you cleared out the gold lode in the Three Rings." Dom sounded resigned. "That right?"

"It's gone. It was rich, but shallow. Paid out $250 per ton for almost a full week. At first, we all thought we'd found the next Phillips lode, but then it dried up. Lately we've been lucky to earn $50 per ton. Been thinking of giving up the Three Rings, but my claim's no better. Even the Phillips Mine is dying, although it still pays out over $300 per ton. If things don't improve, we'll all be leaving Buckskin Joe."

Millie shook her head. Most miners wandered from claim to claim, doing backbreaking work as they searched for their big strike. Few found it. Most earned barely enough to pay for a meal and a night's entertainment. And the way they lived! Glancing around, she decided these miner's accommodations were worse than George's leaning cabin. His cabin had looked uninhabitable, but here she saw wagon boxes converted into makeshift shelters, wagon covers turned into canvas tents, or worse, pine boughs leaned against tree trunks to form rough-looking lean-tos. None of the shelters would keep a man dry in the rain nor warm during a snowstorm.

Why would civilized men choose to live like animals?

Yelling and laughter filtered through the trees as they crossed back over the creek. Millie pulled out her pocket watch, groaned, and braced herself. Even Idaho Springs turned rowdy on a Friday afternoon. The trail climbed away from the creek and through a thick grove of evergreens as male voices grew louder and louder. Finally, the trees opened and Millie got her first view of Buckskin Joe.

"Lor' Almighty!" She stopped and stared. On the edge of town, closest to them, two shirtless men wrestled in the dirt, surrounded by a crowd hollering encouragement. Intermixed with the men were three of the most scandalously clad women Millie had ever seen. Each one showed so much skin, Millie wondered why they bothered to wear their dresses. Worse, the women, like the men, exchanged money as bets were made, sharing swigs of a dark liquid from filthy-looking brown bottles.

"Oh," whispered Hosa, inching forward until he stood beside Millie.

"Look at them purdy ladies." Rachel jumped up and down, clapping her hands.

Dom swore and hurried to Millie's side. Buttercup squeezed between the two children, looked down at the crowds, and fainted.

"Welcome to Buckskin Joe," Milo said, passing them and strolling toward the writhing mass of humanity. He paused and glanced back. "Friday celebrations start early, last most of the night, and tend to be lively."

Millie scooped Rachel into her arms and Dom took a firm hold of Hosa's hand. Peran hurried back to their side, stammering out an apology as he picked up Buttercup—like a fainting goat was an everyday occurrence—and set her across Columbine's loads. "I'll mind the critters," he mumbled.

"This way." Milo disappeared into the crowd.

Millie took a deep breath and followed. They circled around the wrestling match and climbed onto a rough boardwalk. There was no avoiding the smelly miners, but Millie did her best to dodge around the colorfully dressed women. As they fought their way down the street, they passed gaming houses, saloons, dancehalls, billiard rooms, more saloons, and houses of ill repute. Buckskin Joe appeared to have every vice imaginable, and some Millie had never imagined. She wished she had a third hand to cover Rachel's eyes.

"We're almost out of the worst, ma'am," Peran hollered, dodging around a wagon as he pulled the unhappy burros along the dusty street. Buttercup lay sprawled on top of Columbine, her eyes glassy. An ox cart creaked by and Columbine stepped sideways to avoid it. Buttercup slipped from her perch. In slow motion she fell to the ground, landing in a heap underneath the burro, dust puffing up all around her.

Millie cried out, but Dom was already running toward them, dragging Hosa beside him. He scooped Buttercup up and an instant later, the heavy iron tires of a freight wagon rolled over the spot where she'd lain. Dom stumbled back toward Millie, struggling to carry Buttercup and hold Hosa's arm.

The crowd thinned, slightly. Millie's arms ached from carrying Rachel as she squeezed between two men and came upon a woman with half the buttons of her bodice undone. Millie covered Rachel's eyes, but the little girl pushed Millie's hand away and squealed in delight. "Music. I hear music. I wanna dance!"

The woman pushed past, followed by a particularly odious young miner. Behind him stood a woman wearing a dark skirt trimmed excessively with ribbon and other furbelow, a bodice so low her exposed cleavage could swallow a hand, and a ruffled pink petticoat that showed not only her feet, but also most of her ankles and lower legs. Millie gasped at her disgraceful attire, but it was the fancy girl's cold, calculating eyes and garishly painted face that stopped Millie dead.

"Your cheeks are rosy," Rachel said, clapping her hands in delight. "That dress is awfully purdy."

The rouged-cheeked woman stepped forward and pinched Rachel's cheek. "Now your cheek is red too." Her voice was husky and cold, matching her eyes.

Rachel howled in pain and Millie saw red.

"Sard off!" Millie snarled, almost dropping Rachel as she tried to draw her six-shooter. Before she could manage, Dom was beside her, his face flushed with anger. Handing Buttercup to Hosa, he reached over and rested his big hand on Rachel's tiny one, trying to calm the wailing child.

"You ever touch my daughter again," he said in a voice Millie didn't recognize, "and I'll thrash you to within an inch of your life." His expression was murderous. "Get out of my sight, whore." The woman carelessly brushed hair off her face, but she stepped back, her eyes never leaving Dom's face.

"Get outta here, Queeny." Milo appeared and roughly grabbed the woman's arm. He shoved her toward an open door. "Go back inside where you belong."

This was George's Queeny? Millie had met working girls—last year one had even become a friend—but this sullen, angry woman was like none she'd ever seen. Queeny gave Millie a look of pure hatred, spun around, and swept into the saloon, her ruffles flying after her.

"If looks could kill, she'd be Wandering Will's murderer." Milo shook his head. "Sorry about that, Mrs. Drouillard."

A shiver ran up Millie's spine. She had no doubt that Queeny could kill. The fancy girl reminded her of a coiled rattlesnake, ready to strike. Suddenly Rachel's howls quieted and the child squirmed in Millie's arms until her nose was inches from Millie's. "Miss Millie, I think you said a *real* bad word. What does—"

"Miss Rachel. A lady should never use such language, but that woman hurt you." The child opened her mouth and Millie added quickly, "You are never, ever, *ever*, to use those words. Understood?"

Devilment gleamed in the child's eyes as she wiggled free and slipped down until she was standing on the boardwalk. She looked up at Millie and smiled angelically. "Yes, Miss Millie." Cursing her own stupidity and Queeny's cruelty, Millie tightly held Rachel's hand as they continued down the street.

A group of well-dressed men nodded politely before entering a gambling saloon. The door swung closed, but Millie heard a wheel drop and someone yell, "Seven-ty-six, Four-teen, Thirty-three, sixty-five, eight—"

"What's that?" asked Hosa, peeking through cracks in the door.

"Nothing that concerns you." Dom gave Millie a slightly desperate glance. "I told you we shouldn't have brought the children. You should have stayed home. A mother wouldn't want her children exposed to this."

His accusation stung but Millie was too busy keeping track of Rachel to respond. The little girl pulled in one direction and then another, cooing at fancy women's attire and twirling whenever she heard music. "I want a dress just like that one," she said, pointing at a frilly dress worn by a skinny girl who looked just a bit older than Hosa.

Finally, the crowds disappeared, and Milo moved beside Millie, chatting like they were old confidants. "Over there is the Buckskin Joe courthouse. We've been the Park County seat since '62. That's the Grand Hotel, best place to stay in town, but expensive. If you got enough dust and don't like Peran's cabin, I'm sure the Grand's got rooms." He kept talking, pointing out a respectable dry goods store and what looked like a theater, but as they passed a side street, the thunderous pounding of a stamp mill drowned out his voice.

Millie paused to stare at the three-tiered mill. She'd never been inside a working stamp mill, but she'd seen empty mills with their large, iron-tipped stamps and metal-teethed machines that crushed ore—or anything else caught in them. She turned to Rachel and Hosa and yelled over the noise, "You children are never to go anywhere near that stamp mill. Understood?" They nodded but Millie decided she'd emphasize the danger again when she could speak without yelling. The machines could easily kill a man or a child.

As the stamp mill noise dimmed, Peran pulled the burros closer to Millie. "Sorry about that, ma'am. Ain't no other way through town, but I wouldn't want my Angel to see that."

Millie nodded. "I'd like to thank you, sir. We couldn't have gotten the burros through without your help. We are in your debt."

"Not at all, ma'am. My Angel would expect me to help another lady." He sniffed in a most ungentlemanly fashion and licked his cracked lips. "That there's Abner Finch's place." He nodded toward a small cabin. "He's the town sheriff, but he makes the best penny candy around." He grinned, looking childlike and a bit guilty. "My Angel says my sweet tooth is why I've so few teeth."

"I'm looking forward to meeting Mrs. Cornog, sir." She was genuinely curious what kind of woman married a man like Peran. Rachel pulled free of Millie's hold and hurried to the cabin's door, making excited sounds as the sweet smell of bread and cake filled the air.

"Your sheriff runs a bakery and confectionary store?" Dom asked. "Maybe we should go in and meet him." Hosa nodded in agreement.

They'd missed their mid-day meal and Millie felt her own stomach growl, but when she met Buckskin Joe's sheriff, she wanted some time to question him—without the children present. "Tomorrow. I want to get us settled and get supper started."

Reluctantly, Dom corralled Hosa, Rachel, and Buttercup and herded them down the street. "Sheriff Finch makes the best Washington cake I've ever eaten," said Milo, "but he's also a darn good lawman. He found plenty of proof George killed Wandering Will."

"What kind of proof—"

"Later, Millie!" Dom growled. "Not with the children present."

"We will help solve the murder," Hosa said indignantly. He watched a horse-drawn carriage pass by. "After I get a horse."

"I know of a fine animal that might be for sale." Milo

ruffled Hosa's hair and then nudged Dom. "I'll introduce you to Sheriff Finch. He and a colored man play evenings at Buck's Dancehall and Saloon, where Queeny works. We'll go hear him after you're settled. There's also the Odd Fellows Hall. Ever consider becoming an Odd Fellow? We can always use a good man."

Millie wanted to roll her eyes at the man's cajoling, but Dom's curious expression made her pause. Dom had never expressed any interest in the Masons, Odd Fellows, or any other male society. At least not that *she* knew about. Now he nodded and listened as Milo explained about the Odd Fellows membership and meeting schedule. "Everyone in Buckskin wants to be a Fellow," Milo bragged, "but our initiation ceremony keeps all but the bravest out."

"What you do at this ceremony?" Hosa asked. "Arapaho become men by being good hunter, being brave and," he scowled at Millie, "having a fast horse."

"I've heard about the Arapaho military societies, but never heard details." Milo fingered his mustache. "Probably like the Odd Fellows, they keep the initiation ceremony secret."

"Cabin's just up this way a bit." Peran pointed down the dusty street. He paused and touched his hat as a woman hurried toward them. Although she was dressed much more conservatively than Queeny, Millie still found her attire objectionable. "Evening Miss Kate," Peran murmured.

The girl gave Peran a quick nod—briefly glanced at the rest of them—and hurried by.

"What's she doing round here?" asked Milo, turning to watch the girl.

"Kate ain't bad. She's a dancehall girl, but respectable. Not like Queeny."

Millie didn't know there was a difference between a dancehall girl and a fancy girl. She'd ask Dom, when the children weren't listening.

"That's the Tabors' store." Peran pointed at a cabin with a bench out front. Over the door, a sign read *H.A.W. Tabor, General Merchandise*. "And this here's my cabin." Peran pointed at a small log cabin. It wasn't particularly well-built—Millie saw cracks in the walls—but it was a world apart from George's shack. "Wait here while I get my Angel." Peran dropped the burros' leads and hurried down a side alley. "She'll want to show you around."

"Peran's *señorita* is the love of his life." Milo grinned and leaned against the cabin's wall, crossing his ankles. "You say you come to investigate Wandering Will's murder?" Dom nodded. "I think it's George, but Queeny, the working girl with the killer figure, mighta done it. She was one of Wandering Will's former wives. Mean as a rattlesnake—although her charms are worth the risk. Wandering Will went after her any time he was in town. Heard he was with her the night before his death."

"That so." Dom rubbed his chin thoughtfully.

"How many former wives did Wandering Will have?" Millie asked, grabbing Hosa's hand before he wandered into the livery next door.

"Never heard." Milo chuckled. "Two that he spoke of. He had a way with the ladies." Milo ran a finger down his drooping mustache. "Far as I know, Queeny was his last. She followed him here and became jealous as a she-cat when Kate, the dancehall girl we just passed, showed interest in becoming Will's next wife."

NINE

May 5, 1865
Home Sweet Home

Before Millie could ask about Queeny or Kate, Peran arrived and introduced his wife, a petite woman who looked to be anywhere from twenty to forty. Her face showed no lines yet her dark hair—pinned back in a long braid—was streaked with gray. She carried a chubby baby boy in her arms and greeted Millie shyly, her words accented not in Peran's strong Welsh, but in a rolling Spanish melody. Her dress was entirely black and buttoned up tightly around her neck, but her doe-like eyes and milk chocolate skin softened her appearance and emphasized her Spanish heritage. Millie found her a complete contrast to Peran's ruddy exterior and outgoing nature.

"Cabin's not large, but it's solidly built," Peran explained after introductions were made. "It'll keep you dry if we ever get some rain, though Dom might want to repair the holes in the roof." He opened the door and Buttercup bleated and rushed inside. Millie was mortified but Mrs. Cornog just smiled and followed Buttercup. Millie trailed after them, hearing Milo invite Dom to next week's Odd Fellows meeting before taking his leave.

The cabin was small, maybe ten by twelve feet, and grass grew thick near the walls. Cobwebs stretched between the logs, and mice droppings covered the empty shelves. Still, it was better than Millie had expected. Dom could chink the walls and repair the roof, and if the box stove worked, Millie would be satisfied. The shelves could hold her kitchenware and there was room for a bed and table, although it would be tight. A loft extended the entire side of the cabin and Millie thought it would be a perfect place for the children to sleep, assuming it was free from spiders, rats, and snakes.

Peran opened a door on the back wall and pointed outside. "We added a lean-to back here, for a private bedroom. Got to go outside to get there, but it's not too close to the barn and privy so it don't smell too bad."

"Columbine and my Bluebell will have a barn." Rachel clapped her hands. Millie rolled her eyes, dreading the day when George tried to reclaim his burro.

"A private bedroom?" Dom pushed outside, almost knocking Peran over in his haste to view the lean-to. "Millie, look at this!" Peran grinned knowingly and Millie blushed as she passed him and entered the lean-to. It was tiny, almost completely filled with a pole bedstead covered in thick, dusty pine boughs. The roof was so low Dom had to crouch, but that didn't curb her husband's enthusiasm. "Our own bedroom," Dom whispered, lifting his eyebrows suggestively. He brushed past Millie and held out his hand to Peran. "This looks fine, just fine.

We'll take it."

Millie shook her head but after reentering the main cabin, she said politely, "We are pleased, Mr. and Mrs. Cornog, to stay here. Thank you kindly."

Dom handed Peran a teardrop-shaped gold nugget for payment and rudely turned his back on the man, waving the children toward the door. "Let's get Columbine and Bluebell unpacked and settled."

Slightly mortified by his manners, Millie turned to Mrs. Cornog and again offered her thanks. Mrs. Cornog's round-faced son replied with a squeal, like he was celebrating their arrival. The baby had neither the golden-brown skin of his mother nor the white, freckled skin of his father, but instead a complexion that reminded Millie of the almond-skinned Italian immigrants she'd seen in New Orleans. "Your son is darling, and his eyes." She bent closer. "I've never seen brown eyes with gold speckles. They're remarkable. He'll grow up to be quite the handsome young man."

"His name's Gruffy Fernando Miguel Cornog," Peran said, swelling with pride. "He's six months and two days old. Give him a few years and he'll make a fine Welshman."

"*Señora* Drouillard, I am sorry the cabin is so filthy. I am busy with my home and my boy, Gruffy, and did not know of your arrival." Her Spanish accent removed the G and rolled the R's, making the baby's name sound more like Rrriffy.

"The cabin is fine, really. I feel lucky to have it." After reassuring the woman a second time, Millie asked about the stores in town, but their conversation was interrupted when Dom and the children returned, arms wrapped around bundles of supplies. They dumped everything in the middle of the floor and looked at Millie expectantly.

"We leave. You need time to settle." Mrs. Cornog wrapped her son in a long, woven scarf and shooed her husband out the door. "I be pleased if you visit me, *Señora* Drouillard."

"I look forward to it, Mrs. Cornog." The door clicked shut and in the silence that followed, Millie looked at her expectant family and sighed. "Dom, take the water buckets and fill them. See if you can find something cleaner than that dirty Buckskin Creek." Millie looked around and nodded. "Hosa, climb into the loft and make sure there isn't anything dangerous up there. Unless you find a problem, sweep it out. Miss Rachel, see if you can cut some fresh pine boughs, but don't wander too far. We'll want to line the loft with the boughs and then put your straw ticks over them."

"We gonna sleep up there?" Rachel asked, her eyes wide.

"As long as it's safe."

Rachel shrieked and twirled in a circle while Hosa whooped and scrambled up a wood-slat ladder nailed to the wall. Dom dug through their belongings, spilling everything onto the floor as he pulled out the water buckets and hurried out. Soon the cabin was swept out, shelves were washed down, their meager supplies put away, and firewood was chopped and stacked near the box stove. Even Buttercup helped, chewing down the grass growing on the cabin's floor.

Millie pulled out salted pork and bread and they ate a cold supper standing up as the light outside dimmed.

"It's getting chilly. Buckskin Joe's higher in altitude

compared to Idaho Springs." Dom wiped his hands on his pants and bent over the stove, putting kindling into the firebox before lighting it. His fire took, but the smoke didn't go up the chimney. Instead, it poured out, filling the cabin. Dom cursed and doors were flung open. Cold air chilled the room as Dom put out his fledging fire and eyed the stovepipe, looking for the blockage. "I'll have to take it apart."

Millie stepped back as he pulled the stovepipe from the stove. A squirrel dropped onto their floor, followed by a nest holding three babies. Millie screamed, jumped back, and tripped over her own feet, crashing to the ground. The squirrel family darted toward the open front door, but Buttercup blocked their path. The goat's eyes bulged out and she tumbled over in a faint. The squirrels spun around, scurried between Dom's legs, and headed toward Millie.

Hosa pulled out his hunting knife and dove for the adult as Rachel screamed "No!" She tackled her brother as the squirrel family jumped over Millie and dashed out the back door. In the silence that followed, Hosa and Rachel quit struggling and stared wide-eyed at Millie.

"You okay, Miss Millie?" Hosa stood up and lifted Rachel to her feet.

Dom dropped the stovepipe and hurried to Millie's side. "Guess that's why it was blocked."

Millie rubbed her hip and glared at her family. "Miss Rachel, shut the front door. Hosa, the back door. Dom, it's freezing. Finish cleaning the stovepipe and start the blasted fire." Soon all signs of the squirrel nest had been swept outside and Dom's fire was blazing. Millie stretched sore muscles, wanting nothing more than to crawl onto her own down tick and go to sleep. She wished the children a good night—warning Hosa to make sure his sister didn't fall out of the loft—and followed Dom into their private room. Sighing loudly, she changed into her nightdress and crept into the bed. Dom had lined the bed with fresh pine boughs and the smell reminded Millie of their journey, but her down tick felt soft as a feather bed.

She closed her eyes, breathed deeply, and jumped when something banged. "What?" Sitting up, she saw Dom with a hammer near the door. "Dom, what *are* you doing?"

"I'm adding a bar and slat, to keep the children from surprising us. You know how Rachel is." He raised his eyebrows suggestively. "It's been a long trip and we had to share the tent with the children and George." He did a little dance as he finished his work and quickly undressed. "Move over Millie, I've got plans for tonight."

*****

Monday morning, Millie cooked hotcakes for breakfast and served them on the new table Dom had built. As they ate, Hosa and Rachel gave Millie sour looks when she asked Dom if he'd learned the location of Buckskin Joe's school. Rachel was explaining why school wasn't necessary when a knock on their door interrupted her. Hosa, five years older and a head taller than Rachel, jumped from his seat and reached the door first, but Rachel was close behind him. He shoved her aside and removed the locking slat. Millie scolded the boy for his rude behavior as Buttercup rushed over, flanking Hosa like a miniature guard.

"I protect Rachel!" Hosa said indignantly, turning his back on Millie and opening the door.

A boy, somewhere between the ages of Rachel and Hosa, stood outside. He eyed Hosa curiously and smiled as Rachel pushed Buttercup out of the way. "Hi," he said, "I'm Maxcy Tabor. Ma said we had neighbors with children. She sent me here and told me to show you the way to school." He tilted his head to one side. "Though I doubt Mistress Carle, the schoolmistress, will allow an Injun."

Hosa scowled and reached for his hunting knife. Millie quickly hurried over and rested a firm hand on the boy's arm. Hosa didn't take kindly to being called an Indian— he was Arapaho and proud of it.

"Why thank you, Maxcy, that is very kind of you. My husband and I were planning to speak with the schoolmistress this morning. We'll only be here a month or so, but school shouldn't be missed. Won't you come in while we get ready?" Millie didn't comment on the schoolmistress not accepting Hosa. She'd faced the same prejudices at Idaho Springs and, of course, carried the argument. Hosa had attended school—although he hadn't enjoyed it—and he *would* attend Buckskin Joe's school. Millie wouldn't take no for an answer.

Dom and the children questioned Maxcy about life in Buckskin Joe as Millie cleaned up the table, considering her day. After enrolling the children in school, she and Dom would head over to check on George. The two men would want to explore the mine or do something at the Three Rings. Once they were absorbed, Millie could slip away and begin her investigation.

Not that she was a real detective. She knew she wasn't, but since arriving in the Colorado Territory, trouble seemed to follow her like a bad smell. She hadn't had a choice in investigating either of those earlier murders, but with each one, she found she loved the challenge, and the mystery.

The first had been in '63, when she arrived to discover her fiancé—Dom's brother—dead. The second occurred just after she and Dom married when a local Idaho Springs woman had been murdered and Dom was the prime suspect. If Millie hadn't solved that second murder, Dom would have been lynched.

Wandering Will's murder couldn't be as difficult or dangerous as either of those previous murders. Millie figured she could ask some questions, find some clues, and maybe rile up the murderer. He—or she—would do something stupid and the crime would be solved. Dom, of course, would object, which was why she didn't intend to tell him about her plans.

Millie filled the children's lunch tins, smiling as she worked. Soon as she got rid of Dom and the children, she would start her investigation. She couldn't wait.

TEN

May 8, 1865
Mistress Carle, the Schoolmarm

The dueling field beside the small Buckskin Joe schoolhouse looked like any other mountain meadow, but Millie imagined she saw bloodstains on the packed dirt and dying men breathing their last. No way she'd let Dom be part of a duel, neither as a second for George nor standing alone against Tex. She shuddered and turned away. Her eyes were drawn upstream to the three-tiered structure of the stamp mill. It made a cacophony of noise, adding to the unpleasantness of the location. How in the world did the schoolmistress teach with the noise and the ghosts of the field so close?

"What is the schoolmistress's name, Maxcy?" Dom asked. Dom had entertained the children as they walked to the schoolhouse, pointing out a fox print and bobcat track along their path. He was in a much better mood after a weekend filled with busy days and private nights.

"Mistress Carle, sir."

"Excellent. Why don't you children see what tracks you can find while Mrs. Drouillard and I speak with Mistress Carle." Maxcy and Rachel nodded and scurried off, their eyes on the ground, but Hosa just scowled. Millie suspected Hosa's tracking ability was as good, or maybe even better, than Dom's.

"I will not go to school unless I get horse." Hosa stubbornly planted his fists on his hips and glared from Millie to Dom. "I need a horse to escape Utes. Also, father come soon. I need a horse to kill bad soldiers."

Millie felt a surge of panic, again unsure what to do. What would they do if Hosa's father came for the boy? If they gave him a horse, would Hosa leave and search for his father or would it help him to be more content here?

If only Florence Hartley had written a book on parenting, a step-by-step guide to motherhood and its many pitfalls. Knowing she needed to do something, she walked over and knelt beside Hosa, idly wondering when he'd gotten so tall. "Hosa, we'll get you a horse when we get home. For now, you must go to school. Your father would want you to learn our ways. Being able to read and write will allow you to help your people."

The boy harrumphed.

"You'll go to school for me, won't you?" Millie wasn't sure what she'd do if he said no. Hosa hesitated, scowled, and finally nodded. Millie exhaled, ran her hand down his long braid, and stood up. "Thank you, Hosa. Dom, why don't you continue your tracking lesson. I'll go inside and speak with Mistress Carle."

"You sure?"

Millie nodded and glanced around. "Miss Rachel, please pick up your slate and make sure Miss Buttercup doesn't eat your reader." During their journey here, Millie had worked with the children using the McGuffey readers from the Idaho Springs school, thankful for the extra books she'd ordered last January. Thomson's *Mental Arithmetic* and Clark's *Practical Grammar* were bought as bribes to get Hosa into the Idaho Springs school, but on their journey here, she'd found them useful as she became both mother and teacher. "Don't get dirty," she reminded the children.

"This here's a dueling field," Dom said behind her. "I'll be standing over there when I second for George."

"Dom!" Millie glared at him. He smiled, waved pleasantly, and herded the children farther away.

"Why do duelers have seconds, Pa?" Rachel asked.

"Seconds make all the arrangements. They set up the dueling field, mark off the distance between the men, and make sure both duelers carry the same type of weapon. Used to be men dueled with swords, then dueling pistols, but here in the Colorado Territory, six shooters and shotguns are popular. When—"

"Dom! A tracking lesson is far more appropriate than discussing dueling."

"Of course." Dom led the children still farther away until Millie could no longer hear them. She shook her head and turned toward the schoolhouse. After she enrolled the children, she and Dom would discuss which topics were appropriate for children. Pulling open the door, she stepped inside and paused to let her eyes adjust to the dim light.

Long, wooden benches filled most of the room, but along one wall, two boards were laid across sawhorses and several chunks of white limestone rested on them.

Nailed to the wall above them were three whipsawed boards painted black. Beside the doorway was a makeshift desk with a workbook, pen, and an ink well neatly laid out in front of a stool. The schoolhouse was tidy, an indication, Millie hoped, of a structured, efficient schoolmistress.

Movement in the far corner caught Millie's eye and she spotted a scrawny woman dressed in a drab gray skirt bent over a Franklin stove. The woman fed wood into the stove's firebox, her back to Millie. "Good morning," Millie said pleasantly, "I'm Mrs. Drouillard. I have two children to enroll in school."

"Mrs. Drouillard?" The woman straightened and turned, her forehead furrowing. "Any relation to Mr. George Drouillard?"

The woman's nasally voice made Millie's scalp tingle and a new worry assailed her. Would their relationship to George make it *more* difficult to register the children in school? Millie inclined her head in greeting, trying not to show her worries. "A pleasure to make your acquaintance, ma'am." She held out her books, hoping the woman was as desperate for materials as the Idaho Springs schoolmistress. "I know how hard it is to come by books in the Colorado Territory, so I thought you might want to borrow these. This one—"

"You ain't George's wife, are you?"

"Goodness, no. Mr. George Drouillard is my husband's uncle. He's a distant relative. I—"

"Excellent. That man has a fine figure, don't you think? I'm Mistress Carle. Mistress Maude Carle." The woman stepped forward and glanced at Millie's books. The light from an open window gave Millie a better view of her. The schoolmistress looked to be around thirty, her features pleasant, but she'd pulled her hair into a bun so tight, the skin around her eyes and forehead looked shiny and taut. "I'm a widow," she said in her nasally voice. "To make ends meet, I teach here at Laurette."

Millie heard the sour note in the woman's words and felt her smile falter. "Laurette? Isn't this Buckskin Joe's schoolhouse?"

"Buckskin Joe!" Mistress Carle dusted off her hands. "This town's name is Laurette. Named after the first two women settlers here, Laura and Jeanette Dodge." She sniffed. "Everyone called old Joseph Higginbottom, Buckskin Joe, and since he and Mr. Phillips discovered the Phillips lode, the miners thought it amusing to call the town Buckskin Joe. But Laurette is its proper name. That's what the postmaster says and that's what I teach my students."

Mistress Carle sounded cranky, but Millie imagined spending all day teaching children would make even a saintly nun grumpy. "How long have you taught here, ma'am?"

"Next month will be two years. Two *long* years."

"I'm so glad to hear you have experience." After two years, Mistress Carle probably knew all the folks in town, *and* all the gossip. "I'd love to learn more about the history of the town," Millie lied. "Perhaps one day we can have tea together. You can tell me more about Mr. Phillips, Mr. Higginbottom, and the other miners in town." *Like Wandering Will.*

"Higginbottom left before I come. Folks say he traded his claim for a gun and a horse. Gave up his water rights to pay his whiskey bill." She shook her head. "Miners!

Like my dead husband, they're mostly worthless. What I want is a fine-figured man with enough money that I don't have to work in this rotten school."

Millie lifted her eyebrows, concerned for the well-being of her children. "If the school is rotten, perhaps it isn't the best place for my children." Her heart sank. No way could she investigate a murder and school the children at home. Besides, if they were home, they'd want to investigate Will's murder with her.

"It's a good school," Mrs. Carle said quickly. "The only one. And I'm a good teacher. It's just difficult for me, alone, without a man to provide for my needs. But I can teach your children." She narrowed her eyes and added, "Long as you can pay."

Millie considered. Hosa and Rachel weren't easy and this woman and her school might not be the best place for them. Despite wanting to investigate Wandering Will's murder, Hosa and Rachel came first.

Mrs. Carle, apparently seeing her indecision, hurried to her desk and took a seat. She opened her enrollment book and looked expectantly; her pen poised over the page. "Now how do you spell your children's names?"

Maxcy seemed like a nice young man and he hadn't complained about the school. She should give Mrs. Carle a chance. After all, they'd probably only be here for a month or so. How bad could Mrs. Carle be? "Our daughter is Rachel Drouillard. R-a-c-h-e-l D-r-o-u-i-l-l-a-r-d." She watched the woman write the name. "Our son is Hosa. H-o-s-a."

Mrs. Carle looked up, her expression suddenly wary. "What kind of Christian name is Hosa?"

After the woman's eagerness for money, Millie had

hoped enrolling Hosa wouldn't be a problem. "Hosa is our adopted son," she said. "Our adopted Arapaho son."

Mrs. Carle slammed the book shut, her thin lips turning down as she shook her head. "The girl's fine, but I won't take the Indian."

"Hosa is our son," Millie said, tamping down her anger. She understood the teacher's prejudices—she'd had them herself until she'd gotten to know Hosa and his family. "Hosa went to school at Idaho Springs. Yes, he's Arapaho, but he's a good student and very well-mannered." Millie looked away. A decent teacher would know how to make an unruly child behave, wouldn't she? "We'd be willing to pay you twice your normal fee to overcome any difficulties from local families."

"No. His kind ain't welcome by the other children's parents, especially not an Arapaho. Utes come around here, begging eats. They hate them Arapaho. If they find one in my schoolhouse, they'll scalp me."

Millie argued with Mrs. Carle, but their quarrel came to an abrupt stop when the door opened and Dom, Hosa, Rachel, and Maxcy stepped inside. Millie drew in a calming breath and said in a voice barely civil, "Mistress Carle, this is my husband, Mr. Dominic Drouillard, and my children, Miss Rachel and Hosa."

Buttercup bounded inside—like she was going to school too—and jumped onto the nearest bench, her tiny hooves making a clicking sound as she walked down the bench. "So sorry," Millie said, embarrassed as she shooed Buttercup off the bench and outside. She really did need to teach the goat some manners! Slamming the door, she turned and finished her introductions. "Dom, Rachel, Hosa, this is Buckskin Joe's—ah Laurette's—

schoolmistress, Mistress Carle."

"A pleasure to meet you, ma'am." Dom politely doffed his hat. "It's good to know our children will be taught by such an excellent schoolmistress. Maxcy has been telling us all about you." Millie turned and stared. Dom was never polite. Ever. As if to prove her wrong, he stepped over and gently took Mistress Carle's hand, kissing the back before turning it over. "This should pay for the children. We'll only be here a month or so." He placed a teardrop-shaped gold nugget in her palm.

Mistress Carle nodded, not even glancing down at the gold. Her face broke into a wide smile, and she wrapped her free hand around Dom's arm. Leaning forward, she inhaled deeply. "Mr. Drouillard, my, you smell delicious. It will be my pleasure to teach your children." Her tone was low and husky. "Hard to imagine you're related to George Drouillard, but you do have his fine figure." She admired Dom's figure and batted her eyes. "Please, call me Maude. I would be in your debt, *Dom*, if you could help me bring wood in for the stove."

Dom's eyes widened slightly, and he glanced at Millie as Mistress Carle dragged him out the back door. Millie shrugged. If a little infatuation helped enroll Hosa in school, she'd take it. Dom could take care of himself.

"Egads," Maxcy said, shaking his head. "Looks like Mistress Carle's looking for husband number three."

"But Pa's already married," Rachel said, frowning.

"Don't matter none," Maxcy said. "Once Mistress Carle sets her sights on a man, she's like a bugling elk in rut. My pa had to leave town for three weeks to 'scape her."

ELEVEN

May 8, 1865

The Stagecoach's Arrival

"I can't believe you said nothing while that woman groped me like I was a common working girl!" Dom strode indignantly away from the schoolhouse, refusing to even look at Millie. After Dom's arrival, Mistress Carle hadn't complained about Hosa—Millie wasn't sure the schoolmistress had even seen him. She'd had eyes for Dom and only Dom, and her eyes had roamed over him in a most inappropriate way. Still, she hadn't complained when they'd left both children in her schoolhouse.

Millie moved to Dom's side and took his arm. "The important thing is the children will be in school and getting an education."

Dom harrumphed. "You still should have done something. Outside, while I picked up firewood, Mrs. Carle kept squeezing my arm and brushing her fingertips over my biceps." He shuddered. "Then, on the way out for the last load, she accidentally fell." He shook his head and finally glared at Millie. "But it wasn't an accident. I caught her, as any man would, but I wasn't quick enough to grab both arms. That woman's hand landed in a place…" His face reddened. "Well, in a place it shouldn't have landed."

Millie found his embarrassment endearing, although she was shocked by Mistress Carle's behavior. She hadn't realized the schoolmarm had been quite *that* forward. "Gracious sakes! I thought it was just a little harmless infatuation. I don't understand. When I was a single woman, I had every man near Idaho Springs wanting my hand in matrimony. Buckskin Joe must have twice the population of single men. Mistress Carle isn't terrible to look at. Why is she stalking married men?" They neared their cabin and she pulled Dom to a stop, letting Buttercup catch up.

"Even with that red hair and fiery temper," Dom said, his expression softening, "everyone knew you'd make a good wife. You owned a rich mine and were a great cook, but Mistress Carle is different. She's the kind of woman that sucks a man dry. I'd bet most men round here call her the Black Widow, or something worse."

"Shame on you, Dom." Millie hadn't liked the schoolmistress, but no woman deserved such a cruel nickname. Had the townsfolk of Idaho Springs given *her* a nickname, something worse than Red? Pushing away the thought, she added, "I'm sure Mistress Carle was just being friendly, and her fall *was* accidental."

"Her fall, and where her hand landed, was deliberate." Dom opened their cabin door and Buttercup pushed past them, stopping short to look up at the extra sourdough loaf Millie had made that morning.

"I'll grab my shawl and a basket before we head out." Millie took down the bread and wrapped it in a dish towel, ignoring Buttercup's rueful look. "This is for George. I'll accompany you to his cabin and afterwards visit the Tabor store. I'd like to meet Maxcy's mother."

"You don't need to come with me." Dom snagged two left-over hotcakes from their breakfast, offering one to Buttercup. "And you aren't fooling me, Red, but this isn't Idaho Springs. You saw how wild Buckskin Joe can be when we arrived. The kind of men—and women—who live here are the reason that poor schoolmistress is so forward when she finds a decent, good-looking man like me." He grinned and Millie rolled her eyes.

"Your point?"

"You need to leave the murder investigation to me." He waved a hand at her sour look. "Buy supplies, meet Maxcy's mother, or make one of your proper 'morning calls' and get to know Peran's wife. In a place like this, they'll both enjoy some female companionship. Just don't go snooping around. Knowing you, you'll end up on the wrong end of a six-shooter."

Millie appreciated his concern, but not his patronizing words. She planted her hands on her hips and scowled. "You want me to spend my day making calls, buying supplies, and cooking food? To leave the *"men's work"* to you?" Dom had the good grace to look chagrined. "May I remind you that *I've* saved your life at least twice."

"True, but each time the killer was really after you. I just got in the way."

"The killer came after me because I deduced he was a murderer." And maybe because she'd been careless. Knowing Dom was just worried, Millie tried to curb her irritation. She knew she couldn't have solved previous crimes—and survived—without Dom. "I'll come with you and give George the loaf of bread I made as a peace offering. I know you worry, but I promise to be careful. *We'll* investigate this murder, together. I'll tell you everything I learn if you promise to do the same."

Dom threw up his hands. "Fine, then *you* should go back and talk to Mistress Carle."

"Why?" Millie would be happy if she never saw the woman again.

"I think she knows something." Dom set his pack on the table and reached inside. He removed his assay instruments, checked that each item was undamaged, and carefully repacked them.

"What could she know?"

"I'm not sure, but as I gathered wood and deflected her roving hands, I tried to distract her by asking questions. Turns out she knew Wandering Will—hell, she probably knows every single man in town. She said Will visited her class about a month before his death, showing off his prize possession, a Palmetto Armory pistol."

"What was so special about his pistol?" Millie wrapped salted pork left over from last night's meal and handed it to Dom. She had intended to give him the four remaining flapjacks for his midday meal, but at the rate he was eating them, they'd be gone before he left the cabin.

"Don't know. I've heard of the Palmetto Armory. It's located in Reb territory, somewhere in North or South Carolina. Mistress Carle said Will's pistol was special, ornate with a rounded butt."

"Has George mentioned it?"

"No." Dom gave Millie a hard look. "*I'll* ask George about it." He waited until Millie nodded. "Thing is, after Mrs. Carle mentioned the pistol, she paused and got this funny look on her face, like she was just remembering something. And then I swear she lied, saying she knew nothing about Wandering Will's murder."

Millie slipped on her bonnet and wrapped her shawl around her shoulders. If a killer snuck back from the Three Rings mine, he, or she, might bypass the downtown, skirting around closer to Buckskin Creek. Close enough to the dueling field to be seen from the schoolhouse? "Surely Mistress Carle would speak with the sheriff if she saw something suspicious."

"Maybe she didn't realize what she'd seen until I asked her. Anyway, that's just one more reason why it's dangerous for you to ask questions. It's been weeks since Wandering Will's murder. If you start snooping around and get the killer riled up, like you always do, there will be trouble." Dom gave Millie a one-arm hug. "Just promise me you'll be careful, Red. I didn't like Mistress Carle, but I wouldn't want to see her hurt."

Millie kissed Dom to reassure him, and he pulled her into a tighter hug and lengthened the kiss. "Too bad I've got to find George. I could think of several things I'd rather do—all of which would be safer for you." He gave Millie a devilish look that made her stomach flutter, released her, donned his pack, and opened the door.

"Don't you need the burros?"

Dom shook his head as Buttercup hurried outside, part of a flapjack still hanging from her mouth. "Nope. All I plan to do today is assay ore from different sections of the mine. For that, George can lower and lift me by hand."

Millie shuttered and stepped outside, holding a basket in the crook of her arm as they strode down Buckskin Joe's main street. Dom rested his hand on her arm and gave her a concerned look. "I know I can't talk you out of investigating Wandering Will's murder, but will you promise to tell me your plans each day? That way I'll know where to look if you don't come home."

Millie softened at the worry in his voice. "I promise I'll be careful."

"Red, you're as careful as a buffalo stampede. You get some harebrained idea and head off with no worries about killers or harm to yourself. When we arrived, *you* were upset with *me* volunteering to be a second in a duel, but that's nothing compared to some of the things you've done. Remember last year when you broke me out of Denver City's jail? Or when you headed off for a chat with Denver's most notorious Madam? You—"

"May I remind you that I saved you from being lynched."

"You did." Dom reached over and tilted her face up so he could kiss her. Even after a year of marriage, his kiss still made her feel giddy. "But I had to watch a madman drag you away, his gun to your head. I still have nightmares about that."

Lor' Almighty! She *had* been lucky to find a man like Dom. As an orphan, she'd never known love, just friendship. No wonder poor Mistress Carle wanted her husband. "I'll be careful. I promise."

Dom sighed, looking resigned. They passed the Tabors' store and Millie glanced in the open window, pleased to see goods lining shelves and hanging from the ceiling. The sign above the door read "H.A.W. Tabor, General Merchandise" but from Maxcy's description, it sounded like Mrs. Tabor ran the store and post office. As postmistress and storekeeper, Maxcy's momma would certainly have a wealth of information about the town and its inhabitants.

Her thoughts were interrupted by thundering hoofbeats.

Millie turned as a stagecoach clattered into town, scattering riders and pedestrians as the horses skidded to a stop, their hooves—and the stagecoach's iron-ringed wheels—churning up the dusty street. Millie covered her mouth with her handkerchief but slowly lowered it as a group of twenty or so rough-looking miners emerged from a side alley. The men were tightly clustered together, but their eyes were glued on the rocking stagecoach.

Millie felt the hair on the back of her neck rise as the men moved out into the street, causing passing wagons and riders to swerve around them. They spread out, partially surrounding the stagecoach, looking like they were preparing to attack.

Dom's hand dropped until it rested on his six-shooter.

"Do you think they plan to rob the stagecoach?" Millie whispered. "It's broad daylight and the street's busy."

The stagecoach door opened, and a dapper young man dressed in a white linen shirt, fashionable striped trousers, a Prince Albert frock coat, and a black silk top hat climbed out. He looked like an advertisement for a greenhorn, a newcomer without a lick of experience or common sense. The dandy eyed his audience curiously as his shiny brogans disappeared onto the dusty street.

Pausing, he lifted his top hat and politely bowed. "Gentlemen, top of the mornin' to you."

His strong Irish drawl made the words sound like a song but the silence that answered him made his brows draw together. Millie tensed and slipped her hand into her apron, wrapping her fingers around the butt of her six-shooter.

A large, older mountain man standing just to the side of the stagecoach suddenly cried out. He stumbled over his own feet and backed away from the side alley as a large black bear emerged and charged into the street. The bear let out a terrible roar and headed straight for the men and the stagecoach.

Millie jerked her gun from her apron. Buttercup fainted. The stagecoach horses shied sideways. Men ran in all directions as the bear roared again. The stagecoach dandy tried to climb back into the stagecoach, but he tripped and fell backwards. Millie aimed her gun as the bear focused on the downed man and pounced on him.

Men scrambled in all directions, blocking her view, making it too dangerous to take a shot. *Why didn't one of them pull out his weapon?* Millie struggled to get a clear shot, shuddering at the newcomer's terrified screams. The bear lifted his head, the hapless dandy's shiny ankle-high brogan clamped in his mouth. Roughly shaking the man's leg, the bear dragged the screaming man down the filthy street. The stranger's frantic cries were intermixed with…was that laughter?

"Don't shoot." A squat man wearing a flour-covered apron flapping around his thighs ran toward Millie and Dom, his impressive, waxed mustache bouncing, his face a mixture of fury and exasperation. "Don't shoot!" he repeated, knocking Dom's gun arm down. He looked at Millie but didn't touch her. "Please ma'am, put away your six-shooter. The bear won't do the newcomer no harm."

Millie lowered her weapon, her eyes fixed on the screaming dandy. The bear dragged him in front of the older mountain man as the crowd of men hooted, laughed, and slapped each other's backs.

"I'm gonna kill those fools." The man's mustache vibrated with fury. "Wait here." He turned and jogged toward the stagecoach, leaving a trail of white flour. "Kootenay you ass, call off Little Bear. I told you last time this was not funny."

Last time? Millie watched, shocked, as the bear released his victim, turned, and reared up on his hind legs. He set his front paws on the old mountain man's buckskin covered shoulders, stretched out his muzzle, and licked the man's smiling, bearded face.

Shoving aside the mirthful audience, the aproned man strode angrily toward the bear and unmoving dandy. "Make Little Bear sit down, Kootenay, or I'll put a bullet in him."

The big man's smile drooped. His gray hair fluttered in the slight breeze as he snapped his fingers. The bear dropped to the ground like a well-trained dog, ambled to his master's side, and sat down.

Dom swore. Millie couldn't believe the attack had been a joke. What kind of sick men lived in this town?

The dandy lay unmoving in the filthy street, spread out at the old man's feet like a ghastly hunting trophy. The aproned man bent over him and asked, "You okay, son? Let me help you up." Taking the prone man's arm, he lifted him onto his feet, gripping his shoulder firmly. The dandy's fine clothes were filthy, and he swayed unsteadily, looking like he might be sick.

"Howdy, *hombre*," boomed the big mountain man, scratching his bear behind the ears as his smile returned. His deerskin breeches and fringed buckskin shirt made him look like a native, an old, well-worn native. "This here's Little Bear and I'm Kootenay Good. Hope you brought a second pair of britches. Thems, I'm sure, ain't clean no more." The bear turned his head and licked the mountain man's large hand. "Welcome to Buckskin Joe, *hombre*."

TWELVE

May 8, 1865

The Baker-Sheriff

The aproned man let out a string of creative curses and the mountain man, although he was a full head taller than the baker, stumbled backward, his amused expression fading. "Kootenay, you galoot." The baker waved his arms wildly. "You almost got Little Bear shot. Decent folks, like the ones over there…" He pointed at Dom and Millie. "…shoot wild animals."

Kootenay glanced at Dom and Millie, his eyes widening as Millie made sure he saw her six-shooter before she slipped it back into her apron. Dom kept his weapon out, but pointed toward the ground, his handsome face twisted in anger. "That was a joke?" he spat out. "A vulture ain't that mean."

The mountain man's shoulders slumped and several of his cohorts lowered their heads and scurried away. "We were just having a bit of fun, Sheriff." The mountain man's voice no longer boomed. "We didn't do this *hombre* no harm."

"No harm? Kootenay, you scared the bejesus out of this gentleman. Ruined his fine clothes."

"We done him a favor," whined Kootenay. "If he ain't tough, he'll end up buying a salted mine or a painted gold nugget." Several of the men standing nearby nodded in agreement. The dandy's ghost-white face took on a bit of color and he stood up straighter, his shaking hands knocking at dirt and manure clinging to his clothing.

Millie couldn't decide which was more shocking: that these men thought the bear attack was funny or that the sheriff of Buckskin Joe wore a stained, slightly pink apron. At her feet, Buttercup rose from her faint and disappeared beneath Millie's skirt. She felt Buttercup's quivering body press against her leg.

"Sorry, sir," the sheriff turned to the dandy. "These men will happily pay for your hotel and a new set of clothes." A howl of objections rose around him, but he silenced them with a wave of his hand. "They'll pay, or I'll throw them all in the calaboose."

"Now, Sheriff, we ain't—"

"No need, Sheriff," said the dandy in his thick Irish accent. "*Fiat justitia, ruat caelum.*" His voice shook slightly.

"What the heck does that mean?" Kootenay took another step back, looking alarmed. "You a fureigner? You cursing me in your fureign language?" He glanced at the sheriff. "Maybe this *hombre's* soft in the head."

"I am neither, sir." The dandy shook off the sheriff's hand. "My name is Professor O.J. Goldrick. I just said, 'Let justice be done though the heavens fall!' Of course, an imbecile like you won't understand Latin." The man's voice grew stronger, his Irish drawl thickening. "I've come to this cursed cesspool to write a story for the *Rocky Mountain News*. Be assured I'll tell them exactly what kind of ignoramus cretins live here." Professor Goldrick turned, his back straight, and limped toward the stagecoach. Pausing he glanced back at the sheriff. "Jailing such an oaf is useless. He and his creature should be shot."

"Shot?" Kootenay's bushy gray eyebrows shot up.

"But we ain't done nothin' bad." Millie shook her head. She'd read several articles by Professor Goldrick in the *Rocky Mountain News*. She'd found his prose flowery and pompous, although last summer, his summary of Denver's great flood had been fascinating. She could only imagine his description of this incident. Kootenay, looking worried, knelt and hugged his bear. "You won't shoot Little Bear and me, will you, Sheriff?"

"If you ever do anything like this again, I'll turn Little Bear into steaks and throw you in the calaboose."

"We won't do it again." The big man released his bear and rose, shaking his head, his white beard jumping with the movement. Hesitantly, he asked, "Ah, Sheriff, what's an ignoramus cretin?"

The sheriff rubbed his head like he was getting a headache. "Get on out of here, all of you. No more shenanigans!"

Millie could only imagine how hard it must be to enforce the law in a town with men who thought a bear attack was funny. She was impressed that the old mountain man and his bear, along with his motley crew, quickly scurried away. The sheriff turned and headed back toward them, his apron fluttering in the breeze.

When he reached them, he glanced at Dom's gun. "You can put that away, sir."

"You should throw that mountain man in lockup and kill his bear." Dom shoved his weapon back into its holster.

"I would, if I thought it would do any good." The baker extended his hand. "I'm Sheriff Finch. Sorry you had to see that, ma'am. The boys were just having a bit of fun, but that Kootenay's wilder than his bear. Why don't you come into my shop and have a ladyfinger on the house?"

"What's a ladyfinger?" Dom asked suspiciously. "After seeing that bear attack, it wouldn't surprise me if the sheriff of this godforsaken town cooked the fingers of local working ladies."

"Dom!" Millie said sharply, but she kept her fingers tucked in her apron pocket just the same. "Sir, you are the sheriff of Buckskin Joe?" Millie prided herself on her ability to size up strangers, but the short man with his oversized mustache and pink apron didn't look anything like a lawman.

"I am, so I don't cook fingers." He grinned. "Usually I like my job, but days like this make me think about turning in my badge." He led them into a cabin that smelled of sugar, butter, and cinnamon. Dom licked his lips, his eyes glazing over at a counter lined with pies and small cakes. Millie ignored the sweets—although their smell made her mouth water—and took in the cozy bakery. Loaves of flat bread and hard tack were stacked on one side of the counter and on the other sat a plate piled high with oblong biscuits coated in sugar. Between the two were fruit pies surrounded by tins of peaches, oysters, and other delicacies.

Buttercup, who'd stayed hidden under Millie's skirt, poked her head out, bleated, and made a beeline toward the counter. Millie picked up the little goat and backed up slightly as Sheriff Finch stepped behind the counter and fingered his impressive mustache with one hand while he gestured toward the plate of oblong biscuits. "The oval ones are ladyfingers. A French delicacy my customers love. The others are jumbles." Dom eagerly stepped forward, reaching for the plate. He paused when Kootenay Good stomped into the small space. Millie backed up until her shoulders pressed against the wall.

"I need my usual, Sheriff," said the old mountain man.

The cabin was tiny and when Kootenay stepped toward the counter, the fringe of his buckskin sleeve brushed against Millie's hand. She edged toward the door but stopped when the man's bear stuck his head inside. The bear snuffed loudly and Buttercup fainted, her head flopping over Millie's arm.

Sheriff Finch—apparently used to Kootenay and his bear—calmly wrapped up six ladyfingers and handed over the parcel. "I'll add it to your tab, Kootenay, but you need to settle your bill by the end of the month. And no more horseplay."

"It were just having a bit of fun," said Kootenay sullenly. He clutched the treats to his chest like a child protecting something valuable. "I'll pay next week. I got pelts to sell when them traders come through." He glanced at Dom but his honey-colored eyes rested on Millie and Buttercup, his expression curious. Deep wrinkles lined his eyes, although his weather-worn face was mostly hidden under a wild, white beard. His long gray hair flew out like weightless feather down. Up close, Millie thought he looked like a worn-out Father Christmas.

"Thanks for not shooting Little Bear, *hombre*," he said, nimbly slipping past Millie and pushing his bear's head to the side. His movements were graceful, like those of a man half his age, and as the bear turned toward him, he gave the animal a friendly rub behind his furry ears.

Millie gulped down a breath of air, but instead of foul body odor and wild animal scent, she breathed in mountain sage mixed with sugar and butter. She'd always imagined mountain men would be filthy and smelly. After all, they spent their days exploring or hunting, never having time to bathe. Never did she expect to meet a real mountain man—and his pet bear— who smelled like sweet mountain sage.

As the bear and man lumbered away, Kootenay took out a ladyfinger and broke it in half, offering the smaller part to the animal. "Come on, Little Bear," he said, stuffing the rest of the biscuit into his mouth. Side-by-side, bear and man walked down the boardwalk.

Millie shook her head. At Idaho Springs, people considered Buttercup an oddity. She couldn't wait to tell the town matrons about Kootenay and his bear.

"Here, try one." The sheriff held up the plate. "I'm Abner Finch, both sheriff and baker. Although I saw your six-shooter, sir, I didn't catch your name."

"Mighty fine place you got here, Sheriff." Dom took two ladyfingers and offered one to Millie. A bit self-consciously, Millie broke hers in half and offered the smaller piece to Buttercup. "I'm Dom Drouillard and this is my wife, Millie. We'll also take that peach pie—"

"The ladyfingers and the pie should be fine for now," Millie interrupted, knowing Dom's weakness for sweets.

"Drouillard?" The Sheriff eyed them curiously. "Any relationship to George Drouillard?"

Millie took a bite of the biscuit and for a moment her mind went blank. Flavors exploded in her mouth, and she groaned aloud. "This is absolutely the best cake rusk I've ever eaten." If she'd known, she wouldn't have wasted half on Buttercup. "What's in it? Will you share your recipe?" She stepped forward and took another ladyfinger. "How in the world, sir, did you end up here?"

Sheriff Finch laughed, wrapped a peach pie in newspaper, and added a couple more ladyfingers before handing the package to Dom. "I was the baker at the Fuller House in St. Paul. Learned my secret ladyfinger recipe there. The head baker was an amazing cook and teacher, but I was young and wanted an adventure." He twirled his mustache with his finger, reminding Millie of a minstrel show villain. "Hired on as cook for an expedition—they were supposed to make peace with the Sioux. I learned how to handle a gun but found my cooking was my best weapon. The natives loved my sweet biscuits." He chuckled. "They said I was always welcome in their country."

He paused and Millie bit into the second ladyfinger. She'd never tasted anything so good. Buttercup lifted her head and Millie stuffed the last of the treat into her mouth before the goat tried to steal it.

Sheriff Finch picked up a ladyfinger and took a bite, nodding his approval. "In '59, I landed in Denver and later made my way here. Ain't much of a miner, but I make a decent loaf of bread and folks say they'd kill for my pies." He eyed Dom. "You got George Drouillard's build and his eyes. You his kin?"

The man might make the best biscuits in the West, but with the stagecoach debacle, he'd proven he was also a lawman. Millie was impressed on both counts.

"George is my uncle," Dom said, taking another ladyfinger. "We live in Idaho Springs where Millie's the best cook in the area. Her sourdough bread will rival anything you make, except perhaps these." He popped the last of the ladyfinger into his mouth, closing his eyes and sighing happily. "These are worth killing for. Wandering Will wasn't carrying any of them when he met his untimely death, was he?"

The sheriff barked out a laugh. "No ladyfinger crumbs found at the scene of the crime." He turned to Millie. "Did you bring your starter? I'll trade my ladyfinger recipe for your starter. I've made my own twice, but neither would rise. My loaves were as flat and tough as Kansas."

Millie drew closer, but not so close that Buttercup could reach anything. "It is a pleasure to make your acquaintance, Sheriff Finch, and I did bring my starter. I'd be honored to share it with you, but right now I'm afraid we have other concerns. What can you tell us about Wandering Will's murder? We've been told you have proof George killed his partner." Dom gave Millie a dark look, but she ignored him.

If the sheriff thought it was odd to mix sourdough starter and murder in the same conversation, he didn't show it. "No proof, just suspicions. Actually, I'd hoped the whole business was done once George left town. I ain't fond of killings but a few men, like Wandering Will, needed dying." He frowned. "You weren't fool enough to bring George back here, were you?"

"Uncle George didn't kill Wandering Will, so of course he came with us. We arrived last Friday. Left George at his cabin but today—"

"Are you a couple saddle-geese?" Sheriff Finch asked throwing up his hands. "Great horn spoon and dad-sizzle 'snails!'" He added several more creative curses—all with cooking themes—as he untied his apron. Beneath the pink, flour-covered garment, the sheriff wore a six-shooter on each hip. "I apologize for my language, ma'am, but I wish you'd told me George was back in town." He waved Millie and Dom out the door. "I'll come with you, but I imagine it's too late."

"Too late?" Millie hurried outside and set Buttercup on the ground. "What do you mean?"

"Wandering Will was a scoundrel, but he was also an Odd Fellow. When he died and George run off, the Fellows considered the Three Rings Mine theirs. Saturday night, while I was playing my fiddle at the bar, Milo asked me about the mine's ownership. I told him that legally, if George was still alive, half of the Three Rings still belongs to him."

"The Odd Fellows, including Milo, said they'd leave Uncle George alone." Dom's face had gone pale. "They promised to wait until his duel with Milo."

"All of them?"

"We only met a couple."

The sheriff locked his door. "Some Odd Fellows, like that young Tex and his gang, aren't very patient. They wouldn't think twice about ignoring Milo's orders and stringing George up."

THIRTEEN

May 8, 1865

Bayonet Bruises?

The Sheriff hurried down the boardwalk, while Dom rushed out into the street where there were fewer people blocking his path. Millie scrambled to keep up, but couldn't help asking breathlessly, "Sheriff Finch, do *you* think George killed his partner?"

"Millie!" Dom growled.

"Well..."

"George hasn't got an alibi," said the sheriff, slowing his pace slightly, allowing Millie to catch up. He nodded a greeting to two miners as he added, "And he didn't know the Odd Fellows would inherit Wandering Will's half of the Three Rings. In addition, your kin or not, George is a lying meathead with a hair-trigger temper who smells worse than rotting cheese. He's—"

Dom stomped over, his chin jutting out, and blocked Sheriff Finch's path. "Uncle George isn't a gentleman, but that doesn't make him a killer."

"You sure? That quick temper looks like a family

trait." Sheriff Finch's mustache twitched and Millie thought the sheriff was as angry as Dom.

Trying to ease the tension, she took Dom's arm and pulled him away until they were again walking in the direction of the Three Rings mine. "Dom, you know how unpleasant George can be. Also, he has a loose relationship with the truth. Still, I'm sure Sheriff Finch realizes that a temper and motive doesn't make a man a killer."

"You're right, ma'am. I don't have proof George killed Wandering Will, but I'm certain George *is* capable of killing." Millie tightened her hold on Dom's arm when she heard him growl. "I didn't arrest George because I didn't have proof, and there were others who wanted Will dead. Wandering Will was like my sweet cakes; women couldn't resist him. Men, especially those with wives, daughters, or sweethearts, hated him. Problem is, I've got lots of suspects, but not much evidence."

"What evidence did you find?" Millie questioned as Dom spoke over her asking, "Who else wanted Wandering Will dead?"

"I'll tell you about my suspects, but I think it's what I didn't find that's important." They reached the end of the boardwalk and Millie released Dom. He led the way up the trail they'd come down when they arrived. Millie followed and Sheriff Finch politely—or maybe wisely— brought up the rear. "Wandering Will was stabbed twice with a bayonet—a bayonet I never found. Course it could have been tossed down an abandoned mine shaft, but I also never found Wandering Will's prized pistol. I'm sure the killer took it—the pistol was valuable. I've been surprised no one has tried to sell it, or more likely, drink too much and show it off."

"The Palmetto Armory pistol?" Dom asked.

"Does George have Will's pistol, Mr. Drouillard?" Sheriff Finch asked, his voice hard.

"Course not. Uncle George never mentioned the weapon. This morning, the schoolmarm, Mistress Carle, told me about it."

"How do you know the stab wounds were caused by a bayonet?" Millie asked as she held up her skirt—higher than was proper—and tried to keep up with Dom's long strides while also trying to keep her skirt from being caught in the bushes and weeds. Behind her, Buttercup bleated indignantly, obviously also having trouble keeping up. "Wandering Will might have hidden his pistol."

"I considered that, but..." The sheriff's words were drowned out by the sounds of several miners pouring sand and pebbles into a Long Tom. When Millie could hear again, Sheriff Finch said, "...in his cabin. Wandering Will's cabin is upstream from the mine. I searched the whole area between the Three Rings and Will's cabin. Didn't find nothing."

"Millie." Dom stopped and faced her. "Wait 'til tomorrow. We can search Will's cabin together."

The sheriff came up beside them, glancing from Dom to Millie. "Mrs. Drouillard, you aren't going to Will's cabin without an escort, are you?"

"I'm sure she's going to try." Dom's tone sounded sour but resigned.

"I'll be fine. After all, it's just an empty cabin. I'll let you both know what I find." Dom threw up his hands and hurried up the trail. Millie was certain Dom would also search the cabin, but she wasn't so sure he'd share his discoveries, especially if he found anything that implicated George. "Sheriff Finch, how did you know Wandering Will was stabbed with a bayonet?"

"Seen it before when I worked for the Union Army."

"Here in Colorado?" asked Dom. "I was in the First Colorado Volunteers back in '61. Don't remember seeing you there."

"I went back to the states in the summer of '62," said Sheriff Finch as Millie dodged around three miners. The sheriff paused to greet each man before resuming his explanation. "Army placed me in a camp, cooking for a medical unit. It was an outdoor field hospital, treating mostly the sick, but they also tended battle injuries. I'll never forget the screams as them old sawbones cut off arms and legs." Millie glanced back and saw him cringe. "Sorry, ma'am. That isn't a topic for a lady."

"It's not a pleasant topic, sir, but women nurses work with our injured soldiers. If medical schools allowed female students—"

"Millie thinks women should be able to become doctors," Dom interrupted, barely slowing his pace.

"And vote," Millie added.

"You know, Millie, Florence Hartley wouldn't be caught dead voting, and she'd swoon at the thought of investigating a murder." Dom's voice echoed through the trees as he disappeared around a bend.

Millie ground her teeth and paused to turn toward the sheriff. "Please ignore my husband, sir. Dom's worried about his uncle. Still, I believe a lady can remain a lady *and* vote, *or* work as doctor, *or* investigate a murder. It's my duty to determine if George killed Wandering Will."

She placed a hand over her heart. "After all, I wouldn't want a murderer anywhere near my children."

Sheriff Finch laughed. "Of course not."

Millie turned and continued walking. "So please explain about the bayonet. Is that what killed him?"

"No. The bayonet wounds weren't fatal. The one in his leg probably put him on the ground and I imagine whoever stabbed him in the shoulder meant to kill him, but the bayonet struck the shoulder, not the heart. There were clear marks showing Wandering Will struggled against his assailant before he was tossed into the Three Rings shaft."

Millie's stomach gave a little lurch. She couldn't imagine being injured and unable to fight as someone dragged you toward certain death. "That is awful, but still, couldn't the stab wounds be from a hunting knife?"

"I don't think so. There was enough blood I could believe it was a sharp knife instead of a dull bayonet, but I think all the blood came from his fall. It were the bruises near the wounds that made me think they were from a bayonet. They looked like bayonet bruises."

"Bayonet bruises?"

"When I worked the military camp, I often brought supper to the old sawbones. One afternoon, I walked in just as a soldier was brought in. He had a puncture wound that went clear through his shoulder, just like Wandering Will's injury. The head sawbone pointed out a round bruise below the wound, said it was from a socket bayonet, caused when the barrel of the rifle, or more likely the metal ring used to attach the bayonet, struck flesh. Wandering Will had a bruise below both of his stab wounds."

Millie had never considered how a bayonet was attached to a musket, nor imagined that the attachment might leave a bruise. "Are bayonets usually sharp?"

"Usually just the tip. The sides are dull so they don't cut into bone and get stuck."

Millie shuddered. "Aren't bayonets long? It would take a lot of force to send one through a man until the attachment struck flesh." They splashed across the creek just as Dom disappeared up the hill by the mine. "Would a woman have enough strength to wield a bayonet?"

"I've wondered the same thing. She would have to be strong to handle a heavy musket, but I doubt a woman could have dragged Will into the shaft. He wasn't a big man, but he was solid, and the drag marks indicate he fought. A woman wouldn't have had the strength."

Millie considered but refused to eliminate her female suspects. Frontier women were strong and tough. They hauled buckets of water, lifted heavy Dutch ovens, and often cut and split their own firewood. If Will had lost enough blood, he might not have struggled much. "I've been told Queeny, along with a dancehall girl named Kate, wanted Wandering Will dead."

"Wandering Will was as smooth as lemon meringue. Kate, Queeny, and other spurned women hated him." He laughed. "Last year, when Will stopped favoring Kate, she showed up at the Three Rings screaming like a crazy woman. Will told me she pulled out a pepper-box pistol and started shooting. That's the kind of attack I'd expect from a woman. Something—"

Dom's furious bellow interrupted him. Sheriff Finch cursed, passed Millie at a run, and scrambled up the tailing pile.

FOURTEEN

May 8, 1865

Buttercup to the Rescue

Millie lifted her skirt and petticoats and hurried after Sheriff Finch. Scrambling up the hill, she slipped on mine tailings, catching her balance as George bellowed, "*Maudit!* You'll have to toss me in, Tex, just like you did Wandering Will." Millie dropped her skirts and fumbled for her six-shooter.

She reached the Three Rings just as Dom bellowed, "Get away from George or I'll shoot." Millie stopped in her tracks, breathing hard, glancing around. The young Odd Fellow, Tex, stood on one side of the Three Rings shaft, flanked by five rough-looking miners, none of whom looked a day over twenty. The young men were armed and sported black eyes, blood spatters on their filthy clothes, and bruises on exposed skin. George stood on the opposite side of the shaft, blood matting his hair and beard, his hands bound behind his back, a rope tied around his neck.

The rope was secured to a stout pine tree.

"Calm down, the lot of you. Lower your weapons."
Sheriff Finch stood beside Dom. They both had their six-shooters out and their legs spread wide in a solid stance.
"He killed Wandering Will," snarled Tex, waving his gun at George. Millie edged sideways to get a better look at the young man, hearing Buttercup's unhappy bleats somewhere down the trail. She hoped the little goat would get distracted and not come up to the mine.

Tex stood in front of his friends, hatless with his untrimmed beard and sideburns sticking out in all directions, his balding head glistening in the sunshine. "We found Wandering Will's pack and playing cards in the half-breed's cabin." Tex's gun stayed pointed at George as the young man used his free hand to reach into a shoulder bag and pull out a pack of well-used De la Rue cards. "The scoundrel stole them after he killed Wandering Will."

"That's right," hollered a man behind Tex, waving his gun excitedly in the direction of Dom and Sheriff Finch. Millie sucked down a breath. Like a powder keg, these young men just needed a spark for the whole situation to blow to hell. She, Dom, and Sheriff Finch would be killed in the gunfire.

"I didn't kill Wandering Will," George snarled, glancing from Tex to Dom. "Will come by my place the night before he were killed. We had some whiskey, played some poker. He cleaned me out, felt lucky, and headed to town. *Merde!* He planned to pick everything up the next day. He would have too, if you Odd Fellows hadn't murdered him."

"We ain't murdered no one!" Tex excitedly bounced from one foot to the other. Behind him, his gang moved restlessly, obviously itching for action. Millie wanted to tell George to shut up—his words just incited them—but she didn't dare. Tex jammed the playing cards back into his bag and took a menacing step toward George. "Killers should be lynched."

"Stretching your neck down the Three Rings is poetic justice," said a greasy-haired ruffian enthusiastically.

Poetic justice? Millie stared at the young miner. Did he read literature when he wasn't lynching fellow miners?

"Justice is a trial in front of the miners' court." Sheriff Finch's eyes narrowed, and his mouth pinched into a thin line. He didn't look like a friendly baker anymore.

"Millie, get out of here!" Dom glanced at her, beads of sweat trickling down his face. Millie just aimed her six-shooter at Tex and said nothing. Three against six weren't good odds, but they were better than two.

"Lower your weapons, boys." Sheriff Finch's voice was steady, almost calming. "Nobody cares about George, but the miners' court won't take kindly to you killing me and the Drouillards. You'll be hung for that."

Tex's eyes darted to Millie as his gun jerked back and forth with his movements. The fringe on his buckskin coat jumped and swayed, like it was alive. "Drouillard, get rid of your wife. This is man's business."

Millie glared at Tex, but before she said anything, George hollered, "This ain't no tea party, Red. Get lost."

Millie wondered if George was trying to protect or provoke her. She scowled at him, noticing he looked gaunt, his eyes sunken, and beneath the blood, his face looked sallow. "Mr. Drouillard, as I have told you before, my name is—" Buttercup charged up the trail and indignantly rammed Millie in the thigh. She stumbled, almost firing her gun. The little goat gave Millie an indignant glare and then trotted toward Tex.

"Buttercup," Millie gasped. "Come here!"

Buttercup ignored her. Millie stepped forward but Dom—somehow, he was now by her side—grabbed her arm and forced her to stop moving. "Don't go any closer, Millie. These boys are dangerous."

"We ain't boys," Tex sneered. "We're men."

Millie's breathing turned shallow. Buttercup was now a body-length away from Tex. Millie lowered her gun and slapped her thigh. "Buttercup. Please, come here. Buttercup!"

The little goat lifted her nose and stepped directly in front of Tex. He glanced at her, his expression incredulous as Buttercup stretched out her neck and bit off a leather fringe from his buckskin britches. Watching him with bulging eyes, Buttercup chewed on the leather, the end hanging from her mouth like a rattlesnake's forked tongue.

"That goat's eating your pants," said the greasy-haired man.

"She looks hungry," added another young man.

"Go away," Tex stepped back. Buttercup just followed him and stretched out her neck again. Millie frantically called to the little goat, knowing Tex wouldn't hesitate to kill her, but Buttercup ignored Millie and reached up, biting off another leather fringe.

"Don't eat me!" Tex swung his gun downward.

Millie screamed as Tex fired. Buttercup collapsed into a heap as black powder smoke filled the air.

The blast echoed up the valley. Millie jerked free from Dom's hold, her heart broken, and rushed forward.

"Buttercup!" Tears filled her eyes as she dropped to her knees and gathered the dead animal in her arms.

"You low-down, dirty rakehell," Dom spat. "I'm going to skin you alive."

Tex, his eyes wide, backed up until he ran into the greasy-haired man. "I-I didn't mean to kill it. I was just gonna hit it. Make it stop eating me. My finger slipped. It were an accident."

Millie sat on the cold ground, her face pressed into Buttercup's warm fur. She was just a silly goat, but Millie had loved her like one of her children.

"You killed the lady's goat," said a man with a goatee, his stringy beard resembling Buttercup's dirty chin tuft.

The greasy-haired man stepped away from Tex. "Women are crazy about children and critters. She's gonna kill you." He backed away, followed by the others. Tex, wide-eyed and suddenly looking desperate, watched openmouthed as his comrades gave Millie a wide berth, turned, and stampeded down the hill and out of sight.

"I didn't mean to kill the goat," Tex whined. "My gun weren't even aimed at it when it went off."

Millie stopped crying and lifted her head. Her hands shook as she felt Buttercup's warm flank. Beneath her palm, Buttercup was still, but she felt a steady heartbeat. Relief made her feel weak. Buttercup had fainted.

"Now we'll see who gets lynched," George growled. "Let me loose, Nephew, and we can wrap this noose around Tex's scrawny neck."

"There'll be no lynching today." Sheriff Finch slipped his revolver into his holster. "Put away your piece, Tex, and get out of here. You owe Mrs. Drouillard an apology, and the price of a new goat."

"Sorry ma'am." Tex backed away, warily watching Millie. "I'll bring some gold dust by, when I got some."

"You should be ashamed of yourself, Mr. Tex." Millie's voice shook as she fumbled to her feet, Buttercup clasped tightly in her arms. "Killing an innocent animal is cruel. Didn't your mother teach you any manners?"

"Mama taught me good." Tex circled around Millie. "But I were bad. She'd be ashamed of me. I…" He turned and fled.

"I-is she dead?" Dom strode to Millie's side—his own eyes glistening with unshed tears.

Buttercup's eyes remained shut and her head lay still on Millie's arm, but as Millie watched, the rawhide strip slowly disappeared between Buttercup's lips. Millie shuddered. "I think she just fainted." Buttercup opened an eye and burped; the smell so foul Millie gagged.

"I'm impressed, Mrs. Drouillard." Sheriff Finch walked over and patted Buttercup. "I thought for sure there'd be a shootout. Your goat's not hurt."

"No."

Sheriff Finch chuckled. "Never seen a goat and a woman defuse an explosive situation like that. I—"

"*Maudit!*" George hollered. "Quit squawking about the damn goat and get this blasted noose off my neck. I want to see what damage them—"

"George," Dom bellowed, interrupting George's tirade. "My wife just saved your life. You *WILL* be polite, or we'll leave you here to rot!"

For several seconds no one said a word. George glowered at Millie, his whole body shaking in rage, then, like he had done back at Idaho Springs, he seemed to take control of himself and his face went slack. "Sorry, Mrs. Drouillard. Thank you for saving my life." He bobbed his head at Millie and glanced at Dom. "I'd appreciate if you'd turn me loose, Nephew, so I can wipe the blood from my face."

Millie felt a chill run up her spine. Any man who controlled his temper like that was far more dangerous than a bounder like Tex. Despite Dom's adamant denials, Millie easily believed George could have murdered his partner.

FIFTEEN

May 8, 1865

Tex's Surprise

Dom strode over and cut George's hands free. Instead of thanking him, George swore in French as he jerked at the rope around his neck. Dom shook his head and then stopped. He stepped closer to the mine shaft, sniffed, and grimaced, before backing away and giving Millie a baleful look. George yanked the noose from his neck and tossed the rope to the ground. He stomped past the sheriff and disappeared in the direction of the stream. Millie lifted her eyebrows at Dom. "What?"

"You find something?" Sheriff Finch looked from Millie to Dom.

"Not sure, but I think Tex and his buddies may have tossed something unpleasant into the Three Rings." Shaking his head, Dom walked over and gave Buttercup a pat. "Sorry you had to witness that, Millie. I'm even sorrier to say we need to invite George to stay with us for the next couple nights. I don't trust Tex and his cronies."

Millie blew out a long breath and set Buttercup on the ground. "I know." Resigned, she looked around. "What do you think they tossed into the mine?"

"Not sure, but the air in the shaft smells foul."

Millie glanced around, making sure George wasn't in earshot. "Sure it wasn't George?"

Dom grunted and turned as loose tailings clattered and George scrambled into view. His face and hair were wet, but Millie still saw clots of blood in his beard. His knuckles were raw, and a bruise lined his cheek below his left eye. He looked pitiful except for his fury-filled eyes.

"I apologize for my earlier behavior." George's tone was gruff, definitely *not* apologetic. "I had a rough weekend. Saturday morning Tex and his buddies came visiting. Barely got away without my neck being stretched. I spent most of the weekend hiding in a cave with nothing to eat. This morning I crept back to my cabin, but they jumped me while I was grabbing grub. They dragged me here, said they were going to hang me in the Three Rings. They—" He stopped short and gawked at something behind Millie. Uttering a barrage of French curses, he stomped over and kicked a large round boulder with his foot. "I'm gonna kill Tex."

"They'll be no more killing, George." Sheriff Finch rested his hand on his holster. "I want your word on it before I leave, or I'll haul you off to the calaboose."

George scowled and bent, struggling to roll the stone toward a flat outcropping near the creek. "Look what those *pourries* did to my arrastra."

Millie edged closer, curious to see what one of these Mexican ore crushing devices looked like. She smelled

George's body odor and backed up, deciding she wasn't that curious. *Oh Lor'!* She'd invite George into her cabin, but only after he bathed. With soap.

"This is my arrastra's dragging stone." George pushed the stone into a round channel. The channel was six to ten feet in diameter with an upside-down wooden T in the center and a wooden frame over it to hold the T upright. Millie drew closer—despite George's smell—and she saw how the center wooden T shaft could rotate, assuming it was yoked to a burro. The arms on the T almost rested on the ground and would push against the grinding stone, causing it to roll inside the channel and crush the gold ore.

It was a simple device, yet she couldn't imagine the misery of spending one's day carrying ore from the shaft to the arrastra, crushing it, and then using mercury to amalgamate the gold particles out of the crushed ore. It would be backbreaking, wet work—worse than washing clothes—and from what she'd heard, most miners barely made enough to pay for food, lodging, supplies, and dubious entertainment. Worse, these men had left family, friends, and their homes behind.

"We'll fix your arrastra later," Dom said. "I think we've got worse problems, although we can handle them tomorrow if you want to grab a meal and some sleep."

"Later. I want to get down there and see how much of my lode is still there. Tex said they'd cleared it all out. Said the Three Rings was played out." George looked around. "What else did you find?"

Dom pointed into the shaft. "Take a whiff."

George stomped over, sniffed, and snarled an ugly, "*Maudit!*" Shaking his head, causing his tangled beard to jerk, he snarled, "Tex said they left me a surprise, just in case they didn't catch me."

Sheriff Finch strode over but after one shallow breath, he backed away. "I wouldn't have given Tex credit for anything so devious. It's brilliant, really."

Curious, Millie left the arrastra and moved closer to the shaft, but she couldn't bring herself to get too close. Still, even from several steps back, the foul smell made her gag. "It reminds me of meat left too long in the sun."

"Probably a dead, bloated mule, or maybe a deer or a burro," said Dom glumly. "We'll have to remove it piece by stinking piece."

"Even after you do, working down there will be awfully unpleasant." Sheriff Finch grinned. "Sure glad I'm a baker."

Buttercup wandered over, took one sniff, and tumbled over. Dom grabbed the little goat and moved her so she didn't tumble into the shaft. Millie shook her head, but then she had a chilling thought. "Sheriff, Tex didn't have anyone else he wanted dead, did he?"

"Blast it!" The lawman rubbed his forehead. "Sometimes I wonder why I let the miners' court talk me into being sheriff. I'd planned to make dried apple tarts today, but the only thing I'll be doing after this is bathing and washing clothes."

"You won't need to wash clothes," Millie said dryly. "Anything worn near that smell will need to be burned."

"It ain't that bad. I'll go down." George stripped off his blood-spattered coat, revealing tears in his buckskin shirt and pants. "Dom, you and the sheriff handle the whim and lower me down. It's easier with a burro, but with our capstan and pulley system, hand lowering ain't that bad." He stepped forward and picked up the ore bucket.

"I appreciate the offer, George. But as Sheriff, I need to go down, just in case it's a body, not an animal."

"Fine." George placed the ore bucket and rope over the pully and let go. The bucket dropped into the mine, clanking against the walls. He strode over and untied the rope around the whim crossbar. "We'll pull the bucket up so you can climb into it."

Dom joined George, taking a firm hold of the whim's bar. The rope attached to the ore bucket wound over a pully and around a vertical barrel on a shaft, something Dom had called a capstan. Dom and George walked backward, twisting more rope around the capstan until the ore bucket rose into view.

"I told you the vein we found was rich," George said. "Tex said it was played out, but that can't be true. If the Three Rings was worthless, why go to this much trouble?"

"Just to yank on your chain," Sheriff Finch said, inspecting the rope and ore bucket. "Sure this will hold?"

"Course." George glared at him. "A real sheriff would have assumed them Odd Fellows killed Wandering Will. Milo knew they'd inherit the Three Rings, and they're all greedy *pourries.*"

Sheriff Finch eyed George, not bothering to hide his dislike. "I spoke with Tex and Milo after we discovered Wandering Will's body. Tex was at a gaming house all night and most of the morning. Several gamblers confirmed that. Milo was in his cabin. He didn't have an alibi, but he didn't put up a fuss when I searched his cabin. I didn't find Wandering Will's pistol, his poke, or a bloody bayonet."

"He could have hid them."

"Could have." Sheriff Finch lit a candle, took hold of the rope and stepped gingerly into the bucket. When he put one foot in, the bucket sank, but soon held steady. Carefully he stepped into the bucket and wrapped an arm around the rope. Millie cringed and looked away. What if the rope broke? Even without the foul smell, she could never go anywhere near the mine, much less down into it. Just the thought made her feel faint. Stumbling backwards, she glanced over just as Sheriff Finch dropped out of sight.

The rope slowly unwound from the capstan barrel and finally went limp. "It's a burro," Sheriff Finch yelled, his voice muffled. "In bad shape. Get me out of here."

Millie took several more steps back as Sheriff Finch emerged from the shaft, smelling like rotting meat. After climbing from the bucket, he gasped a goodbye and gagging, hurried away. Dom shook his head, locked the whim pole into place and walked over to Millie. "Why don't you take Buttercup back to town. It will take time to remove the carcass." Leaning down, he kissed her.

"Dom!" Millie blushed at his public show of affection, but then she saw his eyes cut toward George. Regretfully, she understood her duty. "Mr. Drouillard, it isn't safe for you to stay in your cabin." Her words were flat, unenthusiastic. "We would be pleased if you would come live with us."

"Sure," he said. "You cook better than me."

Flinching at his rudeness, Millie added, "But before you enter my home, I expect you to bathe and dress in clean clothes."

"Like that's gonna happen."

"It will, if you want supper." Nodding to Dom, she called to Buttercup and snapped her fingers. "Come, Miss Buttercup." The little goat trotted obediently beside her and followed her down the trail toward the stream. Pausing, Millie looked back. "Be safe, Dom."

"We'll be safe." Dom rolled his shoulders. "It's you I'm worried about, Red. Stay away from Tex and try not to cause too much trouble."

SIXTEEN

May 8, 1865
Wandering Will's Cabin

Millie scrambled down the rock tailings and crossed Buckskin Creek. When she reached the trail, she paused. George and Dom would be working in the mine for hours. Hosa and Rachel wouldn't return from school until early afternoon. Millie had time before she needed to start supper and Wandering Will's cabin was just upstream. She considered. Dom had made it clear he didn't want her snooping around the cabin by herself, but she hadn't promised anything.

It was just an empty cabin. When else would she get a chance to search it?

"This way, Miss Buttercup," Millie whispered, turning upstream. She walked up the trail—hoping Buttercup wouldn't bleat as they passed George's arrastra on the far side of the stream. Although she couldn't see them, she heard Dom and George arguing as she hurried by, not stopping until thick evergreens and white-barked Aspen closed in around her. Pausing to catch her breath, Millie glanced around. Beside her, the small stream bubbled, making a left-hand turn just in front of her, but she didn't see a side trail or cabin on her right. Surely Wandering Will's cabin was nearby. Leaving the path, Millie crossed the stream and headed toward a sheer rock wall near the valley floor.

The underbrush was heavy and Millie watched enviously as Buttercup slipped underneath it. Sighing, she pushed through two bushes and squeezed between trees until she reached an open slope covered in uneven boulders. Using her hands and feet, she climbed between two larger boulders, jumping when someone whistled at her. Millie glanced around, expecting to find an angry Dom, but instead, she saw a fat rock chuck sunning itself.

"That wasn't polite." The animal just whistled again as Millie scrambled across the boulder field and edged into the thick foliage, spotting a structure shadowed and hidden by trees. It looked run-down and not particularly friendly, making Millie hesitate. Maybe Dom was right. Surely it was just an empty cabin. Climbing over a downed tree, she cautiously approached.

Wandering Will's cabin was tiny, looking barely big enough for a bed, with no windows and a filthy-looking deer hide covering the door. Millie paused and brushed a pine needle off her arm, imagining the hide wouldn't keep bugs out, much less bears or mountain lions. Knowing she was stalling, she turned and checked on Buttercup. The little goat had stopped to nibble on a bush, looking like she didn't have a care in the world. Millie wished she felt that way.

Around her, the woods were silent. Birds weren't

chirping, the bubbling stream couldn't be heard, and even the gentle breeze was quiet. Millie chided her overactive imagination, took a deep breath, and stepped from the thick underbrush. Gingerly she crept toward the cabin, stopping short when she spotted a clothesline and a washtub. There were fresh drag marks near the tub and a heavy-looking red and black blanket spilled over the washtub's edge. Hesitating, she started when the deer skin moved.

Queeny pushed it aside and strode out.

Without her face paint and dressed in a faded work dress, the fancy woman looked worn and older. Lines creased her cheeks, turning down her mouth into a sour frown, and Millie noticed streaks of gray in her braided hair. She felt a jolt of pity until Queeny—fast as a rattlesnake—spun around and pulled out a derringer.

A leather poke fell to the ground.

Queeny kept her derringer pointed at Millie as she scooped up the poke and shoved it into the folds of her dress, but not before Millie saw two white W's stitched into the narrow leather bag. Wandering Will's poke?

"How very unpleasant to see you again." Queeny glanced around. "Where's your husband?"

Millie swallowed. A derringer was plenty big enough to be deadly and having the action end pointed at her made her stomach feel queasy. "I'm Mrs. Drouillard."

"I know who you are." Slowly she lowered her gun. "I take it you're alone, which is a surprise. Your husband must be busy with George. Did Tex and his buddies succeed in lynching the scoundrel?"

"You knew about that?"

"Tex took an amusement break Saturday night."

Queeny shook her head like it didn't matter. "You're not welcome here, Mrs. Drouillard. Leave." As if Millie wasn't worth the trouble, Queeny's gun disappeared back into the folds of her dress and the woman turned and strode toward the washtub, shooing Buttercup away from the wet wash.

Millie knew she should leave, but when else would she have a chance to question Queeny? "This was Wandering Will's cabin. Why are you here?"

"Why do you care?"

"I'm trying to solve Wandering Will's murder." Millie slipped her hand into her apron pocket and wrapped her fingers around her six-shooter. Its weight helped increase her confidence.

"George murdered Will. Everybody knows that." Queeny lifted the red and black woven blanket from the washtub and threw it over the clothesline, handling the heavy article with ease. Most frontier women were strong, but Millie had assumed a woman in Queeny's line of business wouldn't be chopping wood, hauling water, or doing her own wash. "I thought you lived above the saloon in town."

"Not that it's any business of yours, but I come out here to do my wash."

Millie considered. "You're Wandering Will's ex-wife. Not the only one, from what I hear. This isn't your cabin."

"I told you to leave."

"Not until I get some answers."

Queeny gave Millie a hateful glare and strode over to where Buttercup stood grazing. She knelt and wrapped an arm around Buttercup's neck. Pulling out her derringer, she pointed it at the little goat's head. "Killing you wouldn't be smart, but no one would think twice about me killing this foolish-looking critter. Heard tell you were fond of it."

Millie felt her heart race and her mouth went dry. "You hurt my goat, Miss Queeny, and you'll be seeing Wandering Will sooner than you planned."

Queeny threw back her head and laughed. Buttercup stared up at her, gave a gurgled bleat, and went limp. Startled, Queeny dropped her gun as she released the goat and jumped backward. "I didn't do nothing."

Millie almost laughed. Queeny might be mean as a snake, but she didn't appear to be a killer. "You made my goat faint."

Queeny glared at the goat and shook her head. She picked up her gun and turned back to Millie. "I've always hated weak, fainting females. Why would you teach a goat to swoon?" Her derringer disappeared again into the folds of her dress.

"Did you hate Wandering Will?" Millie asked. "Is that why you killed him?"

"I didn't kill Will!" Queeny fisted her hands on her hips, her eyes flashing. "I loved him and he loved me. I'm the only woman he ever loved!"

Surprisingly, Millie believed her, or at least she believed Queeny had loved Will. "If you both were in love, why'd you become a, ah, fancy woman? Why'd he leave you?"

"He didn't leave me; I left him. He wanted children. I couldn't have any. So I left. Went to work—I don't like being poor. Will loved *me*. *He* followed *me* to Buckskin Joe and wanted me back. Wandering Will spent everything he earned on me. He never visited any other woman."

"What about the dancehall girl? Miss Kate?"

"Kate." Queeny spat out the name. "Kate's nothing but a wanton hussy. Will never cared for her. She got him drunk and he did what any man would do, but a few months later, when she whined about being in a family way, he just laughed. Said he'd take the child and I'd raise it for him."

"Miss Kate had Wandering Will's bastard?" Nobody had mentioned anything like that.

"She claimed it was his, but I doubt it. She's uppity, like you. Likes to pretend she's a proper lady. Says she only works dancehalls to earn her keep, but I know better. I've seen her disappear upstairs with a customer." Buttercup rose from her faint, shook herself, eyeing Queeny with bulging, sorrow-filled eyes.

"What happened to the child?" Millie asked.

Queeny shrugged and turned back to her laundry, hanging up a black dress with red lace. "Who knows. Kate left. Was gone for six, maybe eight months. Probably headed to Denver and got rid of it. Then she came back and someone murdered Will."

"Are you saying Kate killed Wandering Will?"

"Maybe. Maybe George. I don't know, but the night before Will was murdered, he tried to buy a dance and Kate slapped him across the face. She made a scene, even threatened to kill him." Queeny finished hanging her laundry and walked toward the cabin, her back straight. She pushed aside the filthy door covering and paused, giving Millie one final, hateful glare. "Get out of here, Mrs. Drouillard. You don't belong. Unlike your goat, you won't come back from the dead."

SEVENTEEN

May 8, 1865

The Bellyache School

Millie considered all she'd learned as she used the last of her dried meat to make a venison hash. She lit the stove and set her cast iron kettle over the heat, pleased by the pleasant smells that soon filled the cabin. With George joining them, Millie decided additional sourdough biscuits might be needed, along with an extra dose of patience. Buttercup bleated and ran to the front door as Millie reached up for the crock holding her sourdough starter. The door banged open and Hosa and Rachel tromped in. They carried their school readers and slates in one hand and empty lunch buckets in the other.

They wore matching scowls.

Buttercup, pleased to see the children, butted each of them before prancing over and looking at Millie with bulging, expectant eyes. Millie took down the carrot greens she'd saved, amused as Buttercup took her treat and hurried away, the greens hanging from her mouth.

Millie wished it was that easy to make the children happy. Steeling herself, she plastered on a fake smile and said brightly, "Welcome home. Miss Rachel, Hosa. How was your first day at Buckskin Joe's school?"

Hosa glowered at her and said nothing. He'd never liked the Idaho Springs school and his expression indicated today's experience was far, far worse.

Trying not to be deterred, Millie asked, "Did Mrs. Carle have a bell like they use at Idaho Springs? I bet you had to line up, girls on one side and boys on the other. I remember doing that when I was a girl. Back then, girls entered the school first and only after they took their seats were the boys allowed inside." She knew she was babbling, but the children's expressions made her nervous. "Is that how it was today?"

Rachel hung her coat on a nail and stomped over, tossing her planner and slate on the table. "We don't like that teacher. After you left, she taught us a poem about *good* children. Said good children fears God. They obey parents and never lie."

"And love Christ," Hosa added bitterly, tossing his planner onto the table. "I ask about Heisonoonin, the Arapaho Creator. That teacher got mad and make me stand in the corner." His scowl deepened. "She called me a heathen."

Millie blanched and her shoulders slumped. She'd taken the children to church and tried to teach Hosa about Christianity, but he'd never gotten past Christ rising from the dead. Hosa had insisted dead was dead, adding sadly, "Dead people will not come back alive. Not even dead mothers."

"That teacher calls all them children mean names. One

boy is Durty Duncehead and his sister is Bony Broomstick. She called Hosa, The Heathen, and me, Saucy Snip." Rachel looked rather pleased by her name. "She made me stand in the corner, too."

"That was very unkind of her," Millie said, uneasy about what she was hearing. "I'll have a word with Mistress Carle in the morning." Hosa sat down and struggled to take off his moccasins. "Hosa, can I help you?"

"No."

Millie looked away, unsure what to do. Hosa's mother, Sooxei, had made his moccasins days before she'd been killed. They were made of soft deerskin and she'd decorated them with colorful glass beads. Now the shoes were almost too small for Hosa's growing feet, yet the boy refused to wear anything else. Knowing his shoes were an argument for another day, Millie tried to find something—anything—positive about their day. "After your morning lessons, did you make new friends during recess?" Both children looked away. Millie's worries spiked into fear. "Hosa. You didn't do anything improper, did you?"

"No," Hosa said, very, very quietly.

Millie closed her eyes. Would an angry parent soon be knocking on their door? As if reading her mind, Rachel said quickly, "Hosa knocked a mean boy down and cut off some of his hair." She shrugged. "Hosa ain't got no choice. Just like at Idaho Springs, if he don't show 'em he's boss, them big boys turn nasty."

Millie knew it was true—children were not kind—and again she wondered if she should keep the children home. She'd try one more day and then decide. "How about your lessons? Were you both able to keep up with Mistress Carle's instructions in math and reading?" She knew Hosa hated to be placed with the younger children because his reading skills were poor. While they journeyed from Idaho Springs to Buckskin Joe, Millie had worked with him and been pleased with his improvements. The child was bright when he applied himself.

"Did you know they call that place the Bellyache School?" Rachel asked gleefully.

"The Bellyache School? Why in heavens name is it called that?"

"At lunch, Mistress Carle makes one big girl go down and fill the water bucket while we get our lunch buckets. Once she comes back, we get to fill our dippers, but the water tastes like dirt. Them miners upstream have tore up the stream. The girl sitting beside me told me not to drink too much or I'll get a bellyache. Maxcy says even his parents call it the Bellyache School, but that schoolmistress don't like it none, so don't say it round her."

Hosa neatly set his moccasins by the door before sitting on his stool and opening his primer. "That mean Mistress Carle say I read and write bad." He glowered at Millie. "She made me stand in a corner and read a lesson. Five times I read that lesson. Every time she say I read bad. She says I got to read it again at home."

Hosa's furious expression left Millie feeling both fearful and helpless. "Hosa, I know this is difficult for you—"

"A warrior does not need school," he said angrily. "A warrior needs a horse. A warrior does not cut off hair of mean white boy, he takes a scalp."

Dread shivered up Millie's spine. "Hosa, I'm sorry this is so difficult. Mistress Carle is wrong. In less than a year, you've learned to speak excellent English and started reading and writing. I've tried—"

The front door banged open, and George stomped inside. The odor wafting off him was worse than anything Millie had ever smelled. She gagged. Rachel squeaked. And Buttercup fainted.

"Out," Millie cried, waving her arms at the man.

Hosa wrinkled his nose. "Smells like bad meat. Eat bad meat and you get a bellyache."

"Out," Millie repeated. "You'll bathe in the barn." Keeping a hand firmly over her nose and mouth, she shooed George back out the door, her eyes watering. As she slammed the door, Millie felt her own bellyache coming on.

EIGHTEEN

May 9, 1865
Augusta Tabor's Store

The next morning, Dom and George retrieved the burros and left for the Three Rings. Dom thought he could train Columbine to work the whim and George wanted his burro for hauling away the carcass. Rachel hadn't been pleased with George taking "her Bluebell." Wisely, he'd nodded his agreement when Rachel made him promise to take good care of the burro.

After they'd left, Millie asked if Rachel and Hosa wanted to stay home and have her teach them. They'd whispered quietly but when Maxcy arrived, they decided to try one more day at the Bellyache School. Millie was relieved and then immediately felt guilty: a good mother would want her children home, wouldn't she?

Putting it aside—she threw open the cabin's doors and shutters, tying up the hides that insulated the windows. She was happy to have a chilly breeze if it removed the dead animal odor that had accompanied the men home. Unfortunately, even after baths, the odor had clung to both men and this morning, the sour smell lingered like an unwelcome guest.

Shaking her head, Millie went outside and lit a fire under her wash tub. Her eyes watered as she scrubbed Dom's and George's clothes, but she knew the only way to remove the hideous odor would be to burn the garments. Finally giving up, she hung everything on her line, idly wondering how long would she be able to put up with George? In addition to the repugnant smell, last night he'd been barely civil, complaining about how a guest shouldn't have to bathe in a drafty barn, saying her venison hash was dry, and even hinting that a proper hostess—a real lady—would give up her bed to a guest.

The more time Millie spent around George, the more she disliked him. She could easily imagine him attacking his partner with a bayonet or tossing the screaming man down the shaft, but she couldn't think of a single reason why he—or any other killer—would do both. A killer who put a bayonet through someone hard enough to cause a bruise could finish the job with a more precise thrust. Or, if the killer wanted the murder to look like an accident, they could have gotten Wandering Will drunk and pushed him into the mine. Doing both made no sense at all.

If that wasn't bad enough, Millie already had too many suspects. Milo, Tex, and the other Odd Fellows wanted the Three Rings as much as George, giving them all motive for the killing. Queeny had both loved and hated Wandering Will, a dangerous and volatile mix. Kate had been rejected, and if she'd ended up in a family way, she would have been forced to either keep the child or have a dangerous operation. The women's motives were as strong as the men's, but Millie doubted either woman had the strength to drag a struggling Wandering Will into the mine shaft, even if he was badly hurt.

Worse, there were probably other suspects she didn't know about yet. Wandering Will's womanizing meant there could be irate husbands, suitors, and brothers. Millie needed to speak with Kate, yet the woman worked and lived at Buck's Dancehall and Saloon. There was no way Millie could visit such a place, not even to solve a murder. As much as she hated to consider it, she might have to send Dom.

Oh Lor'! The last thing Millie wanted was to send her husband into a saloon to question a loose woman!

Drying her hands on her apron, she glanced at her pocket watch and decided it was late enough for a visit to the Tabor's store. She wanted to meet Maxcy's mother, and she needed supplies. Glancing down at her travel worn and stained skirt, she decided to look for fabric that matched her bodice and buy enough to make a new skirt.

Locking Buttercup in Columbine's empty stall—she didn't dare leave the little goat unattended in the cabin— she headed out. At the Tabor's store, Millie pulled open the heavy wooden door and paused to let her eyes adjust to the dim interior. The shop was large, probably four times as big as Millie's cabin, and every available space contained merchandise. Bolts of colorful lawns, calicos, and other fabrics were displayed in one corner, surrounded by sewing notions, soap, and spices. On the wall behind them hung axes, rawhide gloves, knives, and tobacco pouches. Shelves lining a back wall displayed canned goods, sweets, and barrels of dried goods. One corner appeared to be the local post office, although horse harnesses, pails, and ropes dangled from the ceiling above the space, intermixed with dried vegetables, pots, and pans.

"May I help you?"

Millie turned toward the voice and found a pleasant-looking woman with a long face, curly dark hair that formed ringlets on her forehead, and a womanly figure Millie envied. The woman put down the corn she'd been weighing and looked expectantly at her.

"I'm Mrs. Dominic Drouillard." Millie dipped her head in greeting and took a step deeper into the shop. "My children and your son, Maxcy, have been going to school together. Thank you for sending Maxcy over. He helped us find the schoolhouse and introduced us to Mistress Carle."

"Ah, Mrs. Drouillard. A pleasure. Maxcy said your family was delightful. I'm Mrs. Horace Tabor. Please, call me Augusta." Her words were clipped, and she spoke with a strong Yankee accent. "Ain't many women here in Buckskin Joe so formalities tend to be dropped. I'm pleased to have another lady in town."

"It's a pleasure to make your acquaintance, Miss Augusta. Please, call me Millie."

Augusta looked down at the floor. "Ma'am, did you know there's a goat following you?"

Millie felt her face heat as Buttercup butted her, almost knocking her over. She didn't understand it. On their journey here, Hosa missed his goat and had volunteered to train Buttercup. Now, Buttercup listened to Hosa and did exactly what he wanted, but the little goat still acted like a spoiled child with Millie.

"This is my, uh, goat, Miss Buttercup." Millie quickly

picked up the little goat before she caused any mischief. "I'm sorry, she must have gotten out of the barn and followed me here. Let me lock her up again and I'll be back."

"Your goat's welcome to stay. Long as she don't cause no trouble."

"Are you sure? I can buy a rope and make a lead. That should keep her from wandering. She's usually good about waiting until she's outside to, uh, do her business..." Millie paused and blushed deeper, remembering Dom's explanation about the other, less polite, meaning of the idiom. "I mean...well, she is house trained." *Mostly.*

"She's too small to cause much trouble. Not like them miners' burros." Augusta made a rather unladylike snort. "Those little critters can wreak havoc."

Millie let the outside door close and ducked under an ox yoke, still carrying Buttercup as she skirted around a barrel half-filled with potatoes. "Miners bring their burros into your store?" Millie set Buttercup down and removed a rope from a hook. Gently, she tied the end around Buttercup's neck.

"Mostly the burros just follow their owners in, like your goat followed you. Usually, I can shoo them out before they cause too much trouble, except for Kootenay's bear. He's the worst." Augusta laughed. "Old Kootenay's a local mountain man. Says he came west in '48 and almost froze to death when Frémont got lost trying to find a winter crossing to California. Always brags that he didn't starve 'cause he spiced his mule meat with gunpowder." She shook her head. "No wonder he don't understand why his bear ain't welcome here. Men!

Without womenfolk to keep 'em civilized, they go wild."

"Wouldn't meat spiced with gunpower explode?" Millie asked.

"No idea. Never tried it."

Maybe Millie would try it one night, but just on George's steak. "I saw Mr. Kootenay yesterday." Millie worked her way around several more obstacles until she stood in front of the shop's counter. "He's trained his bear to drag folk around by their boots. He and some miners thought it was funny when they surprised a poor fellow getting off the stagecoach."

Augusta shook her head. "Sounds like Kootenay."

Millie reached for a bolt of fabric, deciding the darker calico wouldn't show dirt as quickly as a lighter fabric. "Has Mr. Kootenay had the bear long? It doesn't live in his cabin, does it?" Buttercup was a nuisance, but Millie couldn't imagine the mess a bear would make in a cabin.

"Little Bear's three or four years old, not that he's little anymore. Old Kootenay killed his mum." Augusta stepped out from behind the counter and came over to pat Buttercup on the head. "Heard tell you're here to find Wandering Will's killer."

Millie sucked in a breath. Word got around quickly. "That's right."

"Bad business that. Can't say for certain George killed Will, but it wouldn't surprise me. George has an untrustworthy streak, least seems to me. Course, also heard Milo's got a gambling problem. Guess with Will's womanizing, lots of folk might want him dead. Even me, since he left an unpaid tab." She cocked her head to one side, dislodging some of the curls stuck to her forehead. "You here for supplies or information?"

"Both." Millie had met many Yankees since coming west, and she hadn't always appreciated their blunt, sometimes pointed, conversation. Still, she found Augusta's short, staccato sentences and directness appealing. The shopkeeper obviously knew everyone in town and could probably add to Millie's list of suspects. She wanted to hear more about Milo's gambling problem and who else might have a motive. "If you have time."

"I'll always make time for another lady. Feel free to shop while I make us tea. Or would you prefer coffee?"

"Tea, please."

Augusta nodded, walked over to a small table near a tiny stove, and talked as she worked. "When I first arrived here, I was the only woman in California Gulch. I missed women's company terribly. Back in my hometown, Augusta, Maine, my mother hosted weekly teas." Her face took on a far-away look. "Lord, I hated them. Ma dressed me in frilly, uncomfortable gowns with tightly laced corsets and insisted I be polite." She shook her head and laughed. "Now I don't even own an evening gown."

Millie set the bolt of material on the counter and added other supplies she needed. "When did you arrive in the Colorado Territory?" she asked politely, enjoying the socializing. After they settled down with drinks, she'd ask the more difficult, less polite questions.

"I'm a '59er," Augusta said proudly as she added wood to her stove and filled her kettle. "Can your goat jump up on my counters? Town pigs sneak in now and then. I've learned to put anything edible out of their reach or to seal it up."

"Miss Buttercup is too well behaved to jump on

counters," Millie lied, tightening the little goat's lead as she opened a jar and took out four peppermint sticks— Dom's favorite treat. A newspaper lay open beside the candy jar and Millie stopped shopping, murder and everything else forgotten. "Is the newspaper recent?" Hungry for news from the States, she turned the pages around and scanned the headlines.

The *Daily Mining Journal* from Black Hawk didn't always have the most accurate news, but Millie hadn't read a newspaper in weeks. Printed on the top of the page was a letter written by J. Wilkes Booth, but Millie didn't need to know the madman's reason for assassinating Lincoln. Instead, she scanned an article about the rebel, General Slaughter. He'd surrendered but now insisted protection for slave property was a term of his surrender. Millie shook her head. The South had been defeated. Slavery was as dead as Lincoln, although with Andrew Johnson as president, the future of former slaves was anyone's guess.

She scanned several more articles, then put the paper aside as Augusta set out steaming cups of tea beside a plate with slices of white cakes. Leading Buttercup over, Millie sat on a wobbly, three-legged stool and picked up her cup. "Was this table a side panel of your covered wagon?"

"Yep. Nothing goes to waste here. This came from the wagon Maxcy and I rode in to cross the plains." Augusta ran a loving finger over the worn wood. "When we crossed the Arkansas River, the water got so deep the whole wagon bed floated up, Maxcy and I with it. We were carried downstream until I managed to stop our motion by clinging to a willow. I held on until the men rescued us." She laughed without humor. "If women knew the perils awaiting them here in the Colorado Territory, they'd never let their menfolk bring them here."

"Do you wish you could go back to your home in Augusta, Maine?"

"Course not. This is my home now. Still, getting into South Park back in February of '60 weren't much fun. We came over Ute Pass and had to build the road as we came. My husband had heard rumors about color discoveries in California Gulch, but we didn't know where it was. After our close call on the Arkansas, we got lost. Like I said, no one but natives here. One day my husband and the other men went out searching for California Gulch. They left me all alone by the campfire with Maxcy. He was just a wee tot then."

Augusta paused and sipped her tea. "A covered wagon and a tent ain't much comfort. Not when you're alone in the wild."

Millie remembered her first few days alone in her cabin in Idaho Springs. It had been spooky and lonely, but she'd had four secure walls surrounding her.

"I waited all day for the men. Kept my fire burning, but then it got dark. Prairie wolves started howling. I got more and more scared. I'm holding Maxcy in one arm, a revolver in my other hand. That's when I heard a noise." She placed her palm on her heart, obviously enjoying the theatrics of her story. "I yelled, scared out of my wits, but no one answered. Almost shot the little burro that walked into camp. Little guy was so cold he burned his fetlocks in my fire. I can laugh now, but not then. When that little burro followed me into my tent, I rested my head on him and wept. Lord, I felt abandoned."

Augusta entertained Millie with more stories about her early life in South Park and it was with true regret that Millie finally turned the conversation to Wandering Will and murder. "You mentioned Mr. Milo had a gambling problem?"

"That's what Mr. Tabor said. Said Milo likes a game called vingt-et-un. Never played, of course, so I'm not sure what it is. Mr. Tabor said something about cards adding up to twenty-one. Said Milo tends to play in Mr. Buck's Dancehall and Saloon. Course if gambling were motive for murder, most of the miners round here would be killers."

"Isn't Buck's where Miss Queeny and Miss Kate work?"

"It is. Those two also don't seem sad he's dead. They both hated him, although I like Kate. She's not a bad girl."

"Which saloon is Buck's?"

"Down the way, third building before the end of town." Augusta gave Millie a sideways glance. "It's Buckskin Joe's most respectable saloon, but a lady wouldn't go in there."

Millie sighed. She'd have to ask for Dom's help, but only if he agreed to her rules of proper conduct. "Do you know anyone else who wanted Wandering Will dead?"

Augusta laughed. "Most everybody, including me. Man left an unpaid bill of over four hundred dollars. I didn't find him the charmer like most ladies, but my husband said to let him have a tab." She shrugged. "Don't know why women, even the respectable ones, fell for Will. Miss Kate had it the worst. You should talk with her. She's sensible, which makes it even harder to understand."

Millie couldn't think of a polite way to ask about Kate's supposed condition, so she hinted at it. "I heard Will and Miss Kate were going to get married."

"Heard that too. Don't know why they split, but I was glad for it. Kate deserves better than Wandering Will. His former wife, Queeny, is ample proof of what happens to a woman who marries him."

"Do you know Queeny?"

"A bit. Even working women need clothes and supplies. She's a mean one. Mr. Tabor said Queeny made Wandering Will's life a living hell. His words, not mine. Course, from what I hear, Wandering Will enjoyed taunting her. Don't know why both stayed in town."

Millie sipped her tea, considering. "What about the Odd Fellows? I heard Wandering Will left them his mining claim."

"Course. The Odd Fellows Society helps all its members write their wills. They'll also pay the fees for burying a member. That's why lots of men join. They…" She paused and cocked her head.

Outside Millie heard men yelling and boots thudding against the walkway. Rising, she hurried to the door and pulled it open. Augusta, just behind her, stopped a man who was limping by. "Alfred, what's going on?"

"A duel! Tex and some newcomer are fighting to the death."

NINETEEN

May 9, 1865
Honorable Murder

Millie didn't wait for Augusta to lock up as she dragged Buttercup toward the dueling field, her heart racing. Had Dom and Tex gotten into it again? No other stranger would be dueling Tex. Silently she cursed the men and their foolish pride, but overriding her anger was a bone-deep fear. What would she do if anything happened to Dom? Choking down her fear, she hurried toward the dueling field.

Breathing hard, she passed a group of miners as the schoolhouse and field came into view. Despite the crowds, Millie saw Tex clutching a rifle, his back to a tall man with a black wool cap. Dom often wore the black cap Mary had knit for him. Millie dropped Buttercup's lead and ran forward as the duelers strode apart. "Six, seven, eight, nine." The crowd shouted each number to the beat of the thudding stamp mill. Between the crowd and the loud mill, no one noticed Millie's cries to stop. She was within twenty feet of the field, clearly able to see Tex's face, when the count reached thirty and the two men spun around. Their rifles cracked and smoke from the black powder darkened the blue sky.

"No!" Millie screamed as both men crumpled to the ground.

Shoving aside bystanders, ladylike behavior forgotten, Millie raced past Tex without giving him a second look. Gasping, she stopped short when she reached the second man. He lay on the ground, facedown and unmoving. Her shaking legs gave out and she landed hard, her eyes glued to the dark wool hat, blood pooling on the ground near his head.

Millie didn't need to see the man's face. She swiped at her tears and asked shakily, "Who-who is he?" The red hair curling out from under the wool hat wasn't Dom's.

A heavyset man lumbered over—Sheriff Finch beside him—and they turned the man over, revealing red hair spilling over a face covered in blood. "How's he look, Doc?" Sheriff Finch asked, his voice emotionless.

Buckskin Joe's dentist—the town didn't have a doctor—knelt and grunted. "He's breathing. Bullet's split the scalp and scraped his skull. Lots of blood that needs staunching. Can you find me something?"

The Sheriff turned and lifted his eyebrows at Millie. "Could you help us out, ma'am?"

Millie wanted to say no—this was not the first petticoat ruined by turning the bottom edge into a bandage—but proper behavior, and her conscience, dictated she acquiesce. Reminding herself the downed man wasn't Dom, she nodded shakily. "Of course. May I borrow your knife, sir?" Millie turned her back on the crowd and glanced toward Tex. Several men surrounded his unmoving body. Looking away, Millie knelt and cut a six-inch strip off the bottom of her petticoat. It was impossible to remove it without improperly showing her lower legs, but if any of the nearby men noticed, they refrained from commenting.

"Thanks." The dentist expertly folded one end into a bandage and wrapped the rest securely around the man's head. "Sheriff, I think he's stable enough for you to take him. Unless the wound fouls, I think he'll live to face the miners' court and a hangman's noose."

"A hangman's noose?" Millie glanced from the dentist to injured man's young face. "Wasn't the duel fair?"

Sheriff Finch didn't respond as he and another miner lifted the injured man by his arms. They left his feet dragging on the ground but stopped moving when the young man groaned and opened pale-blue eyes. Despite the bandage, blood dribbled down his face, making him look ghoulish. His confused gaze landed on Millie and he stared at her.

"Ma?" he mumbled.

"You know him?" Sheriff Finch asked Millie.

"No. Indeed not." She wasn't old enough to be his mother, although there *was* something about him.

"Maybe the wound's done more damage than I thought." The dentist shrugged and looked behind Millie. "Thanks for your assistance, ma'am. I best go check on Tex." Millie watched as Sheriff Finch dragged the stranger away while the dentist strode across the field. The crowd around Tex parted, shaking their heads as the dentist bent down. After a moment he stood up, his expression grim. "Nothing I can do for this one. Get the undertaker to make him a box."

Millie felt ill. She hadn't liked Tex, but no man should die so young. Especially not for sport. She glanced around, looking for Dom as the crowds gradually disbursed. Unable to find him, she slowly made her way back to where Buttercup stood grazing, the end of her lead tangled in a small shrub. She untied the goat and glanced at the school. She needed to talk to Mistress Carle but didn't have the stomach for it right now. Instead, she headed home, entering through the back door just as Dom and George opened the front door.

"You okay," Dom asked, looking concerned.

"Heard Tex got in a duel," George added excitedly.

Despite disgusting smells wafting from them both, Millie burst into tears and threw herself into Dom's arms. "It was awful," she sobbed. "I-I thought it was *you* dueling Tex. H-he's got a wool hat, just like yours."

"Who's got a wool hat?" Dom asked, patting Millie's back.

"The man who dueled Tex." Millie gasped, gagged, and decided she didn't need Dom's comforting support.

She pulled away as George asked, "Did Tex bite the bullet?" Millie found the term appalling, but she nodded. George let out an enthusiastic whoop, strode into the cabin and took down the morning bread, ripping off the end and stuffing it into his mouth.

Millie scowled, wiped the tears from her face, and pulled out a handkerchief to cover her nose. "Mr. Drouillard, as I have asked numerous times, please don't eat the left-over bread with your filthy hands."

"Forgot," George said, unapologetically putting what was left back on the shelf.

Millie just shook her head and turned toward Dom.

"They're talking about hanging the man who won the duel. I don't understand. It looked fair. They both fired at the same time." Millie touched Dom's arm. "I-I thought it was you. It wasn't until I saw the man's red hair that I realized..."

"It wasn't me," Dom said, pulling off his cap and wrapping his arms around Millie.

Despite the awful smell, Millie returned his embrace, drawing from his strength. "How did you know about the duel? Why are you home so early?"

"Milo." Dom released Millie and took off his coat. He sniffed it, scowled, and carried it to the back door, tossing it outside. "Milo's claim is next to Tex's. He said a stranger showed up this morning, aimed his rifle down the hole, and called Tex a "miserable, double-crossing skunk." Tex responded by begging for some fair play. I guess the stranger grabbed Tex's rifle and made Tex march to the dueling field. Forced two men along the way to act as seconds."

"It didn't look like Tex had been forced into the duel."

Dom shrugged. "Milo said it was easy to see the bad blood between Tex and the stranger. Thing is, if Tex was forced into the duel, it'd be murder. The miners' court will decide, but I'd guess we're in for a lynching."

George strode past Millie, bread still sticking out of his mouth, and pushed back the elk skin that blocked the window. "There's a crowd gathering around the jail. Come on, Nephew. You've checked on your wifey, now let's go see a lynching."

"I'm coming too," Millie insisted.

Despite how bad he smelled, Millie didn't object when Dom wrapped his arm around her as they pushed into the crowds. His smell was perhaps why the crowd opened up around them. "This isn't going to be pretty, Millie. Sure you don't want to return to the cabin?"

Millie didn't want to see the red-headed man—or anyone else—lynched, but she wanted another look at the stranger's face. There was something about him. She flinched when a nearby man yelled, "Lynch him!" The call was taken up as Sheriff Finch led the stranger out onto the boardwalk. The injured man kept his face averted; his palms pressed against either side of his temple.

Beside her, George had to holler to be heard over the noisy crowd. "He's got your flaming red hair, Red."

"Mr. Drouillard, as I have told you numerous times, my hair is auburn with a few red streaks."

"Red, your hair is—"

"Mr. Drouillard, do NOT call me Red!"

"But you—"

"Uncle George!" Dom boomed. "Leave Millie alone."

George scowled and pushed deeper into the crowd. Dom and Millie didn't follow. The crowd suddenly quieted as three older men approached Sheriff Finch and his prisoner. The eldest man stepped forward, the creases in his face as deep as sunbaked leather. "What you got to say for yourself, *hombre?*"

A second man stepped forward, rivulets of sweat running down his mostly bald head. "Why'd you go after Tex, stranger?"

The young prisoner stood up, dropped his hands and winced, but he faced the three men with his back straight. "Gentlemen." His pale blue eyes were clear, and he spoke with a slow Texas drawl. "My name is Dave Pemley. The man you called Tex was once my best friend." He paused and pressed his thumb and fingers against the bridge of his nose, like he was battling a terrible headache. Finally, his hand dropped, and he continued. "Tex and me went to school together, along with my younger sister, Ann. When she turned fourteen, she showed a shine for Tex. He was eighteen and my best friend, so I didn't think nothing about it."

He paused and in the silence around them, Millie heard Buttercup's unhappy bleat from inside the cabin. "The day of Ann's fifteenth birthday, Tex suddenly disappeared. He left my Ann heartbroken. A few months later, my parents and I learned he'd also left Ann unmarried and in a family way." He shook his head, winced, and again squeezed the bridge of his nose. "Tex left my Ann shamed. Months later, that shame was too much. The birth killed her. Ma, Pa, and I buried her, and then I took off. My Ann deserved better than what she got."

He turned and spoke directly to the sea of rough miners. "For the past two years I've tracked my old friend. I followed him into Mexico and to the gold fields of California. His trail finally led me here, to Buckskin Joe in the Colorado Territory."

The miners murmured and a few of them shook their heads. The prisoner's eyes scanned over the crowd, widening slightly when he spotted Millie. She squirmed under his penetrating gaze and felt Dom's arm tighten protectively around her shoulder. Finally, he returned his gaze to the three older men who made up the miners' court. "Down the road a ways, I rode through a camp called Fair Play Diggings, a town, folks say, that gives a man a fair deal. I hope you men are as fair-minded. I did what I come to do. I gave Tex fair play, just like he begged for. It's more than he gave my Ann, more than he deserved."

Standing up straighter, he looked around. "I'm ready for your rope or your bullet. Any sentence your fair minds decide, I accept."

Murmurs filled the air and several men shouted out support for the young man. His words had turned the crowd, but Millie kept her gaze on the older men, the miners' court. The man's fate was their decision. They shuffled down the boardwalk and spoke quietly among themselves. The oldest dominated the conversation while the other two nodded, obviously in agreement.

"Isn't Sheriff Finch part of the miners' court?" Millie asked.

"Not here," Dom said. "Hush, they're done."

The three old miners returned and faced the injured man. The crowd stilled as the oldest man began to speak. "Mr. Dave Pemley, we, the miners' court of Buckskin Joe, have given your case due consideration." The man spoke loudly, but his voice quivered with age. "Womern are scarce in these parts. Your story gives us old troublemakers a coveted opportunity to meditate on the sweetness of a plumb fine womern who sometimes trusts a coyote of a man." He turned to face the crowd. "If they's an *hombre* within hearin' of my voice that wouldn'ta done what this red-headed feller did—let him beller out. We'll hang him!"

TWENTY

May 9, 1865

Fancy Women and Dancehall Girls

T he children arrived home while Dom and George were in the barn bathing. Millie set out slices of the raisin pie she'd purchased from Finch's bakery. After all the excitement, she'd had no time to make something herself and the only way to get George to bathe was to bribe him by offering to buy one of Finches pies. Brightly she asked how the children's day had been, hoping it had been better than yesterday, but their expressions and mumbled responses weren't encouraging. Worse, they both ate their pie in silence, their eyes downcast, mumbling one-word responses to her questions.

Even Rachel!

Rachel was never coy, no matter what kind of folly she'd initiated. As Millie's fertile imagination considered one bad scenario after another, a knock on the door interrupted her worries. Hosa jumped up and opened the door to Maxcy, like he'd been expecting him. Mumbling about helping Hosa and Rachel, Maxcy hurried to the table, pulling out his reader. Millie watched in disbelief as the three children huddled together, whispering quietly. They practiced their numbers, spelled words, scribbled diligently on their slates, and read passages aloud to each other.

Millie was thunderstruck. The children had never, ever, worked this hard at Idaho Springs.

Dom came in, his hair wet, and settled down to eat his raisin pie, glancing at the children. "Looks like you all are working hard. Mistress Carle must be a good teacher." Turning to Millie he asked in a whisper, "What'd she do to motivate them?"

"I don't know," Millie said, but she intended to find out. Tomorrow she'd visit the schoolmistress and compliment her on her teaching. That would give her an excuse to ask about Wandering Will's murder.

Dom finished his pie and joined the children, working with them as Millie prepared supper. George came in— still smelling like an outhouse despite his bath. He grabbed his piece of raisin pie and what was left of the loaf of bread, but Millie's only reaction was covering her nose with her handkerchief. After his filthy hands had handled the loaf earlier, she wouldn't have fed it to Buttercup.

Rachel sniffed loudly, glanced at George, and made gagging sounds. "We're done," she said as they quickly put away their school supplies. "Maxcy asked if we want to meet his momma. That okay?"

Millie nodded, wishing she could escape too. "Supper

will be ready in about forty-five minutes. You'll both need to do your chores, so don't be gone too long." They promised to be home soon and scurried out the door. Dom watched them leave, his expression morose. He soon insisted he needed to fix something in their bedroom and quickly disappeared.

George sat at the table like it was his, and silently finished the bread and his raisin pie. Millie politely asked about the Three Rings as she chopped up an onion—unsure if it was the onion or George's smell that made her eyes water. George grunted and Millie gave up on polite conversation. She added the onion to the salted pork on the stove and finished making biscuits. After placing the biscuits in the Dutch oven and checking that her salted pork, onions, and beans weren't scalding, she made her own excuses and left.

In the back bedroom, she found Dom sitting on the bed, his head bowed, his forehead resting in his hands. "Dom, are you ill?" Millie pressed the back of her hand to his forehead.

"I'm fine. Just tired of working in that blasted mine. Never knew a rotting carcass could make a closed-in space so putrid. Tex, or whoever dropped it down there, was brilliant. We've had to take it out, one foul piece at a time. It's the worst work I've ever done."

Millie wondered if Dom was also tired of working with George. Dom was rough and loud, but he had a heart of gold. George was also rough and loud, but his distasteful shiftiness made him feel like he didn't care about anything or anyone but himself. Seeing how miserable Dom looked, Millie decided he deserved something to look forward to. She hated to ask him to spend a night in a dancehall, but *someone* had to investigate Kate. She opened her mouth and then shut it.

How did she bring up such a topic, even with her husband? She considered, but all that came to mind were the rules she'd insist he follow. He could talk, ask questions, and watch, but there would be absolutely *no* hands-on investigating!

"I talked with Mrs. Tabor today. She said that Queeny, the fancy woman, was the last person to see Wandering Will alive."

Dom looked up, interested. "How'd she hear that?"

"Her husband was at the dancehall that night."

"He tell her anything else?"

"He said Wandering Will arrived after dark, had a drink or two, and then tried to buy a dance from Miss Kate. She's the hurdy-gurdy girl who wanted to marry Wandering Will. Mr. Tabor said Miss Kate refused to dance with Wandering Will, threw a fit, and supposedly, even threatened to kill him if he didn't leave her alone."

Dom nodded. "Uncle George mentioned Kate. Said Will broke her heart, none too kindly. I can see why he and George were partners. They probably got along just fine." Millie's eyebrows went up and Dom just shrugged. This was the first negative thing he'd ever said about his uncle. The day must have truly been awful. "She tell you anything else?"

"Mr. Tabor said that after Kate refused to dance with Wandering Will, he threw a fit and yelled at her, right in the middle of the dance floor. After she slapped and threatened him, Will laughed, pulled out his full poke, and said that Queeny would be glad to see him. Apparently Queeny was, since that was the last anyone saw of Wandering Will alive. He and Queeny sashayed up toward her room and he never came back into the dance hall."

Dom's lips lifted into a hint of a smile. "They sashayed, huh?"

She knew the word would amuse him. "Do you remember how Sheriff Finch mentioned he didn't find Will's poke? I think Queeny had it. She dropped it when I saw her at Will's cabin."

Dom ran his fingers through his thick, black hair, saying nothing. Yesterday evening he'd voiced his displeasure, loudly and in detail, at her adventure at Will's cabin. "She might have stolen his poke, but that doesn't mean she killed him. Buck's has a back stair. Just in case a customer doesn't want to be seen." Millie rose as Dom stood up. "We shouldn't leave George alone for too long."

They stepped outside and Millie asked the question she'd been curious about all day. "Dom, are dancehall girls the same as fancy women?"

"A lady wouldn't ask a question like that, Red!" George's voice was muffled, but understandable.

Millie ground her teeth but also felt her face heat. Dom led her into the cabin and she stared at her unwelcome guest. "My name is Mrs. Drouillard." The cabin walls were in bad need of chinking and Millie wondered how much of their conversation George had overheard. "Although my question is perhaps not polite, while investigating a murder, a lady must sometimes ask such things. So I repeat, are dancehall girls the same as public women?"

Dom laid a hand on his heart. "Florence Hartley would

be horrified."

Millie knew he was teasing her and wouldn't have minded if George wasn't watching. She pulled a peppermint stick from her apron pocket and held it out. Sometimes, with both Dom, Buttercup, and the children, bribery was the easiest way to get what you wanted.

Dom's eyes lit up but it was George who stomped over and held out his hand. Reluctantly Millie broke the stick in half. Dom popped his half into his mouth, crunching on the candy as he said, "They're different."

"How? Mrs. Tabor called Miss Kate a decent girl, just hard-up."

"Kate probably is decent. Dancehall girls are paid to dance and sell liquor. That's all." Dom licked his lips.

"That's true, Nephew, although I've met my share willing to supplement their income." George's candy dropped out of his mouth and got stuck in his beard. "You know, either one of them could have killed Wandering Will. They both hated him." He pulled the sticky mess from his beard, taking some hair with it, and popped it all back into his mouth. "Maybe we should go investigate. Spend some time at Buck's and ask some questions." He gave Millie a triumphant glare, like he'd just won an argument.

"I think that's what my proper wife was trying to propose." Dom grinned. "What do you say, Red? Shall I head to the saloon and do some hands-on investigating of Kate and Queeny?"

TWENTY-ONE

May 10, 1865

Hands-on Investigations

After the children hurried off to school—eager to avoid their mother's temper—Millie turned toward her blurry-eyed husband and planted her hands on her hips. Waiting for the children to leave had almost driven her to murder, but no way would she ask about Dom's evening activities with them listening. Not that it hadn't been perfectly obvious that Dom—and George—had a severe case of barrel fever. Dom and George were slouched over the table, their salted pork and fried mush breakfast barely touched, their eyes bloodshot and watery.

"What happened last night?" Millie asked loudly, indifferent to Dom's flinch. "I sent you to gather information, not to carouse and drink too much whiskey." Millie had been furious—and hurt—when Dom staggered into their bed smelling of whiskey, cigar smoke, and cheap perfume. She tried to interrogate him in bed, but he just groaned and was soon snoring, although she suspected the snoring had been an act.

Now she wanted answers.

Dom rubbed his red eyes and poured himself another cup of coffee. George just laid his head on the table. "Well?" Millie asked sharply.

Dom squinted at Millie. "Last night I learned that Miss Kate is a darn good dancer and that ten pinches of gold dust ain't near enough for a night at Buck's. Good thing George spotted me extra."

Millie had emptied most of Dom's poke before he departed. At Idaho Springs, a cup of whiskey cost two pinches of gold dust, so she'd returned ten pinches to his poke. Obviously, she'd been too generous. "What about Will's murder? You were supposed to watch and ask questions, not spend the night carousing and dancing." Millie was jealous, she knew it, but also hurt that Dom had spent the night dancing in the arms of another woman. She trusted him, but still.

"It's easier to interrogate a woman if you've got her trapped in your arms." Millie's face must have shown her hurt because Dom swore and hurried to her side, pulling her into an embrace. "I'm teasing you, Millie. I had to dance with Kate. She's very popular. The only way I could talk with her was to pay for a dance. Or two."

"Or four or five," George mumbled.

Millie tried to pull free from Dom's grasp, but he just squeezed her tighter. "Millie, I love you. Dancing with Kate was fun, but—" Millie glared at him. "But dancing with you is much, much more enjoyable." Millie didn't know if he was being honest, or just trying to appease her. "Millie, I swear, I didn't do anything improper. I danced and I asked questions. Kate said—"

"And he drank whiskey," George added.

"Only a couple whiskeys." Dom scowled at his uncle.

Millie believed—grudgingly—that Dom had danced with Kate to question her. It hurt that he'd enjoyed it so much, but he'd also drunk more than a couple whiskeys. Of course *she* had asked him to visit Bucks, but he'd enjoyed it far too much. "When we return to Idaho Springs, I'll speak with the matrons about starting a temperance society. I'm sure you're not the only husband with a drinking problem."

George barked out a laugh, grabbed his head, and buried his face in his hands. Dom just grimaced. "For every dance with Kate, I had to buy us drinks. It's expected, although I suspect her drinks were just colored water."

"Did you learn *anything* useful?"

"Kate was friendly, but hesitant to talk about her time away. She said she went to Fair Play Diggings and worked there. Said she's never been to Denver City. Maybe Queeny was wrong about Kate's condition. I don't think Fair Play has those kinds of doctors."

Millie pulled free of Dom's hold and cleared the morning dishes. "Why would Miss Queeny lie about something like that?"

"Because Queeny is as mean as a rattlesnake and she hates everyone." George's words were muffled—he hadn't lifted his head from his hands—but his feelings were clear. "Queeny wouldn't think twice about lying if it served her purpose."

Millie set dishes in her wash basin and considered. She might not like George, but she couldn't disagree with his assessment. "Did you ask Miss Kate why she came back to Buckskin Joe?"

Dom turned Millie around and kissed her before refilling his coffee. "Kate said Buckskin Joe paid better, but I'd swear she was lying. Kate's got a temper, and she didn't try to hide that she hated Wandering Will. She even said she was glad he was dead. At the end of our third or fourth dance, she looked me in the eye and said her only regret was that someone beat her to killing him." Dom sipped his coffee thoughtfully. "I think she lied about why she returned to Buckskin Joe, but I don't know why when she was so forward about wanting Will dead."

Why indeed. Millie could think of only one reason. "Do you think Kate killed Wandering Will?"

Dom pinched the bridge of his nose and shook his head. "No. She hated Will, but Kate doesn't feel like a killer."

Millie didn't know what a killer felt like. Would he think she felt like a killer if George and his rude manners drove her to murder? She didn't trust Dom's impressions, not after too much whiskey. She needed to question Kate herself. "And the working woman, Miss Queeny?"

Dom touched Millie's face, his expression serious. "I never got near her. Never even talked to her." He glanced at the table. "But George did."

George slowly lifted his head. Despite his thick beard and tangled hair, he looked a bit green, although the impression might be due to his fading bruises. "Like Kate, Queeny was busy all night. She's a mean one, but she's good at her, uh, profession." His hands shook slightly as he reached up and rubbed his forehead.

Millie felt her face warm. She was a married woman.

She understood how a working woman earned her keep, but how could a woman be "good" at such a profession? Maybe she'd ask Dom, but definitely not in front of George. "I see. So neither of you had a chance to speak with her?"

"I didn't say that. I offered to treat my nephew to a visit—to help with your investigation of course."

Millie narrowed her eyes and folded her arms over her chest, tapping her foot on the ground. She said nothing, just waited.

"He refused," George said sourly. "So I did the job."

Millie's mouth fell open. "You what?"

"I questioned Queeny." He grinned, showing yellow teeth. "She told me lots, while she…" He barked out an ugly guffaw. "She talked while she worked. When—"

"Don't," Dom said sharply. "Just tell Millie what you told me."

"Fine. Queeny told me Wandering Will spent the night with her before he was killed. He was drunk and passed out while she was, uh, working." He grinned lewdly. "Queeny said she took the rest of the night off. Probably because she emptied his poke. The next morning, when Will woke up, she kicked him out. Said he staggered down the back stairs, looking like two wildcats were battering his brain, but alive."

"He might have left alive," Millie considered, "but she could have followed him. Maybe she wanted more pay. Did you ask her if she stole Will's poke?"

"No." George laughed and pulled out his own, empty poke. "After a night at the saloon, a man's poke usually ain't missing, but it's always empty."

"Millie." Dom took her hand. "Queeny might be mean

enough to bayonet Wandering Will, but neither she nor Kate are strong enough to drag him over to the shaft. In addition, neither of them own a bayonet."

George started, groaned, and rubbed his temples. "They could have borrowed one. Old Buck, the bartender, owns a musket with a bayonet. Keeps it under the bar and pulls it out when there's trouble." He nodded like that was exactly what happened. "And Milo brags about his musket and bayonet. Never seen it—I've never been invited to the Odd Fellows Hall—but I hear it's hanging there. Anyway, Queeny or Kate could have found a bayonet if they wanted one. And as for dragging him into the mine, either could have gotten help. Queeny can offer all kinds of unique bribes to her male friends and Kate," he rubbed his forehead. "She and old Kootenay have something going. He'd do anything for her. So, either of them could have killed Will."

TWENTY-TWO

May 10, 1865

The Odd Fellows Hall

Dom kissed Millie goodbye, told her to stay out of trouble, and left with George. He thought today they would finally clean out the last of the carcass and be able to retrieve some ore samples. Only after his assays would he be able to determine if the Three Rings had any value. Millie sighed. If they were going into the mine, she'd again have smelly laundry she'd have to clean. Resigned, she headed to the barn to retrieve yesterday's pile of clothing. Normally she only washed clothes once a week, but like her, Dom had only brought one set of work clothes and one set of church clothes. Reluctantly, she heated water, thinking about what she'd learned and how she should spend her day.

She needed to visit the schoolmistress, wanted to search Wandering Will's cabin without running into Queeny, and was curious if there was anyone she could ask about Kate and the rough mountain man, Kootenay. What kind of relationship did they have? He was old enough to be her father, not that that stopped most miners. Lighting a fire under her wash tub, Millie wondered about the muskets George had mentioned. She'd never handled a musket with a bayonet. Would it be too heavy for her to wield?

The sun was full in the sky when she finished her laundry and wrapped a rope lead around Buttercup's neck. She'd start with a visit to Sheriff Finch's bakery. Her family loved his sweet cakes, and she had a few questions for him.

She stepped into the bakery and the smells delighted her senses and caused her mouth to water. How had Sheriff Finch managed to stay single? Millie was happily married, but even *she* wanted to nibble on his crumb-coated fingers. Blushing at the image, she bent down and picked up Buttercup and approached the counter.

"Mrs. Drouillard. I was hoping someone with refined tastes would come in. Would you do me the favor of tasting my gingerbread soldiers?" He offered her a plate stacked high with gingerbread in the shape of little men carrying what might have been a musket with a bayonet. "Bought the cutter from a little German store in Washington, DC. Soldiers always loved these."

"Thank you, sir." She broke off the musket and offered it to Buttercup before biting off one of the soldier's legs. "Oh! Oh my." Buttercup's eyes bulged out as Millie set her on the ground, placing her foot on the goat's lead rope as she awkwardly fanned her face. "Sir, your gingerbread is incredible." The man's skills were wasted on sheriffing! "I think I need to buy a dozen. For my family." Not that there would be a full dozen left when everyone returned home.

"Excellent." He placed the gingerbread on paper, stacking them all in the same direction, making them look like a miniature gingerbread army. "Anything else I can get for you?"

Buttercup lifted her head and Sheriff Finch stepped around the counter and patted her head. He laughed when the little goat licked his fingers, but Millie felt her face heat. She hoped the sheriff couldn't read minds, although hers at the moment felt blank. "Can you, ah, tell me where to find the Odd Fellows Hall."

Sheriff Finch rose and stared at Millie, his appearance somehow transforming into a lawman. "Mrs. Drouillard. I'm hearing rumblings about you and your husband asking questions. I don't know who killed Wandering Will, but folks round here don't like questions. Most miners have secrets, that's why they came west."

"I understand, sir, but answers are the only way to discover who killed Wandering Will."

"I'll find the killer. I don't want another body for Buckskin Joe's graveyard."

Millie slipped the package of treats into her apron, feeling the solid grip of her six-shooter as she withdrew her hand. "Sheriff, after Wandering Will's death, did you investigate everyone who owned a musket with a bayonet?"

Sheriff Finch rolled his eyes heavenward. "Yes." The word was stretched into at least four syllables. "With the War ripping the States apart, muskets with bayonets are common. All foot soldiers, on both sides, carried them. Most discharged soldiers held on to their weapons. Most of the miners in Buckskin Joe are ex-soldiers, from one side or the other."

Millie felt a bit chagrinned that she hadn't considered that, but she pressed on. "I heard Mr. Buck has one hidden under his bar and there's another on display in the Odd Fellows Hall."

Sheriff Finch frowned. "Your information is accurate, but I examined both weapons. Didn't find blood or anything else on either, although anyone with a brain could have wiped the blade clean."

"True." Millie tilted her head. "So where is the Odd Fellows Hall?"

Sheriff Finch picked up one of his gingerbread men and bit off his head. "Do me a favor, Mrs. Drouillard. Take the gingerbread home before you do anything else. Hard to enjoy eating my soldiers if they're dripping blood."

The Odd Fellows Hall turned out to be located above the town assay shop. The assayer, a thin man with curious eyes, glanced at Buttercup, shrugged at Millie's request, and pointed at a narrow stairway against the wall. Millie climbed up, disappointed to find an open, ordinary-looking room with an elk head mounted on one wall and a musket with a tarnished bayonet on the other.

She stepped over and gingerly took the weapon down from the wall. It was heavy, but if she were angry enough, she could wield it. Well, maybe just as a club. Even angry, she didn't think she could stab someone. Not unless they stood perfectly still, or maybe laid down for her.

If this was the murder weapon, it hadn't been brandished by a woman.

Carefully Millie set the butt of the musket on the

floor—making sure to keep the barrel pointed away from her—and fingered the bayonet. The edge was dull, but the point on the end was as sharp as her kitchen cleaver. The metal band attaching the bayonet to the musket barrel looked rusted, but the round bolt on the bottom would definitely leave a bruise if it struck flesh. Still, the bayonet was long and it would take a lot of force to send it through a body. If she—

"What the hell?"

Millie jumped, the heavy weapon slipping from her fingers as she spun around. The musket fell and the bayonet swung down, almost striking Buttercup. The little goat jumped, fainted in mid-air, and landed in a heap.

"Mrs. Drouillard, this is a men's club. Women are not allowed!" Milo stomped up the last two stairs, blocking the narrow stairway, his expression furious.

TWENTY-THREE

May 10, 1865

Mr. Pemley

"M r., ah, Mr. Milo, w-what a surprise." Millie scooped up Buttercup, loosened the rope around her neck, and ran her fingers over the animal's flank and tail, relieved the bayonet hadn't struck her. "My apology. Dom's been telling me about the Odd Fellows Society. I think he might be interested in joining and since I didn't know anything about them, I was curious. I—"

"You wanted to examine my bayonet to see if I killed Wandering Will." The floor shook as Milo stomped over and picked up his musket. Turning—the bayonet swinging uncomfortably close to Millie's arm—Milo roughly slammed the weapon onto the hand-forged wall hooks. One hook snapped and the weapon clattered to the floor, proving Milo had both the temper and the strength to drive a bayonet clear through a body. As he bent to pick it up, Millie darted behind him and made a hasty escape.

The assay shop was empty by the time she reached the boardwalk she heard Milo tromping down the stairs, calling her name. Taking a deep breath, feeling reassured with Buttercup warm in her arms and people out and about in the street, she turned to face him.

"Mrs. Drouillard. I'm sorry. I didn't mean to frighten you." His tight-lipped expression indicated he wasn't sorry at all. "You surprised me. The Odd Fellows is a man's society and women are forbidden in our lodge."

He might be upset by her trespassing, but Millie thought he might also be upset because he'd killed Wandering Will and didn't like her snooping around. "My apology. I didn't realize that," she lied. "What brings you back to town so early, Mr. Milo? I assumed you'd be working your claim."

"I'm sure you did." He ran a hand down his face as if to wipe away his temper. "Not that it's any of your business, but there's a meeting tomorrow. I came back early to start some preparations. We've got a new member who will be initiated—assuming he passes the ceremony." Milo's unpleasant smile made Millie shiver. "Since your husband is so interested, I'll plan for him to be initiated at the same time."

*****

For a second day in a row, the children looked guilty as sin as they walked inside the cabin, but before Millie could question them, Maxcy knocked on the door and again they set to work on their schoolwork. Millie felt the hairs on the back of her neck rise. They were studying hard, but something was very, very wrong. Hosa, especially, glanced furtively at Millie, guilt written clearly on his face.

Millie eavesdropped on their studies as she prepared the evening meal, wondering how one raised two children, completed daily chores, and investigated a murder. Dom and George soon trudged by the window, leading Columbine and Bluebell. As they passed, Dom yelled, "We're on our way to the barn."

Later, when they entered the cabin, George carried an armful of ore samples, carefully lining them up against the wall, acting like each one was a gold nugget. "Got these from the Three Rings," he said loudly. "Milo and his boys cleared out my vein, but these samples look promising. Dom's gonna do a fire assay on them."

Dom, Millie noticed, didn't look enthusiastic. He could usually tell when ore was high grade. To her, it all looked the same, but Dom had spent years assaying ore at different mining camps. Shrugging, she turned toward the children. "Supper will be ready soon. Are you almost done?"

The three of them nodded, looking like puppets. Maxcy quickly gathered up his slate and reader, said his good-byes, and hurried out the door. Hosa and Rachel slowly put away their school supplies and then sat silently at the table.

Because of her afternoon adventures, Millie hadn't had time to make a decent supper, but she knew Dom and the children would enjoy Johnnycakes. Normally she'd never serve something so mundane to a guest, but she wouldn't mind if George took insult and left. Deciding the children's studying had earned them a treat, she added, "After supper we have Sheriff Finch's gingerbread soldiers for a special dessert." With a flourish, she pulled a towel off a plate, revealing two armies facing each other, ready for battle.

Hosa and Rachel's interest turned to shock as George walked over and helped himself to a soldier, biting off his leg. "Making sure they're good enough for the family," he said as he chewed, shoving the rest of the treat into his mouth. "Mmm. That was good. Wouldn't want uneven armies." He reached over to take a second soldier and Millie cracked her wooden spoon down on his knuckles. "Ouch!" he said, backing away.

"The gingerbread is for dessert." Millie scowled and brandished her spoon.

"Everyone sit down." Dom pulled George toward his stool. "Your hotcakes smell great, Millie. I'm starving."

As they ate, Dom asked about the children's day and they responded with simple yes and no answers. Dom didn't appear overly concerned, but after one particularly evasive answer, Millie could no longer hold her tongue.

"Hosa, tell me about—" A knock interrupted her.

The children jumped to their feet and raced to the door, just as they had done the day Maxcy first arrived. Rachel reached for the locking slat but Hosa rudely pushed her aside, knocking her down. He ignored her outcry and lifted the bar, cracking open the door. Rachel scrambled onto her feet as she snarled something in Arapaho, and then to Millie's horror, she kicked Hosa.

Millie cried out in alarm. Hosa howled. But Rachel calmly ignored them both and pulled the door open, revealing the figure outside. "Who is you?" she asked.

"*Wottowusoo!*" Hosa growled, grabbing Rachel's long

braid and jerking her backward. She shrieked, spun toward him, and punched him in the nose.

What had gotten into these two? Before Millie could do anything, Dom's booming voice shook the cabin. "Children!" They froze. Hosa's fist was wrapped around Rachel's hair, causing the little girl's head to tilt back at an unnatural angle. Rachel's little fists were clenched and blood dripped from Hosa's nose. "Go. Sit. Down." Dom said each word in a tone that cracked like a whip.

The children's arms dropped, and they backed away, but neither returned to the table. Dom glared at them and turned to face the open door. "Mr. Pemley, wasn't it?"

"Yes, sir." The man from the duel stood outside, his features unreadable in the gathering dusk, his soft Texas accent incongruous with his dark profile. Around his face, his red hair gleamed like fire in the dying evening light. "Mr. Drouillard?"

"That's me." Dom's right hand moved slightly until it rested on his six-shooter. "I'm Dominic Drouillard. What do you want?"

The stranger's eyes darted from Dom's hand to Millie's face. In an uncertain voice he said, "I was hoping to speak with your wife, sir."

Millie stared at the stranger and felt a twinge of unease. There was something…

Hosa and Rachel moved like one, circling Dom until they could see Mr. Pemley. "You is the one who killed that man," Rachel said, her eyes narrowing.

"At the dueling field." Hosa glanced uneasily at Millie and quickly added, "We saw you out the Bellyache school's window."

"Children, go sit down." Dom's low, controlled tone

boded no argument. Hosa took Rachel's hand and they hurried back to their stools; their scuffle forgotten. Acting like a gentleman, Hosa helped Rachel sit down, wiping the blood from his face with the back of his hand before he took his own seat. Dom nodded and turned to the stranger. "Why do you want to speak with my wife?"

"Dom, be polite and ask Mr. Pemley inside."

Despite Millie's words and her irritated tone, Dom didn't move.

"I appreciate your reticence, sir. I wanted to thank Mrs. Drouillard for assisting the doctor while he tended my wound." He touched his head. His Texas drawl was less pronounced than Millie's southern accent, but still strong. "I'd be happy to pay for a new petticoat."

"That's kind of you, Mr. Pemley," Millie said with a touch of exasperation. "Dom, please invite the gentleman inside."

Dom frowned and kept his hand on the butt of his six-shooter as the Texan stepped aside. Mr. Pemley walked toward the table, his eyes skittering from Millie to George when the latter took out his six-shooter and loudly slammed it down on the table.

"Mr. Drouillard!" Millie said sharply, but she couldn't look away from Mr. Pemley's face. Why did he look so familiar?

"Can't be too careful," George growled.

Mr. Pemley shook his head, as if his headwound still left him slightly dazed. "Ma'am, I..." He paused and threw up his hands. "God, you look like Ma. I mean, I know that sounds crazy, but look." He reached into his weskit pocket and removed a silver pocket watch.

Millie gaped. The watch was identical to the well-used

one she owned and as he opened the two halves, she suddenly felt cold, knowing what was coming. Mr. Pemley set the opened watch on the table and Millie glanced down, not quite believing her eyes. "*Oh Lor'!*" Pressed into the man's watch cover was a daguerreotype of a smiling woman holding a chubby little boy on her lap. Behind them stood a man with curly hair.

It was an image Millie had seen many, many times.

"How is that possible?" Dom strode around the table and stood behind Millie, resting a comforting hand on her shoulder.

"That's just like the image in Miss Millie's pocket watch," Rachel said, coming over to stand beside Millie.

Feeling numb, Millie slipped her hand into her apron and removed her pocket watch, the only possession she owned from a family she'd never known. Slowly she opened the cover, her hands trembling as she placed her watch beside his. An identical daguerreotype was pressed into her watch's inside cover. She looked up at Mr. Pemley. "Who are you?"

The stranger's pale eyes didn't blink as he glanced from the daguerreotype to her, but his voice shook as he whispered, "Sweet suffering Jesus. I think I'm your brother."

TWENTY-FOUR

May 10, 1865

Family Secrets

*H*er *brother?* The daguerreotypes—along with facial features she now recognized as her own—were ample proof of their relationship, but Millie couldn't believe it. "You're the child. The one in the picture?"

He nodded, looking suddenly uncomfortable. "I've gotta tell you. I don't remember Ma and I haven't seen Pa since a month or so after we left you at the door of that orphanage. He dumped me, too."

Dom's warm hands were the only thing keeping Millie grounded. Her mind churned with shock and questions, but soon one thought crowded out all others. She had a brother, and he didn't know their father had been a criminal. She glanced at Dom. He held her eyes and nodded, seeming to understand she needed time.

"Mr. Pemley, your news comes as a shock to my wife. To all of us." He squeezed Millie's shoulder and reached forward, picking up the man's watch and handing it back. "Millie's tired and I have some assays to do tonight. Why don't you come back tomorrow morning around, uh, nine. We can talk then." He paused, lifting his eyebrows at Millie.

"Yes. Yes, please. Come at nine and I'll make you a late breakfast. We can get to know each other." She glanced from Hosa to Rachel and then at George. "We'll have plenty of time after the children leave for school and Mr. Drouillard heads to his mine."

"Why you want to talk *after* we leave?" Hosa asked, his brow furrowed.

"We should know about any family secrets," Rachel added.

Millie winced, thankful when Dom silenced them with a shake of his head. Mr. Pemley, looking confused and slightly worried, nodded, doffed his hat, and left without another word. His footsteps clattered on the walkway, but as soon as they no longer heard him, the children and George erupted with questions. Millie couldn't focus and was thankful when Dom wrapped his arm around her and helped her to her feet. "I'll tend the children tonight. You look like you need some time alone." He glanced at the plate behind him. "If you want any gingerbread, you best take it now."

Millie was in shock, but not so stunned she didn't grab a gingerbread soldier before she fled. Alone in their bedroom, she sat, biting off the soldier's head, her mind awhirl. She had a brother. A brother who didn't know anything about their family. *Oh Lor'!* She bit off a leg, savored the taste, and wondered how she could explain about their father's terrible past.

The following morning, cranky and sleep-deprived, Millie still didn't know how she'd tell her brother about their father's sordid life. Distracted, she burned the children's cornsticks and felt like the worst mother when Rachel and Hosa began arguing with Dom.

"Children must go to school," Dom said, sounding exasperated. "You'll meet Mr. Pemley later. We'll have him over for supper."

"What's the big secret?" George asked, acting worse than the children. "We're all family. We should know about any problems."

Millie glared at him. "There are no problems."

"Your sleep-deprived face says there are problems," George said.

"Yes. Else why would you want us to leave?" Hosa crossed his arms over his chest. "I stay to protect you. Your brother may be as dangerous as enemy." He glared at George, fingering his knife handle.

"I'm helping Hosa protect you." Rachel defiantly fisted her hands and planted them on her hips. "We ain't leaving."

Millie's temple throbbed and her temper snapped. "Children should be seen but not heard! Off to school, now!" She turned to George. "You too."

"We'll explain after school," Dom said, gently herding Hosa and Rachel out the door. "I appreciate your concern for your ma, but school is important. I'll be here to keep her safe."

A shadow passed over Hosa's face. "School is *not* important. School *not* make a man brave."

"School," Dom said, shutting the door on them. After a long minute, they heard their footsteps walking away, but getting rid of George wasn't so easy. It wasn't until Mr. Pemley arrived that Dom—using bodily force—finally managed to push his uncle out the door. "I'll meet you at the Three Rings."

"You said last night, after assaying that ore, that the Three Rings is worthless," George snarled.

"Goodbye George!" Dom slammed the door and exhaled loudly.

In the silence that followed, Mr. Pemley stood uncertainly in the center of the cabin, glancing from Millie to Dom.

"Please, sit down," Dom waved him toward the table and took a seat.

Millie, feeling too nervous to sit, strode over and tied the window skins back, lightening up the room's gloom. Returning to the table, she noticed her brother had dark rings under his eyes, looking like he hadn't slept any better than she had. "Please, sir, sit down. Would you like coffee?"

"Yes, and I'd be pleased if you'd call me by my Christian name, Dave."

Tears brimmed in Millie's eyes. "Of course. We're family. I'm Miss Millie and my husband is Dom. Please, sit and let's enjoy a meal together." She served up cornsticks and tried to make small talk.

"There's something I need to tell you," Dave suddenly blurted out, interrupting her. "Ma died when you were born and Pa left you at that orphanage, so I know you don't know nothing about them. I was about four years old when he dumped me. I don't remember much, but... well, I'm sorry to say our pa wasn't a good man."

"What?" Relief washed over Millie. "You know?"

"Course. Pa abandoned me at the Pemley homestead; he discarded me like trash. Threw me into a haystack without slowing his horse. It was just after dawn and Mr. Pemley was heading out to feed his cattle. He saw what happened and went to investigate. Good thing. It was winter. I'd have frozen to death if Mr. Pemley hadn't found me. Mr. and Mrs. Pemley were new married and starting their cattle ranch. They took me in, raised me like their own son. They're my real family."

Millie blew out a breath. He didn't know! Bracing herself, she opened her mouth, but George's loud voice interrupted her. "What about that yarn you told to save your neck?" George stuck his head through the window, pushing aside the heavy furs. "The girl you mentioned. You said she were your sister."

"Uncle George!" Dom rose and scowled. "I'll meet you at the Three Rings. Go on now!"

George shook his head, his long beard jerking with the motion. "First I want to know the truth. He's your wife's brother—got to be with that flaming red hair—but then the girl he described weren't his real sister."

"I was raised as her older brother and I loved her."

"I bet you did." George leered. "Were you her lover, the father of her child?"

Mr. Pemley jumped to his feet, knocking his stool over as he drew his six-shooter. George was just as fast. They stood facing each other through the open window, guns pointed at each other, fingers on triggers.

"This is my home," Dom said, his voice low. "Both of you, put away your weapons before someone gets hurt."

George's furious eyes darted between Dom and Dave Pemley. Slowly he lowered his gun. It disappeared, although Millie was certain it was still clutched in his hand. "I'll leave soon as he answers my question. I don't care that he killed Tex, but I want to know if his story were a lie."

"I don't lie, sir. Ann was Mr. and Mrs. Pemley's daughter." Dave shoved his weapon into its holster. "Ann wasn't my blood sister, but I loved her. The Pemley's taught me that family isn't about blood. By the time I was twelve, I was glad Ann weren't my real sister. I knew I wanted to marry her, assuming she'd have me. But I knew I needed to let her grow up, first. She never got the chance."

"Sure." George grunted. "I'll meet you at the Three Rings, not that it's worth nothing. You bring the burros." He scowled and turned to leave. "Welcome to the family, *Dave*," he added before disappearing.

Millie exhaled, strode over, and stuck her head out the window. She watched as George strode away, but suddenly he glanced back, giving her a hateful look. She shivered. George might not have killed Wandering Will, but he was as trustworthy as a bull in heat. She didn't want him learning anything about her family's secrets.

"Sorry about the trouble, Dave. My uncle's a bit of a hothead, but still, I'm glad to know the truth." Dom waved toward the table. "Come, eat. I'm afraid Millie has more to tell you about your pa. He didn't just abandon his children; he was also a criminal."

"What?" Dave stared at Millie. "You were a baby. How could you know anything about Pa?"

Millie returned to her seat, sipped her tea, and haltingly explained about answering a wife-wanted advertisement and traveling to the Colorado Territory. In

Denver City, she'd met a man who, after seeing the daguerreotype in her pocket watch, had recognized their father. He'd turned out to be their daddy's ex-criminal partner and he'd told her all about their daddy's unlawful activities. He also told her about his secrets.

"Our daddy worked for a criminal gang called the Bowe brothers?" her brother asked when she finished. "He stole a fortune in silver coins and ran off with them? That's why we were on the run?" Dave shook his head, looking like he couldn't quite believe it.

"Worse," Millie said quietly, "when he realized his ex-partner was hot on his trail, he hid the coins and made a map that showed where he'd hidden them."

"Our pa stole a treasure of silver coins and then created a treasure map? Sweet suffering Jesus, this ain't real."

Millie gave him a moment to settle by refreshing their drinks, trying to decide how to finish the wretched tale. "Our daddy hid his map in my pocket watch, behind the daguerreotype. He knew his ex-partner was closing in on him. Maybe he dumped you to protect you." After all she'd learned about their father, she didn't really believe that, but the lie might comfort her brother. "Eventually the man I met caught up with Daddy. He killed him."

Mr. Pemley looked down at the table for several heartbeats. Finally, he took out his pocket watch and opened it, staring at the image inside. "I can't imagine any of this is true, but I gotta ask, do you think there's a treasure map hidden in my watch?"

"More importantly." George stuck his head through the window, his eyes glowing like embers. "Is the treasure of silver coins still where he hid them?"

TWENTY-FIVE

May 11, 1865
Angelina Cornog

George knew about the silver coins. The only thing worse, as far as Millie was concerned, was that her brother—unaware of the danger—had pulled out his knife and carefully pried the daguerreotype from his watch. As the image fluttered onto the table, a folded white paper fell with it. George rushed back into the cabin and looked over Dave's shoulder as he unfolded the map. It was identical to the one Millie had found in her pocket watch with lines indicating streets, squares identifying houses, and an X marking the spot where the coins had been buried.

"What does Boone dogs' cave mean?" George demanded. "Where is this? Main Street. Field, Preston, Armstrong, Boone, and Sheffey. This could be any town." George stared at Millie. "Where's the treasure hidden?"

Millie's brother's eyes shone with curiosity, but George's glistened with greed. "Did you ever discover what town this was?" Dave asked.

"No." Millie and Dom answered in unison.

"We didn't," Millie added more quietly, glancing at George. She could see he didn't believe her and she silently cursed. Usually she was a decent liar, but her brother's sudden appearance had thrown her off her stride. "We never figured it out."

Dom rose and stretched. "Millie mentioned last night we could use some fresh meat." Dom slapped Dave's shoulder. "Put away that useless map, Dave, and come hunting. I'd like to get to know my wife's brother."

Dom's nonchalance was so forced, even Millie's brother noticed. He glanced from Millie to Dom and then back at George. Understanding finally lit in his eyes. Quickly he folded the map and put it and the image back into his watch. "Thank you. Hunting and a bit of fresh air sounds fine." He nodded at Millie. "We'll talk again soon."

*****

Millie sighed as the men left, but she couldn't shake off her worry. Her list of problems was growing faster than she could keep track of. Not that there was anything she could do about George and the coins. She cleaned up the dishes and planned her day. She needed to visit her landlady and thank her for the cabin. A word or two with the schoolmistress would put an end to whatever tomfoolery the children had caused, along with learning if the schoolmistress knew anything about Wandering Will's murder.

Millie pulled her pocket watch from her apron and glanced at the time. Eleven was late, but acceptable, for a morning visit. Looking down at Buttercup, she sighed and put everything she could think of out of reach. Hopefully the cabin would do a better job of keeping the troublesome goat contained than the barn had.

Millie closed and tied the window skins, barred the front door, and slipped on her bonnet and coat. Walking away, she heard Buttercup's indignant bleats. The cabin might keep Buttercup contained, but how much damage would she do to it?

"Mrs. Drouillard." Millie turned and saw Sheriff Finch hurrying toward her. "Do you have a moment?"

"What happened? Is Dom okay? The children?"

"Everyone's fine. I wanted to show you this." He reached into his apron's pocket and withdrew an ornate pistol with a rounded handle.

"Wandering Will's special pistol?" Millie carefully lifted the weapon and examined it. "Where did you find it?"

"An Odd Fellow found it in Tex's bedroll. The Odd Fellows buried Tex yesterday and cleaned up his belongings, but Milo recognized Will's pistol and brought it to me this morning."

"Tex killed Wandering Will?" Idly Millie traced the palm tree engraving in the center of the Palmetto Armory stamp. It just didn't make sense. Finally, she looked up at Sheriff Finch. "Why would Tex kill Wandering Will?"

"An excellent question. Tex also had a solid alibi."

Millie considered. "The killer left Wandering Will's pistol in Tex's bedroll to make him look guilty?"

Sheriff Finch shrugged. "Maybe. If he or she did, we have a bigger problem."

"Why?"

"This pistol is worth more than most men make round

here in a couple months. Everyone knew its value since Will was fond of showing it off. If the real killer hid it in Tex's bedroll to make him look guilty, it means you and your husband have the killer worried. Worried enough to give up a valuable weapon. You need to be careful, Mrs. Drouillard. Watch your back."

After Sheriff Finch left, Millie strode toward her landlady's cabin, but her mind wasn't on a social call. She had no idea who killed Wandering Will. Worse, she didn't have a clue what they had done to worry the murderer.

Reaching the Cornog's cabin, Millie knocked and forced her expression into what she hoped was a polite smile. Florence Hartley advised that a morning visit should be no longer then twenty minutes. Millie planned to follow that good advice. She'd say hello, thank you, and goodbye. Her smile dimmed when Mr. Cornog opened the door.

"Ah, Mrs. Drouillard. A pleasure. Come in." He beamed as he wiped egg off his face and stepped back. "We've a bit of cluck and grunt left if you're hungry." He pointed at a dish of ham and eggs.

"Thank you, Mr. Cornog, but I've already eaten." Millie glanced around the small cabin. It was bigger than hers, and much better built, with colorful woven scarves hanging on the walls making it feel homey. "I wanted to come by and thank you both. Our cabin is very comfortable. We appreciate being able to stay there." She didn't mention the mice droppings she swept up each morning nor the hole that kept appearing behind the stove. She'd stomped dirt into the hole every morning, hoping it was a pine mouse, not a rat. "My apology for disturbing your meal. I'll leave you—"

"No reason to rush off, Mrs. Drouillard." Mr. Cornog stepped over and took the baby from his wife. "Gadzooks. Why don't I take little Gruffy off your hands, Angel, and give you ladies time to get acquainted?" He disappeared into the back bedroom.

"*Sí.*" Angelina smiled shyly and cleared the table. "You drink *horchata, señora?*"

Her accent made her words slightly nasally, but not hard to understand. Still, Millie had no idea what she'd just been offered. "Or-cha-da?"

Her hostess laughed, a truly delightful sound, making Millie again wonder about Mrs. Cornog's age. The gray in her hair made her look much older than Millie, yet Gruffy was only six months old and her smooth face had few creases.

"Hor-cha-ta." Angelina pronounced it slowly.

"I'm sorry, Mrs. Cornog, I don't know what that is."

"*Señora* Cornog." Angelina shook her head and frowned. "No, no. My name is Angelina. Yes? We be friends."

They were obviously not friends, but Angelina's hopeful expression made Millie realize just how lonely she must be. Life in a mining town wasn't easy for a woman, and Millie imagined it would be doubly difficult for a foreign woman. Millie set aside formal behavior and smiled. "It would be my pleasure, Miss Angelina. Please, call me Miss Millie."

"*Señora* Angelina. *Señora* Millie. *Sí.*" Angelina cocked her head to one side and smiled. "We drink *horchata* together." She poured a white liquid into two heavy earthenware mugs, indicated that Millie should sit, and offered her the drink. Millie took a seat and cautiously sniffed as Angela sipped her own drink, nodded, and smiled. "You like?"

Millie gingerly tasted the liquid. It was thick, not chewy but textured, sweet, and smelled of cinnamon. "This is good." Millie took a larger drink, savoring the flavors. "It's excellent. I've never tasted anything like it. Do you have a recipe?"

Once again Angelina laughed, sounding delighted. "*Sí.* I teach you, later, but today we..." She paused as her husband came out, carrying their son.

"Got to go work my claim." He handed the baby to his wife and kissed them both on the top of their heads. It was a gentle, loving thing to do—not at all what Millie expected from such a rough-looking man. "You both be safe today." Turning to Millie he touched his slouch hat. "Nice to see you again, Mrs. Drouillard. You have a good day with my Angel."

"Thank you, Mr. Cornog." Millie inclined her head politely.

He opened the door and stepped outside, pausing. "Heard the fellow who killed Tex has your same red hair." He lifted his eyebrows. "Also heard he visited you last night."

"My hair is auburn with a few red streaks," Millie said curtly. Mr. Cornog looked confused, but since Millie had no desire to discuss her hair nor her new relation, she inclined her head. "Good luck with your mining today, sir."

"The Irish have luck, but I'll take what I can get. Gold's getting harder to find and I'd like a bit of happy cabbage for my Angel."

Happy cabbage? Millie had no idea.

Mr. Cornog touched his hat, blew his wife a kiss, and shut the door. Millie turned back to her hostess and saw both love and embarrassment shining in Angelina's dark eyes. "How in the world did you two meet?" She blushed, realizing the rude directness of the question. "I mean...well, he's Welsh and you're from Mexico."

"No, no, not from Mexico. I am American. I was born here." She pointed south. "My Uncle, Manuel Martinez is important man. He get much land from Mexico." She spread her hands wide. "My family own land as far as I can see. *Mi padre* very rich. He hire *señor* Cornog to build a road." She smiled, bouncing her son on her leg. "We fall in love. *Padre* very angry so we run away and marry. We head north, far, far away from my family."

Millie knew disobeying a father, in any culture, wasn't good. "Has your father searched for you? How long have you been married?"

"We leave seven or eight years ago, but I am sure *padre* still searches. If my brothers or *mi padre* find *señor* Cornog, they challenge him to duel." She touched her son's face. "They would kill my *señor*, take away my Gruffy, make me go back." Shaking her head she added fiercely, "I never go. I kill *Padre* and brothers. I die protecting *señor* Cornog and my Gruffy."

Millie admired the woman's conviction. It had taken all the courage Millie possessed to search for a better life by answering a wife-wanted ad. Angelina had left what sounded like a good life, if not a happy one. All because she loved Mr. Cornog. Once Millie might not have understood, but now she had Dom and the children. There was nothing, not even her own life, that she wouldn't sacrifice for them. Finishing her *horchata*, Millie rose. "I should be going."

"No, no, *señora* Millie. You no go." Angelina stood, bouncing her son in her arms. "You come with me. We pick skunk cabbage."

"Skunk cabbage? Heavens, why?" Mary, Millie's neighbor at Idaho Springs, had introduced Millie to several edible mountain plants and berries, but the smelly skunk cabbage wasn't one of them. "Can you eat it?"

"*Sí*. No. If you wrap spring leaves around trout and cook on fire, it tastes good." She licked her lips. "Root makes tea and medicine." She smiled. "You come, *señora* Millie?"

Millie knew she needed to visit the schoolhouse and more importantly, try and make sense of Tex and the pistol, but the woman's gentle, hopeful smile was impossible to refuse. "It would be my pleasure, Miss Angelina."

"*Bueno*. I know where we find lots of skunk cabbage. It is not far, but we must be careful. Bears wake up now and are hungry. They like skunk cabbage, too." She grinned. "In spring, black bears are grumpier than *mi padre*."

TWENTY-SIX

May 11, 1865

Harvesting Skunk Cabbage

Millie breathed hard as she followed Angelina up a steep mountain trail. The small woman scrambled upward like a mountain sheep, her little boy tied neatly on her back in a long, woven cloth she'd called a *rebozo*. The string fringes of the *rebozo* swayed and fluttered with Angelina's movements as the child looked out from his perch, quietly observing his surroundings. After coming west, Millie had wondered why fringed buckskin appeared popular with mountain men and Indians. Last year, before she died, Hosa's mother had shown Millie how fringe actually wicked water away from a garment, allowing it to dry faster. Millie wondered if the Mexicans had learned this from the Indians or the other way around.

The towering evergreen trees opened up to give a view of the valley and Angelina paused. Millie drew beside her, unable to hide her hard breathing. Angelina smiled and pointed at a snow-covered mountain just across from them. "That is Mount Silverheels. Named after the beautiful dancehall girl that wear silver shoes. *Señor* Cornog tell me her story. It is a sad story, but life can be sad." She wrapped her fingers around her son's stockinged toes. "Shall I tell you?"

"Yes, please." Millie appreciated having a moment to catch her breath.

"Years ago, a mysterious woman arrive in Buckskin Joe. She arrive all alone in a stagecoach, wearing a beautiful dress but also a dark veil. She stay at Buckskin Joe's Grand hotel and all miners wonder who she is. Two days after she arrive, she visit *señor* Buck's Dancehall and Saloon—where Kate dances."

"Did Miss Kate meet her?"

"No, no. This woman arrive before Miss Kate."

"Of course. I apologize for interrupting."

"Is okay." Angelina tickled her son's toes and the baby gurgled happily. "The night after the veiled woman visit, *señor* Buck climb on his bar and shoot off his six-shooter. He—"

"He shot off his six-shooter inside his bar? I'm sorry to be so rude and interrupt, but…" Millie blushed. "I thought most saloons had rooms upstairs, for the, uh, fancy women."

Angelina's joyful laugh filled the quiet mountain air. "That *señor* Cornog do not tell me, but he does say *señor* Buck shoot off his gun. All men in saloon go quiet and *señor* Buck say, 'Ladees—and you damned old snortin', cavortin' dirty-whiskered customers of mine who call yourselves men.'" She giggled at her own attempt at a rough miner's accent before continuing the story. "'How many of you can remember when you last saw a genuine, no-fake, beautiful woman?'"

Despite the harsh language, Millie couldn't help laughing. Angelina was obviously repeating the story word-for-word, but her accent was a humorous mix of Mexican, rough miner, and a bit of Welsh. "Miners don't just have dirty whiskers," Millie said. "Most have whiskers thick enough for a mouse to hide in."

"*Sí, sí!* When I meet *señor* Cornog he have long beard." She held her hand below her chin. "It was thick and..." She made a disgusted face. "*Grueso.*"

Millie had been impressed with Angelina's English— the woman was well educated. Still, the meaning of the Spanish word was clear. "So what happened with the mysterious woman? Did she go to the bar, take off her veil, and have a beautiful face?"

"*Sí.*" Angelina scrunched up her face and continued with the story. "*Señor* Buck say, 'If there be a man in Buckskin Joe who would like to give his bloodshot eyes a tonic, let him be at Bill Buck's dancehall next Saturday night. The mysterious, veiled woman will dance in this hall. Her veil will be removed and thrown away forever.'"

"The fine lady was a dancehall girl?" Millie shouldn't have been shocked. Why else would a woman visit Buck's dancehall?

"*Sí.* Silverheels is most beautiful dancehall girl, but she is also kind, like Miss Kate. She dance wearing silver shoes and miners love her." The woman's amused expression faded. "But then pox come to Buckskin Joe." She shook her head sadly, her expression far away. "Many miners get sick and dancehall girls leave. Silverheels stay. She nurse sick miners and bring them food. When they get better, they try to thank her with gold, but Silverheels is gone. No one knows where she go. Many think she get sick, her beautiful face ruined, so she run away and never come back. Miners name Mount Silverheels after her."

The story was like the yarns told by Mr. Griswold in Idaho Springs, but Millie had learned there was often truth in his tales. "Were you here then, Miss Angelina?"

The woman nodded, her fingers caressing her son's toes. "*Sí. Señor* Cornog send me and our children to Fair Play Diggings, to protect us, but that town is still too close. The pox kill my little *niñita*, she was four. It also killed my little *bebé* and almost take my *señor* Cornog."

Millie touched the other woman's arm, unable to imagine the pain of losing children. "I am so sorry, Miss Angelina."

The woman nodded, wiped a tear from her cheek, and turned and headed back up the trail. Millie watched the small woman's lithe body effortlessly climb, but her thoughts turned to Rachel and Hosa. Their antics drove her nuts, but she'd die if anything happened to them. And Dom. Would she have the strength to go on if she lost Dom? Knowing there was nothing she could say or do to lessen such grief, Millie followed Angelina in silence, no longer noticing the beauty surrounding them.

Millie was again breathless when she topped a rise to find Angelina looking down at a beautiful alpine lake. It had crystal clear water and the boulders on the far slope cascaded down like a frozen waterfall. Close to them was an alpine meadow, and on the far side, tall evergreens intermixed with quaking aspens completed the enchanting landscape.

"We pick skunk cabbage here." Angelina led them to the lake's grassy shore and over to a large patch of skunk cabbage.

Millie breathed in the clean, cold air and said quietly, "I am so sorry, Miss Angelina. I can't imagine such a loss."

Angelina looked across the lake, her expression distant. "God take my children and I die of a broken heart. For a long time I want to die, but God give me Gruffy." She took the child off her back, hugged him, and laid him in the grass, wrapping her *rebozo* under and around him like a shield. "God never take my Gruffy away. He know it would kill me."

Angelina bent and kissed her son, her darker skin a contrast to Gruffy's light complexion. "Come, *señora* Millie. I show you how to harvest skunk cabbage." She splashed into the shallow water, bent down, and worked a skunk cabbage free. Turning to Millie, she pulled an ornate knife out from beneath the folds of her skirt. Skillfully, she cut away leaves and rinsed off the plant, showing Millie the root they'd harvest.

"What an unusual knife," Millie said, admiring the ornate decorations on the hilt.

Angelina held out the weapon, letting it glisten in the sunshine. "It belong to *mi madre*. It is a Toledo Jambiya Karud dagger. These." She pointed to the ornate twirled metal decoration protruding from both sides of the hilt crossbar. "These represent *mi madre's* family. When her *madre* was a girl—before they come to New Mexico—a famous knife maker from Yemen visit her family. He get sick and she tend to him. To thank her, he make her this knife. She give it to *mi madre* and she give it to me, before

I leave with *señor* Cornog."

"Your mother knew you were going to run away with Mr. Cornog?"

"*Si*. She help. *Mi padre* want me to marry a rich man." She made a face. "I love *señor* Cornog and *mi madre* understand. She was young when she marry *mi padre*. She have no choice, so she give me a choice and help me run away." Angelina slipped the knife back into its sheath under the folds of her skirt. "I put a knife in your basket."

Millie nodded and moved farther down the shoreline, making sure to keep Gruffy between them. When she again stepped into the lake, icy water soaked through her boots and chilled her feet. Shivering, she bent and pulled on a skunk cabbage. It didn't budge. Millie wrapped both hands around the plant's base and yanked twice before it finally broke free. Just as Angelina had showed, Millie stripped away the leaves and cut off the root. Together they worked in companiable silence, her cold, wet feet offset by the sunshine that warmed her back and shoulders.

As she filled her basket, Millie's mind returned to Wandering Will's murder. What had she done, or had it been Dom who alarmed the killer? Although George was her main suspect, she knew it didn't make sense for him to bring them here if he really was the killer. Milo was as suspicious as Queeny, and then there was Kate and the mountain man Kootenay. Millie glanced over at Angelina.

Angelina knew Kate. Maybe she also knew where Kate went after Wandering Will jilted her. Maybe... A low grunt interrupted her thoughts. Millie felt the hairs on the back of her neck rise as she slowly straightened and turned.

Thirty paces away, a large black bear snorted as it ambled into the marsh, sticking its nose down and ripping out the top, flower-like part of the skunk cabbage. It lifted its head and chewed; its beady eyes focused on Millie.

"Miss Angelina," Millie whispered.

From behind her, Angelina said quietly, "Back away slowly, *señora* Millie. May be *la madre*. Watch out for her *bebés*."

Millie backed out of the lake, her head weaving back and forth. Dom once told her that black bears, unlike grizzlies, were normally not aggressive, unless one got between a mother and her cub. Then they could be deadly. Millie stepped from the lake and the bear ambled in her direction. Were her cubs somewhere behind them, in the dark woods?

"We must climb tree, *señora*," Angelina said urgently. "Drop basket. Let bear eat cabbage. If she climbs tree after you, kick at her nose."

Kick at her nose? Wouldn't the bear bite off her foot? Millie hoped she wouldn't find out. She dropped her basket and backed toward the trees, seeing Angelina sweep Gruffy off the ground and wrap him in her *rebozo*. She tied him onto her back as she moved into the shadows of the thick patch of evergreens.

Just in front of Millie, the bear stuck his nose in the air, snuffed loudly, and splashed through the water toward her basket.

"Quickly. Climb tree, *señora* Millie!" Angelina turned to the closest tree and effortlessly, or so it seemed to Millie, scrambled up into the boughs.

Millie glanced back, relieved to see the bear had stopped at her basket. Hurrying into the thick copse of trees, she searched for one with branches low enough she could reach. Finally, she spotted a thick-trunked pine and hurried over, struggling up one branch after another, cursing when her long skirt got stuck. She reached down for the third time to unhook it just as the bear growled and charged. Millie jerked her skirt free and scrambled up toward the higher branches.

The bear stopped under Millie's tree, but instead of climbing after her, it rose onto its hind legs, stretching out its neck. Suddenly its teeth were much closer to her lower foot. Millie kicked at the bear's nose and tried to scramble higher, but the bear growled ferociously and lunged upward, biting her thick boot sole.

Millie screamed.

She didn't feel the animal's teeth through her boot, but as it shook its head, her foot slipped from the limb. "No!" The bear pulled downward, acting like they were playing tug-of-war with her leg. Millie clung to the tree, feeling the strain in her arms. If she could just reach for her six-shooter, she could shoot the animal, but if she released the branch, she'd fall. The bear wrenched Millie's leg from one side to the other. Suddenly it pulled hard to the left, knocking Millie's other foot off the branch.

For an instant Millie clung there, one foot dangling, the other in the mouth of the bear. The branch she clung to suddenly snapped and she tumbled from the tree. Her foot ripped free from the bear's mouth, and she landed on the animal's back before tumbling to the ground and rolling onto her back.

The large bear pounced on top of her.

TWENTY-SEVEN

May 11, 1865

Black Bear Attack

Millie couldn't scream—the bear's weight pinned her down. She couldn't breathe or even struggle against the weight. Her six-shooter was trapped beneath massive paws, impossible to get. She looked up at the wild animal's beady eyes and waited for death. Her demise would devastate Dom and leave the children orphans. Tears leaked down her face. She didn't want to end her life as a meal for a bear.

The black bear looked down at her, its long, pink tongue lolling out of its mouth. Millie tensed as the animal lowered its head—giving her an up-close view of long, gleaming teeth. She wished she could swoon and not see what was coming, but the bear's teeth held her transfixed. The bear's nose drew closer, but instead of fangs ripping into her neck, the bear's tongue licked away the tears on her face. The tongue felt soft, like a flower petal drawn over her skin.

Was she delirious? Maybe she was already dead.

A call echoed from the distance. She couldn't make out the words, but strangely, it sounded like Hosa's voice. She must be dreaming. The bear lifted its head and looked around. Millie felt the edges of her vision darken as the bear's weight made it impossible to draw breath. A long, shrill whistle broke the silence and the bear again licked Millie's face and bounded off her chest.

Millie inhaled and felt her spinning world slowly normalize. After several more gulps, she shakily lifted her head. Waves of pain throbbed up her back and her skull felt like someone had struck it. Gingerly, she sat up, probing the back of her head with her fingers. It was tender, but she didn't feel blood.

Her hands shook as she lifted her apron and wiped bear drool from her face. She knew she needed to get up—the bear might return any moment—but she didn't have the energy. Angelina suddenly appeared and dropped to her knees beside Millie. "Are you hurt, *señora* Millie?" The woman gently ran her fingers through Millie's hair and down her back. "You bump your head." She looked at Millie's face. "Your eyes look normal. Can you stand?"

"The b-bear?" Her teeth chattered as if she were cold.

"Gone." Angelina pursed her lips, looking angry. "Little Bear will not hurt us." She wrapped her hands around Millie's arms and lifted. Millie's legs shook and wouldn't have held if Angelina hadn't slipped her slender arm around Millie's waist and steadied her. The woman looked so tiny and petite, but her arm was solid.

Millie looked around. "W-where is it?"

In answer, the giant mountain man, Kootenay Good, strode into view. He walked over, standing so close he blocked the sunshine. "Sorry, ma'am, *señora* Cornog. I brought Little Bear up to munch on skunk cabbage." The bear strode over and sat down at the man's side. "Ain't known you were here."

"*Señor* Kootenay, Little Bear was very bad. He scared *señora* Drouillard half to death." Angelina added a string of words in Spanish. Kootenay's eyes widened and he stumbled backward.

At another time, Millie might have found it funny. The top of Angelina's head barely reached Kootenay's shoulder, yet the big man looked like he'd been struck. His lined, weather-worn face turned red—at least in the areas not covered by his gray facial hair—and he stammered, "I-I'm sorry, *señora* Cornog." To Millie's surprise, the man rattled off a long string of Spanish before turning to Millie. "Little Bear ain't hurt you, did he? He were just having a bit of fun."

"*A bit of fun!* Your bear scared me to death!" Millie pulled away from Angelina and stood up straight, squeezing her nose to combat her throbbing head. She wanted to give this idiot a piece of her mind, once she could think clearly.

"How you speak *Española*?" Angelina asked, her tone almost civil.

"Back in '48 I was on Frémont's disastrous expedition. I survived, but twelve other men didn't. Most died from starvation. Afterward, I recovered in a hacienda in New Mexico and learned Spanish." He brushed back his long, gray hair and again broke into Spanish. After a minute of conversation Millie didn't understand, Angelina nodded.

The two turned their attention to Millie. She narrowed her eyes and glared at Kootenay. "Sir, your bear attacked me. You should shoot the animal, or my husband can if you are unable. It should be turned into bear steaks."

"Bear steaks?" He touched Little Bear's head, looking horrified. His head dropped and he looked at his toes as he mumbled, "Little Bear didn't mean no harm, but I'm sorry he ripped your dress."

"My dress?" Millie looked down and gasped. A large flap of material lay partially on the ground, ripped on three sides. The gaping hole exposed her shortened petticoat and more than a little ankle. "It's ruined. My skirt is ruined!"

"I'll bring you some furs," Kootenay said quickly. "I'll buy you a new dress." He looked both remorseful and slightly terrified.

Millie never wanted to see this man or his bear again. Lifting her head, she said curtly, "That won't be necessary. Just keep your bear away from me."

The man's big shoulders slumped and he suddenly looked like a well-chastised, giant child. "Little Bear wanted chow. That's why we come here." Millie felt a twinge of guilt as Kootenay snapped his fingers and turned around, his feet literally dragging in the pine needles. *Lor' almighty!* The mountain man had the manners of a jackanape, but Millie suspected she'd hurt his feelings.

"*Señor* Kootenay." Kootenay looked back as Angelina untied Gruffy from her back and cradled the infant in her arms. "Will Little Bear hurt Gruffy?"

"Course not." Kootenay turned back, his grizzled face brightening. "Little Gruffy has grown." He knelt down and wrapped his massive arm around the bear's neck. The bear turned his head and licked Kootenay's bearded face. "The little stripling can pet Little Bear. He's soft and he don't smell too bad."

"Miss Angelina, I don't think that's a good idea." Millie clearly remembered the bear's sharp, gleaming teeth. One bite—even in play—would kill Gruffy.

Angelina ignored Millie and stepped closer. Gruffy squealed, his arms and legs wiggling wildly as Angelina knelt beside the bear. Gruffy leaned forward and joyfully wrapped his little fists into the bear's fur, pulling until the bear's hide bulged out.

Millie tensed, wanting to snatch the baby away but feared any sudden movement would cause more harm than good. Angelina untangled one of Gruffy's hands, whispering, "*Suave*, gentle." She held Gruffy's hand and showed him how to lightly pet the bear. Gruffy shrieked, grabbed the animal's fur, and pulled himself forward until he buried his chubby face in the dark fur. When he turned his head sideways, his eyes were wide, and soggy fur was matted in his mouth.

Millie gasped, but Little Bear didn't move.

Gruffy fought Angelina as she untangled his fists and mouth from the animal's fur. Beside her, Kootenay grinned, looking as happy as the child. "Mr. Good," Millie said breathlessly. "Your bear is behaving very admirably."

"Little Bear's good. He just plays rough sometimes." Keeping his hold on Little Bear's neck, Kootenay looked up at Millie, his eyes sparkling in the light. "He shouldn't be turned into bear steaks." Gruffy screamed in delight, leaving a streak of drool and spit on Little Bear's coat. Turning his head to rub his fat cheek against Little Bear's fur, the baby's eyes also sparkled.

"Mr. Good, you and Gruffy have the most beautiful golden specks in your eyes," Millie said, unable to believe she was trying to make amends. She sucked in a breath when Little Bear turned his nose toward Gruffy. She saw Angelina tense and try to pull her son away, but Gruffy wouldn't release the bear's fur. The bear moved his nose over until he touched the baby's nose. Little Bear licked Gruffy's face, and the little boy squealed, releasing his fistful of fur and grabbing the long, pink tongue.

Without thinking, Millie bent down and put her hand into the bear's mouth, trying to protect Gruffy's face. She waited tensely, nose-to-nose with Little Bear, while Angelina struggled to pry Gruffy's fingers from around Little Bear's tongue. Finally, Angelina succeeded, and Millie carefully removed her hand. Little Bear turned his head and licked Millie's face. She stumbled backward and stood up, wiggling her fingers in amazement. There wasn't even a scratch on them from the bear's sharp teeth.

"Thank you, *señor* Good. Your bear nice." Angelina, keeping a firm hold on Gruffy, turned to Millie. "We should go."

Kootenay stood up and released Little Bear, looking down at Millie. "Heard you and your man were trying to find Wandering Will's killer."

Angelina glanced at Millie, her expression curious. "*Señora* Millie, why would you care about Wandering Will? I thought *señor* George kill his partner."

"I don't know who killed Wandering Will," Millie said, glancing uncertainly from Kootenay to Angelina, suddenly remembering the sheriff's words of warning and that Kootenay was a special friend of Kate's. Had Kootenay really just accidently come across them? "My husband and I are trying to find the truth."

Kootenay's expression turned sour and Millie took another step backwards. "The truth is George Drouillard's a mean *hombre* well-nigh capable of murder. Wandering Will had it coming, no matter who killed him. Neither man is worth your time. You should worry about your own family and go home before something worse than Little Bear happens to you."

Millie slipped her hand into her apron and wrapped her fingers around the butt of her six-shooter. "Is that a threat, Mr. Good?"

He scowled at her. "Course not. Unlike Wandering Will, I ain't never hurt a woman. Least not on purpose."

Millie knew it was safer for her if she left it alone, but she couldn't help saying, "Mr. Good, you don't sound like you liked Wandering Will. Why is that?"

"Nobody liked the *hombre*. I live upstream from his cabin and had some run-ins with him. Also, he hurt Miss Kate. I ain't sorry he's dead." He dipped his head toward Angelina. "Nice to see you, *señora* Cornog." Turning to Millie, he added in a less friendly tone, "I apologize for Little Bear, but maybe it ain't a bad lesson. Tend to your own family. Forget Wandering Will and go home."

Millie narrowed her eyes as he strode away, but his comment about her family made her feel a twinge of guilt. She should be visiting the schoolmistress, finding out what trouble the children were in, not harvesting skunk cabbage. Tomorrow. It would be her first chore.

Angelina wrapped Gruffy into her *robozo* and waved Millie forward. "Come, *señora* Millie. We go."

Millie looked down at her damaged skirt and sighed. The only way to protect the material was to lift the skirt much higher than was proper. At least they weren't in town. Sighing again, she picked up the folds and lifted as she followed Angelina, struggling to retrieve her empty basket by the lake's shore. A slight breeze chilled her wet feet as she trudged up the trail, stopping when Angelina stopped and looked back.

"*Señor* Kootenay," she hollered.

The big mountain man looked up at them.

"Thank you for helping *señorita* Kate last year."

"Miss Kate ain't deserved what Wandering Will done to her." He glanced at Millie. "For hurting a nice girl like Miss Kate, Wandering Will deserved to die."

"Did you kill him?" Millie asked.

Kootenay just turned and followed his bear back toward the skunk cabbage.

TWENTY-EIGHT

May 11, 1865

Buttercup's Revenge

Millie heard Buttercup's pitiful bleats long before she reached their cabin. Tired and with her head pounding, she resignedly opened the back door. Buttercup charged out, dashed under the clothesline, kicking up her heels. After racing around the area twice, she stopped, eyeing Millie like a bull ready to charge. Millie tensed, expecting a head-butt, but instead, Buttercup darted in, bit the edge of Millie's torn skirt, and jerked backwards.

"No!" Millie cried as the damaged material ripped. Buttercup jumped away and a bread loaf-sized section of Millie's dress tore off. "Give that back!" Millie grabbed for the goat, but Buttercup darted away, the material clenched in her mouth. She charged around the barn, dragging the fabric through the dirt, Millie chasing after her. They zigzagged around the dusty back yard, under the clothesline and around the privy. Finally, near the barn, Buttercup stopped, her sides heaving.

"You bad, bad goat!" Millie gasped. She tried to gently pull the material from Buttercup's mouth, but just managed to tear it more. Buttercup shook her head and the material ripped completely in half. Millie's heart sank as she carefully spread her half open. It was filthy, chewed and covered in prickles. Unusable. The other half was quickly disappearing into Buttercup's mouth. Furious, Millie called the goat several foul names—words if she heard the children or Dom using, she'd wash their mouths out with soap. Her tirade stopped short when she heard laughter.

Turning slowly, she looked toward the cabin.

Dom, George, Milo, and her brother stood by the back door, all clutching portions of a deer. Milo and her brother's eyes were wide with shock, a butchered hind quarter clasped in each of their arms. Dom and George had both dropped their slabs of bloody meat and were bent at the waist, laughing uncontrollably.

Millie was mortified.

Unable to do anything else, she rearranged her skirt, trying to cover the large section of exposed white petticoat. Buttercup, taking advantage of her distraction, jumped forward, jerked the remaining material from her hand, and darted away. The little goat hid behind Dom, peeking out to watch as she devoured the ruined fabric.

Dom stood up, what looked like the deer's heart and liver still clutched in his bloody hands, tears streaming down his wind-blown face. His eyes danced with humor as he said, "Such language, Millie."

Millie stormed past them, went into their bedroom, and slammed the door.

Later, when Dom stepped inside, she didn't look up.

She was dressed in her Sunday dress yet felt totally mortified. Dom, either not noticing her mood or choosing to ignore it, told her about their hunt as he changed clothes. "Oh, by the way," he said, buttoning up his clean shirt, "I've invited George, Milo, and Dave to supper. Seemed polite since they helped butcher and haul the deer back."

"You did what?" she whispered, slowly lifting her head.

Dom saw her expression and stepped back. "It shouldn't be a problem. I'll cook venison steaks on an outside fire."

"No problem? No problem! A last-minute meal for four hungry men after the day I've had." Millie wanted to scream. "When?"

"After the children get home." Dom moved carefully to the door, stepped outside, and paused. "Milo's invited me to become an Odd Fellow. The meeting's tonight. Joining will help our investigation." He fled; the door banging shut behind him.

Millie forced herself to rise and brush and braid her hair. Her muscles ached and her head still pounded but she needed to start cooking, to tell Dom about Wandering Will's pistol and her encounter with Kootenay Good, and whenever she had time, to mend her dress, if that was even possible. She was surprised to find Dom alone in the cabin. "Where's George and Mr. Pemley, ah, Dave?"

"George went back to his cabin. We left a front quarter of the deer there. He and Dave plan to come to supper, but then they'll leave."

"George is leaving? Going back to his cabin?" Millie suddenly didn't feel so bad. "Really?"

"Yep. Tex is dead so I think he'll be safe—especially if I'm an Odd Fellow. Dave plans to visit Buck's Dancehall and Saloon after we eat." Dom laughed. "We met that dancehall girl, Kate, on the walkway before we got to the cabin. I swear, there were sparks flying between those two. Dave was suddenly keen on an evening spent carousing."

Millie shook her head. She wished she knew her brother well enough to advise him about the ills of saloons and dancehall girls, especially since he might be dancing with a potential murderess. She'd have to warn him, somehow, but most men seldom heeded her good advice. Millie sighed. "Did George mention Daddy's treasure map while you were hunting?"

"No, and I'm a bit concerned about that." Dom frowned. "The Three Rings is worthless. George knows it. Unfortunately, I don't see him letting family get in the way when it comes to a treasure of silver coins."

"That is the most cynical thing I've heard you say about your uncle." Millie felt downright elated.

"I know George is a rascal, but I don't believe he killed Wandering Will. Why bring us here to solve the murder if he's the culprit?"

"To get back into his mine. He thought the lode was worth a fortune and couldn't come back without us."

"Maybe." Dom ran his fingers through his hair. "I'll warn Dave to watch out."

Millie nodded and as she prepared potatoes to bake, she told Dom about Wandering Will's pistol and her eventful day. The children returned home just as George arrived and Millie asked about their day, but before they could respond, George interrupted and reenacted Millie and Buttercup's encounter. The children didn't laugh and when Hosa glanced at Buttercup, he cringed. Strands of thread still hung from the goat's mouth.

Milo and Dave soon arrived, dropping their plates and cutlery on Millie's table before joining Dom in back to help with the venison steaks. Soon they were all crowded around the table, the smell of venison steaks and baked potatoes making Millie's mouth water. She was starving, but as she ate, she couldn't help noticing the differences in the four men at her table.

Her brother looked young and inexperienced compared to George. Milo sat between the two, his fancy clothing and slicked back hair reminding Millie of a mountebank, a snake oil salesman, promising to cure all evils. At the end of the table, Dom looked both handsome and decent—the kind of man she was proud to call her husband.

The food quickly disappeared and as plates were scraped clean, Millie's brother finished his coffee, rose, and thanked her for the meal. "I need to be off," he said, his feigned casualness ruined by his excited expression.

"Hope Kate's in a friendly mood," George said, standing and elbowing the younger man.

"You gonna dance with Miss Kate?" Rachel asked, her eyes widening.

Millie turned to her daughter. "Miss Rachel, how do you know about Miss Kate?"

Rachel stammered and Hosa said quickly, "We meet her, after school. She is often at the Cornog's cabin, helping Mrs. Cornog."

Millie couldn't believe it. Hosa had never been a good liar, and this attempt was pitiful. "You met—"

"The Cornogs have kindly taken Miss Kate under their wing." Milo said, interrupting her. "I think she helps Mrs. Cornog with chores and watches their son, Gruffy."

Rachel jumped to her feet and hurried to Millie's brother, grabbing his arm and tugging on it. "Dance with me, Mr. Pemley. Please."

"Miss Rachel!" Millie was shocked by her daughter's behavior. "A lady is never forward."

"I'd be honored to dance with you, Miss Rachel." Her brother winked at Millie, bowed deeply to Rachel, and took the child's hand. They twirled around in the tiny space, Dave showing himself to be an excellent dancer, but Millie's eyes were on Rachel. The child wasn't just following Dave's lead, but actually knew some of the dance steps! Millie pressed her lips together. She was getting a really bad feeling about the children.

Dave took his leave and George soon followed. Millie was ready for the lot of them to be off, impatient to quiz Hosa and Rachel. Her impatience was tempered when Dom asked, "Milo, why don't you tell me about the Odd Fellows' initiation ceremony?" His casual tone didn't fool her for an instant.

"Mr. Milo," she said sharply, "the Odd Fellows' initiation ceremony isn't dangerous, is it?"

Milo smiled so smugly Millie felt a shiver run up her spine. The man was as bad as George—he just hid it better. "Don't you worry none, Mrs. Drouillard. I'll take good care of your husband, but, of course, I can't tell you about our initiation ceremony. It's secret."

"My people have many secret ceremony," Hosa said, showing some enthusiasm for the first time all evening. "We receive first horse after child counting coup ceremony." He pointedly stared at Millie. "Arapaho braves need horses. Arapaho secret ceremony involve horses."

"We'll get you a horse soon," Dom said solemnly, patting the boy's arm the way he did Buttercup's head.

"If he gets a horse, I want a frilly new dress so I can dance like..." Rachel's voice trailed off.

"Like who?" Millie asked.

"Like Arapaho girl," Hosa said quickly.

"Arapaho girls dance?" Millie's stomach clenched.

"Yes." Hosa squirmed. Millie scowled. Soon, very soon, she and the children were going to have a heart-to-heart talk. Something—most likely something she wouldn't like—was definitely going on.

"Of course, the ceremony's a secret, Milo, but surely you can tell me something." Dom laughed and Millie heard his nervousness. "I've heard some interesting rumors, including something about riding a goat."

"Riding a goat?" Millie gave Milo a startled look. "Mr. Milo, there won't be any goats at your meeting, will there?"

TWENTY-NINE

May 11, 1865
Riding the Goat

Milo rose and stretched, his attempt at casual as forced as Hosa's explanation about dancing Arapaho girls. "Couldn't say, but I do want to thank you for an amazing meal, Mrs. Drouillard. Dom, we should get going." Puffing out his chest he added, "As the Noble Grand, I need to be there early, to prepare for the meeting."

Dom nodded, but he didn't get up. "In Denver, I heard a story about an Odd Fellow riding a goat."

Millie felt like her head might explode. Hosa was lying and looked guilty as sin. Rachel appeared to know the dancehall girl, Kate, and Dom was talking about riding a goat. Millie took several deep breaths, deciding to ignore the children for a moment. She turned to Milo, her hand fisted around the knife she'd used to cut her steak. "Sir, the Odd Fellows are grown men. Some with families. Please assure me there will *not* be any goats in your lodge tonight."

Milo squirmed, just as Hosa had. "Like I said, ma'am, the Odd Fellows initiation ceremony is secret."

"That. Isn't. An. Answer." Millie said each word slowly, distinctly.

"Pa, can you tell us the story about riding a goat?" Rachel stepped over to Dom and slipped her hand into her father's, smiling up at him. "Please." Millie ground her teeth. Rachel might have her father wrapped around her finger, but Millie recognized a child's attempt at distraction.

"Of course, sweetheart." Dom lifted the girl onto his lap.

Milo glanced at the door, sighed, and returned to his stool. "Go ahead and tell your little girl a bedtime story, but then we gotta leave."

Dom cleared his throat and brushed Rachel's curly hair out of her eyes. "I met a man in Denver City who told me the story about the Odd Fellows Peak Lodge. Just after they founded the lodge, they had one of their new members ride a goat."

"A real goat?" Rachel's eyes widened. "Why?"

Why indeed? Millie wondered why any man would want to join the Odd Fellows Society. With a name like that, who wouldn't expect goat-riding members.

"The Odd Fellow's name was Mr. Londoner. He—"

"Mr. Londoner's goat riding in Denver City was not part of an initiation ceremony," Milo interrupted, his tone defensive.

"Maybe not, but it's a hell of a story," Dom laughed.

"Language, Mr. Drouillard!"

Dom rested his big hand on Hosa's shoulder. "Do you want to hear Mr. Londoner's story, son?"

"Yes, sir."

Dom smiled indulgently. "Mr. Clark, the man who told me the story, said the first Odd Fellow Lodge in Denver City was established the day before Christmas in 1860. Is that right, Milo?"

"Yes." Milo took out his pocket watch and pointedly looked at it.

"Problem was, when they set up the lodge, there weren't enough members. Seems I'm not the only man wary of the Odd Fellows' initiation ceremony. Anyway, a couple members decided a businessman named Wolfe Londoner would make a fine new member. They enticed him to join by saying he'd look handsomer than General Tom Thumb in the uniform of the order." Dom paused and lifted a thick eyebrow. "You haven't mentioned uniforms, Milo."

"Only the officers, like me, wear uniforms."

"Ahh."

Millie lifted her own eyebrows. Dom's "Ahh" sounded like he was disappointed *he* didn't get to wear a uniform. Sometimes Millie wondered if she truly knew her husband.

"What about the goat riding?" Hosa asked. "In Arapaho ceremonies, men ride horses." He picked up Buttercup and rubbed behind her ears. "Goats are too small to ride. And goats faint."

"You can't ride Miss Buttercup," Rachel said, jumping from her father's lap and hurrying to Hosa's side.

"Of course we won't ride *your* goat," Milo snorted. "She's too small!"

"But you will be riding a goat?" Millie asked.

Milo looked away and Dom frowned. "Anyway, Mr.

Clark said that in 1860, the lodge met in the hall over the J.B. Doyle & Co. Grocery. To get there, members had to climb a flight of rickety stairs. He said a large, smelly goat owned by the livery next door took to laying in the shade on the landing at the top of the stairs. Course the grocery owner tried to drive the animal away—its smell was offensive—but the goat would sneak back whenever someone wasn't around."

"We really need to be going," Milo said. Millie noticed a red flush was working its way up Milo's neck.

"Soon. I have to finish the story for my children." Dom rose and walked to the door, slipping his coat and hat off a nail. "Mr. Clark said he was watching when two Odd Fellows urged Mr. Londoner up the rickety stairs, heading to his initiation. They were halfway up when the smelly goat jumped to his feet on the upper landing and dashed down the stairs. Using his horns, he tossed Mr. Londoner into the air and, as luck would have it, the man landed on the goat's back. Clark said Mr. Londoner shouted, 'By Chaos! This is gallant sport. A League at every breath. Methinks if e'er I have to die, I'll ride this way to death.' He thought the ride was the initiation ceremony."

Millie was horrified. "What happened to the poor man?"

"Was the goat hurt?" Rachel asked, alarmed.

Dom strode to the table and kissed Millie. "Mr. Londoner rode that goat down the street, but when the goat tried to turn a corner, the man's weight unbalanced the animal. Both goat and man crashed through a local drug store's show window. Mr. Clark said Mr. Londoner turned a summersault in the air before landing on his back.

"Mr. Clark, like lots of folks, had chased after the goat and man. He stepped inside the store just in time to see the clerk bend over and ask if Mr. Londoner was okay. Londoner looked at him dazed and said, 'My goat riding is in honor of me being made an Odd Fellow.' Mr. Londoner sat up and rubbed his back and shook his head. 'I would prefer taking my initiation in installments, but that goat is so odorous.'"

"Was the goat hurt?" Rachel asked again.

"No, the goat was fine." He picked up Rachel and gave her a hug, ruffled Hosa's hair, and turned to follow Milo out the door. "I'm hoping the goat tonight doesn't smell quite so bad."

THIRTY

May 12, 1865
The Phillips Lode

Millie awoke before dawn, relieved to feel Dom beside her, although her relief turned to disgust when she got a whiff of him. He smelled like a musky he-goat. Covering her nose, she got out of bed and hurried into the cabin, lighting the box stove, pleased to see an empty corner where George had slept. When her fire caught, she returned to their room and found Dom sitting on the bed, rubbing his shoulder and stretching his back.

"You look like you were in a barfight." Millie's tone was sharper than she intended, but she felt worn down by lack of sleep and worry. After Dom and Milo left, she'd questioned the children, becoming more and more alarmed when they both remained closemouthed. Rachel had defiantly eyed Millie, but Hosa had just silently hung his head. No matter how she tried or what she said, they both had refused to admit any wrongdoing, or to say much of anything. Frustrated, she finally sent them to bed, stewing as she set to work trying to repair her ravaged skirt. Her mending was hideous—there was no way to properly fix a skirt missing a large swath of material—so she'd begun cutting and sewing the fabric she'd purchased at the Tabor store. As she worked, she'd listened, but the children remained quiet as mice.

Hours had ticked by and her fingers became stiff from sewing. After burning down her second candle, she began to truly worry about Dom and this crazy initiation ceremony. Finally, her last candle burned to a nub and she went to bed, falling asleep and not waking whenever Dom returned.

"Why were you out so late?" she asked.

Dom rose and groaned. "Becoming an Odd Fellow takes time. It's also hard on the backside and my shoulder hurts like the dickens."

"You smell like a goat, Mr. Drouillard." She lifted her eyebrows.

He sniffed his undershirt and scowled. "It does smell foul." Sighing, he took down his flannel shirt and slipped it on. "Now that I'm an official Odd Fellow, my fraternity brothers promised to leave George alone—at least until Monday's duel." He yawned. "I'll tell you what I learned last night if you make me coffee."

Monday's duel! She'd totally forgotten about that. She rubbed her face and groaned. "I'll make coffee, but I think you should tell me in here. The children are up to no good and I'd druther they didn't hear whatever you have to say."

"What do you mean they're up to no good?"

"They won't tell me, but Miss Rachel knows more about Miss Kate than she should and Hosa..." She shrugged. "Something is very wrong with Hosa. I'll go to school this morning and try and sort it all out."

Dom nodded and sat on the bed, pulling his trousers over his woolens. "Last night my *brothers* confirmed Milo, and a couple of the officers, knew the Odd Fellows would inherit Wandering Will's half of the Three Rings if Will died." He yawned and Millie saw he had dark circles under his eyes. He sounded as tired as she felt. "The Odd Fellows Society writes holographic wills for any member who wants one, it's one reason single men join the organization. That and if they die, the Odd Fellows will give them a Christian burial. The society does inherit their belongings to help pay for planting them. Milo said Peran found Wandering Will's pistol when he went through Tex's belongings, although I still don't believe Tex was the killer."

Millie didn't either, but when Dom didn't continue, she tapped her foot impatiently. "And the ceremony? Did you ride a goat?" Dom didn't respond and Millie narrowed her eyes. "Mr. Drouillard, tell me about the initiation ceremony."

"I can't," Dom mumbled, averting his eyes just as Hosa had done last night.

"You can't or you won't?"

"I swore an oath of secrecy. I can't tell anyone about the ceremony, not even you."

Millie said something impolite, gave Dom a disgusted look, and stomped from the room. After completing her morning ablutions, she returned to the cabin where she made Dom weak, watery coffee—just the way he hated it—and began cooking a loaf of sourdough bread in her Dutch oven. Cutting up potatoes to fry, Millie's foul mood darkened when she noticed her skirt—the one she'd repaired last night—looked so bad she would be ashamed to wear it in public. Finishing her new skirt was now important, adding one more item on her growing list.

Dom came in, still rubbing his shoulder, poured himself coffee and scowled when he tasted it. "It's not my fault the ceremony's secret." He carried the kettle outside and dumped it, returned, and made a new pot. "The musket and bayonet you described weren't hanging on the wall in the Odd Fellows Hall last night. Interesting that Milo removed it."

"Wonder why he'd hide the weapon now?"

"Because you is investigating the murder," said Rachel, climbing down from the loft. "And asking questions. Maybe he weren't worried before."

"Good morning, Miss Rachel. Good morning, Hosa." Despite their behavior last night, Millie gave each child a hug before sending them outside to the privy.

"After my initiation ceremony," Dom said, putting his coffee on to boil. "I asked how much color the Odd Fellows pulled out of the Three Rings. Everyone said the color lasted only a week or so. The gold vein turned out to be shallow."

"Meaning Wandering Will was killed for nothing?"

"If he was killed because of the gold, yes. After the vein played out, the rest of the Odd Fellows went back to their own claims. Only George, Peran, and Tex continued looking, hoping to find another lode."

"Is there anything promising left in George's mine?" Millie asked as she packed Hosa and Rachel's lunch buckets.

"Not from what I've seen. Last night, after the initiation, my brothers said the whole area is played out. There's talk of moving on."

"Moving on?" Millie turned to stare at her husband. "Where?" She felt cold seep through her. "George won't come back to Idaho Springs with us, will he?"

Dom grinned. "He might." He poured fresh coffee into his cup. "I know you find George so likable."

"He's as likable as a mosquito bite," Millie said, knowing Dom was just getting even for the coffee. She turned her back on him, adding peppermint sticks to both lunches. "George is rude, unpleasant and—"

"And a liar," said Rachel in her high-pitched voice, walking back into the cabin. "Folks say Uncle George is a mean *hombre* well-nigh capable of murder."

Millie froze and slowly turned to stare at the child. "Who told you that?"

"Maxcy," said Hosa, hurriedly pulling Rachel to the table. He pushed her onto her stool and sat beside her, his eyes lowered.

Millie remembered how Mountain Man Kootenay had used those exact words yesterday to describe George. She felt the hair on the back of her neck rise. It was time to get to the bottom of the children's mischief. Maybe she should give *them* something to worry about.

"You two sure have learned a lot from Maxcy," she said sweetly. "And I've been so impressed with all the schoolwork you do at home. I'm planning to come by the schoolhouse this morning to thank Mistress Carle for all her hard work."

"That's kind of you, Millie," said Dom, not appearing to notice the children's matching expressions of horror.

"That is not necessary," Hosa said quickly.

"We is real busy at school," Rachel added.

Millie set her potato fry on the table, poured herself tea, and took her seat. Still smiling, feeling not the least bit guilty at the children's discomfort, she dished food onto their plates. "I'm sure Mistress Carle will make time for me."

"She may not be teaching school here much longer," Dom said as he ate.

"Why?" Millie and the children asked together.

Dom shrugged. "Last night's rumors. If color is getting rare, folks will have to leave and take their kids with them. No kids, no school."

"What about the Phillips lode?" The Phillips lode was the biggest mine in the area, employing dozens of men.

"I'm going by there today, to assay some ore from a new area in the mine, but the Odd Fellow who invited me didn't sound hopeful." He patted Hosa on the shoulder. "This gentleman told me the history of Buckskin Joe last night. I'm sure Mistress Carle would be impressed if you told the class this history."

"She will not be impressed," Hosa said, his voice a whisper.

Dom took a sip of his fresh coffee and cleared his throat. "Buckskin Joe was founded by a man named Joseph Higginbottom. He and Mr. Phillips, along with several others, came here in the fall of '60. They found some color in the creek just down from the town and since Joseph Higginbottom always wore buckskin, they jokingly named the new town after him. Nobody imagined the name would stick or even that there would ever really be a town."

He paused and Millie decided Dom was becoming as verbose a storyteller as Elder Griswold in Idaho Springs. She glanced at her pocket watch and said, "Dom, the children need to be going to school soon."

"Of course. This won't take long but let me tell them the best part. In '60, a miner named Harris went hunting. His ammo was running low—provisions were hard to come by back then—so when he shot at a deer and the animal ran off, he wasn't pleased. Supposedly he stomped over to where his dinner should have been and looked at the ground, hoping to see blood. There was some, but when he squatted to get a better look, he saw a dull yellow color where the buck's hooves had dug into the soil. That's how the Phillips lode was discovered."

"The gold was on the surface and not in a river?" Living near Idaho Springs, Millie had learned of placer gold—flakes of gold panned from a creek—and gold veins in hardrock mining, but she'd never heard of gold found in soft dirt.

"He'd discovered an oxidized ore deposit." Dom finished his coffee and rose. "It's unusual. Harris didn't know what he'd found and sold his claim. The new owner, Mr. Phillips, recognized the surface decompositions and started an open pit mine." He stretched and rubbed his shoulder. "I'll do my assays at the Phillips mine and then I'll check on George." He glanced at Millie. "If George decides to leave town, especially if he disappears before Monday's duel, it may not matter who killed Wandering Will."

"No, it won't." *And if he left, there'd be no duel, but…* "If George decides to leave, my brother could be in danger."

"I'll warn George to stay away from Dave and to forget

about the silver coins. The map does him no good if he doesn't know where the coins are buried."

"Unless he realizes we know."

Dom shrugged. "I'll deal with George, don't worry."

Millie watched him leave just as Maxcy arrived. The children gathered up their supplies and lunch buckets without enthusiasm. Millie wished them a good day, gave them both hugs, and said, "I'll see you in an hour or so."

Maxcy stopped dead, his face turning pale as a snowdrift. "W-what?"

"I'll see you all in an hour or so, when I call on Mistress Carle."

Maxcy looked from Rachel to Hosa, his eyes wide. They left the cabin, but through the open window, Millie heard Maxcy say, "Oh gadzooks! Now whatcha gonna do?"

THIRTY-ONE

May 12, 1865

The South Park Utes

Millie retrieved venison from the barn and started a barley and venison stew. Despite all her other worries, she was looking forward to ending the children's mischief, so much so, she didn't take the time to hike up to the spring for the fresh water she favored. Surely the strong flavors of venison, turnips, and onions would mask the mineral taste of the water from the stream closer to town. After adding the last of Dom's whiskey—it was a Scotch Barley Broth recipe and Millie was almost certain Scotch was another name for whiskey—she put the stew on to cook. Slipping on her bonnet, she turned toward the door.

Buttercup stood in front of it, eyeing Millie like a predator about to pounce.

"I am *not* leaving you here alone, you bad goat," Millie said sourly. She retrieved a rope and tied it securely around Buttercup's neck. "Let's go, and you best behave." Leading the way out the back door and through the barn gate, she paused when she heard a commotion behind her. Hurrying down the dirt road to the main street, she joined a crowd of miners all staring toward the end of town. Millie looked and found a throng of Indians riding into town like an invading force.

Millie gasped and her heart skipped a beat. She pulled out her six-shooter, but suddenly she realized the men around her hadn't removed their weapons. The filthy man beside her hollered, causing Millie to jump and bump into the man on her other side. His tangled beard flowed down over his bulging belly and he laughed as he grabbed her arm to balance her. "Easy does it, darling. I won't let no Injun take your fiery red scalp."

"What in heaven's name is going on?" she asked, not bothering to correct the comment on her hair color.

"They's inviting us to a dance," he answered, releasing her as a slight breeze caused his long beard to flutter up and indecorously wrap around her neck.

She brushed it away and stepped back, her eyes never leaving the street. It was filled with Indians and their ponies, all crowded together, riding side-by-side. Thirty or so warriors led the procession, their well-trained ponies bumping against each other as they moved. Behind them were a tangle of horses and bodies, young and old, men, women, and children. They hollered and cried out in a foreign tongue, colorful bird feathers waved against their sable braids, and red vermillion paint changed their faces into something fearful, almost inhuman.

"They're inviting us to a dance?" she asked, awed by the sight.

As they drew closer, Millie could see that both the men

and the women wore their hair in long braids decorated with beads, feathers, bits of brass, disks of silver made from flattened half-dollars, and what might be colorful bottle glass. Could this be what Indians considered their best Sunday attire? Was this dance they were inviting townsfolk to something like a church social or barn dance?

The warriors clutched weapons, but the women rode their ponies with colorful blankets over their shoulders, their clothing a mixture of animal skins and western attire. Young children, many grasped in their mother's laps, were intermixed in the mayhem. Millie spotted a child Rachel's age riding her own horse, handling it with skill, and behind her rode a child clothed in little besides beads and earrings.

Their voices rose in volume as the mob grew nearer and Millie stared in fascinated horror as a brave mimicked fighting. He pretended to shoot an arrow from an imaginary bow and hollered out a wild cry of victory. His fierce expressions made Millie cringe. Suddenly it hit her. These were the Utes of South Park. Hosa's sworn enemy!

Church social or barn dance, the boy wouldn't be safe with the Utes in town!

Spinning around, Millie froze as something fluttering in the wind caught her eye. Slowly she turned back and stared. Three older men rode front and center, their long eagle-feather headdresses identifying them as chiefs or important tribesman.

Oh Lor'! The center chief—the one with the most impressive headdress—rode a magnificent, prancing palomino stallion, its golden head held high, its white mane dancing with the animal's movement. Above him, flying in the breeze like a war banner, fluttered something long and black. Millie groaned and covered her mouth with her hand.

Above the chief was a bloody scalp with a long black braid.

Hosa!

Millie pushed miners out of her way as she picked up her skirts and ran toward the schoolhouse. *Lor' Almighty!* Her son was safe at school. He had to be. Following a well-worn trail between cabins and other crude dwellings, Millie dodged through clusters of rough miners. Soon noise from the distant stamp mill drowned out the Utes' voices, and the dueling field came into view. Breathless, Millie jerked open the schoolhouse door and hurried inside. The dimly lit interior forced her to stop and squint, searching the children's faces. Each one stared back at her, but none of them were Hosa.

"Hosa? W-where's Hosa!? Where's Rachel?"

Mrs. Carle stepped from the shadows; her hair pulled back into a tight bun. "Hosa? Of course, your little savage isn't here, Mrs. Drouillard. As I wrote in my note, your children are not welcome in my classroom. Not ever."

"Note?" Millie looked around, suddenly terrified. She spotted Maxcy in the back row and the boy ducked his head and looked away. "What note?" Millie turned and grabbed the schoolmistress's arm, shaking her roughly. "Mistress Carle, where are my children?"

Mrs. Carle looked shocked as she jerked free and took a step back. "No wonder they behave like little demons. Control yourself, madam!"

"Where are my children?" Millie screamed. "Where's

Hosa?"

Mrs. Carle pressed her lips together so tightly they formed a single line across her face. "I haven't seen the miscreants since they left Tuesday morning."

"Tuesday morning?" Millie was stunned. "But it's Friday. They said they were here, in school." Despite the pounding in her head, Millie dimly realized the children never said they were in school, they just implied it.

"Mrs. Drouillard, you are a terrible mother. No wonder your children are monsters. I feel sorry for your poor, poor husband. Your children are not here. They lied to you, just as they lied to me."

Along with the terror gripping her heart, Millie also felt shame, and fury. "You should have told me!"

"*I* should have told *you*. Any observant mother would have noticed her children weren't going to school." The schoolmistress shook her head, her disgust clear. "Mrs. Drouillard, your children are dreadful. Tuesday morning was just too much. I tried to whip the wildness out of that savage—his insolence during lessons was intolerable— but he jumped out the window and ran. Your little girl followed him, stomping on my foot when I tried to stop her. She called me...well, she called me a name no little girl should know, much less say."

Millie's head spun. She'd expected trouble, but not this. Hosa and Rachel were supposed to be here, safe. The Utes carried a bloody scalp. Tears filled Millie's eyes as she asked desperately, "Where's Hosa?"

"I don't know, although I'm certain they're the reason for all the trouble I've had since they left. I *know* that bull snake was put in my wood pile. And the dead rat in my cup?" She shook her head. "Vindictive little terrors."

Millie's head spun and she felt like her world was falling apart. Turning, she hurried to the back of the room and knelt before Maxcy. She lifted his lowered face, forcing him to look at her. "Maxcy, where are Miss Rachel and Hosa?"

The little boy braced like he expected Millie to strike him. "They ain't told me where they go. They take off soon as we're out of sight of your cabin. Afternoons, we meet up at the dueling field. As we walk home, I tell them the work we have from the day."

"Maxcy, please, think. The South Park Utes are in town. Hosa is in danger." *Unless he was already dead and scalped.* Millie choked down a sob. "I have to find them."

"I ain't certain." Maxcy hesitated. "One day Rachel mentioned Mountain Man Kootenay and Miss Kate. Ain't sure if they're with 'em, but you might check."

"Mrs. Drouillard," said Mrs. Carle. "You have disrupted my class quite enough. Leave."

Millie rose, furiously wiping away her tears. "Mistress Carle, you are the worst schoolmarm I've ever met. My husband and I entrusted you with our children. We paid for your services. Any responsible adult would have informed us about problems." Millie stomped over until she stood nose-to-nose to the woman. "If anything happens to either of them, I'll-I'll..." She couldn't think of anything bad enough that could be said in front of children. "I'll see you're fired," she ended lamely.

"No need." Mrs. Carle smirked. "Since your children weren't in class, you didn't get the note I sent out yesterday. I'm closing the school as of today." She smiled thinly. "I've come into an, ah, inheritance of sorts, and I don't need to work anymore."

"An inheritance?" Surely Mrs. Carle wasn't stupid enough to blackmail a killer?

"Yes." Mrs. Carle turned to her class. "I'm done. Get out, all of you. School is over." The children whooped and scampered around Millie, grabbing coats and lunch buckets as they left.

Millie had to find Hosa and Rachel, yet she couldn't leave until she was sure Mrs. Carle was safe, no matter how much she disliked the woman. "My husband thought you knew something about Wandering Will's murder. Your sudden inheritance doesn't have anything to do with his murder, does it?" The teacher flinched but said nothing. Millie threw up her hands. "Mistress Carle, blackmailing a murderer can be fatal. Last year a woman in Idaho Springs was killed because she tried just that."

The schoolmistress's face turned crimson. "If you ruin my good name by insinuating such a lie, I'll have Sheriff Finch run you out of town."

Mrs. Carle was in over her head and Millie knew it, but she didn't have time to do more than warn the woman. She had to find Hosa. Once he was safe—dear Lord let them both be safe—she'd come back and talk some sense into the teacher. Hopefully before it was too late.

THIRTY-TWO

May 12, 1865

Missing

Millie rushed toward her cabin, passing Buttercup as she ran out into the dusty street. The Utes were gone, replaced by miners getting an early start to their Friday night revelry. Not able to think clearly through her terror, she hurried into the Tabor's store, impolitely pushing her way through other customers until she reached the front counter. "Miss Augusta, I need your help. My children. They haven't been going to school." She blushed, shamed by her ignorance. "I don't know where they are and with the Utes here, I think Hosa's in danger. The Utes were waving a fresh scalp. An Arapaho scalp. *Oh Lor'!*"

Augusta scrambled out from behind her counter, leaving the customer she'd been helping. "Hosa's Arapaho, isn't he?" Millie nodded miserably. "I'm so sorry, Miss Millie. I thought something was off. Maxcy hasn't been acting like himself. I'll have a word with him when he gets home." She touched Millie's arm. "Any idea where they might be?"

"Maxcy mentioned that mountain man, Kootenay Good, and the dancehall girl, Miss Kate. Do you know where I can find them?"

"We need to find Sheriff Finch. He'll form a posse." Augusta shooed her customers from the store, locked up, and pulled Millie up the walkway. "I hate to say this, Miss Millie, but…" She hesitated and blew out a long breath. "With the Utes showing off that scalp, you, well, you need to be prepared for the worst."

Prepared for the worst? Millie felt cold. The children had only been gone a couple hours. Surely the scalp was older than that. "A man said the Utes were inviting us to a dance. What kind of dance?"

Augusta stopped and rested a hand on Millie's arm. "I'm sorry, Miss Millie. The Utes were inviting us to a scalp dance. The parade was an invitation for townsfolk to attend."

"A scalp dance?" Millie felt sick and slightly hysterical. "They invite spectators and scalp them?"

"Of course not. Calm down!" Augusta slapped Millie smartly across the face. Millie jerked backwards, shocked. "There's no time for hysterics. Are you better now?" Augusta lifted her eyebrows and Millie nodded, but she stepped back, just in case Augusta decided she needed another slap. "The Utes celebrate when they take a scalp. They invited townsfolk so they could show off, and to do some trading. Course their dancing ain't like a square dance, but it's interesting." She pulled open Sheriff Finch's door and paused. "Tonight will be fascinating, unless it's your boy they scalped."

*****

Sheriff Finch assured Millie he and his posse would search the town, starting with the dancehall where Miss Kate worked. While they did that, the sheriff recommended Millie find Dom. If he was at the Three Rings, George could take them to Kootenay's cabin farther up the valley. Millie nodded, suddenly desperate to leave and find Dom. She hurried down the busy thoroughfare, Buttercup bleating as she tried to keep up.

Just as she reached the trail, Peran came striding into view. Breathlessly she explained what had happened and he immediately offered his help, turning around and following Millie upstream. The trail felt like it went on forever, but finally Millie splashed across the creek, hearing Dom yell as she scrambled up the hill.

"Be reasonable, George. You saw me assay ore from five different locations. The Three Rings is played out. It's worthless."

"It weren't when I left," George hollered.

Millie scrambled up the tailing pile. "Forget the gold!" Tears flowed down her cheeks and her voice broke. "Hosa and Miss Rachel are missing. They're in danger."

Dom rushed to her side. "What's happened?"

"Hosa and Rachel. They haven't been going to school. I don't know where they are." She sobbed and buried her face into his broad shoulder. "The Utes came to town today. They…they had a fresh scalp."

She felt his strong hands on her shoulders as he pushed her away. "A scalp? Hosa's scalp?"

"I don't know."

He looked around wildly, like the children would magically appear. Turning back toward her, she felt his fingers dig into her shoulders. "Why didn't you know they weren't in school? Where are they!?"

His rebuke stung but Millie knew there was no time for guilt or recrimination. They had to find the children. Pulling free, she swallowed down her sob and took a deep breath. "Maxcy said they might be with Mr. Good, or maybe with the dancehall girl, Miss Kate. Sheriff Finch is searching town. We need to find Mr. Good."

"I'll take you to Kootenay's cabin." Peran touched Millie's arm, concern creasing his face. "This way. I'm sure we'll find them."

As Millie turned to follow, Dom said, "Come on, Uncle George. We may need your help."

"No," George snarled. "Your brats ain't worth the time. You're better off if the Utes scalped that Arapaho *morveux*."

Millie spun back around, slack-jawed, and saw Dom's face mirrored her own shocked fury. "What did you say?" Dom hissed.

George glared at him. "If my mine's worthless, I need to find some pay dirt. My poke's empty."

"Hosa and Rachel are my children, my family." Dom's voice was low and deadly. "If you won't help find them, George, don't ever darken my doorway again."

"With a wife like yours, I wouldn't want to." George spat at Dom's feet. "You're a disgrace to the Drouillard name." He strode away, giving Millie one final, hate-filled glare before he disappeared.

"This way," Peran said, "Kootenay lives upstream a bit."

Millie nodded, but her eyes were on Dom. He all but vibrated with fury. With clenched fists and a strained face, he passed Millie without a word and strode purposefully after Peran. Millie followed, but by the time she reached the creek, Dom and Peran had disappeared up the trail. She turned to follow but paused when someone called her name. Turning, she found her brother jogging up the trail toward her. "Mr. Pemley, ah Dave, I'm sorry, but I don't have time to talk."

"Sheriff Finch told me what happened. Last night, Miss Kate and I were dancing. She mentioned that mountain man and his pet bear and I got the impression they were friendly." He scowled. "I couldn't find Miss Kate in town, so I headed this way. If she's with the mountain man..." Dave's words petered out.

Millie understood. A single woman visiting an unmarried man was scandalous. But what could one expect from a dancehall girl? "This way." She waved in the direction Dom and Peran had headed. "They may need your help. I'll come as quickly as I can."

"Will you be okay?"

His concern was touching. George was blood kin but he'd never be family. Her brother already was. "I'll be fine, once we find the children." Millie blinked back tears and followed him up the trail.

Within minutes she was alone with only Buttercup as company. Every few steps she was forced to stop and untangle her skirt from a bramble or a branch. She'd always envied Dom's practical pants, but never as much as right now. When she got back to Idaho Springs, she was ordering one of those scandalous, yet practical, bloomers!

The trail climbed higher and the valley narrowed, closing in around her. Had she missed Mr. Good's cabin? Were Hosa and Rachel there? Breathlessly she trudged on, starting when she heard Dom holler. Looking around wildly, she spotted a well-built log cabin hidden in the evergreens.

Twigs and needles tangled in her hair as she squeezed between a quaking aspen and a currant bush, reaching the cabin just as Kootenay Good said, "They were here this morning, like they been every day since Wednesday, but..." His hands gesticulated wildly. "After I told them about the Utes, they lit out of here." Behind him stood the dancehall girl, Kate. She nodded in agreement, but her eyes were on Millie's brother.

"I'm sorry, ma'am," Kate said as Millie moved to her brother's side. "We tried to stop them, but they refused to listen." Millie groaned.

"Where'd they go?" Dom demanded.

"I tried to stop them," Kootenay repeated, his tone desperate. "Really I did. I know it ain't safe for an Arapaho boy to snoop around a Ute camp, but Hosa's as headstrong as, well, as an Indian. He's bound and determined to get a horse. Rachel, she's as cute as a bug's ear, but as stubborn as a mule. When Hosa lit out of here, Rachel was right behind him. Like she always is."

"When did they leave?" Millie demanded. Maybe they'd left after she'd seen the Utes and their scalp.

"Just as soon as they arrived, and I told them those Utes were camped east of town." Kootenay looked miserable. "It was meant as a warning. I know how dangerous them Utes are. I never imagined Hosa would hear my warning and take off. I ain't no good with children." He glanced at Kate. "Never have been."

Millie's stomach roiled. Angry at herself, she yelled at Kootenay. "Was Hosa with you yesterday when Little Bear attacked me?" Kootenay nodded miserably. "Why didn't you tell me?"

The big mountain man's shoulders slumped. "When I found them on Tuesday, Rachel and Hosa said if I told you, they'd run away." He wrung his big hands. "I didn't know what to do."

Millie wanted to scream, but the weight pressing down on her heart told her she was to blame. *She* knew the children were up to mischief. *She* could have checked on them. Kootenay or Kate should have said something, but *she* should have known. She was a terrible mother.

"It's not Koot's fault." Kate stepped beside Kootenay and rested a hand on his arm.

Despite her misery, Millie blinked. In the bright sunlight, with Kate standing so close to Kootenay, the resemblance was clear. It was the eyes. Their honey-brown eyes with brilliant golden speckles.

"Fault doesn't matter," Dave Pemley glanced from Kate to Kootenay, his expression fierce and angry. "We need to find them."

"Before Hosa does something stupid. But how?" Dom strode in circles, pulling on his hair until he suddenly stopped. "Mr. Good, can you track them?"

THIRTY-THREE

May 12, 1865

Miss Kate

K ootenay's brows wrinkled and his expression turned dubious. "Used to think I was a decent tracker, but not after the last couple days hunting with your boy. Hosa's better than anyone I know, including Frémont's Kit Carson. I might be able to follow him, but he knew I weren't pleased. Wouldn't put it past him to lay a false trail." He scratched his head. "Course he's got the little girl with him, so maybe not." As he rambled, Little Bear ambled out the open cabin door and looked around.

Buttercup's eyes bulged out and she fainted, half-disappearing under Millie's skirt. Millie stepped back and scooped her up, anxiously watching as Kootenay stepped over to where the bear stood and squatted. "This here's Hosa's track." He pointed at the ground beside Little Bear's long claws. "His moccasins don't leave much of a print, but the girl's boots got heels. They're clearer."

Dom bent over and nodded. Together they moved

away from the cabin, brushing away tall grass and occasionally pointing at the ground. Little Bear watched them, his big head swinging back and forth between Kootenay and Kate, as if unsure who to stay with. At the edge of the clearing, Dom paused. "Millie, go back to town. If they show up at home, keep them there." It was a command, not a request, but Millie was too distressed to take offense.

"Will you ladies be fine if I accompany Dom and Kootenay?" Peran asked politely, looking from Millie to Kate.

"Of course. Perhaps Dave, uh," Kate looked at the ground. "Perhaps Mr. Pemley would be willing to escort us back to town? After we take Mrs. Drouillard to her cabin, I'll let Mrs. Cornog know where you are, sir."

Millie started as a new realization hit with the force of a blow. How could she have not seen it earlier? The clues had been there. Gruffy didn't have the complexion or coloring of the Cornogs. Kate was a special friend of the couple. Kootenay had helped Kate when she was in trouble.

Had Wandering Will known?

Had Kootenay killed Wandering Will to protect his daughter? Or his grandson? If Wandering Will threatened to take Gruffy away, Millie could add Kate, the Cornogs, or Kootenay to her list of suspects.

"Mrs. Drouillard." Kate touched her arm. "Are you okay? Your face just turned as white as snow. Do you need a drink of water or to sit a moment?"

Millie shook her head, staggered by the truth. "I-I'm fine. Just worried about Hosa and Rachel. We should leave. Maybe they're at the cabin."

"Of course, they'll be there," her brother said soothingly. "Shall we, ladies?"

Little Bear lifted his head, snuffed, and ambled toward Millie. She stepped back but froze when the bear rose up like a man on his hind legs and brought his muzzle so close Millie could smell his breath. Little Bear reached out and licked Buttercup, from her floppy ears all the way down to her tail.

"Little Bear, no!" Kate grabbed the bear and pulled backward. "No, Little Bear, down." Kate pulled the bear backwards and he dropped onto all four feet, but as he went down, Millie heard a ripping sound. Numbly she looked down. The bear's claw had caught in her apron and skirt—her undamaged skirt—and sliced both down the front!

"I'm sorry, Miss Millie," Kate said as she shooed Little Bear back into Kootenay's cabin and shut the door. "Little Bear isn't very well mannered," Kate mumbled, turning back to face them. Millie looked from the girl's honey-brown eyes to the rip in her skirt and could only shake her head.

"Miss Millie, we should go." Dave tugged gently on her arm, guiding Millie away from Kootenay's cabin and Little Bear.

Millie followed slowly, feeling overwhelmed. The children were missing. Miss Kate was Kootenay's daughter. Gruffy was Kate's son. All of her skirts were ruined.

"I'm sorry, ma'am. I should have told you about your children." Kate spoke haltingly as they reached the trail. "On Tuesday, Kootenay found Hosa and Rachel alone in the woods. He was concerned so he brought them to his cabin, but then he wasn't sure what to do. He could entertain Hosa with hunting and tracking, but Rachel…well, he wasn't sure what to do with her. That evening he came and asked me for help, to come to his cabin and watch Rachel. I came on Wednesday and Thursday and again today. Koot looks rough, but he's really quite kind."

Millie's brother made a rude sound and Kate flushed deeper, her eyes widening. Her voice shook as she stammered, "Koot's a friend, that's all. He didn't know what to do with the little girl. He wanted to keep them both safe and worried if he didn't entertain them, they'd run away. Every day, Rachel threatened to leave if we told you. We thought they were safer with us than being alone."

Millie knew Hosa and Rachel and she understood how Kootenay and Miss Kate must have felt. "I appreciate you keeping my children safe, Miss Kate, but you still should have told me."

"You're right." Kate sounded miserable. "I-I don't have children, but I understand a mother's love. When my sister died, it broke my ma's heart. She died six months later."

"What about your father?" Millie asked.

"Pa left when I was little. I never knew him."

Millie waited a beat, but Kate said nothing more. She glanced at the girl and was shocked. Was it possible Kate didn't know Kootenay was her daddy? Millie looked at the girl's face and realized Kate was younger than she'd thought, maybe only seventeen or eighteen. "How old were you when your mother died?"

"Ma died a week after my fifteenth birthday."

Millie felt a wave of compassion as she remembered her own fears on her fifteenth birthday. At fifteen, the nuns at her orphanage sent her to work for the LeGrand family, to earn her keep. She'd been terrified to leave the only home she'd ever known. "How in the world did you end up in Buckskin Joe, Miss Kate?"

"After Ma died, I found an envelope with Buckskin Joe, Territory of Colorado written on it. There weren't no letter, but something Ma once said made me think my pa might live here. I didn't have nowhere else to go, so I came west. I didn't find my pa and when my money ran out, I had to earn a living. I—"

"You did what you had to do," Millie finished.

"Miss Millie," Dave said grudgingly, "Miss Kate dances with men, but she insists on proper behavior."

Millie stumbled as she walked down the trail and paused to set Buttercup on the ground. She groaned as she got a better look at her skirt. The rip went from her knee to the ground and was in the front of the dress, where it would be difficult to hide repairs. Knowing her ruined wardrobe was the least of her issues, she considered Kate and Kootenay. If Kate didn't know Kootenay was her father, it wasn't Millie's place to say anything. "I am sorry for your loss, Miss Kate, but I'm glad Mr. Good has been kind to you."

Kate glanced at Millie's brother. "Koot's a good friend, he helped me when..." she hesitated, "when I was in a bad spot. That's why I couldn't say no when he asked me to help with Rachel."

"Your actions were kind, Miss Kate, but a man should know better than to ask a lady to spend time alone with him in his cabin." Dave gave her a hard look. "It wasn't proper for a lady."

Kate lifted her chin and her voice turned chilly. "A lady wouldn't be caught dead in Buck's saloon, so I guess I'm not a lady."

Dave looked shocked at Kate's words, but Millie could only shake her head. Dave and Kate were obviously in love, but if Dave was upset that Kate spent time alone with Kootenay, he might never forgive her for her other transgression. Millie didn't want to cause more trouble, but she couldn't pass up the opportunity to question Kate about Wandering Will's murder. "Miss Kate, Mr. Good helped you after Wandering Will refused to marry you, isn't that right?"

"Miss Kate didn't plan on marrying Wandering Will," Dave said sharply. "She told me last night she hated the scoundrel."

"I did hate him, in the end, but…" Kate sighed. "Initially I thought Will was different from other miners. He seemed kind and he said he loved me." Her voice dropped lower. "I'm sorry, Mr. Pemley. I'm not a lady. I behaved disgracefully with Will. I knew what I did was wrong, but…" She shrugged and stood up straight, looking miserable but resigned. "After I discovered Will's true nature, when he laughed at my naiveté and discarded me like an empty whiskey bottle, I wanted to kill him. I came back to Buckskin Joe planning to do just that, but someone beat me to it."

THIRTY-FOUR

May 12, 1865
A Ute Scalp Dance

A fter Kate's passionate outburst, Dave's face twisted in shock, hurt, and anger. Without a word he spun around and headed down the trail, not seeing the tears that formed in Kate's eyes. Millie sighed. Young people in love. Dave and Kate were good for each other, but Millie doubted even *her* powers of matchmaking could overcome Kate's disgrace. Silently she followed her brother.

They reached Buckskin Joe to find Sheriff Finch surrounded by a group of men near Buck's Dancehall and Saloon. Millie hurried over, her heart pounding, but the sheriff just shook his head. She choked down a sob and haltingly explained all they'd learned, ending by explaining how Kootenay, Peran, and Dom were trying to track the children.

"Good. That's good." Sheriff Finch looked away. "But I think I'll still head to the Ute encampment. Look around. Ask some questions."

He'd ask if the scalp was Hosa's. Millie swayed unsteadily—actually feeling faint—and Kate stepped forward, encircling an arm around Millie's waist. "Thank you, Sheriff," Kate said quietly. "Perhaps we should check Mrs. Drouillard's cabin first."

"Yes," Millie whispered. "School's out. Surely the children will be home." Barely able to hold herself together, Millie allowed Kate to lead her to her cabin, but when she anxiously opened the door and called out, only silence greeted her. She searched the back bedroom, the barn, and the privy, tears flowing down her cheeks. The children weren't there!

Looking grim, Sheriff Finch nodded and left.

"I've started a fire and put on tea, Mrs. Drouillard. Mr. Pemley will stay while I tell Mrs. Cornog about her husband." Kate laid a comforting hand on Millie's shoulder. "Will you be okay until I get back?"

The simple contact and obvious concern penetrated Millie's numb terror. "Thank you, Miss Kate, you've been very kind." She scrubbed her face with her hands, wiping away her tears. "Excuse me. I need to tack the rip in my dress." She escaped to her bedroom and spent several minutes pulling herself together, adding loose stitches to keep the tear from worsening, and donning a new apron that hid most of the damage. After several deep breaths, Millie sat on her bed and tried to organize her churning thoughts.

No way could she just sit and wait.

Dom was tracking the children. She needed to do something, too. Maybe Hosa and Rachel were prisoners. The Utes might have captured them. The thought gave Millie a surge of fear and hope. She would search the Ute encampment and find her children! The decision made her feel better, more in control, and she strode back into the cabin, finding her brother slouched over the table, looking miserable. Millie sighed. She didn't have time for the two foolish lovers, but she liked Miss Kate and she knew her sisterly duty. "Miss Kate is a fine young lady," she said as she stuffed dried apples and bread into her apron pocket.

"What?" Dave looked up. "What are you doing, Miss Millie?"

"I said Miss Kate is a fine young lady. She'll make some lucky man a fine wife."

"Why are you putting food in your apron?"

"The children will be hungry when I find them." Millie picked up her six-shooter, checked that all the cylinders were loaded except the deadman, and placed the gun on top of the food.

"When *you* find them?" Dave asked slowly.

Millie nodded and slipped into her coat, Buttercup following her every move. Millie opened the door and paused, turning toward him. "Can you tell me where the Utes are camped?"

"The Utes?"

Kate stepped through the back door, glanced at Millie, and nodded. "Are you off to search the Ute camp, Mrs. Drouillard? Excellent idea. I was going to suggest it. Shall we go? We should be able to follow miners heading to the scalp dance."

"You two can't go to the Ute encampment. It wouldn't be proper!" Dave looked from Millie to Kate, his face reddening.

"Some things are more important than proper

behavior," Millie said simply.

Dave threw up his hands. "Of course, I'll accompany you, but Miss Millie, you really should stay here and wait. Miss Kate can go dance, or whatever. I'll stay here with you."

Kate stiffened. Millie just shook her head. "I've never understood why men think waiting is easier than action."

"Shall we go?" Kate asked coldly.

Millie coughed into her hand. She might be a dancehall girl, but Millie liked Kate's spirit. "Yes, but I want to leave Buttercup locked in the cabin; you'll need to step out first."

They stiffly strode outside and after locking an unhappy Buttercup inside, Millie turned and found Kate and Dave with their backs to each other, both in identical stances with their arms crossed over their chests. Their behavior almost made her laugh. They were in love, but too proud to give in. Unfortunately, Millie didn't have time for gently prodding or diplomacy. "Dave, you know everyone makes mistakes. Even your sister, Ann. Miss Kate made a mistake, but—"

"Mrs. Drouillard, this really isn't—"

"And you Miss Kate," Millie said over the woman, "need to remember that men have fragile prides. You can't be surprised that Dave is hurt by your inappropriate behavior. Many men would consider you a soiled dove." Kate's eyebrows shot up and Dave's jaw dropped. "Of course, that's ridiculous. Now apologize and make up. I can follow the miners heading to the Ute camp. After you work out your differences, you can catch up with me." She briskly strode away, following the road in the direction of Buckskin Joe's graveyard.

The dusty road skirted below the graveyard, passing through a thick evergreen grove interspersed with aspen. Late afternoon wind blew up dirt and grime as the tall pines creaked eerily. Millie's ripped skirt flapped, and she heard it tear despite her stiches. Nothing to be done for it now. As she walked, she searched the dark trees, hoping Hosa and Rachel would magically appear. Overhead, dark clouds churned, creating an early dusk as vivid tongues of lightning crackled through the sky.

"Storm's coming," Kate said, hurrying up behind Millie. "It's been an unusually dry spring and we could use the rain, but I only see dry lightning."

Millie glanced behind Kate. Dave followed, but from his expression, Millie couldn't tell if the two had made amends or were still quarreling. Just like fixing her skirt, there was nothing she could do about it now.

Above, thunder boomed, drawing her eyes back to the storm. Despite the threatening black clouds, she could see no rain. The rough road was rutted, making footing difficult, especially as an early dusk descended on them. Millie hurried on, skirting around miners. She stumbled over a rock and bumped into a man.

"Afraid the Utes might scalp you?" he asked as he caught and steadied her with his arm. "Don't worry, darlin', I'll protect you." He tightened his hold and tried to pull her close for a kiss.

Millie gasped, smelling drink on his breath. "Sir, release me!" She struggled against his hold.

"What you got there, Earl?" Another man closed in on Millie's other side. "Remember we're partners. Got to share everything you find."

"Let go!" Millie managed to jerk free and scurried

forward, turning to face the men as she jerked her six-shooter from her apron.

"Now darlin', that ain't very friendly," said the man who'd tried to kiss her.

"Leave her alone, Roger. Vamoose Earl." Kate materialized at Millie's side, pushing Millie's six-shooter down. "That won't be needed, Mrs. Drouillard. These two are harmless."

"He, he tried to kiss me."

"When Earl's had too much to drink, he gets a bit forward, but no need for a gun. A well-placed knee usually does the trick."

A well-placed knee? Millie stared at Kate.

"Miss Kate, that you?" The man called Earl gave Kate a loopy grin. "I ain't done nothing wrong. I caught her. Otherwise she might of falled."

Millie's brother hurried to Kate's side, looking alarmed. Kate just stood up straighter and said, "Roger, Earl, don't either of you recognize a proper lady when you see one?"

"We got real ladies at Buckskin Joe?" asked Roger.

"We was just having a bit of fun," added Earl, swaying unsteadily.

"Mrs. Drouillard's husband is big and jealous. He's got an itchy trigger finger," Kate said, her expression serious. "He won't take kindly to your behavior toward his wife."

"Acting uppity again, Kate?" Millie recognized the voice. Turning, she watched Queeny strut up to the two men, patting one on the rear suggestively as she kissed the other. "Kate ain't no better than the rest of us. Neither is she." She nodded at Millie. "What kind of a proper lady would wear a torn skirt that shows her petticoat almost up to her thigh?"

"At least my dress covers my shoulders," Millie said coldly. Queeny's bodice was so low that with a bit of encouragement, Queeny's bosom would bounce right out.

"These boys like my dress, don't you?" Queeny moved her shoulders suggestively. "Now, which of you was looking for a bit of fun? Fun's my name, long as you got enough color in your poke."

"I got some." Earl pulled Queeny toward the trees.

"Why do you get to go first?" Roger whined, following them.

"Let's go." Dave herded Millie and Kate back down the road. "You two don't need to see the likes of this."

"How can she do that?" Millie felt sick at just the thought.

"It's what she does," said Kate, shrugging. "The two have been drinking whiskey and are well-oiled. Queeny will rob them blind and they won't remember a thing tomorrow morning."

Millie tried to imagine Queeny's life, but she couldn't. "Miss Kate, you have a choice of which men you dance with, right? I mean…"

"My partners know not to treat me like Queeny." Kate pulled Millie around a slow-moving miner. "Roger's okay, his dance is a waltz, and his drink is whiskey. Earl dances well, but after a bit too much drink, his hands get to roving." Kate shrugged. "Like I said, a good, well-placed knee usually solves any problems."

"You really do that to your customers?" Millie almost wished she could visit a dancehall just to watch.

"Not often, but I'm not like Queeny." Kate's words

were said matter-of-factly, but Millie thought they were said for her brother, not her. "Wandering Will hurt me, but he also taught me some tough lessons. Right before I left Buckskin Joe, the week after Wandering Will dumped me like worthless ore, he came round, wanting to dance. When he wouldn't leave me alone, I kneed him just like Kootenay taught me. He doubled over and I struck him on the back of the neck and knocked him to the ground." She stopped walking and turned toward Millie. "I didn't kill Wandering Will, but only because I never got the chance. He almost ruined my life. If it weren't for the kindness of Kootenay and the Cornogs, I would have ended up like Queeny."

"But you didn't." Millie took Kate's arm and placed it over her brother's arm. "You're a fool, brother, if you let her get away." Turning, Millie strode into the darkness. "I hear drums along with thunder. The Utes must be camped just over the next rise."

Millie's footsteps kept beat with the pulsing of the drums as she climbed to the top of the hill. Wind whipped her long braid into her face, but in the distance, campfires flickered, and the sky reverberated with thunder. Millie felt her heart begin to race. What if the scalp was Hosa's? Blood pounded through her temple, but she refused to believe Hosa was dead.

Lightning danced across the sky and thunder rumbled as Millie pushed past clusters of miners trading with Utes. Finally, she reached an open space filled with campfires. Sparks flew into the wind as a line of thirty or forty Ute warriors marched side-by-side, their bare shoulders touching each other. Two of the men carried drums, or maybe they were tambourines, Millie couldn't tell. The background beat of the drums was mixed with a throbbing chant that seemed to keep perfect time with the men's steps. Across from the men, a row of Ute women, their dresses beautifully adorned with beads and silver, moved as one, their steps keeping beat with the men. The lines of men and women slowly approached each other.

"There's the scalp," Kate whispered, pointing.

Millie spotted two women carrying warrior shields and between them, a third woman held a long pole with the Arapaho scalp swinging on the end. *Lor' Almighty. The dark braids looked just like Hosa's.*

Millie swallowed hard and moved closer, trying to see the scalp more clearly, but the chanting and the dancers—if their strange steps could be called a dance—blocked her path. The lines of men and woman joined together and surrounded the scalp, circling it like they were preparing to attack. Lightning lit up the sky, producing phantasmagorical flashes of the strange scene as the scalp's long braids jerked in the night air like it had a life of its own.

Millie edged around the dance area, bumping into miners, and dodging young Indian children. She stopped short when she came upon a Ute horseman sitting calmly on his mustang, his back straight, his head high. Glancing around, she spotted several horsemen watching the dance. Night sentinels, their well-trained mustangs standing still as stone.

In the shadows behind the encampment, Millie heard pounding horses' hooves. She scanned the dark horizon and saw three or four mounted riders racing toward them. The sentry saw the approaching horsemen and hollered something; his cry taken up by other mounted men. The dance stopped as the men rode into camp, their horses scattering slow-moving miners, dancers, and children. The horsemen halted in the center of the dance area and screamed and gestured wildly. Millie didn't understand their words, but the reaction of the dancers was immediate. Their expressions turned ferocious as they cried out in anger.

Dave hollered at Millie and grabbed her arm. He pulled her away from the Utes, taking hold of Kate's arm with his other hand. Together, they backed toward the miners who had formed into a protective group.

"What's happening?" Millie asked.

"Them new Injins," said a miner near her, his weapon drawn. "They say Arapaho are attacking. An Arapaho brave stole their chief's palomino stallion."

THIRTY-FIVE

May 12, 1865

The Ute Chief's Palomino Stallion

D ancers scattered, braves fired guns into the air, horsemen stampeded through the village, and women howled in fury. Dave dragged Millie and Kate away from the angry natives and toward a group of miners. Their jovial, care-free attitudes had been replaced with wide eyes and drawn guns.

"It's safer with others," Dave said, pushing Millie and Kate into the cluster of men.

The miners protectively surrounded them, but Millie felt anything but safe. As men pressed in around her, their foul-smelling bodies jostled against her and she felt like she was being swallowed alive. All her life she'd hated closed-in spaces. Now, as the smell of black powder filled the air and she was squeezed, shoved, and elbowed, Millie felt her chest tighten and her breath come in short gasps. She lost sight of Dave and Kate as she tried to escape. Pushing and shoving, she managed to reach the edge of the group and used her elbows to squeeze between two men, ignoring their indignant cries. Staggering out from the crowd, she bent over and took several deep breaths.

"They're gonna attack!"

Millie stood up and frantically looked around. The Utes did indeed look like they were organizing and preparing to attack.

"Back to Buckskin Joe. We gotta barricade the streets!" hollered another voice.

Stunned, Millie watched as the mass of men edged away from the Ute encampment, moving like they were a single living creature. Bodies suddenly surged around her, and step-by-step, she was forced backward, away from the encampment. In this moving insanity, wind whipped through her hair, men fired weapons into the air, and lightning cut across the sky. Suddenly, Millie heard the shrill cry of a child.

"Momma! Momma!"

She spun around, searching. Again the voice penetrated through the hubbub. "Momma! I'm here!"

A bolt of lightning webbed across the sky, illuminating the frightened faces around her. Floating like a disembodied head above the sea of miners was Rachel. With her hair whipping wildly around her face, the child looked like an unnatural apparition, but Millie's heart lurched at her daughter's terrified expression. Desperately she fought her way toward Rachel, squeezing through bodies as she tried to overcome the backward pull of the mob's motion. Wind kicked up dust and other debris and men knocked Millie from side to side as she fought through the pandemonium calling out to the child. Slowly, painfully, one difficult step after another, she drew closer.

"You should keep better track of your children." Queeny's face suddenly appeared, twisted in a hateful expression, and then it was gone.

Millie gasped and redoubled her efforts. She wedged past one man, ducked under the barrel of a rifle, and pushed away an arm as thick as a log. The dry wind ripped the tears from her face, but Rachel's frantic cries grew louder. Someone bumped Millie and she bounced off another man, feeling a foot strike her shin. Ignoring the shooting pain, she moved, step-by-step, until finally she was beside the man carrying her daughter. "Rachel!"

"Momma!" The man thrust Rachel into Millie's outstretched arms.

"Rachel. My darling. Oh Rachel. Are you okay?" Breathing hard, Millie protectively clutched Rachel's tiny body, trying to protect her and keep her from being ripped away. Rachel wrapped her arms around Millie's neck and her legs locked around Millie's waist. They held each other as the mob again forced Millie to move with it. She dodged and ducked and used her own body to protect Rachel from swinging elbows and hard shoulders. On their left, Millie spotted swaying evergreens. She struggled toward them and finally broke free from the men and stumbled into the dark woods.

Thick branches swayed wildly and cracked like they might break, but Millie bent and pushed deeper into the darkness, protecting Rachel's head as she lurched forward. When she reached a thick trunk, Millie sank down beside it and kissed Rachel's tear-dampened cheek. "Are you okay, sweet pea?"

"Momma, I was so scared."

Rachel's fear made Millie feel sick. A mother should protect her children. "Miss Rachel, where's Hosa? Was the scalp his?"

"No. He were fine when the dance started. But then he went off. He were gonna steal the Ute Chief's horse." Her voice turned indignant. "He left me!"

"Thank the Lord!" Millie sagged against the tree. She buried her head in Rachel's tangled hair and the scent of little girl and soap calmed her racing heart. Hosa was alive, although now he had the entire Ute band chasing after him. She shivered, knowing there was nothing she could do to protect him now. "Are you hurt, sweet pea?"

Rachel hiccupped and pressed her face against Millie's neck. "No." Her tiny body shuddered. "Them miners almost run me over. A man picked me up and I saw you, but I couldn't get to you."

"It's okay. We're safe now." Millie hugged Rachel. "We're safe, but we need to get home. Do you know where Hosa planned to go, after he stole the horse?"

Rachel shook her head, the whites of her eyes glistening in the flashes of lightning. "No. He said he got to hide. Told me not to worry."

Not to worry? Millie suddenly felt exhausted. She was bone tired and Rachel felt heavy in her arms. "We need to get back to the cabin. Do you think you can walk?"

Rachel nodded and Millie set her on the ground. Holding her hand tightly, she pulled the little girl back out into the road. Most of the miners were gone, although there were a scattered few who were too drunk to run. By the time they passed the town graveyard, Millie's feet were dragging, and the cold wind had sucked all the warmth out of her.

"Mrs. Drouillard!" Sheriff Finch ran toward her. Behind him, men dragged trees and brush across the street, blocking it. "Thank goodness you made it back and you found your girl. And the boy?" Millie shook her head. Sheriff Finch nodded grimly and waved her through the blockade. "Go on back to your cabin. The boys and I will protect the town."

Millie staggered to her cabin, pushed open the door, and ignored Buttercup's indignant cries as she shut the door and sank to the floor. She leaned back and pulled Rachel onto her lap. The child shivered but whether from cold or fear, Millie couldn't tell.

"Are you okay, sweet pea?"

"I'm just scared and shaky."

"Oh Rachel, you scared me terribly."

For a long moment, the two silently clung to each other. Buttercup came over to them and licked the tears off Millie's cheeks, as if the little goat understood Millie needed her comfort.

Finally, Rachel looked up. "I'm sorry, Momma." The little girl's voice cracked, and more tears tracked down her blotchy face. "Hosa and me, we was hiding in the trees. We saw you and Miss Kate pass by. He said I gotta find you. Said he were gonna steal a horse. He made me go." The last sentence was said with more heat than fear. "Then he left me."

Millie suspected Rachel was as upset about Hosa leaving her as she was scared. "He didn't say where he would hide with this horse?"

Rachel shook her head. "What are we gonna do? Them

Utes will hurt him if they catch him."

They wouldn't hurt him; they'd kill and scalp him. Millie didn't voice her fears, suspecting Rachel probably knew. To make it worse, Hosa hadn't just stolen a horse, he'd stolen the Ute Chief's prize palomino stallion. The Utes wouldn't give up until they found him. Millie knew they might never see Hosa again.

THIRTY-SIX

May 12, 1865
George's Devious Ways

Wind whipped down the chimney, making it difficult for Millie to light the stove. Finally, she managed and the cabin slowly warmed. Her heartbeat had almost returned to normal when the door burst open and Kate and Dave stumbled inside. Kate took one look at Rachel, moaned, and swept the child off the ground, hugging her.

"Thank the good Lord! I'm so happy to see you both," Dave said, embracing Millie. "Hosa?" Millie shook her head and quietly explained. Dave's relieved expression turned bleak, and he quickly excused himself, heading outside to fill the wood box. Kate kept Rachel in her arms as Millie set out plates and cutlery, trying to reheat her stew without burning it worse.

"We should eat," Millie said as Dave carried in an armload of wood. Despite her words, the smell of her burnt and lukewarm barley and venison stew turned her stomach. Still, she encouraged Kate, Rachel, and Dave to sit at the table as she served up the stew. Taking her own seat, Millie pushed food around her plate, unable to eat even a bite or two. When she looked up, she realized Kate and her brother also hadn't touched their food and the look on their faces made her suddenly fearful. "What? Did the Utes catch Hosa?"

"We don't know about Hosa," Kate said quickly. She paused as wind whistled by the cabin and thunder rumbled. Millie's stomach tightened and she wrapped an arm around Rachel, bracing for the worst.

"At the Ute camp, when all hell broke loose." Her brother flushed, glanced at Rachel and said quickly, "Sorry. Ah, I mean, when the Ute horsemen—"

"What?" asked Millie impatiently.

"After we lost sight of you, we ran into Mr. Drouillard."

"Dom?"

"No," Dave said. "Mr. George Drouillard." Kate leaned against Dave, as if needing his strength, and he wrapped an arm around her shoulders.

Confused, Millie looked from one to the other. "George was at the scalp dance?" She wasn't surprised and didn't really care. "So?"

Her brother sighed. "When the crowd thinned—about half-way back to Buckskin Joe—George ambushed us at gunpoint. Forced us off the road and demanded I give him my pocket watch."

"He would have murdered us if Dave hadn't handed it over," Kate added quickly. "I'm sorry Mrs. Drouillard, but George is a killer. I think he is the one who killed Wandering Will."

Millie lowered her head and pressed her fingers into

J.V.L. BELL 261

her throbbing temples. After the scene at the mine, she should have known. "I'm sorry about your watch, Dave. George is greedy. He wants those blasted silver coins and will do anything to get them."

"He does, and that's the problem. *I* couldn't tell him where they are located. I couldn't, but you can." He held up a hand as Millie opened her mouth. "I understand why you didn't tell me. Probably better that way. But George wants that location. I don't care that he got the watch or the map." He grinned, looking young and slightly reckless. "After I saw how interested George was in the map, I sketched a copy of it, but to be honest, I don't even care about the coins. I care about you and your family." He hugged Kate tighter. "And Miss Kate."

Millie smiled. "I'm glad you two have reconciled."

Kate and Dave both nodded their heads and returned her smile, but soon Dave turned serious. "You know the map isn't useful without a location. I think George knows you know where those coins are hidden. Sister, he'll do whatever it takes, even kill, to get the name of that town."

Millie lowered her head and rubbed her temples, knowing her brother was right. They sat in silence as lightning lit up the edges around the hide that covered the window and a boom of thunder reverberated through the air. She shivered and finally looked back up at Kate and Dave. "Thank you for warning me and I'm sorry George has caused you so much trouble. I'll let Dom know."

"You don't understand, sister. I'm worried George will come by here, tonight. He knows Dom's out looking for Hosa." Wind beat on the roof like angry fists. "I think I should stay until Dom returns."

Tears pricked Millie's eyes. Her brother was a good man. "I appreciate your concern, but Dom will be home soon. Besides, George is ugly, but he's Dom's uncle. I don't believe he'd hurt us." Even as she said it, she knew it wasn't true. George would kill his own mother if the price was right, and a fortune in silver coins, especially after their words at the mine, was well worth George's time. Millie felt her apron, feeling comforted by the heavy weight of her six-shooter. She knew it was safer if Dave remained, but she wanted time alone to talk with Rachel. "I'll be fine, really. I'm armed. I can protect myself."

"Me too," said Rachel, pulling out a small knife from under the folds of her dress.

"Young lady, where did you get that?" Millie tried to take the weapon from Rachel, but the child nimbly pulled away and the knife disappeared back beneath her skirt.

"Miss Millie, please let Dave stay with you." Kate's words drew Millie's attention away from Rachel, a ploy Millie thought was deliberate. Perhaps Kate had given Rachel the weapon. They argued for several minutes, but Millie was firm. They were both exhausted. It was late. The storm would keep George away, and if it didn't, Millie would tell him the truth. The silver coins weren't worth their lives.

Kate and Dave reluctantly left, and Millie added wood to the box stove and moved stools beside it. Sitting on one, Millie patted the stool closest to the stove. Rachel warily sat and didn't move as Millie gently untied her messy braid and tried to comb out the tangles.

"What happened, Miss Rachel?" Millie asked quietly.

Rachel squirmed around until she faced Millie. "I am sorry, Miss Millie, ah Momma." She hung her head. "We shoulda told you we weren't going to school."

"Yes, you should have." Millie wanted to be angry. She wanted to shake the girl and tell her how her lies might cost Hosa his life, but Rachel's frightened expression was proof the child knew the cost of their dishonesty. "Why didn't you? You could have told your daddy. Instead, you lied and added to the lie by doing schoolwork every night. You've hurt me badly. I love you with all my heart, but I'm disappointed."

Tears streamed down Rachel's cheeks. "I-I won't lie no more. I promise."

"Why did you leave school?"

"We…" Rachel hesitated, and Millie braced for another lie. How did one teach a child to be good? Millie always thought the nuns' discipline with rod and strap— quoting Proverbs about how a parent who loves is "diligent to discipline" as they beat a child—just produced angry children. Maybe she was wrong. Maybe a good whipping was the only way to get through to a headstrong child.

"It were that teacher. She were real mean. Hosa hardly did nothing." Rachel's blue eyes—the same sky blue as Dom's—looked imploringly at Millie. "A big boy wanted to see Hosa's hunting knife. He showed it and that teacher gone nuts." Rachel's voice quivered.

Millie rested her palm on Rachel's cheek. "What did Mistress Carle do?"

"She made Hosa come to the front of the class and she took out a horsewhip. She hit him three times on the back 'for he take away the whip from her. He—"

"She used a horsewhip on Hosa?" Millie was horrified and furious. Thunder boomed like a slamming door and

Millie jumped, almost falling off her stool. She glanced at the closed doors. "What did Hosa do?" she asked, slowly.

"Hosa took the whip and said some bad words—in Arapaho. He broke her whip and threw it at her feet. Then he said he were leaving." Rachel looked at Millie imploringly. "I couldn't let him go alone, could I?"

"No, but you should have told us what happened as soon as you got home."

Rachel nodded and Millie turned her head and again tackled the tangled braids. "While you were roaming around, you met Kootenay and Miss Kate? You spent your days with them, right?"

"Mostly."

"Mostly?" *O' Lor'!* Where else had they been?

"Hosa was mad at Mistress Carle," Rachel said slowly. "We went with Max to school and, well, we done some bad things."

As far as Millie was concerned, Mrs. Carle had earned the dead bull snake and rat, although she wouldn't admit that and encourage more inappropriate behavior. "What you did was bad, Miss Rachel. A lady never behaves that way. After Hosa comes home..." She paused and swallowed hard. *If Hosa came home.* "After Hosa comes home, you will both write *I will be nice to my teacher* one thousand times in your planner." Rachel gasped. A letter of apology was also in order, but Millie didn't think Mrs. Carle deserved one. "Do you understand?"

"Yes, ma'am."

"What happened this morning? Did you see the Utes?"

"No. We went to school but couldn't do nothing mean. That man, Mr. Milo, were leaving the schoolhouse just as we got there. We thought him and that teacher done something bad. Mistress Carle was smiling like she were real happy. We ain't never seen her smile so we know something were wrong."

"Mr. Milo visited Mistress Carle this morning?" Millie absently began rebraiding Rachel's hair, giving up on the tangles. In the stove wood crackled, and smoke occasionally puffed out from the cracks in the stovepipe. "I wonder why."

Rachel pulled on Millie's braid. "Momma, we—"

"Ow! That hurts, Miss Rachel. Pulling on my hair is not nice."

"Sorry, but you gotta listen. You and Pa ain't been telling Hosa and me about Wandering Will's murder, but we been listening. We heard you talk about Mr. Milo. Me and Hosa thought he looked sneaky this morning, so we followed him."

"You followed Mr. Milo? Rachel, if you thought Mr. Milo was the killer, you should have stayed away from him."

Rachel nodded seriously. "Hosa and me, we ask each other what you and Pa would do. That's why we followed Mr. Milo."

Millie found no humor in the child's logic. No wonder Dom always worried about her. As Millie struggled with how to respond, the front door banged open. Millie jumped to her feet, fumbling in her apron for her six-shooter, chastising herself for not putting the locking slat in. A dark form filled the doorway. Millie jerked her six-shooter from her apron and aimed at the intruder.

THIRTY-SEVEN

May 12, 1865

Not to Worry?

Millie's hand shook as she aimed her six-shooter at George. "No Momma!" Rachel threw herself at Millie's arm. The child struck her hand and Millie fired the weapon accidentally. The reverberations of the shot deafened her. She choked as black powder smoke filled the cabin, but her skin went cold when she heard a man's violent cursing in a voice she recognized.

She dropped her six-shooter, horrified. "Dom?!" The horror of her actions made her knees buckle and she collapsed. "Lor' Almighty! I-I thought you were George."

"Blast it, Millie!" Dom added several colorful curses as he burst through the door, his eyes wide and wild. "Why—" He caught sight of Rachel and rushed over, sweeping her off her feet. "Thank God! Thank God." He buried his face in her hair, whispering over and over, "Rachel, oh God. I was so worried."

Millie watched them from the floor, unable to stand up. Rachel wrapped her arms around her father's neck and patted him on the back. "It's okay Pa. It's okay."

Millie desperately wanted to be part of that hug. Watching from the outside made her feel empty, but Dom and Rachel didn't seem to notice. Finally, Dom turned toward her, his eyes bleak. "Hosa?"

She shook her head. "W-we didn't find him. I think he stole the Ute Chief's palomino stallion."

Dom nodded darkly. He kept Rachel tightly clutched in his arms as he turned and strode toward the open door. "Kootenay, Peran. Hosa's not here. Millie dropped her gun so she won't shoot you."

Peran and Kootenay peeked cautiously into the door. "You thought your husband was George?" The gold flecks in Kootenay's eyes glinted in the candlelight. "What'd George do to frighten you?"

Millie trembled and needed to take several deep breaths before she could answer. "G-George threatened Miss Kate and my brother. He, he said he'd kill them if Dave didn't hand over his pocket watch. Afterwards, they were worried George would come here. Looking for information."

Dom again cursed, glanced at his daughter, and snapped his mouth shut. "That ass wants the location of those damn coins."

Millie nodded but Kootenay strode into the cabin, stopping just in front of her and looking down as he asked, "Is Miss Kate okay? If that scoundrel hurt her, I'll kill him. I need to check on her. I assume she's with your brother?"

"Or with my Angel," said Peran. "Dom, we'll be back tomorrow morning to search for your boy." Both men turned and slipped out the door, disappearing into the darkness.

Dom shut the door, Rachel still clutched in his arms, and looked down at Millie. "You okay?"

She nodded and pushed herself onto all fours, her legs shaking as she slowly stood up. She couldn't believe she'd almost shot Dom. She could have killed him.

Rachel squirmed in Dom's arms. "You're squeezing too tight, Pa. Let me down. Momma needs me." Dom appeared loathe to release Rachel, but when he set the little girl down, she hurried to Millie and hugged her around the waist. Millie felt lighter with the child's touch, but she wanted, no needed, to feel Dom's strong arms around her. He just looked at her, his eyes cold and distant. "Are you all right, Momma?" Rachel asked.

Millie nodded, feeling almost bereft when Dom knelt beside them and gently pried Rachel free, turning her toward him. Holding her at arm's length, he asked quietly, "Rachel, honey, do you know where Hosa went?"

Rachel shook her head solemnly. "Hosa said he was gonna steal a horse. Said he would need to hide 'till them Utes stop looking for him." She looked earnestly at her father, her expression so like his. "He said to tell you and Momma not to worry."

"Not to worry? Not to worry!" Dom dropped his arms and stood up, his expression furious, his big frame shaking. "You're our children, Rachel. We *always* worry about you." His shouting shook the walls. Turning toward Millie, fury emanated from him like a hot stove. "YOU SHOULD HAVE KNOWN THEY WEREN'T IN SCHOOL!"

Millie understood his fear and rage, but his words cut

her to the quick. The children were their responsibility, not just *hers*. Standing up straighter, she faced him, letting some of her own fear and anger out. "*You* could have checked on them. I knew something was wrong, but *you* never even asked why they didn't answer questions about their school day. All *you* cared about was your uncle and his gold mine!"

"I should have checked? *You* only wanted to solve Wandering Will's murder! At least I worked—"

"Stop!" screamed Rachel. "Don't be mad at each other. It weren't nobody's fault, 'cept Hosa and me." Rachel looked from Millie to Dom, tears sliding down her cheeks. "We were the ones that lied. We pretended we were in school, so Momma wouldn't know. We done schoolwork every afternoon with Maxcy. We lied." She wailed loudly and Dom's furious expression turned to anguish. He'd always been a sucker when Rachel threw a fit. Now he looked at Millie helplessly.

Millie had dealt with Rachel's hysterics often enough to suspect Rachel's current howling was mostly an act. Still, tonight she'd let the child get away with it. Especially if it gave her a chance to show Dom she was a good, loving mother. Picking up the screaming child, Millie held her tight, running a hand down her hair and back. Close to Rachel's ear, she whispered, "Hush. Your screaming will make me deaf."

Rachel quieted and Millie turned toward the box stove. Carefully she sat back down on her stool and rocked Rachel. Dom watched. Now he looked like the outsider. His shoulders slumped and heavily he trod to the table and silently helped himself to Millie's cold stew.

*****

The following morning, Millie slipped out of bed, lighting the box stove and doing her morning ablutions as she prepared for the day. Her eyes felt gritty as she washed her face in cold water, trying to get her thoughts in order. Hosa! She'd worried about him all night, but she feared there was nothing they could do. If they searched for him, they might inadvertently lead the Utes to him.

As the cabin heated, Dom staggered inside, looking as haggard as Millie felt. "I left Rachel asleep in our bed," he said, dark circles and a night's growth of beard adding to his disreputable appearance. He looked at Millie, his eyes haunted. "I'm sorry. I was totally out of line last night."

Millie moved to him and he wrapped his strong arms around her. His strength gave her courage. "I'm sorry, too. I should have kept better track of the children. Can you think of any way to safely find Hosa?"

Dom released her and shook his head. "I thought about it all night. If we search, we might do more harm than good. I don't want to accidently lead the Utes to wherever he's hiding."

"Oh Dom, I'm so scared."

"Me too. But mostly I'm ashamed of my cruel words. You're a good mother, the best. You didn't deserve my criticism. Hosa and Rachel aren't easy and I know you love them. I doubt there was anything either of us could have done to stop Hosa. Once he set his mind on stealing a horse, he was beyond our help."

Millie wiped the tears off her cheeks. "I feel so helpless. I hate feeling helpless!"

"I don't like it either. Least I can deal with George today." Dom's face turned hard. "I'll find him and get your brother's watch back."

A bang on their door interrupted them. Dom rested his hand on his six-shooter and slowly opened the door. The smell of dusty earth and fresh pie wafted inside, followed by Sheriff Finch.

"Sheriff, did you hear something about Hosa?" Millie asked, stepping forward.

"Nothing, but Mr. Pemley came by last night while we were waiting for the Utes. They never came, so I had lots of time to talk to him about his encounter with George. I brought a pie for breakfast. Thought we could eat and plan out what needs to be done, both to find the boy and to make sure George isn't a nuisance."

"Thank you, Sheriff. We should discuss both issues, but I think you also need to check on Mistress Carle."

"Why?" Dom asked, lifting his bushy eyebrows.

Millie hadn't told Dom about Mrs. Carle and Milo, she hadn't had time. As she put coffee on the fire, she repeated what Rachel had told her.

"Couple of my customers mentioned the schoolmarm's sudden announcement. Not that they were sorry to see her go, but she is the only teacher Buckskin Joe's got. And come to think of it, I haven't seen Milo in at least a day. I'll check on both after we eat." Sheriff Finch sliced his pie into four equal sections and served them onto plates Millie set out. "You know, Buckskin Joe used to be a nice quiet place. Sure, we had barfights and duels, Ute trouble, and most nights at least one working woman behaved badly, but that was child's play. Nothing like the trouble your family has brought here."

THIRTY-EIGHT

May 13, 1865
Down the Shaft

L istening to Buttercup's unhappy bleating, Millie pulled on Bluebell's lead as she followed Dom up Buckskin Joe's main street. Over breakfast with Sheriff Finch, Dom had insisted he would visit George and retrieve Dave's pocket watch. Millie had vowed to accompany him, starting an argument. Sheriff Finch had hurried out the door when Dom mentioned he planned to return George's burro and Rachel had loudly thrown herself into the fray. Now, a half hour later, with none of them happy, they headed toward George's cabin. Buttercup's unhappy bleating faded, and Millie glanced back to make sure Rachel was doing okay.

Rachel's tears hadn't swayed her father, but Millie could see the child hadn't given up. She sat on Bluebell's back, just behind the harness, her face blotchy, hugging the little burro and whispering secret plans into the animal's large ears.

Millie tightened her hold on the lead. Returning

Bluebell would take every mothering skill she possessed, facing George again would be even more difficult.

"I'm telling you both to stay home," Dom grumbled for the umpteenth time. "George won't hurt me. I'm his nephew. If he does get unpleasant, having you along won't help."

"We're coming, Dom." Millie tried a new tact. "Accompanying you helps us get our minds off our worries about Hosa."

"And we'll make sure Uncle George don't shoot you," added Rachel. She hugged Bluebell and a tear slipped down her cheek. "But Pa, that mean *hombre* can't have my burro. He'd hurt her."

Dom glared at Millie. "Tell her Bluebell belongs to George. Plus, a lady shouldn't call someone a mean *hombre*."

"A lady should never lie," Millie responded. "And I agree with Rachel. Bluebell is now part of *our* family."

Dom threw up his hands and grumbled incoherently as he strode away.

"We ain't giving her back!" Rachel hollered at her father's back.

Following Dom down the dusty street, Millie dodged around miners who were making an early start to their Saturday revelry. They were on the far side of town when Millie heard Sheriff Finch holler her name. She pulled Bluebell to a stop and turned to wait, her gut clenching from Sheriff Finch's grim expression. The sheriff jogged toward them, his apron flapping around his six-shooters.

"She's gone," he said breathlessly. "Mistress Carle isn't in the schoolhouse or her cabin. Milo's disappeared too."

"Could they be lovers?" Dom asked. Millie stared at

her husband. She'd never considered that. "Maybe they ran off together."

If Mrs. Carle and Milo were lovers, it explained a lot, but Millie didn't believe it. She'd never seen the two even look at each other. But maybe they were lovers and Mrs. Carle *had* inherited some money. Money might have motivated Milo to—

"I don't think they even liked each other," Sheriff Finch said, interrupting Millie's thoughts. "Long before the trouble with Wandering Will, I heard Milo whine about Mistress Carle. He used to call her a nosy old maid." Sheriff Finch sighed. "You all keep an eye out for her. Maybe search around the Three Rings. I'll form *another* posse." He stretched out the word another, emphasizing his displeasure. "We'll search the town, school, and the area around Milo's cabin and claim."

After promising to search for the schoolmistress, Dom and Millie took their leave. They left the crowded town behind, but even on the empty trail, Millie felt the knot in her stomach tighten. Maybe the sheriff was wrong. If Mrs. Carle and Milo had run off together, Mrs. Carle would be alive and well, but if Mrs. Carle had tried to blackmail the killer, the schoolmistress might be dead. Guilt gnawed through her. Would this have happened if she hadn't asked questions and stirred the pot?

"Pa," Rachel hollered as Dom disappeared around a twist in the trail. "Can I ride on your shoulders?"

"Of course, sweetheart." Dom strode back, looking relieved that Rachel was talking to him. He lifted the little girl onto his shoulders, flipping her dress back over his head. Rachel sat with her stockinged feet and legs exposed, showing off the needlework at the bottom of her drawers. Millie shuddered at the impropriety but said nothing. She knew Rachel. The little girl's new position gave her a new angle to work on her father. No way would George be getting Bluebell back, but Millie hoped Dom didn't end up being kicked in the head with her sharp little boot heals during the argument.

"I'll check around the Three Rings for Mistress Carle before we head to George's cabin," Dom said, as he strode up the trail. "A mine's a good place to hide someone."

Millie cringed. A mine was also an excellent place to hide a body. Dom was nowhere in sight when she crossed the creek and paused to catch her breath. From the site of the Three Rings, she heard Dom holler, "Mistress. Carle! George!" Silence answered him.

Millie headed up the trail, but Bluebell pulled back, obviously not wanting to go anywhere near the mine and potential work. Millie dragged her up the incline muttering, "You best behave or I'll let George have you." The little burro snorted, covering the back of Millie's skirt in burro snot.

Millie swore at the little animal but managed to drag her to the top of the hill. She topped the rise just as Dom lift Rachel off his shoulders. Calling Mrs. Carle's name again, he strode closer to the shaft, leaned over the dark hole and called down.

"Dom!" Millie said sharply. "Don't lean that far over. You'll fall in."

He ignored her and called out again. His cry echoed down the shaft, but no one replied. If Mrs. Carle was in the mine, she was in no shape to respond. "I need to go down there," Dom finally said, glancing at Millie.

"You want to go down into the mine?" Millie stammered. Just the thought of watching him disappear into the shaft made her feel ill.

"Bring Bluebell over to the horse's whim and I'll hook her harness to the pole. You'll need to lead her while she's lowering and lifting me."

Millie knew Bluebell didn't like the whim. It was why George always used her on his arrastra. He'd made jokes about Bluebell's poor behavior, laughing about the time she almost knocking Wandering Will out of the ore bucket.

"Dom, we should wait. Bluebell might act up." Millie waved an arm in agitation. "We can search around George's cabin. Wait for Sheriff Finch before you go down there."

Instead of listening to her good advice, Dom walked over and took Bluebell's lead, pulling her toward the whim. The little burro's eyes widened, and she dug in her hooves, but Dom just dragged her over and hooked her harness into the whim's bar. Tentatively he walked the burro in a circle, causing the rope hanging in the shaft to wind around the vertical capstan barrel and the top of the ore bucket to rise into view. "See," Dom said, patting Bluebell. "She'll behave just fine. You'll be able to handle her without a problem."

"And if I can't? Dom, if Mistress Carle was down there, she'd have answered." Millie pulled on her braid, winced, and Bluebell jerked sideways, causing the ore bucket to clang against the shaft wall.

"She might be tied up or gagged." Dom paused and stared at Millie. "I need to go down and look."

Millie sighed. He might be right, but what if Bluebell

continued to misbehave? "Bluebell isn't — "

"Don't worry, Red, you'll be fine." He gave Millie his best, winning smile. "Rachel, help your ma, please."

The little girl smiled sweetly. "I'll happily help Momma, but only if I get to keep Bluebell."

Dom frowned and Millie could see he was doing his own thinking. "If you want to keep Bluebell, show me you can handle her."

Rachel bounded over and took Bluebell's lead. "She'll do anything I want, Pa." Millie followed more slowly, eyeing the ore bucket with distrust. Rachel led Bluebell around in a circle and the ore bucket rose above the rim of the mine. Lowering Dom down the shaft was insane. If Bluebell misbehaved and they dropped him, he'd die. "Dom," she tried again.

"Bluebell will behave, especially with Rachel leading her." He patted the burro's neck. "It'll be fine. Practice a little."

Reluctantly, Millie joined Rachel and together they practiced leading the burro in one direction and then holding the shaft as they turned her around to walk in the other direction. Bluebell behaved well, but Millie had worked with their burro, Columbine, often enough to know burros could be as stubborn as Dom and as unpredictable. Right now lowering him down seemed straightforward, but once Dom put his weight in the bucket... The mine shaft was almost fifty feet deep. "Dom, I — "

"Don't worry, Red. Lowering me down is as safe as a stroll through Buckskin Joe."

"Lotsa folks get shot walking through town," Rachel said, leaning against Bluebell.

"Or attacked by bears when they climb off a stagecoach," Millie added between clenched teeth.

"I'll be fine." He kissed Millie, ruffled Rachel's hair, and strode over to the shaft.

Millie's mouth went dry as Dom sat down, his feet dangling over the edge of the dark shaft. "Dom! You'll fall in." Suddenly her palms felt sweaty and her fingers tingled. "Don't do this!"

"I'll be fine." Dom reached over and pulled the ore bucket toward him. "Lower this down just a bit," he said casually. "I need to put one foot in the bucket and stand up so I can wrap my other leg around the rope."

Millie glared at him, but she knew his expressions. This one meant "I'm doing this." Taking a firm hold of Bluebell's lead, she and Rachel led the burro in a circle, lowering the bucket several inches. They stopped and Millie watched, feeling lightheaded as Dom pulled his miner's hat out and placed a candle in the metal bracket. He doublechecked his tin for extra flint and candles and then nodded at Millie. "I won't be long."

The rope jerked tight, and the pole pushed against Bluebell's harness as Dom carefully put his weight into the bucket and stood up. Millie grabbed Bluebell's halter, her heart racing. Bluebell jerked away from Millie's hand, causing the ore bucket to jump. Dom grabbed for the line and quickly wrapped a leg around the rope. The bucket swayed dangerously.

"Try not to do that, Millie. Let Rachel handle Bluebell." Millie's mouth went dry as she released the burro. "Good. Lower me down, Rachel. Remember, if Bluebell acts up, the bar can be controlled by hand."

"Controlled by hand?" Millie asked, her voice shrill.

"Go away Momma, I'll do it. You is scaring Bluebell." Rachel stroked the burro's neck and started leading her around in a circle.

Millie gasped as Dom began to drop, his sky-blue eyes sparkling in the light. "I love you," she cried out.

Dom's head disappeared into the mine. "I love you both too." His disembodied voice echoed up the shaft.

The whim creaked and Bluebell jerked, trying to pull free, but Rachel kept the animal under control. As she walked beside them, Millie was impressed with Rachel's expert handling. Bluebell wasn't calm, but Rachel kept her in control, except when Millie got too close. The burro seemed to feel Millie's fear and react to it. After one jump that caused the rope to jerk and Dom to yell, Rachel said, "Momma, you is making her scared. Go away."

Reluctantly Millie stepped back and watched the rope play out. Finally, it went slack. Rachel tied Bluebell's lead to a side pole, told the burro to stand still, and walked over to the shaft's edge. "You on the ground, Pa?"

"Miss Rachel!" Millie gasped. "Come here. Get away from the mine's edge."

Ignoring her, Rachel grabbed the bar holding the pully and leaned even farther over the dark hole. "Pa, you okay down there?"

"Miss Rachel!" Millie yelled, feeling almost hysterical. "Step back from the edge."

A tinny voice that didn't sound like Dom echoed unnaturally up the shaft. "I'm good. Nothing here. I'm going to look around, just in case."

"Be careful, Pa."

"Miss Rachel." Millie dragged the name into three long syllables. "Come here." Rachel obeyed and Millie hugged the child tightly. Later, if they survived, she'd strangle her.

"Mrs. Drouillard. Untie the burro and bring the bucket back up." Millie spun around, fumbling for her six-shooter, but Milo just shook his head. "Not a good idea." He stood in a solid stance; his musket pointed at her. The bayonet on the end glistened dully in the light, but the point looked plenty sharp enough to do damage. "Take your pistol out of your apron and toss it here. Do anything stupid and I'll shoot you."

Millie pushed Rachel around until the child was behind her. "Mr. Milo," Millie said as she slowly withdrew her six-shooter and tossed it toward him. "Rachel's a child. Let her leave."

"Get the burro moving. I want the bucket up here. Now!"

Millie's hands shook as she untied Bluebell's lead. The burro backed away from Millie but immediately calmed when Rachel stepped from behind her and took the animal's lead. Rachel turned Bluebell around led the animal in circles around the whim. As the rope wrapped around the capstan, Millie glanced at Milo. He said nothing, but his musket was still aimed in their direction. Finally, the bucket rose into sight and Rachel tied Bluebell to a side post before stepping to Millie's side.

"Let Rachel leave now," Millie said with more confidence than she felt. "She's just a child."

"Whatcha done with Mistress Carle?" Rachel asked.

"Miss Rachel!" Millie said sharply, trying to again nudge the child behind her.

"I didn't do anything with the blasted woman, but I will when I find her." Milo stepped over and picked up

Millie's six-shooter, lowering his musket as he checked to make sure the six-shooter was loaded. Satisfied, he aimed Millie's weapon at her. "Where's Mistress Carle?"

"I don't know," Millie said. "Dom was worried she'd been hidden in the Three Rings. That's why he went down into the mine. You didn't hurt her?"

"Not yet." Milo scowled and glared at Millie. "Yesterday she forced me to give her Wandering Will's pistol."

"Wandering Will's pistol?" Millie's mouth felt dry. Forcing herself to think, she asked, "I thought Sheriff Finch had Will's pistol." If he was talking, he wasn't shooting them.

"The Odd Fellows inherited everything Will and Tex owned. Sheriff Finch returned Will's pistol to me, just as I knew he would, but that old biddy was buying a prune pie when he did." He shook his head and spat. "The next day she showed up at my cabin and tried to blackmail me. Said she remembered seeing me with Will's pistol after his death."

He shook his head and muttered. "Like I had anything to give her. I used all I earned from the Three Rings to pay off my gambling debts. The pistol was the only thing I had left of value. I gave it to her, to keep her quiet until I was ready to leave. Even promised to bring more gold by this morning, but when I come by, the old biddy had disappeared. My pistol was gone, too."

He scowled. "Folks had forgotten about Wandering Will's death until you and your worthless husband started snooping around."

THIRTY-NINE

May 13, 1865

Wandering Will's Murder

Since arriving in the Colorado Territory, Millie had found herself looking at the action end of a six-shooter far too many times—but this was the first time she'd ever seen the wrong end of her own weapon. She didn't like it at all. Especially since Milo looked furious, but not the least bit worried. As she not-so-gently shoved Rachel behind her, she tried to deflect Milo's anger. "Mr. Milo, I don't know where Mistress Carle is hiding. Dom went into the mine to look for her."

"We thought you pushed her in, just like you done to Wandering Will," Rachel said, sticking her head out from behind Millie's skirt.

Millie shoved the child back and told her to shush, but Milo scowled, and his mustache started quivering. "You got the scariest children I've ever met, Mrs. Drouillard. Course you're pretty bad yourself. None of this would have happened if you and your meddling family hadn't come to Buckskin Joe. That old schoolmarm didn't realize what she seen until your husband started talking."

"She saw you sneaking back with a bloody bayonet?" Maybe if Millie could keep Milo talking, Sheriff Finch would show up.

"You think I'm a dunderhead?" He blew out a breath that made his mustache flutter. "The old biddy remembered walking by my cabin one night and saw me messing with Wandering Will's pistol. Your husband's questions reminded her of that night. When she saw Sheriff Finch give me the pistol, she realized I'd had the pistol a week *after* Will's death." He spat in the dirt. "Women. None of you, not even Queeny, are worth this trouble."

"I didn't find her," Dom's voice echoed up the shaft. "Miiillllee, lower the bucket."

Milo glanced at the mine shaft and then narrowed his eyes. "An excellent idea."

"You want me to lower the bucket and haul Dom out?" Millie worried Milo might hesitate to kill a woman and a child, but not a man.

"Course not." He twirled the end of his mustache with his free fingers. "Heard you weren't fond of dark, underground places." Moving closer to the edge of the shaft, Milo kept the six-shooter pointed at Millie as he yelled, "No need to come up, Dom. Your wife and little girl want a tour of the Three Rings. The little girl is coming first."

"What? Milo, that you? What—" Millie didn't hear the rest of Dom's hollering. Every inch of her had gone cold at Milo's words. No way could she go down into the mine. She'd faint, like Buttercup, and fall to her death. "If you hurt my family, Milo," boomed Dom. "I'll hunt you down. By the time I'm done, you'll wish you were in hell. Let 'em go. Millie can't come down here. She's too afraid."

Milo scowled, but Millie saw fear in his eyes. Maybe he would let them go. Her hopes died when Milo said harshly, "Brat. Get into the bucket or I'll shoot your ma."

"No!" Millie screamed, grasping the child's arm. "She's just a little girl. She'll fall. Just let her go. She won't tell anyone."

Rachel squeezed Millie's hand and pulled free. She walked over to the mine shaft, her head high, looking just like a child-version of Dom. "Don't worry, Momma. I ain't afraid."

"Rachel, no!" Millie gasped, fear paralyzing her as Rachel grabbed the rope and without hesitation—like she was playing on a swing—swung her feet into the bucket.

Holding the rope with both hands, Rachel winked at Millie. "I'm good, Momma. Be nice to Bluebell as she lowers me down."

"Do it," Milo snarled.

Millie's hands shook as she untied the burro and tried to turn her around. Bluebell backed away from Millie, causing Rachel and the bucket to drop. "Bluebell, no!"

"Just pet her, Momma. Keep her calm."

Millie took a deep breath. If she didn't calm her fears, Bluebell might shy or do something crazy. If she did, Rachel could fall out of the bucket. "Hold on, sweet pea," she said as she pulled the burro toward her. It took some work but finally Bluebell allowed Millie to stroke her. As Milo impatiently told her to hurry, Millie managed to turn the burro and get her walking around the whim. Tears blurred Millie's vision as Rachel sank out of sight.

"Love you, Momma!"

"I love you too, Rachel." Millie walked Bluebell in a circle, wincing every time the burro jumped or jerked. Each time, Rachel yelled out "I'm fine!" and Millie somehow got the burro moving again. It wasn't a particularly warm day, yet Millie felt sweat run down her back. When the rope finally went slack, she leaned over to tie up Bluebell, but Milo stopped her.

"Bring the bucket back up."

Millie wiped perspiration off her face and managed to turn Bluebell back around. "You got Rachel, Dom?" she hollered.

"Yes. She's safe." Dom's disembodied voice wobbled up the shaft.

Milo stepped closer and looked down into the darkness. "Dom, the bucket is coming back up. If it looks like there is something heavy in the bucket, I'll cut the rope and let you fall to your death. Understood?"

"I understand." Millie knew Dom was scared for her, but as Bluebell reluctantly brought the bucket back up, Millie's own fears outweighed every other thought. Even with Milo threatening to kill her, she wasn't sure she could climb into the bucket, much less descend into the dark shaft. Just the thought made her tremble and feel faint.

Millie tried not to think as Bluebell skittered around the whim, the rope wrapping again around the capstan and jerking the ore bucket back up. When it rose into view, Millie tied Bluebell to the structure's frame and slowly turned to look at Milo. Her mouth was dry but her skin was drenched in sweat. "W-why bother bayonetting Wandering Will before you threw him into the Three

Rings?" she asked, her voice shaking.

Milo snorted. "I didn't bayonet Wandering Will. Hadn't even planned on killing him that morning. Will kept bragging about this rich lode he'd found. My gambling debts had put me in a tight spot and my debtors were gettin' unfriendly, so when Will complained about George, I fed his fears. I convinced him *we* should become partners. We planned to get rid of George that morning, but when I got here, Will was rolling around on the ground, bleeding from his leg and shoulder. He was madder than a wet hen but was getting sloppy. Lots of blood around him. I doubted he'd survive long enough for me to get help."

"You didn't stab him?" For an instant Millie forgot her own fear.

"Didn't I just say that?"

"Who did?"

"Probably George, although Will was cursing women. Not that it mattered. I knew everyone would blame George. Figured after the law lynched George, the Odd Fellows would inherit the Three Rings. I'd get the whole mine." He laughed. "I'll never forget Wandering Will's face when he realized I wasn't gonna help him. He screamed like a girl as I dragged him toward the shaft."

"And then you told everyone I done it."

Millie spun around. George Drouillard stepped out from behind a tall pine tree, his six-shooter aimed at Milo. "You're a coward, Milo. When you kill a man, you should look him in the eye." Without another word, George fired his gun.

FORTY

May 13, 1865
Betrayed

illie screamed as Bluebell jerked back, bucking and kicking. Her halter rope snapped and she bolted, breaking the whim's shaft and charging past Milo before disappearing from sight. The broken pole struck Millie's side as she watched Milo sway unsteadily and slowly drop to his knees. For an instant he stared at Millie, his expression blank, and then he tumbled forward, striking the ground with a dull thud. A pool of blood formed around his still form.

Deep in the mine, Millie heard Dom frantically call out, but she couldn't manage to speak, to answer. George strode past, his boots crunching against the gravel. He paused to kick Millie's six-shooter out from Milo's hand before stepping closer and none too gently kicking Milo's side. Apparently satisfied Milo was no longer a threat, George looked up, his eyes cold and calculating.

"Millie, what's happening?" Dom's words echoed with fear. "Who fired a gun? Are you all right?"

"Your wife's fine," George said sarcastically. "I saved her life."

"Millie?"

Millie swallowed. "Milo's dead," she croaked. "George shot him." George might have saved her from Milo, but Millie didn't feel safe.

"Thank God! George, send the bucket down and pull us out."

"Can't. Burro broke the whim's pole and ran off." His eyes glued on Millie, George removed Dave Pemley's pocket watch from his weskit. He held it by the chain and let it swing back and forth, an unpleasant smile on his face. "Maybe Milo was right, Red. First time I've ever agreed with the *imbécile*." He sneered. "*Mrs. Drouillard*, how about a tour of the Three Rings?" He laughed. "Heard you really enjoy dark, underground places."

"George, what are you doing?" Dom hollered. "Lower the bucket and get me out. We're family, remember."

"That's right, family." George pointed his six-shooter at Millie as he slipped the pocket watch back into his weskit. "Tie the rope around what's left of that whim's pole so the bucket doesn't fall. Family helps family so I'm gonna help you face your worst fears."

"George, what are you doing? What do you want?" Dom screams sounded demonic as they echoed up the shaft. "You hurt Millie and I'll come after you. I won't ever give up."

"I believe you would, Nephew, which is why I'm sending her down to you. Alive. Unfortunately, I'll have to lower her by hand." He glared at Millie. "Do it, now, and then go stand by the mine shaft."

Millie licked dry lips and secured the whim pole, but

forcing her legs to move toward the mine shaft was much more difficult. One slow step at a time, she approached the dark shaft, but as she got close her legs began to shake. She took two more steps and then her feet refused to obey her mind. Swaying slightly, she turned toward George. "Milo confessed to killing Wandering Will. I'll tell Sheriff Finch you saved my life. You don't have to do this."

George just shook his head, the end of his thick beard jerking with the motion. "Climb into the ore bucket, Red. Either that or I'll shoot you."

Millie heard Dom's curses, but she could only stare at the ore bucket. Her palms tingled. Her stomach churned. Her legs wobbled as she managed to take another step closer. The gaping shaft was in front of her, looking like a black opening into hell. Her breathing turned shallow and she found she couldn't move. She just couldn't.

From what felt like a long, long distance, Dom cried desperately, "Millie, do as he says. I'm down here. Sit on the edge and put your feet in the bucket. Wrap your arms around the rope and hold on."

Sit on the edge of the shaft? Was he crazy? She couldn't even force herself to step close to the edge. Knowing George would kill her if she didn't follow his orders, she dropped onto her hands and knees. Crawling, she moved until she could look down into the black emptiness. She shuddered. Tears spilled down her cheeks. She didn't want to die. Hand shaking, she reached out, but the bucket hung in the middle of the shaft, out of reach.

"I-I can't," she whimpered, hating George, hating feeling this scared and helpless.

"I knew it!" George hollered excitedly. "Just knew it!

Except for that big mouth of yours, you're a coward."

"She's terrified, George. Let her go." The deep shaft made Dom's voice reverberate. "Let her go, and I'll tell you the location of the hidden silver coins."

"So you do know." George's smile turned feral. "Where?"

"First let her go. Then I'll tell you."

Millie was having trouble thinking, much less speaking, but when she glanced up at George, she knew he wasn't going to let her go. He was playing with them. And enjoying it. She cowered against the ground when he jammed his pistol into his holster and strode toward her. She screamed when he grabbed her arm.

"Shut up!" George carried her forward, dropping her down until she sat with her legs dangling into the shaft. She tried to roll over and crawl away, but he held her firm as he jammed her feet into the bucket. Then he lifted her up, forcing her to stand in the bucket. It swung wildly, dropping under her weight. Millie screamed and grabbed wildly for the rope, her whole body shaking violently. Wrapping her arms around the rope, she squeezed her eyes shut and waited.

"Hold on, Millie," Dom yelled desperately. "Hold on. Close your eyes and don't faint."

Millie's knees felt weak and her vision tunneled. She bit her lip, tasting blood, knowing if she fainted, she'd die. Pressing her face against the rough rope, she told herself to breathe. In and out. The bucket swayed erratically beneath her but with her eyes closed, Millie thought she was gaining control.

And then the bucket dropped.

Her eyes flew open. "No!" she screamed as George,

holding what was left of the whim's pole, slowly backed in a circle. The ground rose up around her. "No! *Oh Lor'!* Please, no!"

"Enjoy the ride, Red," George said as her head dropped below the surface.

Millie's body shook violently. Death couldn't be this terrifying. Dirt and stone surrounded her and the daylight dimmed. Millie tried to control her racing heart, her gasping breath, but she was losing the battle. She felt light-headed and her knees began to buckle.

"Look up, Momma. Look at the purdy blue sky. Just like Pa's eyes." Rachel's words penetrated Millie's terror. She tilted her head back. Above her, the circle of sky was a deep blue, just like Dom's eyes. The lower she dropped, the smaller the blue circle appeared, but it was enough. She had to hold on. Just a little longer. Then she'd be with Dom and feel his strong arms around her. He'd cloak her in his strength and protect her from the darkness.

"Hold on Millie. Breathe, and keep looking up." Dom's voice sounded just a bit less panicky.

The circle of sky grew smaller. Surely, she was almost to the bottom of the shaft. A shiver of hope went up her spine until the bucket jerked to a stop. The motion caused Millie's feet and the bucket to swing sideways. The bucket struck the wall, knocking Millie off balance. She shrieked and almost tipped over backwards. Her wet palms slipped on the rope and her body convulsed. No! She was so close. Somehow, she managed to rebalance herself. Looking up, a dark head spoiled her circle of blue sky.

"Where is it Dom? Tell me or I'll cut the rope." Beside George's head, Millie saw the glint of his hunting knife.

FORTY-ONE

May 13, 1865

A Quick Drop and a Sudden Stop

Millie felt her sweat-covered hands slip. Her shaking legs caused the bucket to jerk and swing wildly. She couldn't hold on much longer. Her breathing turned ragged, and she couldn't seem to take in enough air. Death had to be kinder than this searing terror. No! She was too close to fall now. Trying to regain control, she focused on George's head and her hatred of the man.

"Tell me where the silver coins are, Nephew. Best be quick or you'll be needing a new wife." He laughed. "Course, that could be a good thing. This one's nothing but a sniveling anchor. Now, where are they?"

"Abingdon," Millie whispered.

"Abingdon," Dom hollered. "Abingdon, Virginia."

"Abingdon, Virginia. See, that wasn't so hard." George's head disappeared.

Moments later Millie's stomach lurched as the bucket dropped. For an instant she thought George had cut the rope, but finally, she realized she was descending much faster than before, but not falling.

"You're almost down, Millie," Dom said, his voice sounding so close. "Just another twenty feet."

Darkness smothered her and her teeth chattered. She looked up at the sky and focused on her memories of Dom's warm embrace. The blackness wouldn't be overpowering if he was holding her. And Rachel too. Suddenly the bucket jerked to a stop again. Millie moaned. Below her, Dom cursed viciously.

"What about Boone Dogs' Cave?" George hollered.

"It's the cave where Daniel Boone's dogs were attacked," Dom snarled. "Now lower her down."

"Sure." There was a loud thud and the rope in Millie's hand went slack. She dropped like a stone.

Her shoulder bounced off the wall and the bucket crashed to the floor. It made a terrible noise as Millie hit something hard but warm. Dom grunted, his strong arms protecting her as they both tumbled to the ground.

"Millie," he said breathlessly. "Millie, are you all right?"

Millie couldn't answer. Her shoulder felt like it had been split by a sledgehammer and Dom's arms were so tight, she couldn't breathe.

"Millie! Millie, talk to me." Dom's shrill voice split the air as he released her and frantically patted her arms and body. "Millie, where does it hurt?"

"Not so loud." Millie lifted her arm. Her shoulder exploded in pain.

"Momma!" Rachel jumped into Millie's lap, knocking

out the little air she'd managed to breathe in. The child wrapped her arms around Millie's neck and more pain erupted in her shoulder, but Millie ignored it. She felt Rachel's shaking body. Carefully she wrapped her uninjured arm around the child.

"I'm okay," she whispered, gently squeezing Rachel.

"Sure?" The child squirmed closer and her spindly arms and legs became entangled with Millie and Dom's.

"Millie, are you hurt?" Dom sat up and lifted both Millie and Rachel onto his lap. "Anything broken?" He squeezed her thigh before probing farther down her leg.

"Dom!" But it wasn't the impropriety of his probing that made Millie gasp. She'd recovered her wits enough to realize they were in the mine. She was in a dark, ugly pit. One that smelled like rotten meat. Bile rose in her throat as a weight pressed down on her chest.

"Your breathing doesn't sound right." His big hand moved up, feeling her cheek and pressing against her injured shoulder.

"Ouch! Stop!" Millie wriggled off his lap, falling onto a rocky floor. "Rachel, take Rachel." As if by magic the child's weight disappeared. Millie squirmed onto her knees, ignoring the sharp stones that bit into her flesh. She looked up at the small circle of blue and tried to inhale.

Dom rubbed her back. "Calm down. You're fine. We're together."

"Breathe in, Momma. Out. In. Out." Rachel chanted quietly, continuing the mantra until Millie found she was breathing to the child's commands.

"I'm okay." Millie felt for Dom's hand. Her shoulder throbbed and as her mind cleared, she gagged on the foul air. Releasing Dom, she covered her mouth and nose. "Lor' Almighty!" she mumbled. "Hell couldn't smell this awful."

"Thank goodness. You're complaining so you must be okay." Dom exhaled loudly. "You scared me half to death." Millie turned toward his voice and in the shadowy light could see his sparkling blue eyes. "You're breathing better." He pulled her into a heartfelt hug.

"Ow!" Millie jerked back and bumped into the rocky wall. Gingerly she rubbed her shoulder.

"You're hurt!" He reached up and probed her face and forehead, his big finger poking her in the eye. "Where? What about—"

"I'm okay, Dom." Millie appreciated his concern, but she didn't want him poking and prodding her. She needed to feel his strength, so she wrapped her hands around his. "I hit my shoulder on something." She gingerly rolled her shoulder. It hurt, but she didn't think anything was broken. "I'm okay." She wasn't sure if she was trying to reassure him, or herself.

"Here." Rachel scrambled around them and overturned the ore bucket. "You can sit here, Momma."

"Thank you, Miss Rachel. That's very thoughtful." Millie was relieved Rachel was holding up so well. Thank goodness the child had been down in the mine when George killed Milo. Dom helped Millie stand up and Rachel shoved the bucket near her. Cautiously she sat down, thankful for Dom's steadying hold. She took a deep breath, trying to control the fear that threatened to overwhelm her, but only managed to gag on the foul air. "Are you both okay? The ore bucket didn't hit either of you, did it? Dom, did I hurt you when I landed?"

"You knocked him over." Rachel came over and cuddled against Millie. "He's moving sore."

"Dom?"

"I'm fine. I'll have a couple new cuts and bruises, nothing to worry about." He laughed. "Just a scratch."

Millie winced. Last time Dom had said "just a scratch," he'd had a bullet wound in his hip. Millie knew Dom could be dying and he'd still confidently assure her there was nothing was wrong. She sighed. Nothing she could do about it right now. Wrapping her good arm around Rachel's thin shoulders, Millie whispered, "At least we're together." *Except for Hosa,* her mind responded. She felt a tear trickle down her face. Was Hosa still alive?

"Kootenay said George was one mean *hombre.*" Rachel's indignation rang out clearly. "But I thought family were family." She huffed and looked up at the sky above. "Now whatta we gonna do?"

Millie followed Rachel's gaze and shivered. The light looked so close, but the surrounding mine walls were rough, almost vertical. "We can't climb out." Millie turned to Dom. "Is there an air shaft or a back exit?"

"No." He kicked at the rope that lay twisted around their feet. "This shaft's the only way out."

"Sheriff Finch knows we're here. He'll come looking." Millie tried to sound confident, trying to comfort Rachel. The sheriff *would* find them, *eventually.* Maybe. But would it be before nightfall? Just the thought made Millie's breathing uneven and her palms tingle.

"Breathe, Momma. Breathe." Rachel patted her arm. "Out. In. Out. In. Out."

Again the childlike chant calmed Millie's breathing, but her heart continued to race. They would get out, sometime, but until then, Millie needed to control her fear. *But what if nobody found them?* Would they die in this terrible place?

"Stop it, Millie!" Dom shook her slightly. "You're heart is racing like a runaway train. Turn off that overactive imagination. We'll get out. We will!"

Millie nodded and ran a shaking hand down Rachel's hair, but her fingers got stuck in the tangles. Squinting, she realized Rachel looked like a homeless, motherless waif. Dom rubbed his backside, obviously in pain, and Millie gulped down a sob. This was all her fault. *She* wanted to play detective. Hosa was in danger because *she* refused to stay home, to be a mother. They would all suffer, maybe even die, all because of *her* selfish behavior. "I'm so sorry. I should have stayed at Idaho Springs with the children."

"I should have seen George for the liar and thief he is," Dom replied.

Millie lowered her head, her fear replaced by self-loathing. She was a terrible mother! No one would search for them, the Utes would scalp Hosa, and they would all starve to death. All because of her.

"It ain't your fault, Momma," Rachel said quietly, as though she could read Millie's thoughts. "We's a family and finding that man's murderer were the right thing to do." She stomped her foot, little stones crunching under her heel. "Now stop feeling bad. It ain't doing no good."

"She's right, Millie." Dom put one hand on Rachel's head, the other gently on Millie's hurt shoulder. "This is George's fault. And mine for trusting him. You're an amazing mother. Now stop worrying. We'll find a way out somehow. Or someone will find us."

"Hosa will find us," Rachel said confidently. "After them Utes stop looking for him, he'll rescue us."

"Of course, he will." Millie hugged Rachel tightly, resting her forehead against Rachel's. Hosa *would* search for them *if* he was alive. But what if George lied to Sheriff Finch? He could say they'd left town, gone after Hosa. Sheriff Finch would believe him. They'd never be rescued. They'd starve to death, or worse.

Unbidden, the story of Daniel Blue and his brothers popped into Millie's mind. The Blues had headed west with two other men in February of '59, deciding to take the Smoky Hill route—touted the shortest route by newspapers, despite the lack of a marked trail. Without a river to guide them, the group became lost west of Fort Riley. Their conditions worsened and as one man after the other died, the survivors resorted to cannibalism. In the end, only Daniel survived. He'd eaten his brothers. Millie shivered. She would gladly give her life so that Rachel could live, but what became of a child who survived by devouring her family?

Her dark thoughts were interrupted when Dom said confidently, "We'll rescue ourselves. I've got my pick down here. I can use it to cut steps into the shaft's walls and climb out." His hand lifted off Millie's shoulder as he knelt. He struck his flint and the flame was so bright Millie had to look away. As her eyes adjusted, she saw Dom had lit the candle in his hat bracket. The flickering light illuminated his worried expression and Rachel's bedraggled appearance.

Rachel squirmed free from Millie's embrace as Dom leaned over and gently probed Millie's shoulder. "Sure it ain't broken?" He touched Millie's face. "Okay now?"

Her shoulder throbbed, but she imagined the pain was nothing compared to starving to death. "I'm fine."

"My pick is near the back of the mine. I'll be gone a couple minutes. Will you two be okay?"

Millie nodded. Rachel eyed her tentatively and then took her father's hand. "If Momma's okay, I want to come with you and see the mine."

"G-go ahead," Millie encouraged, her voice shaking. The thought of being left alone made her skin crawl, but she tried to smile. "B-be careful. Miss Rachel, you listen to your daddy."

Dom gently touched Millie's face. "We'll only be gone a few minutes. You just sit tight."

"And breathe," Rachel added.

Millie nodded, but as the dark mineshaft swallowed them, fear threatened to overwhelm her. She clamped a hand over her mouth so they wouldn't hear her whimper. The thick darkness pressed around her, making her feel alone and helpless. She tipped her head back and stared up at the light and the round patch of blue. The edges of the shaft blurred as her eyes filled with tears.

They would die in this horrible place.

"If it gets bad, Pa." Rachel's disembodied voice wobbled eerily from the black shaft, like a voice from hell. "You gotta promise to kill us. That's better than starving or eating each other."

Millie gasped. Her six-year-old daughter was asking Dom to kill them. Putting her face in her hands, Millie sobbed.

FORTY-TWO

May 13, 1865
Family

By the time Dom and Rachel returned, Millie had gotten herself under control and was wiping her tears from her filthy face. Rachel came and stood beside her as Dom lifted his candle, examining the wall. Millie hugged Rachel, watching as Dom began chopping holes into the wall. He cut hole after hole, each one above the last, making steps as high as he could reach.

"That should work," he said, carrying his pick back into the shaft. "Why don't you and Rachel move a little deeper into the shaft, just in case I fall."

Millie wanted to tell him the foot holes were a terrible idea, but what other choice did they have? Silently she stood and thanked Rachel for dragging the heavy bucket back into the shaft.

"Come on, Momma. I'll help you."

Taking a deep breath, Millie forced her feet to move into the gaping black hole. Each terrible step took all the courage she possessed, but with Rachel holding her hand, pulling lightly, Millie managed. Sinking back onto her bucket, Millie felt her body tremble. Her voice shook as she said, "W-we're out of the w-way, D-Dom. B-be careful."

He came over, kissed her on the forehead, and handed her his hat, the shimmering candle lighting up the grim mine. "I'll be careful, Red." Millie imagined he was using the nickname to try and help her forget her fear, but it didn't work. The light flickered as she watched him put his boot into the lowest hole and search for a hand hold.

The wall wasn't sheer, but to Millie's eyes, it didn't look climbable. She held her breath as Dom ascended one, two, and then three steps. Maybe he could do it. But how would he cling to the wall and cut steps higher above him? Just as she had the thought, something cracked and Dom cried out. His arms windmilled and he uttered a vile curse as he tumbled back down to the ground. He landed on his feet, but his back struck the wall with a muffled thud.

"Dom!" Millie rushed over, relieved to see he didn't appear hurt. Trying to ease his temper, she said sharply, "Such language."

"Sorry." Dom glanced guiltily at Rachel.

"I ain't heard that one before, Pa. What's it mean?"

Millie choked out a laugh. "Miss Rachel, you are never, ever to repeat that word." Noticing Dom was rubbing his back, she asked, "Did you hit it hard?"

"Just bumped it." He sounded dejected.

"Cutting steps isn't going to work, Dom. The wall's too steep."

Dom grunted and used his foot to clear the sharp rocks near the wall. He slid down, landing with his back covering the first foot hole he'd cut, his long legs spread out before him.

Millie's heart went out to him. According to her etiquette books, she was supposed to be the caring mother, the considerate wife. Dom was expected to be the family provider and protector. Right now, those society roles felt like hogwash, but Millie had no doubt—despite Dom's dislike of her etiquette books—that he was feeling all the weight of their predicament. Bending down, she brushed away the worst of the sharp stones and carefully sat down beside him.

Rachel curled up on Dom's lap and Millie rested her head on his shoulder. In silence, they watched the shadows at the top of the shaft move across the wall. Time passed and Millie's breathing slowed until it was almost normal. She started when Rachel's voice broke the silence.

"When them men come and killed my family, I-I didn't want to live no more. When I climbed out of that chimney and saw my momma and pa." She shuddered. "There were blood all over and nobody moved."

She paused and Millie felt a lump rise in her throat. Rachel had never spoken of the massacre that had killed her family. Rachel's mother had been Dom's first love— a woman he'd wanted to marry before he came west. He hadn't known about his daughter's existence until last year. Before he could head east to find her, Confederate guerrillas attacked her family's cabin, killing everyone but Rachel. The girl had survived only because her mother had shoved her up into the chimney and told her not to make a sound.

Reaching over, Millie used her filthy bodice sleeve to

wipe at the tears sparkling on Rachel's face. "We are so sorry, sweet pea." She took Rachel's tiny hand in both of her own and wrapped her fingers around it.

"Strangers come and took me to that orphanage." Rachel looked down at their clasped hands and gently squeezed Millie's. "It were a terrible place, but I didn't care. I didn't care 'bout nothing. Not even when that man come and said I got another Pa. I don't wanna go, but he just packed me up and shipped me off. Finally, after a long stagecoach ride, that smelly man brought me to you."

Dom wrapped both his big hands around theirs, protecting them both. Millie smiled weakly at him, but her thoughts turned to the day Rachel arrived. They were hosting a dinner party when Mr. Poor carried Rachel into their cabin and dumped her into Dom's arms. The bond between father and daughter had been instantaneous. For those first few weeks, Rachel had clung to Dom like he was her salvation, not letting anyone, including Millie, come between them.

Millie's insecurities about motherhood began at the Big Sandy when she'd witnessed Hosa's mother's death. After risking her own life to save the boy, she made herself a promise. She would do whatever she could to care for the child and keep him safe, to make him a welcome part of her family. She'd soon discovered that fulfilling that promise was almost impossible. She could keep Hosa safe and fed, she could love him, but she didn't know how to make him feel like he was a member of their family. He'd been respectful, but never called her momma, or Dom, pa. And he'd constantly reminded them he needed a horse so he could join his father and go to war.

After Rachel arrived, bonding with Dom but not her, Millie's insecurities only worsened. She'd been raised in an orphanage and had never known her mother. She had no idea, no examples on how to become Hosa and Rachel's mother, to make them part of her family. Baffled, she'd struggled with loving the children yet teaching them manners and discipline. Hosa and Rachel were strong-willed and they'd both experienced horrendous tragedies. She loved them with all her heart, but she'd always worried and wondered if they loved her.

"I always wanted a daughter," Dom said softly. "Rachel, you are everything I ever wanted."

"We both feel blessed to have you," Millie added.

"I were so scared," Rachel whispered, "but after a bit, I knew I had a new pa."

"And I had a daughter," Dom said, his voice breaking. "An amazing, wonderful, beautiful daughter. I love you so much."

"I love you too, Pa." She pulled her hands free from theirs and rose up to kiss Dom's cheek. He wrapped his arms around her, hugging her tightly.

Millie felt her heart break. She was happy for them, she really was, but she wanted to be a part of that love. Suddenly Rachel wiggled free of Dom's hold and crawled into Millie's lap. "And I got a new Momma, too." She snuggled against Millie and kissed her cheek. "And a wild Indian for a brother."

Millie choked out a half-laugh, half-sob, gently caressing the child's face. "I love you so much, Miss Rachel. I couldn't ask for a better daughter."

"Course you could, Momma. I love you, but I ain't that

good of a daughter. I ain't told you the truth."

"It doesn't matter," Millie said.

Dom wrapped his arms around them and pulled them close. "We're a family. We won't die here." His voice cracked. "We won't die because if Sheriff Finch doesn't find us, Hosa will. Or your brother, Dave, will come looking. George could never understand what we have, and that's his loss. Families stick together. Always. They help each other, no matter what."

Millie clutched Dom and Rachel, almost wishing Hosa was with them. Not trapped in a mine shaft, but together with them. He was part of their family. An important part, whether he realized it or not. "Someone will find us. I'm sure of it."

"Miss Millie?"

Millie looked up, so quickly her head cracked against the cold wall. Above them, two dark shapes looked down. One was a round human head; the other a long and lean horse's nose.

"Miss Millie?" repeated the voice.

"Hosa? *Oh Lor'!*" Millie scrambled to her feet as Rachel bounded out of her lap. "You're alive. Thank the Almighty!"

"Hosa!" Bouncing up and down, Rachel clapped her hands and yelled the boy's name. "Hosa! We is rescued! Now we don't gotta eat each other!"

FORTY-THREE

May 13, 1865
Hosa to the Rescue

"**E**at each other? Yuck! My horse and I help you out." Hosa patted the long nose near his head. "Mr. Milo is not alive."

Millie swallowed. Milo's body was up there where Hosa could clearly see it. Would it bring back memories of the horrors they'd experienced at the Sand Creek Massacre? Beside her, Dom hollered, "Hosa. It's great to see you, son. We've been worried. Are you safe?"

Millie gasped. "Hosa! If you're in danger, you should leave." She urgently waved the boy away. "Take care of yourself." Her stomach lurched. "Someone else will find us." *Surely someone else would find them.*

"I have little time. My *Neeyoooxetiineese* is fast." Hosa rubbed his face against his horse's long cheek. "Strong too. He can pull you out. Then we leave."

"Is there enough rope up there?" Dom kicked at the rope at his feet. "If you can secure one end of the rope and drop the other end down, I'll climb out by myself."

Hosa's head disappeared and moments later a rope snaked over the pulley and dropped down toward them. "Tie this around you, Mr. Dom. My horse will pull you out. That is faster."

As soon as the end of the rope was within reach, Dom grabbed it and made a loop. He slipped his arms inside the loop and hollered, "I'm ready." His words were barely out of his mouth when the rope went taut and his feet were jerked off the ground. He yelped as he was lifted upward at an alarming speed. Spinning, he kicked at the walls to keep from scraping against them.

"Hold on, Dom!" Millie anxiously watched Dom rise higher and higher, his feet flailing. If the rope slipped or broke... Millie didn't breathe until Dom reached the top and climbed from view. Except for her long exhale, everything went silent.

And stayed silent.

"Don't forget us, Pa!" Rachel yelled. Millie knew Dom wouldn't forget them, but as the seconds ticked by, she felt the darkness close in around her. "Breathe, Momma, breathe." Rachel jerked on her arm. "In. Out. In. Out."

"I'm lowering the rope down." Dom's head suddenly appeared. "Tie it to the ore bucket and ride the bucket up. Just make sure the knot won't give."

Millie watched the rope snake down, feeling her palms begin to sweat. Suddenly getting out of this terrible place felt as imperative as breathing. She grabbed the rope as Rachel retrieved the ore bucket. Awkwardly, Millie tied the end around the thick metal handle, unsure what kind of a knot to use.

"That ain't no knot, Momma, it's a tangle." Rachel scratched her head. "Sure it ain't gonna come undone?"

"Maybe I better check," Dom bellowed. "Move out of the way while I haul the bucket up. I'll check the knot and lower it back down." Rachel dragged Millie toward the dark tunnel as the bucket rose, clanging against the walls. Soon it was coming back down and Dom was yelling, "Okay. One of you climb in and I'll haul you up."

"You go." Millie nudged Rachel toward the bucket. The last thing she wanted was to be left alone, but she wouldn't abandon Rachel.

"No Momma, you go. I ain't scared."

Their argument grew louder in volume until Dom finally hollered, "Both of you get in. With the pulley system, I can haul you both up."

Surely the two of them weighed less than Dom. The rope would hold. Lor' Almighty, it had to hold. The next few minutes, as they rose up the shaft, were some of the worst in Millie's life. Almost as bad as when she'd been lowered. Finally, she crawled from the bucket, ignoring the pain in her shoulder, and scurried away from the mine's gaping hole. Never had she been so relieved to be someplace. After wiping sweat and grime from her face, she stood up and looked around. "Where's Hosa?"

"Ick." Rachel plugged her nose with her hand. "That Milo musta pooped himself. He smells bad."

Dom hurried over and enveloped Millie and Rachel in his arms. Holding them tightly, he herded them away from the Three Rings mine, past Milo's body, and down the hill. He didn't release them until they were beside the creek. As they washed their hands and faces, Dom explained that Hosa had left as soon as he'd hauled Dom out. "Said he'd meet us at Idaho Springs. He looked good, Millie. Happier than I've ever seen him. That horse he stole is something else. Golden like the sun and he follows Hosa around like a well-trained puppy." Dom patted Millie's good shoulder, leaving dirty wet streaks on her sleeve. "I think Hosa will be fine. We need to head to town and tell Sheriff Finch about what happened. We can leave George to him. I want to pack up and leave for home immediately."

Millie nodded. She wanted to hug her son. They could be on their way within hours. Wrapping her good arm around Rachel, she followed Dom down the trail, already considering how she would pack and the supplies she'd need to purchase. For an instant, her thoughts turned to Wandering Will. Milo hadn't stabbed him. Millie suspected she knew who had.

Not that it mattered anymore.

They reached the edge of town and Millie shuddered at the wild Saturday celebrations already in full swing. She wouldn't miss this town, although she had enjoyed getting to know Miss Augusta, Miss Kate, and Miss Angela. They pushed past the masses of drunk men and scantily clad women. Finally, they reached the less crowded side of town, but Millie paused and stared. "There's something going on at the stagecoach stop."

A crowd of maybe twenty people surrounded an obviously angry Queeny and an equally upset Mrs. Carle. The schoolmistress's face was pinched, and she clutched something in her arms. Queeny screamed at her and when she grabbed for the woman, Sheriff Finch stepped between them, looking like he wished he was anywhere else in the world.

"Miss Queeny. Mistress Carle. Behave!" The sheriff tried to keep the two angry women apart as Dom, Millie, and Rachel drew closer.

"She murdered my Will! I want his pistol." Queeny reached around the sheriff and grabbed for the schoolmistress.

Sheriff Finch pushed Queeny's arms away as Mrs. Carle cried. "This is my pistol. Milo paid me with it." Even as she said it, she glanced around warily.

Millie kept a firm hold of Rachel's hand as she moved until she stood beside Dave Pemley, Miss Kate, and Kootenay Good. From there, she could see Wandering Will's pistol clenched in the schoolmistress's arms.

"Milo should have given it to me. It belonged to my Will!" Queeny cried. "I—"

"Milo killed Wandering Will!" Dom's booming voice quieted both women and caused every eye to turn toward him. The crowd parted as he strode up beside Sheriff Finch, although Millie noticed he didn't move in between the two angry women. "Milo confessed to killing Wandering Will," Dom repeated, his voice dropping a notch in volume. "And then George killed him."

"George killed Milo?" Sheriff Finch's eyebrows shot up. "In self-defense?"

Dom glanced at Millie. She shook her head and said, "George murdered Milo. Afterwards, he forced us into the Three Rings and left us there to die."

"Son of a chocolate nugget!" Sheriff Finch exclaimed. "George Drouillard is worse than burnt butterfingers. I'll have to round up some men and form *another* posse." He shook his finger at Millie. "Hope you folks are leaving town soon. Never seen so much mischief. I've hardly had time to bake since you arrived."

FORTY-FOUR

May 13, 1865

Why do you Wanna Get Married?

The stagecoach rumbled into town, causing the crowd around Queeny and Mrs. Carle to scatter. Millie pulled Rachel off the street and stepped closer to Dom. The coach came to a stop beside them and Millie saw Queeny slip behind the sheriff and grab for Wandering Will's pistol. Mrs. Carle let out a screech and pivoted, managing to keep hold of her prize as Sheriff Finch caught Queeny and shoved her into Dom's arms. Millie might have laughed at Dom's shocked expression if she wasn't so worried about Queeny scratching his eyes out. Fortunately, Queeny jerked free and stepped away, her expression murderous.

The stagecoach door opened, and a well-dressed man appeared. He made to step down from the coach but never got the chance. Mrs. Carle—Wandering Will's pistol clutched to her breast—knocked the man back as she scrambled into the stagecoach and disappeared inside. Queeny howled and clambered after her.

The women's angry voices rose in volume and Millie stepped back as the stagecoach began to rock and passengers tumbled out the door. As the last passenger escaped, she caught a glimpse of Queeny and Mrs. Carle wrestling on the floor of the coach, their screamed obscenities shocking in their vulgarity. She covered Rachel's ears as Sheriff Finch stepped forward, slammed the stagecoach door shut, and pulled out his six-shooter, aiming it at the wide-eyed driver. "Get your stagecoach out of my town, now!"

"But the luggage in the boot," voiced the confused driver. "And I need fresh horses."

"Now!" The sheriff's mustache quivered.

Millie had never seen the mild-mannered man look so menacing. The stagecoach driver swallowed, his prominent Adam's apple bobbing. He jerked on his horses' reins and yelled, "Haw! Get on, Betsy. Let's go, Ross." The horses turned the coach around and the driver flicked his whip.

"I'm gonna kill you, Queeny!" yelled Mrs. Carle as the horses broke into a gallop and headed out of town.

After reassuring the stagecoach passengers that their bags would be returned tomorrow, Sheriff Finch turned to Dom. "You're with me. If I have to search for your burnt-whiskered uncle, you're gonna to help." The sheriff stomped away, calling out over his shoulder, "Peran, find some Odd Fellows. You all need to retrieve Milo's body and bury him. Kootenay, I want you too. I might need a tracker."

Dom glanced at Millie and she nodded. "We'll be fine,

go ahead." He nodded and hurried after Sheriff Finch and Kootenay. Millie took Rachel's hand and turned toward their cabin, but she paused when her brother called out.

"Miss Millie, may I have a word with you?"

Dave hurried to her side; Kate's hand clasped in his. In a whisper he asked, "Did George force you to tell him the location of the silver coins?"

"Abington in Virginia," Rachel blurted out before Millie could answer. "Pa had to tell George or he would have dropped Momma down the shaft."

"Abington, Virginia." Dave frowned and scratched his head like he was trying to make up his mind. Finally, he turned toward Kate and took her other hand. "I know you've only known me a couple days, but I adore you, Miss Kate. Will you marry me? We could marry tomorrow morning and catch the afternoon stagecoach. We'll beat George to Virginia. The coins should give us enough to buy a ranch."

"Get married?" Millie asked, stunned.

"Yes!" Kate jumped into Dave's arms. "Yes, yes, yes!"

After a passionate kiss that made Millie blush and cover Rachel's eyes, Millie asked, "Mr. Dave, I know you made a sketch of the map, but is it detailed enough to find them?" Millie could see it was already too late to talk her brother out of a hasty marriage. She liked Miss Kate, but the two had only known each other for a couple days.

Dave gave Kate another exuberant kiss and then held her tightly by his side as he turned toward Millie. "I think so. If not, I'll have the Abington sheriff get the original back from George, after he arrests him."

"After our marriage!" said Kate breathlessly.

Millie nodded and paused. She didn't want to do it—she wanted to pack up and find Hosa—but Dave was her brother and family was family. "Mr. Pemley, Miss Kate. Would you care to have your wedding in our cabin?"

Dave smiled broadly. "That's mighty kind of you, Miss Millie. We'd be honored. Assuming I can find a preacher, we could marry early tomorrow morning. You can head out right after the ceremony."

"Father Dyer was in town two nights ago." Kate smiled mischievously. "Preaching in Buck's."

"In a saloon?" Millie was horrified.

Rachel interrupted their discussion by rudely stomping her little foot. "Miss Kate. You is a dancehall girl. A purdy one. Why do you wanna get married?"

"Miss Rachel!" Millie said sharply, horrified by the child's impolite words.

"A dancehall girl gets to dance. A wife just works," Rachel insisted.

"Miss Rachel!" Millie said, wondering if she would ever understand parenting and children. "That's enough." After they were home, she would need to have a long talk with the child. Rachel's aspirations to become a hurdy-gurdy girl needed to be nipped in the bud.

"Rachel." Kate released Dave and knelt so her eyes were level with the child. "Mr. Pemley and I are in love and people in love get married. We would be honored if you would be a flower girl in our wedding."

The frown lines in Rachel's forehead smoothed and she cocked her head. "What's a flower girl?" Millie could only shake her head at her daughter's suspicious tone.

"A flower girl wears a pretty dress and leads the bride and groom to the preacher." Kate kissed the little girl's forehead. "She strews flower blossoms on the floor, but since there aren't many flowers this early in the spring, you'll just dress up pretty and walk before us."

"I get to wear a purdy dancing dress?" Rachel's face lit up but then immediately fell. "But I don't got no purdy dancing dress."

"Young lady, that is not a polite way to respond to such a kind offer." Millie used her sternest mother tone. "You have your Sunday dress."

"That ain't no dancing dress," Rachel sulked, looking at her feet. "Not like Miss Kate's purdy green one."

Despite *all* they'd been through this morning, Millie wanted to scream. Would being a mother ever get easier? "Rachel." Millie stretched out the name. "Your Sunday dress is very nice."

Kate stood up and turned to Millie. "Ma'am, if you wouldn't mind, I could ask Miss Angelina if we could borrow one of her daughter's dresses. She has several that are quite lovely. I'm sure there is one that would fit Rachel."

"Please, Momma. Please!" Rachel took Millie's hand and looked up, looking every inch a dirty street urchin.

Millie softened, remembering how brave Rachel had been in the mine. "That would be kind, Miss Kate. Miss Rachel, you'll have to be very, very careful of the dress, and be on your best behavior."

"Course," Rachel said, jumping up and down.

"If I'm not being too forward, Mrs. Drouillard." Kate's face turned a bit pink. "I have a dress you could borrow for yourself. We are about the same size."

Millie had only seen Kate in low-cut, barely respectable dresses, and she didn't want to hurt the girl's feelings. Still, her current dress was filthy and the repaired one in the cabin was almost as bad. She truly had nothing in her wardrobe to wear, much less for a wedding. "I'd be please to try one on to see if it would fit."

Kate's face turned even redder. "It will fit, but you, ah, might have to wear a shawl."

Oh Lor'!

*****

Millie was bone-tired as she pulled open the cabin door and was greeted by a very disgruntled Buttercup. Thankfully the little goat hadn't done too much damage, but as she butted Millie in the thigh—none too gently— Millie knew even extra victuals for the journey home probably wouldn't improve the goat's mood.

"I can take Buttercup to the barn and see if Bluebell is there," Rachel said sweetly. "After, can I go find some flowers for Miss Kate's wedding? I can take Buttercup with me."

Where did the child find the energy? Millie just wanted to clean up and take a nap. She glanced at her daughter and shook her head. "You need a bath, first."

"I'll wash up later. Please? I want to gather some of them little white flowers so I can throw them on the floor like Miss Kate said."

Millie finally shrugged. Without Rachel underfoot, she could clean up and get started on the food they'd need for the journey. "There may be Windflowers, or Pasqueflowers, close to the creek near the schoolhouse." She thought about George and added, "Please ask Maxcy to go with you and be careful. I don't want you wandering any farther than the dueling field."

"Yes, Momma."

Millie watched the little girl and goat skip around the cabin and disappear. Sighing, she went into the cabin and lit her box stove. Sleep would have to wait. She had food to prepare, a wedding to think about, and she needed a bath.

An hour and a half later, feeling clean and almost normal, Millie grunted as she lifted her Dutch oven and set it on the stove. She'd decided to make Rachel's favorite, Fairy Cakes sprinkled with sugar, as a treat for the wedding. Standing up, she sniffed, smelling smoke, but she didn't see any new, noticeable leaks in her box stove. Stretching, she strode toward her front door, but before she could open it, Maxcy burst inside, dark smoke wafting in behind him.

"Mrs. Drouillard. The mountain is on fire. Buttercup got scared and ran toward the stamp mill. Rachel chased after her."

"Rachel and Buttercup are near the stamp mill?" Millie sucked in a breath. "That mill is deadly!"

FORTY-FIVE

May 13, 1865

Fire!

illie shoved her feet into her boots and raced out the door, following Maxcy. Black smoke billowed from the hillside on the far side of the valley, flames jumping from one pine tree to the next. The spring had been dryer than normal, but not so dry a fire should have started—unless it was deliberate.

George! Had he lit the fire as a distraction, or just to be ugly?

The trail they'd arrived on was near the blaze. She prayed Dom, Kootenay, and Sheriff Finch weren't caught near the flames, but she had no time to worry about them. She dodged around men rushing toward Buckskin Creek carrying buckets, shovels, rakes, saws, and axes. As she neared the creek, she saw other miners frantically clearing brush and trees, forming a twenty-foot-wide break on the far side of the creek. She knew if the fire jumped the water, it would destroy the town. The wood buildings—many of them dry and coated in resin—

would burn, along with everything in them.

"Maxcy, wait!" Millie hollered breathlessly. The little boy paused and looked back. "Did Miss Rachel run toward the stamp mill or into it?"

"I ain't sure. I saw her run toward the mill. I didn't follow. Ma told me never to go near the mill."

Rachel too knew the mill was dangerous. She would never enter the building and Buttercup would faint dead anywhere near the noise. Rachel wouldn't go there unless she had no other choice. Uneasily, Millie glanced around. Could George be hiding nearby?

"Maxcy, I'll find Miss Rachel. You run back to my house and let the burros out. We'll catch them later. Then go help your mother protect her store." Maxcy hesitated, nodded, and hurried back toward Buckskin Joe.

Millie ran up Buckskin Creek, ignoring the men who yelled at her to get back to town. In the distance, she saw the stamp mill, the loud thumping reverberating up the valley. The huge, three-tiered structure had been built into a hill and she saw open doorways at each level. The building was located beside the stream, needing the water both to drive the heavy, ore-crushing stamps and to wash out the gold.

The stamp mill would be the first building to burn if the fire crossed the stream.

Breathing hard, Millie stepped through the mill's lowest level's doorway and looked around. The noise from the pounding stamps reverberated off the walls, filling the open space—about the size of three dining halls—with ear-splitting noise. The horrendous battering of the stamps thundered in Millie's head, making it hard to think. How did men work in such a building, especially with all the chaotic motion?

Doors on all three levels, on both sides of the mill, stood open, spilling sunlight into the building. Cracks in the walls and ceiling added to the natural light, but there were plenty of dark corners and machines to hide behind. She stood on the lowest level, and in front of her were numerous ten-foot-high stamps with diameters the size of a man's head. Each stamp quickly rose and fell, crushing a steady stream of finger-sized ore chunks into wet slag. Water washed the slag out from under the stamps and onto flat tables surrounded by groups of men. These men glanced at her and waved, indicating she should leave. Instead, Millie stepped deeper into the room, stopping when a giant man with a close-cropped beard strode toward her. He looked furious.

"Get out," he shouted above the noise. "The fire… close… Go!"

Millie only heard some of his words, but she understood enough to shake her head. "I'm looking for a child," she screamed. "A girl with a goat."

"Hurl a goat?"

Millie stepped closer, yelling each word. "Girl. Goat. Missing!"

His thick eyebrows shot up and he spun around, striding toward the men surrounding the flat tables. Millie couldn't hear his words, but his arms swung wildly as he spoke. One man pointed upward. Millie turned, jumping in alarm when a long belt flapping beside her slowed and then stopped. Ignoring the machinery and ear-splitting noise, Millie eyed the upper floors. The second floor looked like it was just a wide walkway, going between large machines and behind the huge stamps. The third floor looked wider and she could see piles of ore stacked near the far wall. If she were inside and hiding, Rachel could be anywhere. Surely she could see Millie and would come out. Unless she was hurt or being held hostage.

"Disturbance... third..." Millie spun around. The man was again beside her, shouting and pointing upward. "Shut... workers... fire."

Millie prayed she'd understood correctly as she hurried toward a rickety, steep stairway. She climbed up to the second floor, dodging around a man shoveling larger chunks of ore into metal jaws that opened and closed, breaking the chunks until they fell through a grate and slid downward, feeding the stamps. Millie shivered. The jaws were large enough to crush a man's head, or an entire child.

If Rachel was inside this building, she had to be running, or hiding, from George. No way she and Buttercup would have come inside willingly. Millie turned and swept her eyes around the room below. Huge machinery and dark corners provided ample places to hide. Could George be down there? Perhaps he was waiting for all the workers to leave, to help put out the fire, before making his escape. Or maybe he was holding Rachel hostage. *O' Lor!* Smoke poured into the room from the doors closest to the river.

The roar of machinery dropped in volume and Millie saw a big metal wheel stop turning. As she watched, another belt stopped flapping and two spinning wheels slowed and came to a stop. One-by-one, the giant stamps stopped crushing oar. Beside her, the metal jaws closed and didn't reopen. Millie's ears rang as the room quieted and soon the only sound was the splash of water and the crackle of fire.

"Outside," yelled the large man who had spoken with Millie. "Out! Grab a shovel, pick, or rake. The fire has almost reached the mill!"

Millie lifted her skirt and hurried up the stairs as men charged outside. The higher she went, the worse the smoke became. Coughing, she reached the upper walkway and hollered, "Rachel. Miss Rachel!"

"Hide Momma!" A muffled voice came from somewhere to her left. "Hide."

Millie stumbled toward the voice, circling behind a man-sized pile of ore. She dropped to her knees when she saw Rachel huddled near the wall, Buttercup clasped in her arms. "Miss Rachel, thank God. What happened?" Pulling Rachel into her arms, she kissed the child. "I—"

"George. He's down there." Rachel squirmed out of Millie's embrace and pointed toward the main floor. "I was gathering flowers outside and saw him. He ran toward us, so Buttercup and me runned to the mill. Buttercup fainted when we got near that door." She pointed at an open door down the walkway. "George followed us. I think he were being chased, but he seen me. I picked up Buttercup and come inside. Then I seen him. He sneaked in the same door you come through."

"George is down there?" Millie shivered. She scanned the room and realized all the workers were gone. The mill was empty, and the room was very, very smoky. The fire outside crackled loudly, sounding close, and black smoke poured in through the open doorways.

Below her, a shadow moved. Millie squinted into the smoke and the shadow became George!

"I know you're up there, *pute*. You and my worthless kin have caused me no end of trouble." George's voice crackled like the fire outside. Millie saw him edge toward the open door. She released Rachel and quietly scooted around the ore pile, pulling out her six-shooter. "Wish I had time to teach you a lesson, but I got to go, before Dom and Finch find me again."

He moved into the light, planning to make his escape. After all he'd done, Millie couldn't let him escape. She lifted her weapon and fired. George dove back into the shadows, his cursing loud and vile. Millie hadn't aimed to kill, she hadn't aimed at all. She just wanted to keep him trapped until someone heard her gunfire.

"You're crazy." George fired his own weapon and Millie lunged behind the ore pile. When she dared to peek around it again, she saw George disappear outside.

"Did you get him, Momma?" Rachel asked.

"No. He's gone." Millie coughed and slipped her six-shooter back into her apron. Reaching over Rachel, she picked up Buttercup. The little goat appeared comatose, except for her open eyes. "We need to get out of here."

Rachel's eyes widened. "Momma, the walls are on fire!" Millie turned toward where Rachel pointed and saw the lower wall, the one closest to the stream, had flames licking up its sides.

The fire had jumped Buckskin Creek.

Millie struggled to her feet, pushing Rachel in front of her. The little girl darted around the pile of ore, stumbled, and regained her balance as she ran toward the open door. "Come on, Momma! We have to get outside."

FORTY-SIX

May 13, 1865
Escape

As she ran, Millie glanced at the wall, horrified by how quickly the dry wood was being consumed. Flames climbed up toward the ceiling and expanded the breadth of the large front wall. It was still well below them—although she could feel the heat from the flames. Millie hugged Buttercup tightly as she followed Rachel toward the open door, darting around ore piles and cursing her long skirts. Half-way to the door, she stumbled on loose ore and fell to one knee. She struggled back onto her feet, ignoring the pain, and choked on thick smoke. She glanced over to see the entire lower wall was now engulfed in flames. The flickering firelight, crackling fire, and churning smoke made the room feel alive.

"Hurry, Momma. Hurry!" Ahead of her, Rachel darted out the door. Millie crouched low, trying to find less smoke-filled air, and lurched forward. She tasted fresh air and saw sunshine. Just three, maybe four more steps away. Suddenly Rachel burst back inside, screaming as she collided with Millie. They fell, arms and legs and goat hooves tangled. "Back," Rachel screamed. "We've got to go back!"

"What?" Millie grabbed Rachel's arm as the girl jumped to her feet and tried to run farther back into the smoke-filled room. Before she could ask more, a gunshot exploded outside, splintering the wood just above Rachel's head. On hands and knees, they scrambled back as a cacophony of gunfire filled the air. Holes appeared around the doorway and struck the ore pile they cowered behind. "Why—"

"He's coming," Rachel cried, her whole body shaking. She shrank against Millie's side.

He's coming? Millie didn't understand. A shot exploded close to them and hard shards of rock tore into Millie's skirt. She ducked lower, trying to protect Rachel and Buttercup. Then, she realized what was happening.

George. They were shooting at George. They had no idea Millie and Rachel were in the burning stamp mill.

Thick smoke scorched Millie's lungs, making her feel like she was breathing fire. She could breathe, but she didn't want to. Her eyes felt raw and her nose ran, the secretions mixing with sweat that poured down her face and ran down her back. The fire was close, much too close.

Millie choked down one burning breath after another, wiped her eyes, and removed her six-shooter as she peered around the ore. George lay just inside the doorway, slowly crawling deeper into the building, clutching his side. His movements stopped right in front of the ore pile they hid behind. Breathing hard, coughing and choking on the smoke, he swore, promising over and over again to kill Dom.

Millie gently pushed Rachel and Buttercup toward the back wall. The crackling and falling of timbers hid their movement, but sooner or later George would hear their hacking coughs. Millie could see blood glistening on the hand George pressed against his side. He was injured, but his gun arm was steady.

The fire crackled and burned closer. Closer. Closer.

They had to get out, but how? George would shoot them as soon as he saw them. Death by George's bullet, burn to death, or rush the door and risk being killed by whoever was shooting outside.

Millie's six-shooter felt hot and heavy in her hand. She had to shoot George. Oh Lor', she'd never killed another person. But even if she managed, how could they get outside without being shot and killed by accident?

They were trapped.

A burning timber crashed through the floor twenty feet away. Buttercup suddenly jolted to life and rammed Millie's arm. Her six-shooter went flying. Buttercup, her red eyes reflecting the fire, jumped forward like an insane demon. She landed on George, kicked him in the face, and charged out the door.

"What?" George twisted around, his gun turning with him. His eyes widened when he spotted Millie.

She didn't think. There was nothing to think about. Springing forward, she rammed into George, knocking his gun from his hand and kneeing him. He grunted as she rolled on top of him, and she screamed at Rachel to run. To get out. The little girl darted past, but as Millie tried to flee after her, George's thick arm encircled her waist and jerked her backwards.

George might be hurt, but he was still stronger than she was. Kicking wildly, Millie struck out blindly, choking on smoke, perspiration coating her. She managed to squirm out of his grasp, but before she could run, he grabbed her wrist. Blood and sweat were her friend and as she pulled and twisted her arm. His hand slipped but he still firmly held her hand. She twisted and finally managed to pull free.

She was free. Pushing herself toward the door, she saw Rachel disappear outside. They were going to make it. On hands and knees, she scrambled forward. George grabbed her ankle and jerked her backward. Falling flat on her belly, she felt herself being dragged back.

She rolled over and looked back, intending to use her free foot to kick him, but she froze in shock and awe.

Flames licked so close she could have touched them.

For an instant she was too stunned to react, but as heat singed her face, Millie burst into action. She kicked out wildly, striking George in the shoulder. Behind him, flames crept along the wooden walkway, illuminating him in a red glow, making him look inhuman.

Suddenly he howled and released her ankle. Rolling away, Millie crawled onto her hands and knees and dragged herself toward the door. She waited for a bullet or for George's hand to again grab her ankle. Instead, all she heard were his inhuman screams.

Then she smelled burning flesh.

Her knee struck a chunk of ore and she skidded onto her belly, her face landing just inside the door. With the last of her energy, she shoved herself forward, glancing back as she choked and coughed. George lay on his back,

328 MURDER AT BUCKSKIN JOE

rolling wildly from side to side, slapping at his face as flames consumed his beard.

Millie slithered forward, squinting at the bright sunlight, hacking up bile as she tried to breathe. Her lungs felt burned and her arms gave out. Lying prone on the rough ground, she closed her eyes, no longer able to move. Heat scorched her legs. Fire would soon consume her skirts.

Strong arms suddenly wrapped around her and lifted her off the ground, dragging her away from the burning building. "Millie. Dear God. Millie. Are you okay? Please, answer me."

She couldn't answer. She felt overwhelmed with relief and love as Dom carried her across the open field, his big hands shaking. "Are you shot?" His voice cracked and she saw tears streaking his filthy cheeks. "Please, honey. You've got to be okay."

Millie choked, trying to fill her scorched lungs with fresh, clean air, but only managing to hack and cough. For a long moment, she couldn't respond. Her eyes teared and she coughed uncontrollably. When her fit subsided, she choked out, "Rachel?"

"Safe. Thank goodness you sent out Buttercup. We might have shot you by mistake."

FORTY-SEVEN

May 14, 1865

A Smoky Wedding

D ave and Kate squeezed through the guests in Millie's cabin, smelling of smoke and looking exhausted, despite their clean Sunday clothes. Millie felt like she'd been trampled by a stampede of buffalo and then scalped alive, but the dark rings under her guests' eyes told her she wasn't the only one hurting. The town had managed to put out the fire, but it hadn't been easy. The stamp mill had burned to the ground, yet by sheer determination, the miners had saved the town of Buckskin Joe. Still, it had been touch and go most of the night.

Despite their tired expressions, Kate and Dave smiled radiantly, boosting Millie's flagging energy. Finally the last, but most important guest arrived. There was clapping and hoots of approval as Father Dyer pushed through the crowded room to his place behind the altar. Father Dyer was large and more rough-looking than Millie thought proper, but if he knew how to say wedding vows, she wouldn't complain. She wanted to get her brother married, to change out of Kate's low-cut dress, and to leave Buckskin Joe.

And she would never return.

Father Dyer stared down at the makeshift altar Rachel had made as Millie encouraged her guests to assemble. Every time she bumped into anyone, she had to pull her shawl back up to cover her very low bodice. Finally, the room quieted and Dom took Millie's hand. He leaned over and whispered, "You should take Miss Kate up on her offer and keep that dress. I like how it looks on you."

Millie rolled her eyes. Rachel twirled around and led Dave and Kate down the aisle between their guests. The little girl's fancy dress flew out as she spun around and threw flower petals at everyone. Behind the happy couple, Millie spotted Buttercup and scowled. She'd specifically given instructions that Buttercup was to remain in the barn with Columbine and Bluebell.

The little goat followed the happy couple, devouring any petals that made it to the floor. Shrugging, knowing no one but her cared, Millie turned her attention back to Dave and Kate. Rachel reached the altar, spun around several times, and threw the last of her flower petals at Father Dyer. After smiling like she was the star of the show, she skipped to Millie and Dom's side and wiggled in between them.

Kate and Dave stopped in front of the altar and looked at the minister expectantly, totally unconcerned as Buttercup hurried around them and began chewing on the fringe of Father Dyer's trousers. The minister nudged Buttercup aside and stood up straight. In the silence that followed—while Millie held her breath, hoping the man knew some kind of wedding vows—Augusta leaned over and whispered, "Don't worry none, Miss Millie. He don't look like much, but Father Dyer's a real Methodist preacher."

And he was. Using a strong voice that filled the cabin, Father Dyer preached against the evils of gambling, drinking, and other vices. Dave and Kate listened attentively while Buttercup nosed around their feet, devouring flower petals and parts of the altar. The service was quick—Buttercup hadn't devoured all the greenery—but by the end, Millie was impressed with Father Dyer's words and passion. He pronounced Dave and Kate man and wife, oversaw the signing of the marriage certificate, and accepted a dollar as payment.

"He's a real Methodist preacher, but he don't earn much," Augusta told Millie as Father Dyer made a bee-line to the food table. "To supplement his wages, he delivers mail all over South Park. Said he had a forty-pound bag to carry over Mosquito Pass to California Gulch this afternoon. He's loading up before he goes."

Standing beside the food table, Father Dyer stuffed pies into his pockets as quickly as he crammed them into his mouth. If Kate hadn't asked Sheriff Finch to bring extra food, there would be nothing left when the bride and groom reached the table. Turning away, Millie discreetly tugged up her bodice, covered her exposed bosom with her shawl, and glanced around.

Kate and Dave looked like two young people in love. They were surrounded by their guests—Kootenay, the Cornogs, Sheriff Finch, and the Tabors—and were happily receiving congratulations. Rachel danced around the room, bumping off one person and being twirled by another, grinning madly.

Millie was anxious to begin their journey back to Idaho Springs, but since she couldn't leave until the celebration ended, she decided she might as well clear up one or two issues. Taking a shallow breath—her lungs still hurt from yesterday's smoke—she approached Kootenay. "Mr. Good, may I have a word with you?"

Kootenay eyed Millie suspiciously. Yesterday, the big mountain man had been surprised when she invited him to Kate's wedding, but not Little Bear. Now he lumbered outside after her, looking suspicious. The air smelled of smoke, causing Millie to cough, but the sky was blue and the sun warm. Kootenay dipped his head at Millie, the gold specks in his eyes sparkling. "Thank you, ma'am. Kate's wedding were beautiful."

Millie had never met a man like Kootenay. He was a mixture of a joker, a simpleton, and a mountain man with the joy of a child. He had all the good and bad that came with each. Still, he'd helped Kate when she needed him. The girl deserved to know the truth. "You're welcome, sir. I'm happy for them both. I wanted to…" She hesitated, finally deciding to be blunt. There was no polite way to phrase her words. "Mr. Good. You should tell Miss Kate that you're her father."

The big man stumbled backward like she'd struck him. "How, how'd you know?"

"Your eyes. You, Kate, and Gruffy all have beautiful golden speckles in honey-colored eyes. They're quite remarkable and unique."

He looked down at his toes and shuffled his feet. "I can't. I left her and her ma when Kate were little. I meant to go back, to send money. But I ain't never done either."

Millie patted his big shoulder. "That may be true, but you've been her friend. She's leaving later today. Family is important. You need to tell her, or I will." She herded him inside, his shoulders hunched, and his feet dragging.

Kootenay slowly approached Kate and although Millie couldn't hear what he said, she smiled when Kate's eyes widened, and she let out a whoop. Kootenay hunched down, as if expecting a blow, and he almost fell over when Kate jumped into his arms.

"That was kind of you, *señora* Millie." Angelina Cornog moved beside Millie, her son bouncing in her arms. "*Señor* Good need to tell her. Now Kate has a husband and father."

"You knew?"

"*Sí.*"

Millie hesitated and held up a finger, smiling when Gruffy wrapped his chubby fist around it. "Has Miss Kate told my brother about Gruffy?"

"*Sí*, we all talk last night. *Señorita* Kate, no, now *señora* Kate, she love my Gruffy, but she know, Gruffy is my boy. He stay with me and *señor* Cornog."

"I'm glad." Millie pulled her finger free and tickled Gruffy. "He's a fine boy. You're lucky to have him."

"*Sí.* I am very lucky."

Millie looked at the woman and Angelina smiled encouragingly, like she knew what Millie wanted to ask. "This week has taught me a lot about family. I've learned that I would do anything, absolutely anything, to protect my children. I'd even kill for them if I had to."

Angelina's doe-like eyes stayed steady. "*Sí.* I protect my Gruffy. Always."

Millie nodded and glanced around to make sure

Sheriff Finch wasn't anywhere within earshot. He and Dom were near the food table, each sampling a pie. "Do you have your special knife with you, *señora* Angelina?" Millie asked. "The one your mother gave you."

"*Sí*." Angelina balanced Gruffy on her hip and slipped a hand into the folds of her dress, withdrawing the ornate knife she'd shown Millie the day they'd harvested skunk cabbage. Millie eyed the weapon. It would have produced a wound like a bayonet and the ornate metal twirls on either side of the blade would have caused bruising when they'd struck flesh.

"Wandering Will threatened to take Gruffy away?" Millie asked.

"*Sí*." Angelina scowled. "He say Gruffy is his. He take him unless I pay, but I have no money."

"Did you tell *señor* Cornog?"

"No. I know *señor* Cornog. He would try to kill Wandering Will, but maybe my *señor* is killed instead. I go alone. Wandering Will is at his mine and he laugh at me. Says tomorrow he come for my Gruffy. He will give my boy to Queeny to raise. I go crazy. I stab him in the leg and when he falls, I try to kill him. But my knife strikes his shoulder, not his heart. Before I can stab him again, I hear someone yell." She shrugged. "I hide in trees and watch Milo kill the bad man. Then I leave."

Millie sighed. So much for her detective skills. She'd never really suspected Angelina—not until Milo's confession. Angelina skillfully slipped the knife back under the folds of her skirt as Millie said, "It has been a pleasure to meet you, *señora* Angelina. Take good care of Gruffy. If you and *señor* Cornog ever visit Idaho Springs, please call on us."

FORTY-EIGHT

June 4, 1865
Goodbye

Millie had never been so happy to see anyplace before. Their cabin looked just like it had when they'd left, except the meadow had turned green and colorful. Lush grass was spotted with blooming silver Lupine, red Indian paintbrush, and yellow Arrowleaf, but best of all, a beautiful palomino stallion grazed near the cabin. Rachel ran in front of them, looking neither footsore nor exhausted as she screamed, "Hosa! Hosa, we're here!"

The door burst open and Hosa rushed outside. He looked more grown-up than Millie remembered, although maybe the tears in her eyes were blurring her vision. Rachel jumped into Hosa's arms and soon all four of them were enveloped in a family hug.

"O Lor! Hosa, it's so good to see you." Later Millie might discuss his transgressions. Stealing a horse and causing such worry was not acceptable behavior, but for now she was simply thankful they were all safe and together. Never, ever again, would she take her family for granted.

"*Héébee Kooníini'íini, Niibeeseitit Wox.*"

Millie spun around, breaking free from her family's embrace. Mounted on a painted pony sat Woonbisiseet, Hosa's father. Millie hadn't seen the man in eight or ten months, but the changes in him were shocking. A year ago, he'd been a young brave in his prime, proud of his wife and son. Now his wife was dead, his people massacred. Woonbisiseet looked old beyond his years. His broad shoulders were gaunt—like he hadn't eaten a decent meal in months—and several red sores and scars disfigured his strong features.

"Woonbisiseet," Dom said slowly. "It's good to see you, old friend."

There was an awkward silence until Woonbisiseet said something. Millie didn't understand the words, but Dom's drawn expression spoke volumes. She tensed, wanting to scream and fight, but she knew she could do nothing.

"Three days." Dom nodded and glanced at Hosa. The boy stood up straighter, his gaze steady. Obviously, he'd already spoken with his father. Woonbisiseet nodded, reined his horse, and cantered away.

"Three days?" A sick feeling twisted in Millie's stomach.

"I will stay three days," Hosa said, gently touching Millie's face. "Then I leave and go to war. I fight against white men with my father."

Millie didn't cry—her tears would come later. She didn't yell or insist Hosa was still just a child, although Lord she wanted to. She knew he was now a man and there was no way she would insult him. Instead, she nodded and cherished every second they spent together over the next three days. Only at night did she burrow into Dom's strong arms and cry.

Three days passed quickly, and Millie couldn't stop her tears when Woonbisiseet rode out into the meadow. She handed him food before enveloping Hosa in a long, desperate hug. She couldn't seem to let go until Hosa gently pulled away, kissed her on the cheek, and bid farewell to Dom and Rachel. Holding on to each other, Rachel, Dom, and Millie watched Hosa mount his fine horse, wave goodbye, and ride away.

"We'll see him again," Rachel said, hiccupping through her sobs. "He's gonna come back, someday."

Millie felt Dom squeeze her shoulder. She'd read enough about the Indian Wars to know Hosa would be lucky to survive, but Rachel didn't need to know that. If they were fortunate, someday they would be reunited—like Kate and Kootenay. God willing, someday they'd be a family again.

Acknowledgements

I thought after all I'd learned from *The Lucky Hat Mine* and *Denver City Justice*, writing would get easier. I was wrong. Each book has unique issues and the more I write, the more I appreciate all the people who help me turn a manuscript into a published work. With *Murder at Buckskin Joe*, I first want to thank my critique group, 30th Street Fiction. Kate, Rick, Caitlin, Ian, Jess, Lezly, Juli, Maggie, Evan, Stan, and Matt. You guys are the best! There is no way I could do this without your encouragement, friendship, and amazing critiques. I'd also like to give a special thanks to my editors, Caitlin Berve of Ignited Ink Writing, LLC and Doug Lang, English connoisseur and history expert.

As with other books, I did tons of research while writing *Murder at Buckskin Joe*, but the mining details were difficult. I want to thank my mining experts, Lisa and Thom Fisher, for all their corrections and clarifications on stamp mills, Mexican Arrastras, Long Toms, the amalgamation process, and vertical shaft mining. I also want to thank Dr. Richard Sauers and the folks from the Western Museum of Mining & Industry for answering my questions, allowing me to use their amazing library, and letting my photographer shoot the cover in their incredible stamp mill.

My critique group helps flesh out and polish chapters, but beta readers give a ton of their time and energy to offer suggestions and improvements to the overall story.

Their feedback is invaluable to help with story flow, character arc, and readability. I can't express how much I appreciate each of my amazing beta readers: my writing buddy, Liz Crawford; my neighbor and friend, Jane Evans; mountain man extraordinaire (who I hope someday to meet!) HL Miller; and my Sister-In-Crime, Donnell Bell. You all gave me invaluable feedback—I can't tell you how much I appreciate each of you.

I'd like to thank the people who helped polish and create the final book. Mary George used her incredible wordsmithing for the back cover blurb and Annie Carter created the fabulous sketch of the arrastra. Final proofs were read by Jan Gunia, Skippy Rollins, and Jean Rosar who each helped me spot last-minute typos.

For the cover, Clifford Conklin, photographer extraordinaire, experimented with all sorts of cover ideas, including using the amazing model, Kristian Reynolds. Nikki Rasmussen, artist and designer, used Cliff's photos along with a photo of a Civil War Era Palmetto Pistol from Old South Military Antiques (www.oldsouthantiques.com) to create my amazing cover.

Finally, and most importantly, I couldn't write without the love and support of my family, John, Tess, and Corrie. Thanks to everyone who has made this book possible.

Made in the USA
Monee, IL
25 October 2021